Dear Target Book Club Reader,

What a great pleasure it is to meet you on this page, to have the opportunity to introduce myself and my work to you. My novel *One Thousand White Women: The Journals of May Dodd* has enjoyed a wonderfully gratifying word-of-mouth success over the past decade—passed from bookseller to reader, from one reader to the next, from one book club to another. I've always believed that writing and reading are collaborative processes. It is you, the reader, who brings an author's work to life in your imagination. When you open the cover of our books and enter the world we have created there, reader and writer complete each other. To have my novel honored by the Target Book Club as one of its picks opens up a whole new source of willing, fertile imaginations to me, a new set of connections, a kind of continuous electrical conduit running between us. Readers: without you writers wouldn't exist.

Set in the 1870s, at the height of the Plains Indian Wars, *One Thousand White Women* is the story of a diverse collection of courageous young women who travel west to live and marry among the Cheyenne Nation. Part of a bold, secret U.S. government program to bring peace at last to the Great Plains, these women are both volunteers and recruits—some felons, some diagnosed as insane and committed to lunatic asylums, some simply lonely souls with nothing left to lose. What they have in common is that they all live on the fringes of society, now forced by their respective circumstances to leave the so-called "civilized" world behind and enter the strange, terrifying, exhilarating world of the "savages." Narrated in the first-person journal format by a feisty young woman from Chicago named May Dodd, *One Thousand White Women* is a love story and an adventure tale. It is a variation on the time-honored theme of the American melting pot, an attempt to meld cultures and races and religions, the wild and the civilized, an attempt for human beings of vastly different worldviews and realities to know each other, to understand each other. It is, finally, an American tragedy.

I spent seven years, on and off, working on this novel, researching the historical era and Native American history and culture, writing and imagining the lives of my characters. In that time, as happens with writers, the characters in the novel became as real to me as actual people. I knew exactly what they all looked like, I saw them and they spoke to me in my dreams. I laughed and I wept with them. In an odd way, they took over the novel, and wrote it for me, acting out their own inexorable fates.

I hope as you, the reader, enter these pages, and come to know the people living here, that *One Thousand White Women: The Journals of May Dodd* catches you up and sweeps you away as it did me.

Thank you. And thank you, Target.

With gratitude and all best wishes,

Jim Fergus

"Fergus is gifted in his ability to portray the perceptions and emotions of women. He writes with tremendous insight and sensitivity about the individual community and the political and religious issues of the time, many of which are still relevant today. This book is artistically rendered with meticulous attention to small details that bring to life the daily concerns of a group of hardy souls at a pivotal time in U.S. history." —*Booklist*

"[May] and the other brides rise from the underbelly of society, becoming the most noble characters in this imaginative tale of the American West reeling under the decline of one culture and the forcible ascent of another." —*Publishers Weekly*

"In a word, *One Thousand White Women* is terrific! What Jim Fergus has done within these pages is give life and voice to an aspect of the American West and its native peoples that has been, if not covered up, too long overlooked. It is a tremendous achievement by a remarkable writer." —David Seybold, editor of *Boats* and *Fathers and Sons*

"*One Thousand White Women* is definitely a fresh twist on the traditional Western. Fergus has started his career as a novelist with a book rich in the results of personal fervor and study, and one that reflects a sensitive imagination. Fans of Western fiction and students of American frontier history can confidently add this novel to their summer reading list." —*San Antonio Express News*

"Jim Fergus's powerful first novel is a surefire winner. I read it non-stop and would now like to propose a hundred-year moratorium on all books about white women in the Old West, since it will take the rest of us at least that long to amass the research—not to mention the compassion—needed to equal this fine work. A masterful job!"
—Robert F. Jones, author of *Tie My Bones to Her Back*

"This is a rich, beautifully conceived, rollicking novel, literally bursting with original characters and with the profound joy and heartbreak of the real history of the American West. May Dodd may be the most compellingly alive fictional character of that history since Little Big Man."
—Charles Gaines, author of *A Family Place, Stay Hungry, Pumping Iron,* and *Survival Games*

ONE THOUSAND WHITE WOMEN

The Journals of May Dodd

Jim Fergus

ST. MARTIN'S GRIFFIN

NEW YORK

ONE THOUSAND WHITE WOMEN. Copyright © 1998 by Jim Fergus. All rights
reserved. Printed in the United States of America. For information, address
St. Martin's Press, 175 Fifth Avenue, New York, N.Y. 10010.

www.stmartins.com

Bird drawings by Loren G. Smith
Design by Nancy Resnick and Heidi Eriksen

The Library of Congress has catalogued the hardcover edition as follows:

Fergus, Jim
    One thousand white women : the journals of May Dodd / Jim Fergus.
        p. cm.
    ISBN 978-0-312-18008-9
    1. Cheyenne Indians — Fiction. I. Title.
PS3556.E66054   1998
813'.54 — dc21
                                                                    97-37118
                                                                    CIP

ISBN 978-1-250-00464-2 (Target Book Club Edition)

First Target Book Club Edition: July 2011

10 9 8 7 6 5 4 3 2 1

To Dillon

→ ACKNOWLEDGMENTS ←

Writing careers in general, and the writing of novels in particular, can be accurately, if somewhat unromantically, likened to rolling large boulders uphill. Sometimes the writer needs a little help, and if we're very lucky, people come along at opportune moments and not only offer a word of encouragement, but actually put their shoulder to the boulder and help us to move it forward. I have been that lucky, and owe thanks to many people—friends, family, and colleagues—for the existence of this book. So special and grateful thanks to all of the following:

To Barney Donnelley, without whose faith and generosity I couldn't have been a writer. To my agent, Al Zuckerman, the quintessential pro, whose unfailing instincts culled this story out of the rockpile. To my editor, Jennifer Enderlin, for her constant enthusiasm for this project, her hard work, good cheer, and impeccable editorial judgment. To Laton McCartney, for years of wise counsel and boundless optimism. To Jon Williams, whose early turn at this particular boulder encouraged me to continue pushing. To Bob Wallace, who gave me my first magazine assignment almost twenty years ago, and, remarkably, stepped back into my professional life once again as editor in chief just in time to oversee this much-belated "first" novel. To Bonny Hawley and Douglas Tate, for invaluable insights and information on British place, name, and character. To Laurie Morrow, for her precise woman's perspective on the subject of romantic attraction. To Rev. Rolland W. Hoverstock, for critical information about the Episcopal church and ceremonies circa 1875. To Sister Thérèse de la Valdène, for providing always cherished retreats at Dogwood Farms, and to Guy de la Valdène, for wonderful dinners and a large vote of confidence when it was most needed. Finally, thanks to Dillon for cheerfully occupying over the past fifteen years the nearly always thankless role of writer's spouse.

While the author acknowledges the help and support of all of the above people in the creation of this novel, he accepts full responsibilities for any of its shortcomings.

Five percent of the author's royalties earned on the sale of *One Thousand White Women* will be donated to the St. Labre Indian School, Ashland, Montana 59004.

Women will love her, that she is a woman
More worth than any man; men that she is
The rarest of all women.

— William Shakespeare,
The Winter's Tale, Act V, Scene 1

→ AUTHOR'S NOTE ←

In spite of efforts to convince the reader to the contrary, this book is entirely a work of fiction. However, the seed that grew into a novel was sown in the author's imagination by an actual historical event: in 1854 at a peace conference at Fort Laramie, a prominent Northern Cheyenne chief requested of the U.S. Army authorities the gift of one thousand white women as brides for his young warriors. Because theirs is a matrilineal society in which all children born belong to their mother's tribe, this seemed to the Cheyennes to be the perfect means of assimilation into the white man's world—a terrifying new world that even as early as 1854, the Native Americans clearly recognized held no place for them. Needless to say, the Cheyennes' request was not well received by the white authorities—the peace conference collapsed, the Cheyennes went home, and, of course, the white women did not come. In this novel they do.

Certain other historical events are here rendered, but in an entirely fictitious manner. At the same time, the real names of certain actual historical figures are used in this novel, but the characters themselves are fictional creations. In all other respects this book is a work of fiction. Names, characters, places, dates, geographical descriptions are all either the product of the author's imagination or are used fictitiously.

Any resemblance to actual persons, living or dead, or to actual events or locales is entirely coincidental.

Finally, while a genuine attempt was made to render the Cheyenne language as accurately as possible, certain misspellings and misuses inevitably occur in this book. For these errors, the author offers sincere apologies to the Cheyenne people.

→ INTRODUCTION ←

by J. Will Dodd

As a child growing up in Chicago, I used to scare my kid brother, Jimmy, silly at night telling him stories about our mad ancestor, May Dodd, who lived in an insane asylum and ran off to live with Indians—at least that was the fertile, if somewhat vague, raw material of secret family legend.

We lived on Lake Shore Drive and our family was still quite wealthy in those days, descendants of "old" money—a fortune and a dynasty begun by our great-great-grandfather, J. Hamilton Dodd, who as a young man in the mid–nineteenth century began plowing up the vast Midwestern prairies around Chicago in order to cultivate grain in what was some of the most fertile farmland in the world. "Papa," as he is still known by his descendants, was one of the original founders of the Chicago Board of Trade; he was friend, crony, business partner, and competitor, as the case might be, of all the most prominent entrepreneurs in that booming Midwestern metropolis—among them Cyrus McCormick, inventor of the reaper, Philip Armour and Gustavus Swift, the famous pork and beef packers, and the brothers Charles and Nathan Mears, lumbermen who bought up and single-handedly destroyed the great old-growth white pine forests of Michigan.

No one in our family spoke much about my great-grandmother May Dodd. Among the wealthy, ancestral insanity has always been a source of deep-rooted embarrassment. Even these many generations later, when the razor-sharp robber-baron genes have been largely blunted by line-breeding and soft country-club living, by boarding school and Ivy League educations, even now no one in our social milieu likes to admit to being directly descended from a crazy woman. In the heavily edited official family history, May Dodd remains little more than a footnote: *"Born March 23, 1850 . . . second daughter of J. Hamilton and Hortense Dodd. Hospitalized at age 23 for a nervous disorder. Died in hospital, February 17, 1876."* That's it.

But even old-money taciturnity—for which there is no competition on earth—and the equally unparalleled ability of the rich to keep dark secrets, could not completely obscure the whispered rumors that trickled down through the generations that May Dodd had actually died under somewhat mysterious circumstances—not in the hospital as officially stated, but somewhere out West. This was the story that fueled my and my brother Jimmy's imaginations.

By the time I was a junior in college, our father had squandered most of the family fortune, which had by then already been vastly diluted by a couple of generations of unproductive heirs—what people used to call "wastrels." Pop finished it off with a series of bad investments in Chicago commercial real estate just when that market was collapsing, and then he managed to break a trust and drink away the last bit of money that was to pay for his sons' higher education. Partly as a result of this Jimmy got drafted—which was almost unheard of in our circles—and sent to Vietnam, where he was killed when he stepped on a land mine in a rice paddy in the Mekong Delta. Less than six months later, Pop drank himself to death.

I was luckier than my brother and managed to stay in college, drew a high lottery number, and graduated with a degree in journalism, armed with which I eventually became the editor in chief of the city magazine *Chitown*.

It was while researching a piece for the magazine about the old scions of Chicago that I happened to come again across May Dodd's name. I remembered the tales that I used to tell Jimmy, and I wondered where I had first heard the rumor that she had gone "out West to live with Indians"—which in our family had become a kind of euphemism for insanity.

I started poking around in the family archives, casually at first, then with greater and greater interest—some might even say obsession. One letter, reportedly written by May Dodd from inside the asylum to her children, Hortense and William, who were just infants at the time of her incarceration, had survived. Source of both the old family rumor, as well as proof positive of how crazy May really was, this letter was for me the beginning of a long, strange journey.

I took a leave of absence from my job at the magazine in order to devote myself full-time to following the convoluted trail of May Dodd's life. My research led me eventually to the Tongue River Indian reservation in southeastern Montana. It was here, armed with my family letter as proof of my ancestry, that I was finally granted access to the following journals, which have remained among the Cheyennes—a sacred tribal treasure for well over a hundred years. I need hardly add that the tale they tell of U.S. government intrigue *cum* social experiment has also remained one of the best-kept secrets in Western American history.

The following prologue to the journals briefly describes the historical events that led to May Dodd's story, and is based on several sources, including newspaper accounts of the time, the *Congressional Record*, the *Annual Report to the Commissioner of Indian Affairs*, correspondence from the files of the Adjutant General's Office in the National Archives in Washington, D.C., as well as various materials available in Chicago's Newberry Library. The Indian point of view pertaining to Little Wolf's visit to Washington in 1874 and the subsequent chain of events is based on Northern Cheyenne oral history recounted to me by Harold Wild Plums in Lame Elk, Montana, in October 1996.

→ PROLOGUE ←

➤⃔

In September of 1874, the great Cheyenne "Sweet Medicine Chief" Little Wolf made the long overland journey to Washington, D.C., with a delegation of his tribesmen for the express purpose of making a lasting peace with the whites. Having spent the weeks prior to his trip smoking and softly discussing various peace initiatives with his tribal council of forty-four chiefs, Little Wolf came to the nation's capital with a somewhat novel, though from the Cheyenne worldview perfectly rational, plan that would ensure a safe and prosperous future for his greatly beseiged people.

The Indian leader was received in Washington with all the pomp and circumstance accorded to the visiting head of state of a foreign land. At a formal ceremony in the Capitol building with President Ulysses S. Grant, and members of a specially appointed congressional commission, Little Wolf was presented with the Presidential Peace Medal—a large ornate silver medallion—that the Chief, with no intentional irony, a thing unknown to the Cheyennes, would later wear in battle against the U.S. Army in the Cheyennes' final desperate days as a free people. Grant's profile appeared on one side of the medal, ringed by the words: LET US HAVE PEACE LIBERTY JUSTICE AND EQUALITY; on the other side an open Bible lay atop a rake, a plow, an ax, a shovel, and sundry other farming implements with the words: ON EARTH PEACE GOOD WILL TOWARD MEN 1874.

Also in attendance on this historic occasion were the President's wife, Julia, who had begged her husband to be allowed to attend so that she might see the Indians in all their savage regalia, and a few favored members of the Washington press corps. The date was September 18, 1874.

Old daguerreotype photographs of the assembly show the Cheyennes dressed in their finest ceremonial attire—ornately beaded moccasins; hide leggings from the fringe of which dangled chattering elk teeth; deerskin war shirts, trimmed at the seams with the scalps of enemies and elaborately ornamented with beads and dyed porcupine quills. They wore hammered silver coins in their hair, and brass-wire and otter-fur bands in their braids. Washingtonians had never seen anything quite like it.

Although over fifty years old by this time, Little Wolf looked at least a decade younger than his age. He was lean and sinewy, with aquiline nose and flared nostrils, high, ruddy cheekbones, and burnished bronze skin that bore the deep pockmarks of a smallpox epidemic that had ravaged the Cheyenne tribe in 1865. The Chief was not a large man, but he carried himself with great bearing—head held high, an expression of innate fierceness and defiance on his face. His demeanor would later be characterized by newspaper accounts as "haughty" and "insolent."

Expressing himself through an interpreter by the name of Amos Chapman from Fort Supply, Kansas, Little Wolf came directly to the point. "It is the Cheyenne way that all children who enter this world belong to their mother's tribe," he began, addressing the President of the United States, though he did not look directly in Grant's eyes as this was considered bad manners among his people. "My father was Arapaho and my mother Cheyenne. Thus I was raised by my mother's people, and I am Cheyenne. But I have always been free to come and go among the Arapaho, and in this way I learned also their way of life. This, we believe, is a good thing." At this point in his address, Little Wolf would ordinarily have puffed on his pipe, giving all those present a chance to consider what he had thus far said. However, with usual white man bad manners, the Great White Father had neglected to provide a pipe at this important gathering.

The Chief continued: "The People [The Cheyennes referred to themselves simply as *Tsitsistas*—the People] are a small tribe, smaller than either the Sioux or the Arapaho; we have never been numerous because we understand that the earth can only carry a certain number of the People, just as it can only carry a certain number of the bears, the wolves, the elks, the pronghorns, and all the rest of the animals. For if there are too many of any animal, this animal starves until there is the right number again. We would rather be few in number and have enough for everyone to eat, than be too many and all starve. Because of the sickness you have brought us (here Little Wolf touched his pockmarked cheek), and the war you have waged upon us (here he touched his breast; he had been wounded numerous times in battle), we are now even fewer. Soon the People will disappear altogether, as the buffalo in our country disappear. I am the Sweet Medicine Chief. My duty is to see that my People survive. To do this we must enter the white man's world—our children must become members of your tribe. Therefore we ask the Great Father for the gift of one thousand white women as wives, to teach us and our children the new life that must be lived when the buffalo are gone."

Now a collective gasp rose from the room, peppered with scattered exclamations of astonishment. To interrupt a man while he was speaking, except to utter soft murmurs of approbation, was an act of gross impoliteness to the Cheyennes, and this outburst angered Little Wolf. But the Chief knew that white people did not know how to behave, and he was not surprised. Still, he paused for a moment to let the crowd settle and to allow his chiefly displeasure to be registered by all present.

"In this way," Little Wolf continued, "our warriors will plant the Cheyenne seed into the bellies of your white women. Our seed will sprout and grow inside their wombs, and the next generation of Cheyenne children will be born into your tribe, with the full privileges attendant to that position."

At exactly this point in Little Wolf's address, President Grant's wife, Julia, fainted dead away on the floor, swooned right from her chair with a long, gurgling sigh like the death rattle of a lung-shot buffalo cow. (It was unseasonably hot in the room that day, and in her memoirs, Julia Dent Grant would maintain that the heat, not moral squeamishness at the idea of the savages breeding with white girls, had caused her to faint.)

As aides rushed to the First Lady's side, the President, reddening in the face, began to rise unsteadily to his feet. Little Wolf recognized that Grant was drunk and, considering the solemnity of the occasion, the Chief felt that this constituted a fairly serious breach of etiquette.

"For your gift of one thousand white women," Little Wolf continued in a stern, louder voice over the rising clamor (although at this point interpreter Chapman was practically whispering), "we will give you one thousand horses. Five hundred wild horses and five hundred horses already broke."

Now Little Wolf raised his hand as if in papal benediction, concluding his speech with immense dignity and bearing. "From this day forward the blood of our people shall be forever joined."

But by then all hell had broken loose in the room and hardly anyone heard the great leader's final remarks. Senators blustered and pounded the table. "Arrest the heathens!" someone called out, and the row of soldiers flanking the hall fell into formation, bayonets at the ready position. In response, the Cheyenne chiefs all stood up in unison, instinctively drawing knives and forming a circle, shoulders touching, in the way that a bevy of quail beds down at night to protect itself from predators.

President Grant had also gained his feet, swaying slightly, his face scarlet, pointing his finger at Little Wolf, and thundering, "*Outrageous! Outrageous!*" Little Wolf had heard that the President was a great warrior and a man much respected by his enemies. Still, the Sweet Medicine Chief did not care to be pointed at in this impertinent manner, and if he'd had his quirt with him, he'd have knocked the Great Father, drunk or not, to his knees for this behavior. Little Wolf was infamous among his people for his temper—slow to be aroused but grizzlylike in ferocity.

Order was finally restored. The Cheyennes put their knives up, and the guards quickly ushered the Indian delegation out of the hall without further incident, the great chief striding proudly at their head.

That night doors were locked all over Washington, shades pulled, wives and daughters forbidden to go outside as word of the Cheyennes' blasphemous proposal swept the capital. The next day's newspaper headlines further fanned the flames of racist fears and civic hysteria: **"Savages Demand White Women Love Slaves!," "White Brides for the Red Devils!," "Grant to Swap Injuns: White Girls for Wild Horses!"** In what must surely have been every

nineteenth-century American man's worst nightmare, those
few citizens who did venture out with women on their arms
over the next few days cast furtive glances over their shoulders, keeping an anxious watch out for the hordes of mounted
redskins they secretly feared might swoop down upon them,
wailing like banshees as they lifted scalps with a single slash
of glinting knife blade, to carry off their shrieking women-
folk and populate the earth with half-breeds.

Official response to Little Wolf's unusual treaty offer
was swift; a tone of high moral outrage dominated the proc-
lamations of the Congress, while the administration itself
moved quickly to assure a nervous citizenry that *no*, white
women would certainly not be traded to the heathens and,
yes, immediate steps were being taken by the U.S. military
to ensure that the virtue of American womanhood would be
well protected.

Two days later Little Wolf and his entourage were packed
inside a cattle car and escorted by armed guard out of the nation's capital. Word of the Indians' peace initiative had leaked
out over the telegraph wires, and angry citizens wielding de-
nunciatory placards turned out in lynch mob–like crowds
along the way to taunt the Cheyennes as they passed, pelting
their train car with rotten fruit and racist epithets.

At the same time that the Northern Cheyennes were being booed from train platforms across the Midwest, another
parallel, and far more interesting national phenomenon
was gaining momentum. Women from all over the country
were responding to the Cheyennes' marriage proposal—
telegraphing and writing letters to the White House, volun-
teering their services as brides. Not all of these women were
crackpots, and they seemed to cut a wide socioeconomic
and racial swath: everything from single working girls in
the cities looking to spice up their drab lives with some

adventure; to recently emancipated former slaves hoping to escape the sheer drudgery of post-slavery life in the cotton mills, sweat shops, and factories of newly industrialized America; to young women widowed in the War Between the States. We know now that the Grant administration did not turn a deaf ear to their inquiries.

In private and after the initial uproar had abated, the President and his advisors had to admit that Little Wolf's unprecedented plan for assimilation of the Cheyennes made a certain practical sense. Having already implemented his Indian Peace Policy, which gave over management of the Indian reservations to the American Church, Grant was willing to consider any peaceful solutions to the still explosive situation on the Great Plains—a situation that impeded economic progress and promised yet more bloodshed for frontier settlers.

Thus was born the "Brides for Indians" (or "BFI" program, as its secret acronym became known in the President's inner circle). Besides placating the savages with this generous gift of brides, the administration believed that the "Noble American Woman," working in concert with the church, might also exert a positive influence upon the Cheyennes—to educate and elevate them from barbarism to civilized life.

Other members of the President's cabinet continued to champion the original plan for resolution of the "Indian problem," and it was understood by all concerned that any recalcitrant tribes would still be subject to the "final solution" of military annihilation.

Yet while the genocide of an entire race of native people was considered by many to be morally palatable and politically expedient, even the more progressive members of the Grant cabinet were aware that the notion of white women interbreeding with the savages would never wash with the American public. Thus, in a series of highly secretive, top-level meetings on the subject, the administration decided, in age-old fashion, to take matters into its own hands—to launch its own covert matrimonial operation.

Grant's people assuaged their political conscience with the proviso that all of the women involved in this audacious experiment be volunteers—really little different than mail-order brides—with the added moral legitimacy of being under the wing of the church. Official rationale had it that if these socially conscientious and adventuresome women chose to go West and live with the Indians of their own volition, and if in the process, the Cheyennes were distracted from their warlike ways, then everyone benefited; a perfect Jeffersonian example of government greasing the wheels of social altruism and individual initiative.

If the "Brides for Indians" program had an Achilles' heel, the administration knew that it lay in its plan to supplement an anticipated shortage of volunteers by recruiting women out of jails, penitentiaries, debtors' prisons, and mental institutions—offering full pardons or unconditional release, as the case might be, to those who agreed to sign on for the program. One fact that the government had finally learned in its dealings with the natives, was that these were a literal people who expected treaties to be fulfilled to the letter. When the Cheyennes negotiated for one thousand brides, they meant exactly that number—and in return would deliver exactly one thousand horses to fulfill their end of the bargain. Any discrepancy in these figures would be sufficient cause to send the Indians back on the 'warpath. The administration intended to ensure that this did not occur— even if it meant early release of a few low-level felons or minor mental defectives.

The first trainload of white women bound for the northern Great Plains and their new lives as brides of the Cheyenne nation left Washington under a veil of total secrecy late one night the following spring, early March 1875—just over six months after Chief Little Wolf made his startling public request of President Grant. Over the next several weeks trains departed stations in New York, Boston, Philadelphia, and Chicago.

On March 23, 1875, a young woman by the name of May Dodd, age twenty-five years to the day, formerly a patient in the Lake Forest Lunatic Asylum, a private facility thirty miles north of Chicago, boarded the Union Pacific train at Union Station, with forty-seven other volunteers and recruits from the Chicago region—their destination Camp Robinson, Nebraska Territory.

[NOTE: The following journals are largely unedited, and, except for very minor corrections in spelling and punctuation have been here transcribed exactly as written by their author, May Dodd. Contained within May Dodd's journals are several letters addressed to family members and friends. There is no indication that any of these letters were ever mailed, and they appear to have served the author primarily as a way for her to "speak" to individuals in her notebooks. It is also probable that May left this correspondence, as she says of the journals themselves, to be read later by her family in the event that she not survive her adventure. These letters, too, are presented in the order and form in which they appear in the original notebooks.]

THE JOURNALS OF MAY DODD

→ NOTEBOOK I ←

A Train Bound for Glory

"Frankly, from the way I have been treated by the so-called 'civilized' people in my life, I rather look forward to residency among the savages."

(from the journals of May Dodd)

HEF

[NOTE: The following entry, undated, appears on the first page of the first notebook of May Dodd's journal.]

I leave this record for my dear children, Hortense and William, in the event that they never see their loving mother again and so that they might one day know the truth of my unjust incarceration, my escape from Hell, and into whatever is to come in these pages . . .

23 March 1875

Today is my birthday, and I have received the greatest gift of all—freedom! I make these first poor scribblings aboard the westbound Union Pacific train which departed Union Station Chicago at 6:35 a.m. this morning, bound for Nebraska Territory. We are told that it will be a fourteen-day trip with many stops along the way, and with a change of trains in Omaha. Although our final destination was intended to have been concealed from us, I have ascertained from overhearing conversations among our military escort (they underestimate a woman's auditory powers) that we are being taken first to Fort Sidney aboard the train—from there transported by wagon train to Fort Laramie, Wyoming Territory, and then on to Camp Robinson, Nebraska Territory.

How strange is life. To think that I would find myself on this train, embarking upon this long journey, watching the city retreating behind me. I sit facing backwards on the train in order to have a last glimpse of Chicago, the layer of dense black coal smoke that daily creeps out over the beach of Lake Michigan like a giant parasol, the muddy, bustling city passing by me for the last time. How I have missed this loud, raucous city since my dark and silent incarceration. And now I feel like a character in a theater play, torn from the real world, acting out some terrible and as yet unwritten role. How I envy these people I watch from the train window, hurrying off to the safety of their daily travails while we are borne off, captives of fate into the great unknown void.

Now we pass the new shanties that ring the city, that have sprung up everywhere since the great fire of '71. Little more than cobbled-together scraps of lumber they teeter in the wind like houses of cards, to form a kind of rickety fence around the perimeters of Chicago—as if somehow trying to contain the sprawling metropolis. Filthy half-dressed children play in muddy yards and stare blankly at us as we pass, as if we, or perhaps they, are creatures from some other world. How I long for my own dear children! What I would give to see them one last time, to hold them . . . now I press my hand against the train window to wave to one tiny child who reminds me somehow of my own sweet son William, but this poor child's hair is fair and greasy, hanging in dirty ringlets around his mud-streaked face. His eyes are intensely blue and he raises his tiny hand tentatively as we pass to return my greeting . . . I should say my farewell . . . I watch him growing smaller and smaller and then we leave these last poor outposts behind as the eastern sun illuminates the retreating city—the stage fades smaller and smaller into the distance. I watch as long as I can and only then do I finally gain the courage to change seats, to give up my dark and troubled past and turn around to face an uncertain and terrifying future. And when I do so the breath catches in my throat at the immensity of earth that lies before us, the prairie unspeakable in its vast, lonely reaches. Dizzy and faint at the sight of it, I feel as if the air has been sucked from my lungs, as if I have fallen off the edge of the world, and am hurtling headlong through empty space. And perhaps I have . . . perhaps I am . . .

But dear God, forgive me, I shall never again utter a complaint, I shall always remind myself how wonderful it is to be free, how I prayed for this moment every day of my life, and my prayers are answered! The terror in my heart of what lies ahead seems of little consequence compared with the prospect of spending my lifetime as an "inmate" in that loathsome "prison"—for it was a prison far more than a hospital, we were prisoners rather than patients. Our "medical treatment" consisted of being held captive behind iron bars, like animals in the zoo, ignored by indifferent doctors, tortured, taunted, and assaulted by sadistic attendants.

My definition of LUNATIC ASYLUM: A place where lunatics are created.

"Why am I here?" I asked Dr. Kaiser, when he first came to see me, fully a fortnight after my "admittance."

"Why, due to your promiscuous behavior," he answered as if genuinely surprised that I dare to even pose such a query.

"But I am in love!" I protested, and then I told him about Harry Ames. "My family placed me here because I left home to live out of wedlock with a man whom they considered to be beneath my station. For no better reason than that. When they could not convince me to leave him, they tore me from him, and from my babies. Can you not see, Doctor, that I'm no more insane than you?"

Then the doctor raised his eyebrows and scribbled on his notepad, nodding with an infuriating air of sanctimony. "Ah," he said, "I see—you believe that you were sent here as part of a conspiracy among your family." And he rose and left me and I did not see him again for nearly six months.

During this initial period I was subject to excruciating "treatments" prescribed by the good doctor to cure me of my "illness." These consisted of daily injections of scalding water into my vagina—evidently intended to calm my deranged sexual desires. At the same time, I was confined to my bed for weeks on end—forbidden from fraternizing with the other patients, not allowed to read, write letters, or pursue any other diversion. The nurses and attendants did not speak to me, as if I did not exist. I endured the further humiliation of being forced to use a bedpan, although there was nothing whatsoever physically wrong with me. Were I to protest or if I was found by a nurse out of my bed, I would be strapped into it for the remainder of the day and night.

It was during this period of confinement that I truly lost my mind. If the daily torture weren't enough, the complete isolation and inactivity were in themselves insupportable. I longed for fresh air and exercise, to promenade along Lake Michigan as I once had . . . At great risk I would steal from my bed before dawn and stand on a chair in my room, straining to see out through the iron bars that covered the tiny shaded window—just to catch one glimpse of daylight, one patch of green grass on the lawn outside. I wept bitterly at my fate, but I struggled against the tears, willed them away. For I had also learned that I must not allow anyone on staff to see me weep, lest it be said in addition to the doctor's absurd diagnosis of promiscuity, that I was also victim of Hysteria or Melancholia . . . which would only be cause for further tortures.

Let me here set down, once and for ever, the true circumstances of my incarceration.

Four years ago I fell in love with a man named Harry Ames. Harry was several years my senior and foreman of Father's grain-elevator operations. We met at my parents' home, where Harry came regularly to consult with Father on business matters. Harry is a very attractive man, if somewhat rough around the edges, with strong masculine arms and a certain workingman's self-confidence. He was nothing like the insipid, privileged boys with whom girls of my station are reduced to socializing at tea and cotillion. Indeed, I was quite swept away by Harry's charms . . . one thing led to another . . . yes well, surely by the standards of some I might be called promiscuous.

I am not ashamed to admit that I have always been a woman of passionate emotions and powerful physical desires. I do not deny them. I came to full flower at an early age, and had always quite intimidated the awkward young men of my family's narrow social circle.

Harry was different. He was a man; I was drawn to him like a moth to flame. We began to see each other secretly. Both of us knew that Father would never condone our relationship and Harry was as anxious about being found out as I—for he knew that it would cost him his job. But we could not resist one another—we could not stay apart.

The very first time I lay with Harry I became with child—my daughter Hortense. Truly, I felt her burst into being in my womb in the consummation of our love. I must say, Harry behaved like a gentleman, and assumed full responsibility. He offered to marry me, which I flatly refused, for although I loved him, and still do, I am an independent, some might say, an unconventional woman. I was not prepared to marry. I would not, however, give up my child, and so without explanation I moved out of my parents' home and took up residence with my beloved in a shabby little house on the banks of the Chicago River, where we lived very simply and happily for a time.

Naturally, it was not long before Father learned about his foreman's deception, and promptly dismissed him. But Harry soon found work with one of Father's competitors and I, too, found employment. I went to work in a factory that processed prairie chickens for the Chicago market. It was filthy, exhausting work, for which my privileged upbringing had in no way prepared me. At the same time, and perhaps for the same reason, it was oddly liberating to be out in the real world, and making my own way there.

I gave birth to Hortense and almost immediately became pregnant again with my son William . . . sweet Willie. I tried to maintain contact with my parents—I wished them to know their grandchildren, and not to judge me too harshly for having chosen a different path for myself. But Mother was largely hysterical whenever I arranged to visit her—indeed, it is she, perhaps, who should have been institutionalized, not I—and Father was inflexible and refused to even see me when I came to the house. I finally stopped going there altogether, and kept up only a tenuous contact with the family through my older married sister, also named Hortense.

By the time I gave birth to Willie, Harry and I had begun to have some difficulties. I wonder now if Father's agents were already working on him, even then, for he seemed to change almost overnight, to become distant and remote. He began to drink and to stay out all night, and when he came home I could smell the other women on him. It broke my heart, for I still loved him. Still, I was more than ever glad that I had not married him.

It was on one such night when Harry was away that Father's blackguards came. They burst through the door of our house in the middle of the night accompanied by a nurse, who snatched up my babies and spirited them away as the men restrained me. I fought them for all I was worth— screaming, kicking, biting, and scratching, but, of course, to no avail. I have not seen my children since that dark night.

I was taken directly to the lunatic asylum, where I was consigned to lie in bed in my darkened room, day after day, week after week, month after month, with nothing to occupy my time but my daily torture and constant thoughts of my babies—I had no doubt they were living with Father and Mother. I did not know what had become of Harry and was haunted by thoughts of him . . . (Harry, my Harry, love of my life, father of my children, did Father reward you with pieces of gold to give me up to his ruffians in the middle of the night? Did you sell your own babies to him? Or did he simply have you murdered? Perhaps I shall never know the truth . . .)

All of my misery for the crime of falling in love with a common man. All of my heartbreak, torture, and punishment because I chose to bring you, my dearest children, into the world. All of my black and hopeless despair because I chose an unconventional life . . .

Ah, but surely nothing that has come before can be considered unconventional in light of where I am now going! Let me record the exact events that led me to be on this train: Two weeks ago, a man and a woman came into the ladies dayroom at the asylum. Owing to the nature of my "affliction"—my "moral perversion," as it was described in my commitment papers (a sham and a travesty—how many other women I wonder have been locked away like this for no just cause!), I was among those patients strictly segregated by gender, prohibited even from fraternizing with members of the opposite sex—presumably for fear that I might try to copulate with them. Good God! On the other hand, my diagnosis seemed to be considered an open invitation to certain male members of the asylum staff to visit my room in the middle of the night. How many times did I wake up, as if suffocating, with the weight of one particularly loathsome attendant named Franz pressed upon me, a fat stinking German, corpulent and sweating . . . God help me, I prayed to kill him.

The man and woman looked us over appraisingly as if we were cattle at auction, and then they chose six or seven among us to come with them to a private staff room. Conspicuously absent from this group were any of the older women or any of the hopelessly, irredeemably insane—those who sit rocking and moaning for hours on end, or who weep incessantly or hold querulous conversations with their demons. No, these poor afflicted were passed over and the more "presentable" of us lunatics chosen for an audience with our visitors.

After we had retired to the private staff room, the gentleman, a Mr. Benton, explained that he was interviewing potential recruits for a government program that involved the Indians of the Western plains. The woman, who he introduced as Nurse Crowley, would, with our consent, perform a physical examination upon us. Should we be judged, based on the interview and examination, to be suitable candidates for the program, we might be eligible for immediate release from this hospital. Yes! Naturally, I was intrigued by the proposal. Yet there was a further condition of family consent, which I had scant hope of ever obtaining.

Still I volunteered my full cooperation. Truly, even an

interview and a physical examination seemed preferable to the endless hours of agonizing monotony spent sitting or lying in bed, with nothing to pass the time besides foreboding thoughts about the injustice of my sentence and the devastating loss of my babies—the utter hopelessness of my situation and the awful anticipation of my next "treatment."

"Did I have any reason to believe that I was not fruitful?"—this was the first question posed to me by Nurse Crowley at the beginning of her examination. I must say I was taken aback—but I answered promptly, already having set my mind to passing this test, whatever its purpose. *"Au contraire!"* I said, and I told the nurse of the two precious children I had already borne out of wedlock, the son and daughter, who were so cruelly torn from their mother's bosom.

"Indeed," I said, "so fruitful am I that if my beloved Harry Ames, Esq., simply gazed upon me with a certain romantic longing in his eyes, babes sprang from my loins like seed spilling from a grain sack!"

(I must mention the unmentionable: the sole reason I did not become with child by the repulsive attendant Franz, the monster who visited me by night, is that the pathetic cretin sprayed his revolting discharge on my bedcovers, humping and moaning and weeping bitterly in his premature agonies.)

I feared that I may have gone too far in my enthusiasm to impress Nurse Crowley with my fertility, for she looked at me with that tedious and by now all too familiar expression of guardedness with which people regard the insane—and the alleged insane alike—as if our maladies might be contagious.

But apparently I passed my initial examination, for next I was interviewed by Mr. Benton himself, who also asked me a series of distinctly queer questions: Did I know how to cook over a campfire? Did I enjoy spending time outdoors?

Did I enjoy sleeping out overnight? What was my personal estimation of the western savage?

"The western savage?" I interrupted. "Having never met any western savages, Sir, it would be difficult for me to have formed any estimation of them one way or another."

Finally Mr. Benton got down to the business at hand: "Would you be willing to make a great personal sacrifice in the service of your government?" he asked.

"But of course," I answered without hesitation.

"Would you consider an arranged marriage to a western savage for the express purpose of bearing a child with him?"

"Hah!" I barked a laugh of utter astonishment. "But why on earth?" I asked, more curious than offended. "For what purpose?"

"To ensure a lasting peace on the Great Plains," Mr. Benton answered. "To provide safe passage to our courageous settlers from the constant depredations of the bloodthirsty barbarians."

"I see," I said, but of course, I did not altogether.

"As part of our agreement," added Mr. Benton, "your President will demonstrate his eternal gratitude to you by arranging for your immediate release from this institution."

"Truly? I would be released from this place?" I asked, trying to conceal the trembling in my voice.

"That is absolutely guaranteed," he said, "assuming that your legal guardian, if such exists, is willing to sign the necessary consent forms."

Already I was formulating my plan for this last major hurdle to my freedom, and again I answered without a moment's hesitation. I stood and curtsied deeply, weak in the knees, both from my months of idle confinement and pure excitement at the prospect of freedom: "I should be deeply honored, Sir, to perform this noble duty for my country," I said, "to offer my humble services to the President of the United States." The truth is that I would have gladly signed on for a trip to Hell to escape the lunatic asylum . . . and, yet, perhaps that is exactly what I have done . . .

As to the critical matter of obtaining my parents' consent, let me say in preface, that although I may have been accused of insanity and promiscuity, no one has ever taken me for an idiot.

It was the responsibility of the hospital's chief physician, my own preposterous diagnostician, Dr. Sidney Kaiser, to notify the families of those patients under consideration for the BFI program (these initials stand for "Brides for Indians" as Mr. Benton explained to us) and invite them to the hospital to be informed of the program and to obtain their signatures on the necessary release papers—at which time the patients would be free to participate in the program if they so chose. In the year and a half that I had been incarcerated there against my will, I had, as I may have mentioned, been visited only twice by the good doctor. However, through my repeated but futile efforts to obtain an audience with him, I had become acquainted with his assistant, Martha Atwood, a fine woman who took pity on me, who befriended me. Indeed, Martha became my sole friend and confidante in that wretched place. Without her sympathy and visits, and the many small kindnesses she bestowed upon me, I do not know how I could have survived.

As we came to know one another, Martha was more than ever convinced that I did not belong in the asylum, that I was no more insane than she, and that, like other women there, I had been committed unjustly by my family. When this opportunity presented itself for me to "escape," she agreed to help me in my desperate plan. First she "borrowed" correspondence from Father out of my file in Dr. Kaiser's office, and she had made a duplicate of his personal letterhead. Together we forged a letter in Father's hand, written to Dr. Kaiser, in which Father explained that he was traveling on business and would be unable to attend the proposed meeting at the institution. Dr. Kaiser would have no reason to question this; he was aware of Father's position as president of the Chicago and Northwestern Railroad, for which Father had designed and built the entire grain-elevator system—the largest and most advanced such warehouse in the city, as he is forever reminding us. Father's job involved nearly constant travel, and as a child I rarely saw him. In our forged letter to Dr. Kaiser, Martha and I, or I should say "Father," wrote that the family had recently been contacted directly by the government regarding my participation in the BFI program and that Agent Benton had personally guaranteed him my safety for the duration of my stay in Indian territory. Because Martha had been privy to the entire interview process, I knew that I had passed all the necessary requirements and had been judged to be a prime candidate for the program (not that this represents any great accomplishment on my part considering that the main criterion for acceptance was that one be of childbearing age and condition, and not so insane as to be incapacitated. It is, I believe, safe to say that the government was less interested in the success of these matrimonial unions than they were in meeting their quota—something that Father, ever the businessman and pragmatist could appreciate).

Thus in our letter, Father gave his full blessing for me to participate in, as I believe we wrote "this exciting and high-minded plan to assimilate the heathens." I know that Father has always viewed the western savages primarily as an impediment to the growth of American agriculture—he detests the notion of all that fertile plain going to waste when

it could be put to good Biblical use filling his grain eleva-
tors. The truth is, Father harbors a deep-seated hatred of
the Red Man simply for being a poor businessman—a short-
coming which Father believes to be the most serious character flaw of all. At his and Mother's endless dinner parties he
is fond of giving credit to his and his wealthy guests' great
good fortunes by toasting the Sac Chief Black Hawk, who
once said that "land cannot be sold. Nothing can be sold but
for those things that can be carried away"—a notion that
Father found enormously quaint and amusing.

Too—and I must acknowledge this fact—I believe that
secretly Father might actually have appreciated this opportunity to be rid of me, of the shame that my behavior, my "condition" has brought on our family. For if the truth be known,
Father is a terrible snob. In his circle of friends and business
cronies the stigma of having a lunatic—or, even worse, a
sexually promiscuous daughter—must have been nearly unbearable for him.

So he went on in his letter, in his typically overblown but
distracted manner—in the same tone he might employ if he
were giving permission for me to be sent off to finishing
school for young ladies (perhaps it is simply due to the fact
that the same blood flows through our veins, but it was almost diabolically simple for me to imitate Father's writing
style)—to state his conviction that the "bracing Western air,
the hearty native life in the glorious out-of-doors, and the
fascinating cultural exchange might be just what my poor
wayward daughter requires to set her addled mind right
again." It is an astonishing thing, is it not, the notion of a
father being asked (and giving!) permission for his daughter to copulate with savages?

Enclosed with Father's letter were the signed hospital
release papers, all of which Martha had delivered by pri-

vate messenger to Dr. Kaiser's office—a tidy and ultimately perfectly convincing little package.

Of course, when her part in the deception was discovered, as it surely would be, Martha knew that she faced immediate dismissal—possibly even criminal prosecution. And thus it is, that my true, intrepid friend—childless and loveless (and if the truth be told rather plain to look upon), facing in all probability a life of spinsterhood and loneliness—enlisted in the BFI program herself. She rides beside me on this very train . . . and so at least I do not embark alone on this greatest adventure of my life.

24 March 1875

It would be disingenuous of me to say that I have no trepidations about the new life that awaits us. Mr. Benton assured us that we are contractually obligated to bear but one child with our Indian husbands, after which time we are free to go, or stay, as we choose. Should we fail to become with child, we are required to remain with our husbands for two full years, after which time we are free to do as we wish . . . or, at least, so say the authorities. It has not failed to occur to me that perhaps our new husbands might have different thoughts about this arrangement. Still, it seems to me a rather small price to pay to escape that living Hell of an asylum to which I would quite likely have been committed for the rest of my life. But now that we have actually embarked upon this journey, our future so uncertain, and so unknown, it is impossible not to have misgivings. How ironic that in order to escape the lunatic asylum I have had to embark upon the most insane undertaking of my life.

But honestly, I believe that poor naive Martha is eager

for the experience; excited about her matrimonial prospects, she seems to be fairly blooming in anticipation! Why just a few moments ago she asked me, in rather a breathless voice, if I might give her some advice about carnal matters! (It appears that, due to the reason given for my incarceration, everyone connected with the institution—even my one true friend—seems to consider me somewhat of an authority in such matters.)

"What sort of advice, dear friend?" I asked.

Now Martha became terribly shy, lowered her voice even further, leaned forward, and whispered. "Well . . . advice about . . . about how best to make a man happy . . . I mean to say, about how to satisfy the cravings of a man's flesh."

I laughed at her charming innocence. Martha hopes to carnally satisfy her savage! "Let us assume, first of all," I answered, "that the aboriginals are similar in their physical needs to men of our own noble race. And we have no reason to believe otherwise, do we? If indeed all men are similarly disposed in matters of the heart and of the flesh, it is my limited experience that the best way to make them happy—if that is your true goal—is to wait on them hand and foot, cook for them, have sexual congress whenever and wherever they desire—but never initiate the act yourself and do not demonstrate any forwardness or longings of your own; this appears to frighten men—most of whom are merely little boys pretending to be men. And, perhaps most importantly, just as most men fear women who express their physical longings, so they dislike women who express opinions—of any sort and on any subject. All these things I learned from Mr. Harry Ames. Thus I would recommend that you agree unequivocably with everything your new husband says . . . oh, yes, one final thing—let him believe that he is extremely well endowed, even if, especially if, he is not."

"But how will I know whether or not he is well endowed?" asked my poor innocent Martha.

"My dear," I answered. "You do know the difference between, let us say, a breakfast sausage and a bratwurst? A *cornichon* and a cucumber? A pencil and a pine tree?"

Martha blushed a deep shade of crimson, covered her mouth, and began to giggle uncontrollably. And I, too, laughed with her. It occurs to me how long it has been since I really laughed . . . it does feel wonderful to laugh again.

27 March 1875

My Dearest Sister Hortense,

You have by this time perhaps heard news of my sudden departure from Chicago. My sole regret is that I was unable to be present when the family was notified of the circumstances of my "escape" from the "prison" from which you had all conspired to commit me. I would especially have enjoyed seeing Father's reaction when he learned that I am soon to become a bride—yes, that's right, I am to wed, and perforce, couple with a genuine Savage of the Cheyenne Nation!— Hah! Speaking of moral perversion. I can just hear Father blustering: "My God, she really is insane!" What I would give to see his face!

Now, truly, haven't you always known that your poor wayward little sister would one day embark on such an adventure, perform such a momentous deed? Imagine me, if you are able, riding this rumbling train west into the great unknown void of the frontier. Can you picture two more different lives than ours? You within the snug (though how dreary it must be!) confines of the Chicago bourgeoisie, married to your pale banker Walter Woods, with your brood of pale offspring—how many are there now, I lose track, four, five, six of the little monsters?—each as colorless and shapeless as unkneaded bread dough.

But forgive me, my sister, if I appear to be attacking you. It is only that I may now, at last—freely and without censor or fear of recriminations—voice my anger to those among my own family who so ill-treated me; I can speak my mind without the constant worry of further confirming my insanity, without the ever-present danger that my children will be torn from me forever—for all this has come to pass, and I have nothing left to lose. At last I am free—in body, mind, and spirit . . . or as free as one can be who has purchased her freedom with her womb . . .

But enough of that . . . now I must tell you something of my adventure, of our long journey, of the extraordinary country I am seeing. I must tell you of all that is fascinating and lonely and desolate . . . you who have barely set foot outside Chicago, can simply not imagine it all. The city is bursting at its very seams, abustle with rebuilding out of the ashes of the devastating great fire, expanding like a living organism out into the prairie (well, is it any wonder then that the savages rebel as they are pushed ever further west?). You cannot imagine the crowds, the human congress, the sheer activity on what used to be wild prairie when we were children. Our train passed through the new stockyard district— very near the neighborhood where Harry and I lived. (You never did come to visit us, did you, Hortense? . . . Why does that not surprise me?) There the smokestacks spew clouds of all colors of the rainbow—blue and orange and red— which when they enter the air seem to intermingle like oil paints mixed on a palette. It is quite beautiful in a grotesque sort of way, like the paintings of a mad god. Past the slaughterhouses, where the terrified cries of dumb beasts can be heard even over the steady din of the train, their sickening stench filling the car like rancid syrup. Finally the train burst from the shroud of smoke that blankets the city, as though it had come out of a dense fog into the clear-plowed farm country, the freshly turned soil black and rich, Father's beloved grain crops just beginning to break ground.

I must tell you that in spite of Father's insistence to the contrary, the true beauty of the prairie lies not in the perfect symmetry of farmlands, but where the farmlands end and the real prairie begins—a sea of natural grass like a living, breathing thing undulating all the way to the horizon. Today I saw prairie chickens, flocks of what must have been hundreds, thousands, flushing away in clouds from the tracks as we passed. I could only imagine the sound of their wings over the roar of the train. How extraordinary to see them on the wing like this after the year I spent laboring in that wretched factory where we processed the birds and where I thought I could never bear to look at another chicken as long as I lived. I know that you and the rest of the family could not understand my decision to take such menial work or to live out of wedlock with a man so far beneath my station in life, and that this has always been spoken of among you as the first outward manifestation of my insanity. But, don't you see, Hortense, it was precisely our cloistered upbringing under Mother and Father's roof that spurred me to seek contact with a larger world. I'd have suffocated, died of sheer boredom, if I stayed any longer in that dark and dreary house, and although the work I took in the factory was indeed loathsome, I will never regret having done it. I learned so much from the men and women with whom I toiled; I learned how the rest of the world—families less fortunate than ours, which, of course constitutes the vast majority of people—lives. This is something you can never know, dear sister, and which you will always be poorer in soul for having missed.

Not that I recommend to you a job in the chicken factory! Good God, I shall never get over the stink of it, my hands even now when I hold them up to my face seem to reek of chicken blood, feathers, and innards . . . I think that I shall never eat poultry again as long as I live! But I must say my interest in the birds is somewhat renewed in seeing the wild creatures flying up before the train like sparks from the wheels. They are so beautiful, fanning off against the setting sun, their tangents helping to break the long straight tedium of this journey. I have tried to interest my friend Martha, who sits beside me, in this spectacle of wings, but she is very soundly asleep, her head jostling gently against the train window.

But here has occurred an amusing encounter: As I was watching the birds flush from the tracks, a tall, angular, very pale woman with short-cropped sandy hair under an English tweed cap came hurrying down the aisle of our car, stooping to look out each window at the birds and then moving on to the next seat. She wears a man's knickerbocker suit of Irish thornproof, in which, with her short hair and cap it might be easy to mistake her for a member of the opposite sex. Her mannish outfit includes a waistcoat, stockings, and heavy walking brogues, and she carries an artist's sketch pad.

"Excuse me, please, won't you?" the woman asked of each occupant of each seat in front of which she leaned in order to improve her view out the window. She spoke with a distinct British accent. "Do please excuse me. Oh, my goodness!" she exclaimed, her eyebrows raised in an expression of delighted surprise. "Extraordinary! Magnificent! Glorious!"

By the time the Englishwoman reached the unoccupied seat beside me the prairie chickens had set their wings and sailed off over the horizon and she flopped down in the seat all gangly arms and legs. "Greater prairie chicken," she said. "That is to say, *Tympanuchus cupido*, actually a member of the grouse family, commonly referred to as the prairie chicken. The first I've ever seen in the wilds, although, of course, I've seen specimens. And of course I have studied extensively the species' eastern cousin, the heath hen, during my travels about New England. Named after the Greek *tympananon*, 'kettledrum,' and *'echein,'* to have a drum, aluding both to the enlarged esophagus on the sides of the throat, which in the male becomes inflated during courtship, as well as to the booming sound which the males utter in their aroused state. And further named after the 'blind bow boy,' son of Venus— not, however with any illusion to erotic concerns, I should hasten to add, but because the long, erectile, stiff feathers are raised like small rounded wings over the head of the male in his courtship display, and have therefore been likened to Cupid's wings."

Now the woman suddenly turned as if noticing me for the first time, and with the same look of perpetual surprise still etched in her milk-pale English countenance—eyebrows raised and a delighted smile at her lips as if the world itself were not only wonderful, but absolutely startling. I liked her immediately. "Do please excuse me for prattling on, won't you? Helen Elizabeth Flight, here," she said, thrusting her hand forward with manly forthrightness. "Perhaps you're familiar with my work? My book *Birds of Britain* is currently in its third printing—letterpress provided by my dear companion and collaborator, Mrs. Ann Hall of Sunderland. Unfortunately, Mrs. Hall was too ill to accompany me when I embarked on my tour of America to gather specimens and make sketches for our next opus, *Birds of America*—not to be confused, of course, with Monsieur Audubon's series of the same name. An interesting artist, Mr. Audubon, if rather too fanciful for my tastes. I've always found his birds to be rendered with such . . . caprice! Clearly he threw biological accuracy to the wind. Wouldn't you agree?"

I could see that this question was intended to be somewhat more than rhetorical, but just as I was attempting to form an answer, Miss Flight asked: "And you are?" still looking at me with her eyebrows raised in astonished anticipation, as if my identity were not only a matter of the utmost urgency but also promised a great surprise.

"May Dodd," I answered.

"Ah, May Dodd! Quite," she said. "And a smart little picture of a girl you are, too. I suspected from your fair complexion that you might be of English descent."

"Scottish actually," I said, "but I'm thoroughly American, myself. I was born and raised in Chicago," I added somewhat wistfully.

"And don't tell me that a lovely creature like you has signed up to live with the savages?" asked Miss Flight.

"Why yes I have," I said. "And you?"

"I'm afraid that I've run a trifle short of research funds," explained Miss Flight with a small grimace of distaste for the subject. "My patrons were unwilling to advance me any more money for my American sojourn, and this seemed like quite the perfect opportunity for me to study the birdlife of the western prairies at no additional expense. A frightfully exciting adventure, don't you agree?"

"Yes," I said, with a laugh, "frightfully!"

"Although I must tell you a little secret," she said, looking around us to see that we were not overheard. "I am unable to have children myself. I'm quite sterile! The result of a childhood infection." Her eyebrows shot up with delight. "I lied to the examiner in order to be accepted into the program!

"Now you will excuse me, Miss Dodd, won't you?" said Miss Flight, suddenly all business again. "That is to say, I must quickly make some sketches and record my impressions of the magnificent greater prairie chicken while the experience is still fresh in mind. I hope, when the train next stops, to be able to descend and shoot a few as specimens. I've brought with me my scattergun, especially manufactured for this journey by Featherstone, Elder & Story of Newcastle upon Tyne. Perhaps you are interested in firearms? If so, I'd love to show it to you. My patrons, before they ran into financial difficulties and left me stranded on this vast continent, had the gun especially built for me, specifically for my travels in America. I'm rather proud of it. But do excuse me, won't you? I'm so terribly pleased to have met you. Wonderful that you're along! We must speak at greater length. I have a feeling that you and I are going to be spiffing good friends. You have the most extraordinarily blue eyes, you know, the color of an Eastern bluebird. I shall use them as a model to mix my palette when I paint that species if you don't terribly mind. And I'm fascinated to learn more of your opinion on Monsieur Audubon's work." And with that the daffy Englishwoman took her leave!

While we are on the subject, and since Martha is proving at present to be exceedingly dull company, let me describe to you, dear sister, some of my other fellow travelers, who provide the only other diversion on this long, straight, monotonous iron road through country that while beautiful in its vast and empty reaches, can hardly be described as scenic. I've barely had time yet to acquaint myself with all of the women, but our common purpose and destination seems to have fostered a certain easy familiarity among us—personal histories and intimacies are exchanged without the usual period of tedious social posturing or shyness. These women—hardly more than girls really—are all either from the Chicago area or other parts of the Middle West, and come from all circumstances. Some appear to be escaping poverty or failed romances, or, as in my case, unpleasant "living arrangements." Hah! While there is only one other girl from my asylum, there are several in our group from other such public facilities around the city. Some are considerably more eccentric even than I. But then it was my observation in the asylum that nearly every resident there took solace in the fact that they could point to someone else who was madder than they. One, named Ada Ware, dresses only in black, wears a widow's veil, and has perpetual dark circles of grief beneath her eyes. I have yet to see her smile or make any expression whatsoever. "Black Ada" the others call her.

You will, perhaps, remember Martha, whom you met on the sole occasion when you visited me in the asylum. She is a sweet thing, barely two years younger than I, though she seems younger, and homely as a stick. I am forever indebted to her, for it was Martha who was so invaluable in helping me to obtain my liberty.

As mentioned, one other girl from my own institution survived the selection process—while a number of others declined to accept Mr. Benton's offer. It seemed remarkable to me at the time that they would give up the opportunity for freedom from that ghastly place, simply because they were squeamish about conjugal relations with savages. Perhaps I will live to regret saying this, but how could it be any worse than incarceration in that dank hellhole for the rest of one's life?

This young girl's name is Sara Johnstone. She's a pretty, timid little creature, barely beyond the age of puberty. The poor thing evidently lacks the power of speech—by this I do not mean that she is simply the quiet sort—I mean that she seems unable, or at least unwilling, to utter a word. She and I had, perforce, very little contact at the hospital, and therefore hardly any opportunity to get to know one another. I have a suspicion that this will all change now, for she seems to have attached herself to me and Martha. She sits facing us on the train, and frequently leans forward with tears in her eyes to grasp my hand and squeeze it fiercely. I know nothing of her past or the reason why she was originally confined in the institution. She has no family and according to Martha had evidently been there long before I arrived— ever since she was a young child. Nor do I know who supported her there—as we both know that wretched place was not for charity cases. Martha has intimated that Dr. Kaiser himself, the director of the hospital, volunteered the poor girl for the program as a way of being rid of her—what Father might recognize as a cost-cutting measure—for according to Martha, the girl was treated very much like a "poor relation" in the hospital. Furthermore, though we are hardly free to discuss the matter with the poor thing sitting directly in front of us, Martha has suggested that the child may, in fact, have had some familial connection with the Good Doctor—possibly, we have speculated, she is the product of his own romantic liaison with a former patient? Although one must wonder what kind of man would send his own daughter away to live among savages . . . Whatever the child's situation, I find it troubling that she was accepted into this program. She is such a frail little thing, terrified of the world, and so obviously ill prepared for what must certainly prove to be an arduous duty. Indeed, how could she be prepared for any experience in the real world, having grown up behind brick walls and iron-barred windows? I am certain that, like Martha, the girl is without experience in carnal matters, unless the repulsive night monster Franz visited her, too, in the dark . . . which I pray for her sake that he did not. In any case, I intend to watch over the child, to protect her from harm if it is within my power to do so. Oddly, her very youth and fearfulness seem to give me strength and courage.

Ah, and here come the Kelly sisters of Chicago's Irish town, Margaret and Susan, swaggering down the aisle—redheaded, freckle-faced identical twin lassies, thick as thieves, which in their case is somewhat more than an idle expression. They take everything in, these two; their shrewd pale green eyes miss nothing; I clutch my purse to breast for safekeeping.

One of them, I cannot yet tell them apart, slips into the seat beside me. "'*Ave* ya got some tobacco on ye, May?" she asks in a conspiratorial tone, as if we are the very best of friends though I hardly know the girl. "I'd be *loookin'* to roll me a smoke."

"I'm afraid I don't smoke," I answer.

"*Aye*, 'twas easier to get a smoke in prison, than it is on this damn train," she says. "Isn't that so, Meggie?"

"It's *sartain*, Susie," Meggie answers.

"Do you mind my asking why you girls were in prison?" I ask. I tilt my notebook toward them. "I'm writing a letter to my sister."

"Why, we don't mind *at-tall*, dear," says Meggie, who leans on the seat in front of me. "Prostitution and Grand Theft—ten-year sentences in the Illinois State Penitentiary."

She says this with real bravado in her voice as if it is a thing of which to be very proud, and as I write she leans down closer to make sure that I record the details correctly. "*Aye*, don't forget the Grand Theft," she repeats, pointing her finger at my notebook.

"Right, Meggie," adds Susan, nodding her head with satisfaction. "And we'd not have been apprehended, either, if it weren't for the fact that the gentleman we turned over in Lincoln Park '*appened* to be a municipal *jeewдge. Aye*, the old reprobate tried to solicit us for sexual favors. 'Twins!' he said. 'Two halves of a bun around my sausage' he desired to make of us. Ah ya beggar!—we gave him two halves of a brick on either side of his damn head, we did! In two shakes of a lamb's tail we had his pocket watch and his wallet in our possession—thinking in our ignorance what great good fortune that he was carrying *sech* a large *soom* of cash. No doubt His *Jeewдgeship's* weekly bribe revenue."

"It's *sartain*, Susie, and that would've been the end of it," chimes in Margaret, "if it weren't for that damn cash. The *jeewдge* went directly to his great good pal the Commissioner of Police and a *manhoont* the likes of which Chicago has never before seen was launched to bring the infamous Kelly twins to *juicetice!*"

"'*Tis* the God's own truth, Meggie," says Susan, shaking her head. "You probably read about us in the newspaper, Missy," she says to me. "We were quite famous for a time, me and Meggie. After a short trial, which the public advocate charged with our defense spent nappin'—the old bugger—we were sentenced to ten years in the penitentiary. *Aye*, ten years just for defendin' our honor against a lecherous old *jeewдge*, with a pocketful of bribe money, if you can believe that, Missy."

"And your parents?" I ask. "Where are they?"

"Oh, we *'ave* no idea, darlin','" says Margaret. "We were foundlings, you see. Wee babies left on the steps of the church. Isn't that so, Susie? Grew up in the city's Irish orphanage, but we didn't really care for the place. *Aye*, we been living by our wits ever since we *roon* away from there when we were just ten years old."

Now Margaret stands straight again and scans the other passengers with a certain predatory interest. Her gaze comes to rest on the woman sitting across the aisle from us—a woman named Daisy Lovelace; I have only spoken to her briefly, but I know that she is a Southerner and has the distinct look of ruined gentry about her. She holds an ancient dirty white French poodle on her lap. The dog's hair is stained red around its butt and muzzle, and around its rheumy, leaking eyes.

"Wouldn't *'appen* to *'ave* a bit of tobacco, on ye, Missy, would *ya* now?" Margaret asks her.

"*Ah'm* afraid *naught*," says the woman in a slow drawl, and in not a particularly friendly tone.

"*Loovely* little dog, you've got there," says Margaret, sliding into the seat beside the Southerner. "What's its name, if you don't mind *me* askin'?" The twin's insinuating manner is transparent; it is clear that she is not interested in the woman's dog.

Ignoring her, the Lovelace woman sets her dog down on the floor between their feet. "You go on now an' make *teetee*, *Feeern Loueeese*," she coos to it in an accent as thick as cane molasses, "*Go wan* now, sweet*haart*. You make *teetee* for Momma." And the wretched little creature totters stiffly up the aisle sniffling and snorting, finally squatting to pee by a vacant seat.

"Fern Louise, is it then?" says Meggie. "Isn't that a grand name, Susie?"

"*Loovely*, Meggie," Susan says. "A *loovely* little dog."

Still ignoring them, the Southern woman pulls a small silver flask from her purse and takes a quick sip, which act is of great interest to the twins.

"Is that whiskey you've got there, Missy?" Margaret asks.

"No, it is *naught* whiskey," says the woman coolly. "It is *mah nuurve* medicine, doctor's order, and *no*, you may not have a taste of it."

The twins have met their match with this one I can see!

Now here comes my friend, Gretchen Fathauer, bulling her way down the aisle of the train, swinging her arms and singing some Swiss folksong in a robust voice. Gretchen never fails to cheer us all up. She is a big-hearted, enthusiastic soul—a large, boisterous, buxom, rosy-cheeked lass who looks like she might be able to spawn single-handedly all the babes that the Cheyenne nation might require.

By now we all know Gretchen's history almost as well as our own: Her family were immigrants from Switzerland, who settled on the upland prairie west of Chicago to farm wheat when Gretchen was a girl. But the family farm failed after a series of bad harvests caused by harsh winters, blight, and insect attack, and Gretchen was forced to leave home as a young woman and seek employment in the city. She found work as a domestic with the McCormick family—yes, the very same—Father's dear friend Cyrus McCormick, who invented the reaper . . . isn't it odd, Hortense, to think that we probably visited the McCormicks in our youth at the same time that Gretchen was employed there—but of course we would never have paid any attention to the bovine Swiss chambermaid.

Gretchen longed to have a family of her own and one day she answered an advertisement in the *Tribune* seeking "mail-order" brides for western settlers. She posted her application and several months later was notified that she had been paired with a homesteader from Oklahoma Territory. Her intended was to meet her at the train station in St. Louis on an appointed day, and convey her to her new home. Gretchen gave notice to the McCormicks and two weeks later boarded the train to St. Louis. But alas, although she has a heart of gold, Gretchen is terribly plain ... indeed, I must confess that she is rather more than plain, to the extent that one of the less kind members of our expedition has referred to the poor dear as "Miss Potato Face" ... and even those more charitable among us must admit that her countenance does have a certain unfortunate tuberous quality.

Well, Gretchen's intended had only to take one look at her, with which he excused himself under pretense of fetching his baggage, and Gretchen never laid eyes on the miserable cur again. She tells the story now with great good humor, but she was clearly devastated. She had given up everything—and was now abandoned at the train station in a strange city, with only her suitcase, a few personal effects, and the meager savings from her former employment. She could not bear the humiliation of going back to Chicago and asking the McCormicks for her old job. Nor was the possibility of returning to her family, shamed thusly by matrimonial rejection, any more appealing to her. No, Gretchen was determined to have a husband and children one way or another. She sat on the bench at the train station and wept openly at her plight. It was at that very moment that a gentleman approached her. He handed her a small paper flyer on which was printed the following:

If you are a healthy young woman of childbearing age, who seeks matrimony, exotic travel, and adventure, please present yourself to

*the following address promptly at 9:00 a.m., Thursday morning on
the twelfth day of February, the year of our Lord, 1875.*

Gretchen laughs when she tells the story—a great hearty
bellow—and says in her heavy accent, "*Vell*, you know, I *tought*
this young fellow must be a messenger from God, I truly do.
And *ven* I go to to *dis* place, and *dey* ask me if I like to marry a
Cheyenne Indian fellow and have his babies, I say: '*Vell*, I *tink
de* savages not be so *chooosy*, as *dat* farmer *yah*? Sure, *vy* not? I
make *beeg*, strong babies for my new *hustband*. *Yah*, I feed *da*
whole damn nursery, *yah*?'" And Gretchen pounds her massive breast and laughs and laughs.

Which causes all the rest of us to laugh with her.

Unable to break the Southern woman's steely indifference
to them, the Kelly sisters have moved on to try their luck in
the next car. They remind me of a pair of red foxes prowling
a meadow for whatever they might turn up.

Just now as I was writing, my new friend, Phemie, came
to sit beside me. Euphemia Washington is her full name—a
statuesque colored girl who came to Chicago via Canada.
She is about my same age, and quite striking, I should say
nearly fierce, in appearance, being over six feet in height,
with beautiful skin, the color of burnished mahogany—a
finely formed nose with fiercely flared nostrils, and full Negro lips. I'm sure, dear sister, that you and the family will find
it perfectly scandalous to learn that I am now fraternizing
with Negroes. But on this train all are equal, at least such is
the case in my egalitarian mind.

"I am writing a letter to my sister at home," I said to her,
"describing the circumstances of some of the girls on the
train. Tell me how you came to be here, Phemie, so that I
may make a full report to her."

At this she chuckled, a rich warm laugh that seemed to issue from deep in her chest. "You are the first person who has asked me that, May," she said. "And why would your sister be interested in the nigger girl? Some of the others seem quite distressed that I am along." Phemie is very well spoken, with the most lovely, melodic voice that I've ever heard—deep and resonant, her speech like a poem, a song.

It occurred to me that, truth be told, you, dear sister, probably would not be interested in hearing about the nigger girl. Of course, this I did not say to Phemie.

"How did you happen to go to Canada, Phemie?" I asked.

She chuckled again. "You don't think that I look like a native Canadian, May?"

"You look like an African, Phemie," I said bluntly. "An African princess!"

"Yes, my mother came from a tribe called the Ashanti," Phemie said. "The greatest warriors in all of Africa," she added. "One day when she was a young girl she was gathering firewood with her mother and the other women. She fell behind, and sat down to rest. She was not worried, for she knew that her mother would return for her. As she sat, leaning against a tree, she fell asleep. And when she woke up, men from another tribe, who spoke a tongue she did not understand, stood round her. She was only a child, and she was very frightened.

"They took her away to a strange place, and kept her there in chains. Finally she was put in the hold of a ship with hundreds of others. She was many weeks at sea. She did not know what was happening to her, and she still believed that her mother would come back for her. She never stopped believing that. It kept her alive.

"The ship finally reached a city the likes of which my mother had never before seen or imagined. Many had died en route but she had lived. In the city she was sold at auction to a white man, a cotton shipper, who owned a fleet of sailing vessels in the port city of Apalachicola, Florida.

"My mother's first master was very good to her," Phemie continued. "He took her into his home where she did domestic duties and even received a bit of education. She learned to read and write, a thing unheard of among the other slaves. And when she became a young woman, her master took her into his bed.

"I was the child born of this union," Phemie said. "I, too, grew up in that house, where I was given lessons in the kitchen by the tutor of Master's 'real' children—his white family. Eventually the mistress discovered the truth of my parentage—perhaps she finally saw some resemblance between the kitchen nigger's child and her own children. And one night when I was not yet seven years old, two men, slave merchants, came and took me away—just as my mother had been taken from her family. She wept and pleaded and fought the men, but they struck her and knocked her to the ground. That was the last time I ever saw my mother, lying unconscious with her face battered and bleeding . . ." Phemie paused here and looked out the train window, tears glistening in the corners of her eyes.

"I was sold to the owner of a plantation outside Savannah, Georgia," she continued. "He was a bad man, an evil man. He drank and treated his slaves with terrible cruelty. The first day that I arrived there he had me branded on the back with his own initials . . . Yes, he burned his initials into the flesh of all his slaves so that they would be easily identified if ever they ran away. I was still just a child, eight years old, but after the first week that I was there, the man began to have me sent to his private quarters at night. I do not need to tell you what happened there . . . I was badly hurt . . .

"Several years passed this way," she went on in a softer voice. "Then one day a Canadian natural scientist came to visit the plantation. He came under the guise of studying the flora and fauna there—but he was an abolitionist and his true purpose was to spread the word to the slaves about the underground railroad. He carried excellent letters of introduction and was unwittingly welcomed at all the plantations. Because I had a little education, and because I had always been fascinated with wild things of all kinds, my master charged me with accompanying the naturalist on his daily excursions to collect specimens. Over the several days of his visit, the man spoke to me often of Canada, told me that every man, woman, and child lived free and equal there—that none was owned by another. The scientist liked me and took pity on me. He told me that I was too young to attempt to escape alone but that I should encourage some of the older slaves to take me with them. He showed me maps of the best routes north and gave me the names of people along the way who would help us.

"I spoke to some of the others, but all were too terrified of the Master to attempt such an escape. They had seen what Master did to runaway slaves who were returned to him.

"One night a week or so after the man left, after I had returned weeping and in great pain to the slaves quarters from Master's bedroom, I made a bundle of a few clothes and what little food I could gather and I left alone. I did not care if I died trying to escape. Death seemed welcome compared to my life.

"I was young and strong," Phemie said, "and over the next several nights I ran through the forest and swamps and canebrakes. I never stopped running. Sometimes I could hear the hounds baying behind me, but the naturalist had instructed me to wade up streambeds and across ponds, which would cause the dogs to lose the scent. I ran and I ran.

"For weeks I traveled north, moving by night, hiding in the undergrowth during the day. I ate what I could scavenge in the forest and fields, wild roots and greens, sometimes a bit of fruit or vegetables stolen from farms or gardens. I was hungry and often I did not know where I was, but I kept the North Star always before me and I looked for landmarks which the scientist had described to me. Often I longed to go into the towns I passed to beg a little food, but I dared not. Upon my back I still wore Master's brand, and if captured I would surely be returned to him and terribly punished.

"In those weeks alone in the wilderness, I began to remember the stories my mother had told me of her own people, of the men hunting and the women gathering from the earth. I would never have survived my journey to the land of freedom were it not for what my mother had taught me about the wilds. My grandmother's knowledge, passed down through my mother, saved my life. It was as if, all these years later, my mother's mother came back for me just as she had always believed she would come for her . . .

"It was several months before I finally crossed into Canada," Phemie continued. "There I called on people whose names the naturalist had given me and eventually I was placed in the home of a doctor's family. I was well treated there and was able to continue my education. I lived with the doctor and his family for almost ten years—I worked for them and was paid an honest wage for my labors.

"One day I happened to see a small notice in the newspaper requesting young single women of any race, creed, or color to participate in an important volunteer program on the American frontier. I answered the advertisement . . . and, here we are . . . you and I."

"But if you were happy with the doctor's family in Canada," I asked Phemie, "why did you wish to leave there, to come on this mad adventure?"

"They were fine people," Phemie said. "I loved them and will be forever grateful to them. But you see, May, I was still a servant. I was paid for my work, that is true, but I was still a servant to white folks. I dreamed of more for myself, I dreamed to be a free woman, truly free, on my own and beholden to no others. I owed that to my mother, and to my people. I know that as a white woman, it must be difficult for you to understand this."

I patted Phemie on the back of her hand. "You'd be surprised, Phemie," I said, "at how well I understand the longing for freedom."

But now an ugly thing has occurred, spoiling the moment. As Phemie and I were sitting together, the Southern woman Daisy Lovelace, seated across the aisle, set her ancient miserable little poodle down on the seat beside her and said in a voice so loud that we couldn't help but turn to look. "*Feeern Loueeese*," she said, "would you rather be a *niggah*, or would you rather be *daid*?" upon which cue the little dog teetered stiffly and then rolled over on its back with its little bowed legs sticking straight in the air. Miss Lovelace shrieked with mean-spirited laughter.

"Wretched woman!" I muttered. "Pay no attention to her, Phemie."

"Of course I don't," Phemie said, unconcerned. "The poor soul is drunk, May, and believe me, I've heard far worse than that. I'm sure that such a parlor trick was a source of great amusement to her plantation friends. And now she finds herself among our motley group, where she must at least assert her superiority over the nigger girl. I think we should not judge her just yet."

I have dozed off, with my head on Phemie's shoulder, only to be rudely awakened by the shrill voice of a dreadful woman named Narcissa White, an evangelical Episcopalian who is enrolled in the program under the auspices of the American Church Missionary Society. Now Miss White comes bustling down the aisle of the train passing out religious pamphlets. "'Ye who enter the wilderness without faith shall perish' said the Lord Jesus Christ," she preaches, and other such nonsense, which only serves to further agitate the others—some of whom already seem as skittish as cattle going to the slaughterhouse.

I'm afraid that Miss White and I have taken an instant dislike to one another, and I fear that we are destined to become bitter enemies. She is enormously tiresome and bores us all witless with her sanctimonious attitudes and evangelical rantings. As you well know, Hortense, I have never had much interest in the church. Perhaps the hypocrisy inherent in Father's position as a church elder, while remaining one of the least Christ-like men I've ever known, has something to do with my general cynicism toward organized religion of all kinds.

The White woman has already stated that she has no intention of bearing a child with her Cheyenne husband, nor indeed of having conjugal relations with him, and she assures us that she signed up for this mission strictly as a means of giving herself to the Lord Jesus—to save the soul of her heathen intended by teaching him "the ways of Christ and the true path to salvation," as she puts it in her most pious manner. Evidently she intends to distribute her pamphlets among the savages, and seemed not in the least deterred when I pointed out to her that very likely they won't be able to read them. It may be blasphemous for me to say so, but personally, I believe that our Christian God as He is represented by the likes of Miss White may be of somewhat limited use to the savages . . .

I will write to you again soon, my dearest sister . . .

31 March 1875

We crossed the Missouri River three days ago, spending one night in a boardinghouse in Omaha. Our military escort, or "guard" as I prefer to call them, treat us more as prisoners than as volunteers in the service of our government—they are contemptuous and snide, and have a gratingly familiar air that suggests some knowledge of the Faustian bargain we have struck with our government. None of us was permitted to go abroad in Omaha, nor even allowed to leave the boardinghouse—perhaps they fear that we might have a change of heart and seek to escape.

The next morning we boarded another train, which for the past two days has followed along a bluff overlooking the Platte River—not much of a river really—wide, slow-moving, and turgid.

We passed through the little settlement of Grand Island, where we took on supplies but were not permitted to disembark, westward through the muddy village of North Platte, where we were once again forbidden to so much as stretch our legs at the station. We did witness a remarkable spectacle yesterday morning at dawn—thousands, no I would more accurately guess, millions of cranes on the river. As if by some signal, perhaps simply frightened by the passing of our train, they all suddenly took flight, rising off the water as one being, like an enormous sheet lifted by the wind. Our British ornithologist, Miss Flight, was absolutely beside herself, rendered all but speechless by the spectacle. "Glorious!" she said, patting her flat chest. "Absolutely glorious!" Truly I thought the woman's eyebrows were going to shoot right off the top of her head. "A masterpiece," she marveled. "God's masterpiece!" I found this at first to be an odd remark, but soon realized how accurate a description it really was. The birds made a noise we could hear even over the roar of our locomotive. A million wings—imagine it!— like the sound of rumbling thunder or a waterfall, punctuated by the strange, otherworldly cries of the cranes, their wingbeats at once ponderous and elegant, their bodies so large that flight seemed improbable, legs dangling awkwardly beneath them like the rag tails of a child's kite. God's masterpiece . . . and perhaps after my long, spartan confinement behind four walls and a locked door such a spectacle of freedom and fecundity seems even more wonderful. Ah, but on this morning the earth seems like an especially fine place to be alive and free! I think that I shall not mind living in the wilderness . . .

I have no true sense of this strange new country yet. Compared to Illinois, the vast prairies hereabouts seem more arid, less productive, and the few farms that we pass down in the river floodplain appear poor—boggy and undeveloped. The people working in the fields look gaunt-eyed and discouraged as if they have given up already any dreams of success or prosperity. We passed one poor fellow trying futilely to plow a flooded field with a team of oxen; it was clearly a hopeless endeavor, for his oxen were mired up to their chests in the mud, and the man finally sat down himself and put his head dejectedly in his arms, looking as though he was going to weep.

I suspect that the uplands are better suited to the cattle business than are these marshy lowlands to agriculture. Indeed, the further west we move the more bovines we encounter—a variety of cattle that is quite different from anything I have ever seen back in Illinois, longer-legged, rangier, and wilder, with long, gracefully arced horns. Yesterday we saw a colorful sight—a herd of what must have been several thousand cows being driven across the river by "cowboys." The engineer had to stop the train for fear of a collision with the beasts, thus giving us a wonderful opportunity to observe the scene. Of course, I have read about the cowboys in periodicals and I have seen artists' renderings of them and now I find that they are every bit as colorful and festive in the flesh. Martha blushed quite crimson at the sight of them—a charming habit she has when excited—and an exciting scene it was, too. The cowboys make a thrilling little yipping noise as they drive their charges, waving their hats in the air cheerfully. It all seems rather wild and romantic, with the herd splashing across the river, urged along by these gay cowboys. We are told by one of the soldiers that these men are on the way from Texas to Montana Territory, where a prosperous new ranching industry is springing up. Who knows, perhaps we "Indian brides" will also visit that country in time—we have been forewarned that the savages are a nomadic people, and that we are to be prepared for frequent and sudden moves.

3 April 1875

Today our train has been stopped for several hours while a number of the men aboard indulge in a bit of "sport"—the shooting of dozens of buffalo from the train windows. I fail to see myself where exactly the sport in this slaughter lies as the buffalo seem to be as stupid and trusting as dairy cows. The poor dumb beasts simply mill about as they are knocked down one by one like targets at a carnival shooting gallery, while the men aboard, including members of our military escort, behave like crazed children—whooping and hollering and congratulating themselves on their prowess with the long gun. The women for the most part are silent, holding handkerchiefs to their noses while the train car fills with acrid smoke from the guns. It is a grotesque spectacle and seems terribly wasteful to me—the animals are left where they fall, many of those that aren't killed outright, mortally wounded and bellowing pitifully. Some of the cows have newborn spring calves with them and these, too, are cheerfully dispatched by the shooters. I have noticed during the past day that the country we are passing through is littered with bones and carcasses in various stages of decay and that a noticeable stench of rotting flesh often pervades the air. Such an ugly, unnatural thing can come to no good in God's eyes or anyone else's for that matter. I can't help but think once again what a foolish, loutish creature is man. Is there another on earth that kills for the pure joy of it?

Now we are finally under way again, the bloodlust of the men evidently sated . . .

8 April 1875—Fort Sidney, Nebraska Territory

We have reached our first destination, and are being lodged in officers' homes while we await transportation on the next leg of our journey. Martha and I have been separated, and I am staying with the family of an officer named Lieutenant James. His wife Abigail is tight-lipped and cool and seems to have adopted the superior attitude with which those of us enrolled in this program have been treated by virtually everyone with whom we have come in contact since the beginning of our journey. Although "officially" we are going among the heathens as missionaries, everyone seems to know the real truth of our mission, and everyone seems to despise us for it. Perhaps I am naive to expect otherwise— that we might be accorded some measure of respect as volunteers in an important social and political experiment but of course small-minded souls like the Lieutenant's wife must have someone to look down upon, and so they have cast us in the role of whores.

Shortly after our arrival, my hostess knocked on the door to my room, and when I answered, refused to enter but demanded in a haughty tone that I not speak of our mission in front of her children at the dining table.

"As our mission is a secret one," I answered, "I had no intention of discussing it. May I ask why you make such a request, madam?"

"The children have been exposed to the drunken, degenerate savages who frequent the fort," the woman replied. "They are a filthy people whom I would not invite into my home, let alone allow to sit at my dinner table. Nor will I permit my children to fraternize with the savage urchins.

We have been ordered by the fort commander to house you women and to feed you, but it is not by our choice, nor does it reflect our own moral judgment against you. I shall not have my children corrupted by any discussion of the shameful matter. Do I make myself clear?"

"Perfectly," I answered. "And may I add that I would rather starve to death than to sit at your dining table."

Thus I spent my short time at Mrs. James's home in my room. I did not eat. Early one morning I went out to walk on the fort grounds, but even then I was leered at by a group of soldiers and by some very rough-looking brigands in buckskin clothes who frequent the fort. Their lewd remarks caused me, however reluctantly, to give up even the small diversion of walking. Our mission appears to be the worst-kept secret on the frontier, and seems to threaten and terrify all who know of it. Ah, well, this is of scant consequence to me; I am rather accustomed to doing the unconventional, the unpopular . . . clearly to a fault . . . Frankly, from the way I have been treated by the so-called "civilized" people in my life, I rather look forward to residency among the savages. I should hope that at the very least they might appreciate us.

11 April 1875

We are under way again, on a military train to Fort Laramie. We have lost several more of our number at Sidney. They must have had a change of heart with our destination now so close, or perhaps the army families with whom they were lodged convinced them to abandon this "immoral" program.

Or perhaps—and most likely of all—they took to heart the pathetic sight of the poor savages who inhabit the environs of the fort. I must admit that these are as scurvy a lot of beggars and drunkards as ever I've witnessed. Filthy and dressed in rags, they fall down in the dirt and sleep in their own filth. My God, if I were told that one of these poor unfortunates was to be my new husband, I, too, would reconsider. How they must stink!

While at Fort Sidney, my friend Phemie was put up by the Negro blacksmith and his wife. Many of our women have refused to be housed with Phemie during our journey because she is a Negro. As we are all of us off to live and procreate with heathens of a different race and a darker color, such fine distinctions strike me as especially pointless—and I wager that they will become less and less pronounced once we are among the savages themselves. Indeed, I suspect that Phemie will come to seem more and more like one of us . . . like a white person.

The blacksmith and his wife were very kind to Phemie and gave her extra clothing for her journey. They told her that the "free" Indians with whom we will be living are not at all like these "fort sitters," and that the Cheyennes are regarded as among the most handsome and cleanly of the various plains tribes, and their women considered to be the very most virtuous. We were all greatly relieved by this news.

The new train is a considerably more spartan affair, the seats mere benches of rough wood; it is as if we are being slowly stripped of the luxuries of civilization. Martha seems increasingly anxious; the poor mute child Sara practically hysterical with anxiety—she has chewed her finger nearly raw . . . even the usually boisterous and cheerful Gretchen has fallen oddly silent and apprehensive. And all the others are in various states of distress. The Lovelace woman drinks her "medicine" furtively and silently from her flask, clutching her old white poodle to her bosom. Miss Flight still wears her perpetual expression of surprise, but it is now tinged with a certain anxiety. Our woman in black, Ada Ware, who rarely speaks, looks more than ever like an angel of death. The Kelly sisters, too, seem to have lost a good measure of their street-urchin cheekiness in the face of these endless, desolate prairies. The twins have stopped prowling the train and sit across from each other like mirror images, quietly staring out the window. Of great relief to all, the evangelist, Narcissa White, who is usually preaching loudly enough for everyone to hear, is now lost in fervent, silent prayer.

Only Phemie, God bless her, remains, as always, calm, unperturbed, her head held high, a slight smile at her lips. I think the trials and tribulations of her life have given her a nearly unshakable strength; she is a force to behold.

And just now she has done a very fine thing. Just as we have all sunk to our lowest ebb, exhausted from the long journey, discouraged and frightened of what lies ahead; riding silently, and staring out the window of the train, and seeing nothing but the most dreadfully barren landscape—dry, rocky, treeless—truly country with nothing to recommend it, country that increases our anxieties and seems to presage this terrible new world to which we are being born away. Just then Phemie began to sing, in her low melodic voice, a Negro slave song about the underground railroad:

> *This train is bound for glory, this train.*
> *This train is bound for glory, this train.*
> *This train is bound for glory,*
> *Get on board and tell your story*
> *This train is bound for glory, this train.*

And now all eyes were watching Phemie, and some of our women smiled timidly, listening spellbound while she sang:

This train don't pull no extras, this train,
This train don't pull no extras, this train,
This train don't pull no extras,
Don't pull nothing but the midnight special,
This train don't pull no extras, this train . . .

The proud brave sorrow in Phemie's lovely voice gave us courage, and when she took up the first verse again: *"This train is bound for glory, this train"* . . . I, too, began to sing with her . . . *"This train is bound for glory, this train. . . ."* And a few others joined in, *"This train is bound for glory, Get on board and tell your story"* . . . and soon, nearly all the women—even I noticed "Black Ada"—were singing a rousing and joyous chorus, *"This train is bound for glory, this train . . ."* Ah, yes, glory . . . isn't it fine to think so . . .

→ NOTEBOOK II ←

Passage to the Wilderness

"A peace is of the nature of a conquest;
For then both parties nobly are subdu'd,
And neither party loser."

(William Shakespeare,
Henry VI, Part Two, Act IV, Scene 2,
from the journals of May Dodd)

><

13 April 1875

Well, here we are at last, Fort Laramie, a dusty godforsaken place if ever there was one. It seems a hundred years ago that we left the comparative lushness of the Chicago prairie to arrive in this veritable desert of rock and dust. Good God!

We are housed here together in barracks, sleeping on rough wooden cots—all very primitive and uncomfortable . . . and yet I should not speak those words just yet. How much more uncomfortable will our lives become in the ensuing weeks? A week's rest here, we are told, at which time we are to be escorted north by a U.S. Army detachment to Camp Robinson, where we are finally to meet our new Indian husbands. Sometimes I am convinced that I really must be insane—that we all are. Would not one have to be insane to come to a place like this of one's own free will? To agree to live with savages? To marry a heathen? My God, Harry, why did you let them take me away . . .

13 April 1875

My Dear Harry,
 You have perhaps by now heard the news of my departure

from the Chicago area. Of my relocation to the West. Or perhaps this news has not yet reached you? Perhaps you are dead, done in by Father's hooligans ... Oh Harry, I have tried not to think of you, tried not to think of our sweet babies. Did you give us all up, Harry, for a handful of coins? I loved you so, and it tortures me not to know the answer to these questions. Were you with another woman on the night of our abduction from your life, drinking and unaware of our plight? I prefer to believe so, Harry, than to believe that you were in league with Father. Was I not your faithful lover, the mother of your children? Were we not happy for a time, you and I? Did we not love our dear babies? How much money did he give you, Harry? How much was your family worth to you?

I'm sorry ... surely I have unjustly accused you ... perhaps I shall never know the truth ... Oh, Harry, my sweet, my love, they have taken our babies ... God, I miss them so, I ache for them at night, when I awaken with a start, their dear sweet faces in my dreams. I lie awake wondering how they are getting on, wondering if they have any memory of their poor mother who loves them so. If only I could have some news of them. Have you seen them? No, surely not. Father would never allow it, nor even allow the fact that such a lowborn man such as yourself could be the father of his grandchildren. They will grow up spoiled and privileged as I did, insufferable little monsters who will look down on the likes of you, Harry. Strange, isn't it? That our lives could be torn from us so suddenly, our children swept away in the middle of the night, their mother incarcerated in an insane asylum, their father ... God only knows what has become of you, Harry. Did they kill you or did they pay you? Did you die or did you sell us to the highest bidder? Should I hate you or should I mourn you? I can hardly bear to think of you, Harry, without knowing . . . now I can only dream of someday returning to Chicago, after my mission here is fulfilled, of coming home to be again with my children, of finding you and seeking the truth in your eyes.

As it is, Harry, how fortunate that you and I were never officially married, for I am presently betrothed to another. Yes, that's right, I know it seems sudden. But my general objections to the institution of marriage notwithstanding, I have struck a strange bargain to purchase my freedom. And although I do not as yet know the lucky gentleman's name, I do know that he is an Indian of the Cheyenne tribe. Yes, well, I can only make this admission in a letter which even if I knew how to reach you, I would be forbidden to mail. This is all supposed to be very secret, though of course it is not . . . And while it may sound insane to say so, I felt that I had a duty to write to you, to tell you this news . . . even if I cannot post this letter. Having discharged my obligation, I remain, if nothing else . . .

The loving mother of your children,
May

17 April 1875

After a week here at Fort Laramie, I shall be happy to be under way at last. The boredom has been unrelieved. We are kept under virtual lock and key, prisoners in these barracks, allowed only an hour to walk around the grounds in the afternoons, escorted always by soldiers. Perhaps they fear that we will fraternize with the agency Indians and all of us have a change of heart. I must say these are every bit as abject as those at Sidney—a sorrier more disgraceful group of wretches could not exist on earth. Primarily Sioux, Arapaho, and Crows we are told. The men do nothing but drink, gamble, beg, and try to barter their poor ragged wives and daughters to the soldiers for a drink of whiskey, or to the half-breeds and other criminal white men who congregate around the fort. It is all unsavory and pathetic—many of the women are themselves too drunk to protest and, in any case, have very little say in these vile transactions.

Yet we must keep heart that these fort Indians are in no way representative of the people to whom we are being taken. At least so I continue to maintain for the sake of the child Sara and my friend Martha. As I pointed out to Martha, even in the unlikely event that her husband were to trade her to a soldier for a bottle of whiskey, it would only mean that she would be free, relieved of her duty, back among her own people. Ah, but then I had forgotten that dear Martha's heart is now firmly set on finding true love among the savages, and thus my attempt to comfort her with the possible failure of her union had quite the opposite effect.

The only other diversion in our otherwise tedious stay at Fort Laramie comes during the communal meals held in the officers' dining hall. We have been, presumably for reasons of security, isolated from the general civilian population at the fort, but some of the officers and their wives are allowed to take their meals with us. Once again the "official" version of our visit here is that we are off to do "missionary" work among the savages.

Today I had occasion to be seated at the table of one Captain John G. Bourke, to whose care our group has been assigned for the remainder of this journey. The Captain is aide-de-camp to General George Crook himself, the famous Indian fighter who recently subdued the savage Apache tribe in Arizona Territory. Some of our ladies had read about the General's exploits in the Chicago newspapers. Of course, I did not have access to such luxuries as newspapers in the asylum . . .

I am very favorably impressed with Captain Bourke. He is a true gentleman and treats us, finally, with proper courtesy and respect. The Captain is unmarried, but rumored to be engaged to the post commander's daughter, a pretty if somewhat uninteresting young lady named Lydia Bradley, who sat on his right at table, and tried to monopolize the Captain's attention by making the most vapid conversation imaginable. Although he was most solicitous of her, she clearly bores him witless.

Captain Bourke was far more interested in our group, and asked many penetrating, if delicately phrased, questions of us. He is clearly privy to the true nature of our mission — which is not to say that he approves of it. Having spent a good deal of time among the aboriginals during his former posting in Arizona Territory, the Captain prides himself on being something of an amateur ethnographer and seems quite knowledgeable about the savage way of life.

Apropos of nothing, I shall, by way of personal aside, mention my observation that the Captain appears to have rather an eye for the ladies. I confess that he is a most handsome fellow, with fine military bearing and a manly build. He is dark of hair that falls just over his collar, wears a moustache, and has deep-set, soulful, hazel eyes, with a fine mischievous glint to them as if he were perpetually amused about something. Indeed his eyes seem less those of a soldier than they do those of a poet—and are shadowed, somewhat romantically, by a slightly heavy brow. He is a man of obvious intelligence and sensitivity.

It amused me and pleased my vanity to notice further that Captain Bourke directed more of his conversation to me than to any of the other women at the table. This fact was not lost on his fiancée and only served to make the poor thing prattle on ever more inanely.

"John, dear," she interrupted him at one point just as he was making an interesting observation about the religious ceremonies of the Arizona savages. "I'm sure that the ladies would prefer conversation about more civilized topics at the dining table. For instance, you have very cavalierly neglected to compliment me on my new hat, which just arrived from St. Louis and is the very latest fashion in New York."

The Captain looked at her with a distracted and mildly amused air. "Your hat, Lydia?" he asked. "And what does your hat have to do with the Chiricahuas' medicine dance?"

Her efforts to turn the conversation to the topic of her hat thus rebuffed, the poor girl flushed with embarrassment. "Why, of course, nothing whatsoever, dear," she said. "I thought only that the ladies might be more interested in New York fashion as a topic of dinner conversation than in the frankly tedious subject of savage superstitions. Is that not so, Miss Dodd?" she asked.

I could not help uttering an astonished laugh. "Why yes, Miss Bradley, your hat is perfectly lovely," I said. "Tell me, Captain, do you think that we women might be able to impart to our savage hosts a finer appreciation of New York fashion?"

The Captain smiled at me and nodded gallantly. "How very deftly, madam, you have married the two topics of ladies headwear and savage customs," he said, his eyes sparkling with good humor. "Would that your upcoming missionary work among them be accomplished as smoothly."

"Do I detect a tone of skepticism in your voice, Captain?" I asked. "You do not believe that we might teach the savages the benefits of our culture and civilization?"

The Captain adopted a more serious tone. "It has been

my experience, madam," he said, "that the American Indian is unable, by his very nature, to understand our culture—just as our race is unable fully to comprehend their ways."

"Which is precisely the intended purpose of our mission," I said, treading rather closely to the subject of our "secret." "To foster harmony and understanding among the races—the melding of future generations into one people."

"Ah, a noble notion, madam," said the Captain, nodding in full acknowledgment of my meaning, "but—and I hope you will forgive me for speaking bluntly—pure poppycock. What we risk creating when we tamper with God's natural separation of the races will not be one harmonious people, but a people dispossessed, adrift, a generation without identity or purpose, neither fish nor fowl, Indian nor Caucasian."

"A sobering thought, Captain," I said, "to a prospective mother of that generation. And you do not believe that we might exert any beneficent influence whatsoever over these unfortunate people?"

The Captain reddened in embarrassment at the boldness of my admission, and Miss Bradley looked confused by the turn in the conversation.

"It has been my unfortunate experience, Miss Dodd," he said, "that in spite of three hundred years of contact with civilization, the American Indian has never learned anything from us but our vices."

"By which you mean," I said, "that in your professional opinion our mission among them is hopeless."

The Captain looked at me with his intelligent soulful eyes, the furrow between his eyebrows deepening. I thought I detected in his gaze, not only concern, but something more. He spoke in a low voice and his words chilled me to the bone. "It would be treasonous for an officer to speak against the orders of his Commander in Chief, Miss Dodd."

A hush fell over the table, from which all parties were grateful to be rescued finally by Helen Flight. "I say, Miss Bradley," she said, "were you aware that the feathers on your hat are the breeding plumes of the snowy egret?"

"Why, no, I wasn't," answered Miss Bradley, who seemed relieved and somehow vindicated by the fact that the conversation had come back, after all, to the subject of her hat. "Isn't that fascinating!"

"Quite," Helen said. "Rather a nasty business, actually, which I had occasion to witness last spring while I was in the Florida swamps studying the wading birds of the Everglades for my *Birds of America* portfolio. As you correctly stated, the feather-festooned hat such as the one you wear is very much the vogue in New York fashion these days. The hatmakers there have commissioned the Seminole Indians who inhabit the Everglades to supply them with feathers for the trade. Unfortunately the adult birds grow the handsome plumage that adorns your chapeau only during the nesting season. The Indians have devised an ingenious method of netting the birds while they are on their nests—which the birds are reluctant to leave due to their instinct to protect their young. Of course, the Indians must kill the adult birds in order to pluck the few 'aigrettes' or nuptial plumes as they are more commonly known. Entire rookeries are thus destroyed, the young orphaned birds left to starve in the nest." Miss Flight gave a small shudder. "Pity . . . a terribly disagreeable sound that of a rookery full of nestlings crying for their parents," she said. "You can hear it across the swamp for miles . . ."

Poor Miss Bradley went quite ashen at this explanation and now touched her new hat with trembling fingers. I feared that the poor thing was going to burst into tears. "John," she said faintly, "would you please escort me back to my quarters. I'm feeling a bit unwell."

"Oh, dear, did I say something wrong?" asked Helen, her eyebrows raised expectantly. "That is to say, I'm frightfully sorry if I upset you, Miss Bradley."

I was anxious to speak to Captain Bourke at greater length, and in private, about his obvious objections to our mission among the savages, and after dinner I spied him sitting alone in a chair on the veranda of the dining room, smoking a cigar. The bald truth is, I am undeniably drawn to the Captain, which attraction perforce can come to naught . . . but what harm can there be in an innocent flirtation?

I must have startled the Captain, for he fairly leapt from his seat at my approach.

"Miss Dodd," he said, bowing politely.

"Good evening, Captain," I answered. "I trust that Miss Bradley is not too ill? I'm afraid Helen's remarks upset her."

The Captain waved his hand, dismissively. "I'm afraid that Miss Bradley finds many things upsetting about life on the frontier," he said with an amused glimmer in his eye. "She was sent here last year from New York, where she has lived most of her life with her mother. She is discovering that army forts are hardly suited to young ladies of refined sensibilities."

"Better suited, perhaps," I said jokingly, "to we rough-and-ready girls from the Middle West."

"Not well suited, I should say," answered the Captain, his brow knitted thoughtfully, "to womankind in general."

"Tell me, Captain," I asked, "if life at the fort is difficult for women, how much harder will our life be among the savages?"

"As you may have guessed, Miss Dodd, I have been fully briefed by my superiors about your mission," he said. "As I suggested in our dinner conversation on the subject, I would prefer not to express my opinion."

"But you already have, Captain," I answered. "And in any case, I do not ask your opinion. I merely ask you, as an expert on the subject of the savage culture, to describe something of what we might expect in our new lives."

"Am I to understand," said the Captain, his voice tightening in anger, "that our government did not provide you ladies with any such information when you were recruited for this mission?"

"They suggested that we should be prepared to do some camping," I said—not without a trace of irony in my tone.

"Camping . . ." the Captain murmured. ". . . madness, the entire project is utter madness."

"Would this be a personal or a professional opinion, Captain?" I asked with an attempt at a laugh. "President Ulysses S. Grant himself has dispatched us on this noble undertaking, and you call it madness. Perhaps this is the treason to which you referred."

The Captain turned away from me, his hands crossed behind his back, the fingers of one still holding the smoldering cigar. His strong profile with long straight nose was outlined against the horizon; his nearly black hair fell in curls over his collar. Although this was hardly the time for such observation on my part, I confess that I could not help but notice again what a fine figure of a man the Captain is—broad of back, narrow of hip, straight of carriage . . . the breeches of the soldier's uniform displayed the Captain's physique in a most favorable light . . . watching him now, I felt a stab of something very like . . . desire—a sensation which I further attribute to the fact that I have been, for over a year, confined to an institution without benefit of masculine company, other than that of my loathsome tormentors.

Now Captain Bourke turned around to face me, looked down upon me with a penetrating gaze that quite literally brought the blood to my cheeks. "Yes," he said, nodding, "the President's men in Washington sent you women here, consigned you to marriage with barbarians as some sort of preposterous political experiment. Camping? The very least of your worries, Miss Dodd, I assure you. Of course, the Washingtonians have no idea what sort of hardships await you—and probably don't care. As usual, they have not bothered themselves to consult those of us who do know. Our orders are simply to see that you are delivered safely to your new husbands—offered up, as it were, as trade goods. To be traded for horses! Shame!" said the Captain, whose anger had come up now like a fast-moving squall. "Shame on them! It is an abomination in the eyes of God."

"Horses?" I replied in a small voice.

"Perhaps they neglected to mention that the savages offered horses for their white brides," the Captain said.

I recovered my composure quickly. "Perhaps we should be flattered," I said. "I understand that the savages hold their horses in the very highest esteem. Furthermore, you must remember, my dear Captain, that no one forced us to participate in this program. We are volunteers. If there is shame in our mission, then some of it must rest with those of us who signed up of our own free will."

The Captain looked at me searchingly, as if trying to ferret out some possible motive that might make such a thing comprehensible to him. His broad brow cast a shadow like a cloud over his eyes. "I watched you at table tonight, Miss Dodd," he said in a low voice.

"Your regard did not escape my attention, Captain," I said, the blood rising again in my cheeks . . . a certain tingling sensation.

"I was trying to understand what had possessed a lovely young woman like yourself to join such an unlikely enterprise with such a motley assortment of cohorts," he continued. "Some of the others . . . well, quite frankly it is easier to speculate why some of the others had signed up. Your British friend, Miss Flight, for instance, clearly has a pressing professional need to visit the prairies. And the Irish sisters, the Kelly twins, why they have the look of rogues about them if ever I've seen it—I'll wager that they were in trouble with the police back in Chicago. And the big German girl— well, surely her matrimonial prospects among men of her own race are somewhat limited . . ."

"That is most unkind, Captain," I snapped. "You disappoint me. I took you for too much of a gentleman to make such a remark. The fact is that we are none of us any better than the next. We all entered into this for our own personal reasons, none of which is superior to that of the others. Or necessarily any of your concern."

The Captain straightened his back and clicked his heels together with smart military precision. He inclined his head in a slight bow. "You're quite right, madam," he said. "Please accept my apology. My intention was not to insult your companions. I only meant that a pretty, intelligent, witty, and obviously well-brought-up young lady such as yourself hardly fits the description of the felons, lonely hearts, and mentally deranged women that we had been notified by the government to expect as volunteers in this bizarre experiment."

"I see," I said, and I laughed. "So this is how our little troupe was billed; no wonder that we have been treated with such disdain by all we encounter. Would it salve your conscience, Captain, to know that you were handing over only such misfits and riffraff to the savages?"

"Not in the least," said the Captain. "That isn't at all what I meant." And then Captain Bourke did a peculiar thing. He took me by the elbow, grasped my arm lightly but firmly in his hand. The gesture was at once oddly proprietary and intimate, like the touch of a lover, and I felt again the pulse of my own desire. He stepped closer to me, still holding my arm, close enough that I could smell the aura of cigar smoke about him, could smell his own rich manly odor. "It would still be possible for you to refuse, madam," he said.

I looked into his eyes, and stupidly, as if in a kind of trance, as if paralyzed by his touch, I took his words to mean that it would still be possible for me to refuse his amorous advances.

"And why would I do that, Captain?" I asked in a whisper. "How could I refuse you?"

And then it was the Captain's turn to laugh, releasing my arm suddenly and pulling away, clearly embarrassed by this misunderstanding . . . or was it? "Forgive me, Miss Dodd," he said. "I meant . . . I only meant that it would still be possible for you to refuse to participate in the Brides for Indians program."

I must have turned very red in the face. I excused myself then and returned forthwith to my quarters.

18 April 1875

Captain Bourke was noticeably absent at the dining table yesterday, as was his fiancée Miss Bradley . . . I suspect that they must have dined privately, perhaps in the Captain's own quarters . . . Hah! It suddenly occurs to me that my journal entries—like my entirely inappropriate romantic longings of the past twenty-four hours—begin to sound like those of a lovesick schoolgirl. I seem quite unable to get the good Captain out of my mind. I must be insane! . . . betrothed to a man whom I have not met, infatuated with a man whom I cannot have. Good God! Perhaps my family was correct in committing me to the asylum for promiscuity . . .

19 April 1875

Dear Hortense,

It is very late at night, and I write to you by the dim light of a single candle in our spartan Army barracks at Fort Laramie. I am unable to sleep. A very strange thing has happened tonight of which I can not breathe a word to any of my fellow brides. Yet I am bursting to confide in someone, and so I must write you, my sister . . . yes, it reminds me of when we were little girls and still close, you and I, and I would come into your room late at night and crawl into your bed and we would giggle and tell each other our deepest secrets . . . how I miss you, dear Hortense . . . miss the way we once were . . . do you remember?

Let me tell you my secret. At dinner this evening I was seated once again, and I think not by accident, at the table of one Captain John G. Bourke, who has been chosen to escort us to Indian territory. Indeed, we are scheduled to depart tomorrow for Camp Robinson, Nebraska Territory, where we are to meet our new Indian husbands.

Although he is only twenty-seven years of age, Captain Bourke is a very important officer, already a war hero, having won the Medal of Honor at the bloody battle of Stones River, Tennessee. He comes from a good middle-class family in Philadelphia, is well-educated and a complete gentleman. He is at once extremely witty, with a mischievous sense of humor, and truly one of the handsomest men I've ever set eyes on—dark with intelligent, piercing hazel eyes that seem able to gaze directly into my heart. It is most disconcerting.

Under the circumstances you might think that there is little opportunity for gaiety or flirtation among our group of lambs off to slaughter, but this is not so. Dinnertime especially offers us some diversion from the boredom and inactivity of fort life, and in the manner natural to any group of unmarried women, all have been vying for the Captain's attentions. And all are green with envy that he only has eyes for me.

Our mutual, and perforce, perfectly innocent attraction and good-natured banter has not been lost on Miss Lydia Bradley, the post commander's pretty, if vapid, daughter, to whom Captain Bourke is engaged to be married this summer. She watches her fiancé like a hawk—as I would if he were mine—and misses no opportunity to divert him from his attentions toward me.

As a painfully obvious tactic toward this end, Miss Bradley goes to great lengths to cast me in an unfavorable light in the Captain's eyes. Unfortunately she's not a terribly clever girl, and her efforts so far have been distinctly unsuccessful. Tonight at table, for instance, she said: "Tell me, Miss Dodd, as a member of the church missionary society, I am curious to know with which denomination you are affiliated?" Ah, so her first gambit would be to expose me as a Protestant in front of the Captain who, is himself, as he had just informed us, Catholic, having been educated as a boy by the Jesuits.

"Actually, Miss Bradley, I am neither a member of the missionary society," I said, "nor affiliated with any particular denomination. Truth be told, I'm a bit of an agnostic when it comes to organized religion." I have found that the best, and certainly simplest defense of one's faith, or lack thereof, is the truth. And while I hoped that this information did not prejudice the good Captain against me, it has also been my experience that the Roman Catholics often prefer those of no faith to those of the wrong faith.

"Oh?" said the girl, feigning confusion. "I would have thought that to go among the heathens as a missionary, membership in the church would be the very first requisite."

It was again obvious where Miss Bradley was trying so clumsily to lead me. I'm certain that the Captain's sense of duty and discretion would have prevented him from discussing professional matters with his fiancée, but clearly she had by now deduced the true nature of our enterprise.

"That would depend," I answered lightly, "on what sort of mission one was fulfilling, Miss Bradley. Of course, I am not at liberty to discuss the details of our upcoming work among the savages, but suffice it to say that we are . . . shall we say . . . ambassadors of peace."

"I see," said the girl, visibly disappointed that she had elicited from me no hint of embarrassment for being a wanton woman off to couple with heathens. Having spent over a year in a lunatic asylum for roughly this same "sin," I am scarcely intimidated by the transparent interrogations of a twit such as Miss Bradley. "Ambassadors of peace . . ." she added, trying for a trace of sarcasm in her voice.

"That's right," I said, and I quoted:

> "'A peace is of the nature of a conquest;
> For then both parties nobly are subdu'd,
> And neither party loser.'

So saith the great Shakespeare."

"*Henry VI*, Part Two, Act IV, Scene 2!" boomed the Captain, with a broad smile. And then he quoted himself:

> "*You did know
> How much you were my conqueror, and that
> My sword, made weak by my affection, would
> Obey it on all cause.*'"

"*Antony and Cleopatra*, Act III, Scene 11," I said, with equal pleasure.

"Wonderful!" the Captain said. "You're a student of the Bard, Miss Dodd!"

I laughed heartily. "And you, too, sir!" And poor Miss Bradley, having inadvertently led us, like horses to water, toward yet another common interest, fell silent and brooding, as we embarked upon a lively discussion of the great Shakespeare, joined enthusiastically by Miss Flight. The Captain is bright and extremely well read—altogether a perfectly charming dinner companion, and the evening was very gay, without further mention of our rapidly approaching fate . . .

Yes, yes, I know, Hortense. I can hear your objections already. I am fully aware that this is hardly the time to be embarking upon romantic liaisons—especially as both Captain Bourke and I are, shall we say, "bespoke." On the other hand, perhaps there is no better time for just such innocent flirtation—which is certainly all that it can be. After my ghastly ordeal in the asylum, where I fully expected to die lying in a dark, sunless room, you cannot imagine how wonderful it is to be in the company of a dashing Army officer who finds me . . . desirable. You would have no way of knowing this dear, but often forbidden love is the sweetest of all . . . ah yes, I can just hear you saying, "Good Lord, now she speaks of love!"

After dinner, poor Miss Bradley was "unwell"—the second time she has fallen ill since she's dined with our group. The Captain maintains that she is simply too delicate for frontier life, but as we women well know, feigning illness is the last refuge of one who lacks imagination.

I was already on the porch waiting for him when, after escorting Miss Bradley home, Captain Bourke returned to smoke his evening cigar. It was a lovely spring evening, warm and mild. The days are lengthening and dusk was just beginning to settle over the land, so that the bare rocky buttes of this godforsaken country were softened in gentle outline against the horizon. There was still a bit of color in the sky where the sun had set over the western hills. I stood facing the day's last fading light when the Captain approached.

"Would you care to take a stroll around the fort grounds, Miss Dodd?" he asked, stepping beside me so that his arm brushed lightly against mine. His touch was like that of flesh on flesh. It made my knees weak.

"I'd be delighted, Captain," I said, but I did not move away from his touch . . . indeed, could not. "Are you certain that your fiancée would approve," I added only half-jokingly, "of your keeping company with another woman?"

"Unquestionably she would not," the Captain said. "I'm sure you must find her to be a silly thing, Miss Dodd."

"No, not silly," I said. "Quite charming actually. Perhaps only rather young for her years . . . a bit callow."

"And yet she is not, I suspect, very much younger than you, madam," he said.

"Ah, tread cautiously, Captain!" I said "—a delicate subject, a woman's age. In any case, I am old for my years. As you are for yours."

"In what way old, Miss Dodd?" he asked.

"In the way of experience, Captain Bourke," I said. "Perhaps you and I can more fully appreciate the great Shakespeare because we have both lived enough of life to understand the truth and wisdom of his words."

"In my case war was a stern teacher of truth, if not wisdom," said the Captain. "But how is it that a young woman of your obvious breeding knows so much of life, madam?"

"Captain, it is quite likely that you and I will not know each other long enough for my personal history to matter," I said.

"It matters to me already, Miss Dodd," he said. "Surely, you are aware of that."

I still stared at the horizon, but I could feel the Captain's dark eyes on my face, the heat of his arm against mine. My breath came in shallow draughts as if I could not take sufficient air into my lungs. "It is late, Captain," I managed to say. "Perhaps we should take our stroll another time." Where our arms had touched and now parted it was like tearing my own flesh from the bone.

My candle burns down, dear Hortense, I must rest my pen . . .

I am,

Your loving sister, May

20 April 1875

Under way at last, we ride in mule-drawn wagons, escorted by a very snappy company of cavalry, at the head of which

Captain John G. Bourke, with perfect military carriage, rides a smart-stepping white mare. That the Army has entrusted us to the care of such an illustrious Indian fighter as the Captain is testament, I believe, to the fact that our safety is of the utmost concern to the authorities.

A number of the fort residents have gathered to watch our procession out the gates, including the Captain's pretty young fiancée, Lydia Bradley, who is dressed in a lovely pale pink spring dress and a matching bonnet (noticeably unadorned by feathers) and who smiles and waves a white handkerchief at her Captain as he passes. He tips his hat to her gallantly. How I envy them, the life they will lead together. How drab she makes me feel . . .

Then we are through the gates, and beyond the fort and into the great prairie itself. Here the road rapidly deteriorates until it is little more than two ruts and then seems to disappear altogether. The ride is rough, the wagon itself exceedingly uncomfortable, with only the most unforgiving benches on which to sit. We are constantly jostled, often so violently that it seems to shake our teeth loose in our heads. Dust seeps up through the floorboards so that a perpetual cloud roils inside. Poor Martha has been sneezing since we got under way. With fully a fortnight yet to go I fear that it will be a long, desperately unhappy journey for her.

21 April 1875

Spring is in full bloom today, which offers a bit of cheer to this otherwise difficult passage. Much to the shock of some of the other ladies, I have decided to ride up on the buckboard alongside our teamster, a rough-spoken young man named Jimmy. I prefer the open air to choking on dust in-

side the wagon, and I am able to see something of the countryside as we pass, to enjoy a bit of the springtime.

Beyond the vastly improved view, another advantage to
riding up top with Jimmy is that he can educate me about
this new country of ours. While he is a rough lad, he seems
quite knowledgeable on the subject, and I think that secretly he rather enjoys the feminine company.

Whereas the country on our first day of travel was flat,
tedious, and largely without vegetation of interest, we seem
today to be gaining a more varied topography of gently rolling hills intersected by rivers and creeks.

It has been a damp spring and the grass is as green as
mother always described Scotland to be when she was a girl—
the prairie wildflowers are just now coming into bloom, the
birds everywhere in full song, the meadowlarks trilling joyously as if announcing our passage. There are ducks and
geese by the thousands in every pothole of water and upon
every flooded plain. Helen Flight is terribly pleased with the
fecundity of bird life, and periodically begs the Captain to
halt our procession so that she may descend with her shotgun to shoot one of the poor things—which she first sketches
and then expertly skins to keep as a specimen for her work.

The Captain, a sportsman himself, so enjoys watching
Miss Flight's prowess with the shotgun that he hardly objects to the delays caused by our frequent stops. Jimmy, my
new muleskinner friend, is equally admiring of our accomplished gunner, and takes every opportunity to halt the
wagon when birds are in range so that Miss Flight can display her considerable skills.

Thus she swings to the ground with masculine authority,
all business, standing with her legs firmly planted, slightly
apart, toes pointing out, to charge her muzzle loader. Even
though the weather is warming daily, Miss Flight still wears

her knickerbocker suit and particularly from the rear looks far more like a man than a woman. From a flask she carries in her jacket, she pours gunpowder into the barrel; this she rams home using wadded cotton from discarded petticoats. This is followed by a measure of very fine shot and then another wad made of card, which prevents the shot from rolling out the gun barrel. To her credit Miss Flight will only shoot the birds on the wing—believing it "unsporting" to do otherwise.

Not only does she collect her specimens in this manner, but she is filling our larder with all manner of game birds and waterfowl, which we surprise out of the plum thickets or spring potholes along the route. These include ducks, geese, grouse, snipe, and plover—which fare will undoubtedly provide a much welcome addition to our Army rations.

In only the first two days out from Fort Laramie, we have also seen deer, elk, antelope, and a small herd of bison grazing, and while the Captain will not permit the soldiers to hunt at too great a distance from the wagon train owing to the threat of Indians, we should have no want of fresh game en route.

Because of the spring floodwaters, we try to keep to the higher ground, though sometimes we are forced to drop down into the bottoms to ford the rivers and streams. It is hard going for the mules, who do not like to walk in thick mud, or even to get their feet wet. "There ain't nothin' an old mule hates worse," Jimmy instructs me, "than to put their *goddamn* feet down in water. They ain't like a horse that way. They's just *goddamn* prissy about water is all. But in every other way, you can give me an old mule over a horse any day. *Any day.*" A strange, rough boy, Jimmy, but he seems to have a good heart.

Traversing these drainages is a wet, muddy experience

for us all. Several times already today we have had to descend to lighten the mules' load, hike our dresses up, and make our own way across the streams on foot, soaking our feet through to the bone.

And yet the river bottoms strike me as the loveliest country, for everything lives here, or passes by here or comes to water here from the long empty reaches of desert plains between.

At night we make camp as near to the water as possible while still being on dry ground. The mules are hobbled or picketed in the grass meadow, which is already lush with tender green shoots. It is very pretty. I think that one day I should like to live in such a place . . . perhaps one day I shall return home to reclaim my dear babies and we shall all come here together . . . to live in a little house on the banks of a creek, on the edge of a meadow, surrounded by a grove of cottonwood trees . . . ah, sweet dreams keep me alive . . .

Yes, indeed, and instead I shall soon be living in a tent! Think of it! Camped out like a nomad, a gypsy! What an astonishing adventure we have embarked upon!

To my great disappointment, Captain Bourke has hardly met my eye and barely spoken to me since we departed Fort Laramie. I sense that he is intentionally avoiding me. Perhaps because he is officially "on duty" now, his strict, military deportment appears to have completely supplanted his charming social demeanor. I confess to preferring the latter.

Tonight at dinner in the "mess" tent as the Army insists upon calling it, the conversation turned as it does with ever greater frequency to the subject of our Cheyennes. The Captain admitted, if rather grudgingly, that the tribe is a superior race as the American Indians go—a handsome, proud, and independent people, who have kept to themselves as much as they have been able in these times, avoiding the missionaries, the agencies, and general commerce with the whites more than any of the other tribes. This, the Captain stated, has allowed them to remain less "spoiled" than the others.

"I find that to be an unfortunate choice of words, Captain," objected our official church representative Narcissa White, "for it implies that contact with Christian civilization is the root cause of the spoilation of heathens, rather than the ladder by which they might climb from the muck of paganism."

"I consider myself to be a devout man, Miss White," answered the Captain. "But I am also a military man. It is the lesson of history that in order for Christian civilization to extend her noble boundaries, barbarians must first be roundly defeated on the battlefield. By spoiled I mean only that in giving the Red Man gifts—rations and charity that are not earned by the sweat of his own brow—our government has never accomplished anything other than to encourage him, like a dog fed scraps at table, to beg more gifts, rations, and charity."

"And brides," I interjected good-naturedly. "Give the damn heathens one thousand white women, and soon they'll want a thousand more!"

"Although I think you mock me, Miss Dodd," said the Captain with an amused glint in his eye, "that is exactly correct. Such well-intentioned gifts will only make them bolder in their demands. The savages will never be convinced of the benefits of civilization until they are first subdued by superior force."

"Yes, and isn't that why the government is sending us among them?" I said, with a bit of false bravado.

"*Yah*, May, I *tink* so," Gretchen Fathauer said. "I *tink дey* not seen superior force until *ðey* seen us!" And we all laughed. For what else is there to do?

22 April 1875

This evening after dinner our muleskinner Jimmy called at the tent in which I share extremely close quarters with Phemie, Martha, Gretchen, and the girl Sara. Jimmy asked me to step outside for a word, and then proceeded to inform me that Captain Bourke should like to see me in his own quarters. There is little opportunity for privacy in our camps at the end of the day's travels, and I must say his request startled me, especially given the Captain's recent coolness toward me. The lad led me there. He is such a strange boy . . . I cannot put a finger on it . . .

The Captain greeted me at the entrance to his tent, and seemed genuinely pleased that I had come. "I hope you will not consider my invitation to be too forward, Miss Dodd," he said, "but evening bivouacs in the field can be exceptionally dull, particularly to an old Army man such as myself who has endured so many of them. I always carry with me in the field my cherished volume of Shakespeare, which I amuse myself by reading at night. I thought this evening you might be willing to join me—far more interesting to read aloud with a fellow enthusiast."

"Why thank you, Captain, I'd love to," I answered. "And shall I invite Helen Flight to join us, to play yet a third part?"

I had set this small trap for the Captain, just to gauge his reaction. And I was not displeased to see that he was unable to mask the flicker of disappointment that crossed his brow.

But he recovered quickly and was, as usual, the perfect gentleman. "Yes . . . yes, by all means, Miss Dodd, a fine idea, do please ask Miss Flight to please join us. Shall I send Jimmy to fetch her?"

And then our eyes met and we stared for some time at one another, and the charade melted away in the heat of our gaze like parchment paper held over a candle flame. "Or possibly, John," I said in a low voice, "may I call you John?—possibly, John, it might, after all, be more amusing if it were just the two of us reading tonight."

"Yes, May," he whispered, "I was thinking so myself. Though I fear to expose you in any way to the appearance of impropriety."

"Ah, yes, the appearance of impropriety," I said. "Certainly that dreadfully sanctimonious woman Narcissa White will have her spies abroad. She misses nothing, and no opportunity to meddle in the affairs of others. But truthfully, Captain, at this point the appearance of impropriety is quite low on my list of immediate concerns."

And so I entered John Bourke's tent, an event which caused, as we had both suspected, no small scandal among our traveling party—although the evening was passed in perfect . . . I should say near perfect . . . innocence, for both of us are well aware of the other's feelings and to spend such time alone in company is only to fan the embers of that which cannot be. But this night we read Shakespeare together—nothing more. Nothing less. The fact is that nothing else has transpired between us besides a mutual but unspoken longing. It hangs between us, as palpable as a spider's web connecting our fates. Possibly it is simply due to the bizarre circumstances, or the fact that we must be denied one another, but I have never in my life known such a powerful stirring of feelings . . .

When I returned several hours later to my tent, Martha lay awake in her cot beside mine. "May, dear God, are you quite mad?" she whispered, as I slipped beneath my blanket.

I smiled and moved my head close to hers, and quoted, also in a whisper, " 'Love is merely a madness, and, I tell you, deserves as well a dark house and a whip as madmen do.' *As You Like It*, Act III, Scene 2. Perhaps this is why each time I have fallen in love, I am accused of madness, Martha."

"Love? Good God, May," Martha said, "it's impossible! The man is engaged. You are engaged. It can never be."

"I know, Martha," I answered. "Of course it can't. I only play. 'We that are true lovers run into strange capers.' As you may have guessed we amused ourselves by reading from *As You Like It* tonight."

"You're not going to quit us, May?" Martha asked with a tremor in her voice. "You're not going to abandon me to the savages while you run off with the Captain, are you?"

"Of course not, dear," I said. "All for one and one for all. Isn't that the vow we made?"

"Because I never would have come, May, if it weren't for you," said poor timid Martha, and I could tell that she was near to tears. "Please don't leave me. I've been worried sick about it, ever since I noticed how you and the Captain look at each other. Everyone has noticed. All have spoken of it."

I reached out and took Martha's hand in mine. "All for one and one for all," I repeated. "I'll never leave you, Martha. I swear. Never."

23 April 1875

As I had suspected, the White woman has already been spreading lies about my so-called "tryst" with the Captain.

She is abetted in these efforts by the Southerner, Daisy Lovelace, with whom Miss White seems to have struck up an unlikely friendship—possibly because they are both generally disliked by the others. But what possible difference can their opinion of me make? The scurrilous gossip they spread is fueled by dull envy, and I shall not let it concern me.

Everyone has also noticed that both Miss White and Miss Lovelace try at every opportunity to curry favor with the Captain—unaware apparently that he, being a strict Catholic, dislikes Protestants on general principle—and, by reason of his wartime experience in the Union Army, is equally prejudiced against Southerners.

It is a pathetic thing, indeed, to listen to the poor Lovelace woman trying to impress the Captain at the dining table with stories about her "Daddy" and the plantation they once owned with the two hundred *"niggahs."* Such information serves no other purpose than to offend the Captain further. One night at dinner, he asked her politely what had become of her father's plantation.

"Why Daddy lost everythin' during the *wah, suh,*" she said. "Damn Yankees burned the house to the ground and set the *niggahs* free. Daddy never did recover from the shock; he took to drink and died a broken and penniless man."

"I'm very sorry to hear that, madam," the Captain said with a polite incline of his head, but not without the usual spark of amusement in his eyes. "And did your father fight in the great war?" he asked.

"No *suh*, he did not," said the dreadful woman, who clutched her old decrepit poodle, Fern Louise, to her breast. She allows the wretched little creature to sit on her lap at meals, fussing over it like a baby and feeding it morsels of food from her plate. *"Mah* daddy felt that his *fust duty* was to stay home and protect his family and his property from the vicious rape and pillage for which the Yankee army was so infamous. And so Daddy sent two of his best buck *niggahs* to fight in his stead. Course, straightaway they run off to join the Union, like all *niggahs*'ll do given the very *fust* opportunity." An unseen glance passed between the Captain and me; already we have a way of communicating wordlessly and we were both thinking at that moment that the Bard himself could scarcely have penned a more deserved end for this woman's dear departed daddy.

24 April 1875

We have now entered Indian country, and are forbidden to venture away from the wagons unescorted by soldiers. We have just been informed that last month Lt. Levi Robinson, after whom the new camp to which we are being conducted was named, was ambushed and murdered by hostile Sioux Indians from the nearby Red Cloud Agency while accompanying a wood train from Fort Laramie on this very same route. Evidently this news has been kept from us until now, for fear of causing panic among our women, and, of course, further explains our large military escort and the fact that Captain Bourke is in command of it.

The proximity of danger has imparted a new sense of immediacy to our mission, almost as if until this very moment, we had been but half-aware of the true nature of our destination—or perhaps only half-willing to think about it. I suspect that this may also be the cause of the increasing gravity I have noticed in John Bourke's countenance since we departed Fort Laramie. Onward we go, closer and closer to our appointed fate . . .

25 April 1875

I have made an extraordinary discovery. This afternoon I went into the willows to do my business and there I surprised our teamster "Jimmy" in the same act. By obvious means I now know that "he" is a "she"—yes, not a young man at all, but a woman! I knew something was peculiar about him . . . her . . . from the beginning. Her real name, she has confessed to me, is Gertie, and she is known on the frontier as "Dirty Gertie." We have heard stories of this woman's escapades at the forts and trading posts all along the way. A saloon girl, turned gambler, turned gunslinger, turned muleskinner, she's as rough and eccentric a woman as ever I've encountered, but not at all a bad sort, I believe, only a bit rough around the edges. She has begged me not to tell her secret as the other muleskinners are entirely ignorant of her true identity, and she would surely lose her position if they knew of the deception.

"I'm just tryin' to make my way in the world, honey," she explained. "Ain't a mule outfit in the country that'll hire on a gal skinner—especially one named Dirty Gertie. And I *learnt* some time ago that if I go around as a boy, it keeps most a them fellas from tryin' to crawl into my bedroll all night long— and those that does is roughly served by their compadres. Now a gal can holler all she wants and *probly* the *only* thing'll happen is the others'll line up behind the first. But if they think you're a boy and one 'em tries to get in your britches, why the others enjoy to inflict hurt on that kind of pervert. Men are strange creatures, honey, that's all I know for sure."

Although I had some difficulty imagining the men beat-

ing a path to Dirty Gertie's bedroll, I do enjoy riding up on
the buckboard with "Jimmy" all the more for knowing "his"
secret. I have not told another soul. Not even the Captain—
although I have a suspicion he already knows.

5 May 1875

Camp Robinson is just as it sounds—a camp, a tent camp.
We are housed in large communal tents where we sleep
upon wooden and canvas cots with the same coarse woolen
Army blankets to which we have grown accustomed on the
trail. Great security measures are being taken here as well,
with guards posted everywhere at all hours—to the extent
that we have less privacy than ever.

By all accounts there has been much unrest among the
Indians at the agency throughout the spring. On the same
day in February that poor Lieutenant Robinson was killed,
the agent here, a man named Appleton, was murdered at Red
Cloud and fourteen mules stolen from the government sup-
plier's string. Our own Cheyennes have been implicated in
these depradations, along with the Sioux. We seem to have
arrived at a volatile, if perhaps timely moment, and Captain
Bourke is all the more concerned for our welfare. Soon we
shall have full opportunity to put to the test the notion that
we women may exert some civilizing influence over the wayward savages.

After regular defections en route our little group now numbers well under forty women. We have been informed that we
are the first installment of "payment" to the savages—thus we
are truly pioneers in this strange experiment. Reportedly,
more will immediately follow, as other groups have currently

embarked to various forts across the region. As the first, we are to be "traded" to a very prominent band of the Cheyenne tribe—that of the great Chief Little Wolf. Vis-à-vis the Captain's ethnographic expertise, we are told that the Cheyennes live in small communal bands that come together at certain times of year, somewhat like the great flocks of migratory geese. This makes the logistics of such an exchange rather complex, for these nomadic people follow the buffalo herds hither and yon during the spring, summer, and fall months and then maintain more or less permanent winter villages along some of the major river courses. We will be going first to one of these winter encampments, the exact location of which is unknown, but the Captain warns that we must be prepared to be on the move almost constantly. This sounds ever more foreign and terrifying to those of us who have been accustomed to a generally sedentary existence. Indeed, I wonder if there could have been any preparation made to ready us for our coming ordeal. Perhaps the Captain is right and this is all madness. Thank God we have Phemie and Helen Flight along. And Gretchen, too. Their close familiarity with the wilds of Nature should be invaluable to us all on this adventure, for many of our women are strictly "city girls" with little knowledge of the out-of-doors. I begin to understand why the recruiter Mr. Benton asked if we enjoyed camping out overnight . . . the least of our worries as the Captain pointed out . . .

6 May 1875

Good God, we saw them today! Our adoptive people. A contingent of them rode in to inspect us as though we were trade goods . . . which, indeed, is precisely what we are.

They quite succeeded in taking my breath away. I counted fifty-three in the party—although it was somewhat like trying to count grains of sand on the wind—all men, mounted, they rode as if they were extensions of the horses themselves, rode in together like a dust devil, like one being, whirling and wheeling their horses. Our guards, alarmed, stood at the arms-ready position, surrounding our tent quarters, but it was soon clear to all that the Indians had only come to inspect the trade goods.

They are, I am relieved to report, nothing at all like those pitiable wretches around the forts. They are a lean and healthy race of men, dark of face, brown as chestnuts, small-boned and with sinewy, ropy muscles. They have a true animal litheness about them, and a certain true nobility of countenance. My first impression is that they are somehow closer to the animal kingdom than are we Caucasians. I mean this not in any disparaging sense; I mean only to say that they seem more "natural" than we—completely at one with the elements. Somehow I had imagined them to be physically larger, hulking creatures—as the artists render them in the periodicals—not these slender, nearly elfin beings.

Which is not to suggest that the savages are unimposing. Many of our visitors had their faces painted in bizarre designs, and were resplendently attired in leggings and shirts made of hide, with all manner of fantastic adornment. Others were bare-chested and bare-legged, their torsos, too, painted fantastically. Some wore feathers and full headdresses and carried brilliantly decorated lances that flashed in the sunlight. They wore beads and hammered silver coins in their braided hair, necklaces of bones and animal teeth, brass buttons, and silver bells so that their grand entrance was accompanied by a kind of low musical chattering and tinkling that contributed to a general effect of otherworldliness.

They are magnificent horsemen and handled their small, quick-stepping ponies with perfect precision, the horses themselves spectacularly painted with designs, their manes and tails decorated with feathers and beads, pieces of animal fur, brass and copper wire, buttons and coins.

Some of the savages wore little more than loincloths in the way of clothing—these are immodest garments that leave little to the imagination and caused some of our young ladies to turn their heads away out of a sense of modesty. Not so I, having never been of a particularly modest disposition. Indeed, among the many other contradictory emotions that I experienced upon first laying eyes upon these whirling creatures—man and horse—I admit to having felt an eerie, terrifying sense of exhilaration.

The apparent leader of this contingent of Cheyennes, a proud and handsome man, conferred in rapid sign language with the sergeant in charge of our guard troops. We have been advised that we must all learn the sign language as soon as possible, and pamphlets prepared by Lt. W. P. Clarke describing some of the most common gestures have been distributed among us. Captain Bourke, who is well-versed himself in this skill, has been teaching us a few of the rudimentary gestures. In jest, the Captain and I have even attempted to act out a passage from *Romeo and Juliet* in sign talk—and not without some success, I might add—and a great deal of merry laughter—which activity seems ever more precious as our fate approaches!

Having heard the speech of some of the hangs-around-the-fort Indians and that of the Army's own native scouts, I do not very well see how we shall ever be able to learn the spoken language of these people. It sounds so primitive to the ear—grunting and guttural—obviously a tongue without familiar Latin roots . . . we may as well try to learn the speech of coyotes or cranes for all it has in common with ours.

Now some of our women could only bring themselves to peek timidly from behind the tent flaps as the Indians milled about making these dreadful sounds. Those more bold among us came out to stand in the yard in front of the tents for a better look at our new gentlemen friends. It was a peculiar moment, I can assure you: the women gathered together in small clusters facing these savage mounted men, both parties inspecting the other like packs of dogs sniffing the wind.

Poor Martha blushed crimson and was rendered completely speechless by the sight of the Indians.

Our Englishwoman, Helen Flight, her eyebrows raised as always in pure astonishment, was, as usual, at a less total loss for words. "Oh . . . my goodness! Colorful lot, aren't they? That is to say, the Indians of the Florida swamps with whom I had brief acquaintance were usually covered with a terribly unattractive brown mud against the ubiquitous mosquitos. But these chaps are an artist's dream!"

"Or a *guurl's wuuust naaghtmare*," said Daisy Lovelace, who I'm certain had been drinking, and clutched her old tiny French poodle to her breast, her hooded eyes narrowed to slits. "Why they are as *daahk* as *niggahs, Feeern Loueeese.* Wouldn't Daddy *jest* die if he knew his little girl was going to marry a damn *niggah* Injun boy?"

The cheeky Kelly twins were also completely uncowed by the spectacle of savages, and pushed directly to the front of our group to face the Indians boldly. For their part the Cheyennes seemed fascinated by the sight of the twin redheads; the men grunted and sneaked furtive looks at them. The savages have the oddest way of looking at you, while not appearing to look at you. It is difficult to describe but the men did not stare directly at us in the same way that white men might, but rather seemed to study us in their peripheral vision. "Look, Meggie," said Susan. "See how charmed that one is with me! That handsome laddy there on the spotted white pony. *Aye*, I believe he *loykes* me!" And with this, the brazen girl hiked her dress up to reveal her bare leg to the young man. "*'Ave* a peek at that then, darlin','" she said with a raw laugh. "How'd ya like to rest your lance in that sweet *cooontry?*" Her bold gesture seemed to cause the poor fellow great distress, and he wheeled his horse in a tight circle.

"Ah, but you're a naughty girl, Susie, ye are!" said sister Margaret. "*Aye, lookit* how you've got the poor lad *roonnin'* in circles already! It's *sartain*, though, that he's got eyes for you."

Gretchen Fathauer stood, solid as a house, her hands on her broad hips, eyes squinted against the sun. Finally she raised her fist in the air, and shook it as if to get their attention, and cried out. "*Yah!* All you fellas there! I am a *goot* woman! I make someone of you a *goot* wife." And she pounded her breast. "I *yam* not a pretty girl but I make *bick*, strong babies!" And she laughed, bellowing like a cow.

Phemie, as always perfectly serene, only chuckled in her deep good-natured way and shook her head, seemingly quite pleased at the spectacle. Her dark Negro skin seemed to cause a bit of commotion among the savages, as well, for several milled around her, making sounds like conversation and touching their own faces as if discussing her skin color. Then someone called out to the crowd and a moment later a large Negro Indian rode to the front and presented himself to Phemie. I mean to say that he was dressed exactly like the savages but he was very clearly a black man, and a large black man at that, who, seated on his little Indian horse, made the thing look like a child's pony. "Well, I'll be," Phemie said, chuckling, "I thought I'd seen everything, but just look at you. What you doin' dressed up like an Indian, nigger?" But the black man did not appear to speak English any more than the other savages, and he only grunted something incomprehensible to her in their language.

There then ensued a spirited discussion among the heathens. Some began to shout out to one another; it reminded me a bit of the atmosphere of a cattle auction at the Chicago stockyards; I believe that the men were actually staking their claims to us! They never pointed their fingers, but studied us intently and called out. We could only imagine their discussion: *"I'll take that one with the yellow hair! I'll take the redhead. I'll take the big one! I'll take the black-skinned woman. I choose the one in the blue dress! I'll take the one with the white dog!"* Had it not all been so perfectly dreamlike, perhaps we might have taken offense at their presumption. But it has been clear from the beginning, and never more so than at this moment, that we are in the process of entering a new world, that the civilization which we have inhabited all our lives is crumbling away beneath us like an enormous sinkhole opening under our feet.

I looked about trying to ascertain who, if anyone, had claimed me, when my eyes met the averted glance of the one who had ridden in at the head of this contingent, and now sat on his horse, perfectly motionless and silent. He held a lance and an elaborately decorated shield, and wore a magnificent headdress of eagle feathers that spilled down his back and across his horse's rump. White zigzag lightning bolts ran down the legs of his black horse, but he wore no paint on his own face. He looked somewhat older than most of the others, or perhaps more accurately only seemed older, for he owned a certain stillness and confidence that suggested maturity. He had dark skin and very fine features with a fierce set to his jaw. Nor did he call out as the others had, but sat his mount like a statue. Now he raised his lance, and made with it a single short shake toward me, an imperious, kinglike gesture of taking, a kind of feudal ownership by right, and I knew beyond a shadow of a doubt that this one, the headman, had chosen me to be his bride. I nodded . . . less to my future husband personally, than in simple resignation, a kind of final acceptance of this terrible bargain we have struck, and I confess that I thought to myself with pure womanly calculation and my bedrock sense of practicality: *I could do worse than this one.*

At that precise moment I looked across the yard at the company of mounted soldiers who watched over these strange proceedings in nervous formation. They were trying to control their nervous horses, who snorted and whinnied, pranced and pawed—the air pungent and dangerous with the foreign scents and sights of their wild counterparts. And there at the head of his battalion, standing straight in his stirrups as his own white mount slipped sideways, Captain John Bourke stared at me with a look of unbearable sadness in his eyes.

As suddenly as they had ridden in and as if by some unknown signal, the savages wheeled all as one in perfect synchronization, like a covey of blackbirds rising from the ground, and galloped off as they had come . . .

7 May 1875

This morning, Colonel Bradley, the post commander, came to see us, accompanied by Captain Bourke—the purpose of their visit, to explain to us the procedures of our impending "transfer." How little romance there is in that word! This is to be effected in the morning. The Cheyennes will come for us just past daybreak; we are advised to travel with as little luggage as possible—trunks are not a thing understood by the savages, and they have no practical means of transporting them. They have not yet, as the Captain points out wryly, invented the wheel.

More in our group have had eleventh-hour changes of heart—I'm certain from having viewed the aboriginals yesterday. Indeed, one poor girl, who like me was recruited from an institution in Chicago—to which she had been committed for "Nervousness"—seems to have had a complete mental breakdown, sobbing and uttering gibberish. She has been taken to the camp hospital tent. I suppose this behavior may be expected of one who did, after all, come from an asylum. Truly this is no place for the Nervous. Several others deserted in the middle of the night, but soldiers returned them to us this morning. The women had been found by the Indian scouts wandering in the hills, dazed and half-dead from exposure—for it is still quite cool at night. I do not know what is to become of them now. As far as I'm concerned, we have struck our bargain and now must live with it. God knows we've all had second thoughts . . .

Yes, tomorrow they come for us . . . Good God . . . what have we done?

A postscript to this day's entry: Late this evening "Jimmy" came again to our quarters and called me outside.

"Cap'n needs to see you at his tent, honey," Gertie said to me. "I better warn you, he's in a terrible state."

I had noticed earlier at our briefing with Colonel Smith that the Captain seemed silent and preoccupied, but I had never seen him so agitated as when I arrived at his tent. He was seated in a chair with a glass and a bottle of whiskey before him, and when I arrived he stood and began to pace the floor like an angry caged lion.

"Do you know why I have sent for you?" he asked, without any of his usual civility.

"Presumably not to read Shakespeare," I answered.

"You may mock me all you like, May," he snapped angrily, "for you are a proud and foolish girl. But this is not a game. You are no longer an actor in a farce."

"I resent your words, John," I said. "No one knows that better than I. Let me restate my answer to your question: I suspect that you have asked me here in order to entreat me not to participate in tomorrow's transfer."

He stopped pacing and turned to face me. "To entreat?" he bellowed. "To entreat? No, madam, not to entreat—to forbid! You must not go through with this insanity! I will not permit it."

I confess that I did laugh then at the Captain's distress . . . but mine was purely the false bravado of a desperate woman. For if the truth be told, I, too, was beginning to lose heart for this venture, was nearly paralyzed with fear and apprehension for myself and my fellow travelers. Ever since we have seen the savages in the flesh, our morale has been shaken to its core. But I could not let the others, or the Captain, see my loss of faith, my failure of courage.

"My dear Captain," I answered. "May I remind you that I am not one of your soldiers, that it is hardly your position to forbid me to do anything. In any case, our orders come from a higher authority."

The Captain shook his head in something like disbelief, but his anger seemed to drain away. "How can you still laugh, May?" he asked in a soft voice of wonder.

"Do you honestly believe, John, that my laughter is light-hearted?" I said, "That I mock you? That I consider this to be a game, or myself a player on a stage? Don't you know that I laugh because it is my last defense against tears?" I quoted: "'I will instruct my sorrows to be proud—'"

"'For grief is proud and makes his owner stoop,'" John Bourke finished for me. And then he knelt beside me. "Listen to me, May," he said, taking my hands and pressing them hard in his. "You cannot imagine the hardship that will be yours. You will not survive the life these people live—cannot survive—any more than you could survive life with a pack of wolves or in a den of bears. This is how different they are from us. You must believe me when I tell you this. The savages are not just a race separate from ours; they are a species distinct."

"Are they not human beings, John?" I asked. "May we not at least hope to find some common ground as fellow men and women?"

"They are Stone Age people, May," said the Captain, "pagans who have never evolved beyond their original place in the animal kingdom, have never been uplifted by the beauty and nobility of civilization. They have no religion beyond superstition, no art beyond stick figures scratched on rock, no music besides that made by beating a drum. They do not read or write. I ask you this: Where is the savages' Shakespeare? Their Mozart? Their Plato? They are a wild, indolent race of men. Their history is written in blood, centuries of unrelieved savagery, thievery, and butchery, murder and degeneracy. Listen to me, May: they do not think as we do. They do not live as we do . . ." He hesitated, and seemed to struggle for the words . . . "They do not . . . love as we do."

The breath caught in my throat in terror and apprehension at the starkness of the Captain's words. "Love?" I asked, nearer than ever to breaking down completely. "Tell me, John, in what way do the savages not love as we do?"

Now he could only shake his head and avert his eyes from mine. "Like animals . . ." he finally murmured. "They make love like animals."

"Good God, John . . ." I said softly, with a sense of despair as complete as any I have ever known . . . or so I allowed myself to think for a brief moment. But then I remembered again the despair that I had escaped—and this brought me back from the abyss of my own cowardice.

"You wondered once why I had agreed to participate in this program," I said, "and now I must tell you, Captain. Perhaps it will help to put your mind to rest. I was recruited by our government from a lunatic asylum—given the choice between the very real possibility of spending the rest of my life locked up in that place, or going to live among the savages. Which would you have done, John, given such a choice?"

"Why you're no more insane than I, May," the Captain protested. "What was the nature of your illness if I may be so forward as to ask?"

"Love," I answered. "I was in love with a man whom my family found unsuitable. I bore his children out of wedlock."

I did not miss the flicker of disappointment that crossed John Bourke's face at this moment—his good Catholic rectitude clearly offended by news of my "sin." He looked away from me in some confusion. "People are not committed to lunatic asylums for making such mistakes," he said at last.

"Mistakes, John?" I said, "Love is no mistake. My dearest children, with whom I pray nightly to be reunited after this present adventure is over, were not mistakes."

"And what official diagnosis of your illness did the doctors give in order to have you committed?" he asked.

"Moral perversion," I answered directly. "Promiscuity, my family called it."

Now the Captain released my hand and stood from his

kneeling position. He turned away from me again, a look of even greater distress on his face. I knew what he must be thinking.

"John," I said, "I feel no need to defend myself again against such lies, or to justify my behavior, past or present. You and I are friends, are we not? We have become, I think, in a short time, dear friends. Unless my feelings deceive me, had the circumstances of our meeting been different, we might have been much more than that. I may be a woman of strong passions, but I am not promiscuous. I have been with only one man in my life. He is the father of my children, Harry Ames."

"I could intervene with the authorities on your behalf, May," the Captain interrupted, turning back to me. "Perhaps I could arrange that you be excused from the program."

"Even if you could do so," I said, "you could not prevent my family from putting me back in that ghastly place. Just as you tell me that I cannot imagine life among the savages, so you cannot imagine the life that was mine there. Where every day was exactly like the last—an endless string of sunless, hopeless days, one after another after another. Whatever is to come in this strange new world we enter cannot be worse than the tedium and monotony of existence in the asylum. I will never go back, John. I will die first."

Now I stood and went to him. I put my arms around his waist and my head on his chest. I held him, felt his beating heart. "Perhaps you hate me now, John," I said, "now that you have learned the truth. Perhaps you think that I deserve to be sent off to live with savages."

The Captain closed his arms around me, and for that moment and for the first time in longer than I could remember I felt completely safe, as if I had found there against his chest sanctuary at last from the tumult and heartbreak of my life. I smelled his strong man's scent like a forest in the fall and felt the muscles of his back and arms like the sturdy walls of a well-made house. The rhythmic beat of his heart against my own breast was like the pulse of the earth itself. Would that I could rest there forever, I thought, in the safe haven of this good man's arms.

"You must know that I am in love with you, May," he said, "that I could never hate you, or judge you. If I were able to stop this madness, I would. I would do anything to save you."

"You are engaged to marry another, John," I said. "As I am. Even if I required saving, it is too late."

But now I believe that perhaps it was John Bourke, after all, who required saving from me, from my own terrible need, my desire to disappear within him, and him within me, as one being together, inseparable. Who falls swifter or harder from grace and with such splendid soul-rending agony than an Irish Catholic boy raised by Jesuits? An honorable soldier engaged to another? What sweeter love is there than that which cannot be?

When John Bourke kissed me, I tasted the faint sweetness of whiskey on his lips, and felt his deep moral reluctance giving itself up to my more powerful need for him. I felt us both being swept away together, and I held tight, held on for dear life, as if only the contact of our bodies could fix me in this time and place, as if only when his flesh and mine became seamless, seared together as one, would I be truly anchored to this world, the only world I know. "Will you show me now, John," I whispered into his mouth, "dear John, will you show me now," I implored, "how a civilized man makes love?"

8 May 1875

My Dear Harry,

I must try to write you the breeziest, the chattiest letter possible this evening, for if ever I am to go completely mad it will be on this strange night, our first in Indian country. And if I write to you and imagine that you will actually read this letter, perhaps I can pretend for this one moment longer that all is well, that I am simply having a dream from which I will awaken in your arms, in our apartment, our babies sleeping beside us . . . and all will be well . . . yes . . . all will be well . . .

I am to be a Chief's wife. That's right, the head savage has chosen me to be his bride. His rank being the savage equivalent of royalty, this will make me something like a Queen, I should think . . . Hah! And what would you think of that, Harry, if you could only know where our actions have led me? A Chieftain's wife, Queen of the Cheyennes, future mother of the royal savage children. . . .

The man's name is Little Wolf—he is much celebrated among the Plains Indians and has had a personal audience in Washington, D.C., with President Ulysses S. Grant himself. Even my Captain admits that the Chief is by reputation a fearless warrior and a great leader of his people. And I must say, as savages go he is not altogether unpleasant to look upon. It is impossible to guess how old he is. Not a young man, certainly, and quite a bit older than I, but not old either . . . perhaps near forty years of age. But very fit and healthy-looking, with dark, almost black eyes, and strong features set in a kind of wolflike demeanor. Yet he strikes me as a gentle man with a soft pleasant manner of speaking that makes even the hideous Indian language seem less ugly.

They came early this morning, Harry, driving a herd of horses ahead of them with unimaginable fanfare, making strange yipping, animal-like sounds—exactly the noises one might expect savages to make. The horses were herded into the camp corral, where they were counted by the camp comptroller.

Yes, well, naturally, I have mixed feelings about being traded for a horse . . . although I suppose I should take some consolation from the fact that the mount Little Wolf presented to the post commander for my hand was, by all accounts, one of the finest in the string . . . not that I, personally, am any great judge of horseflesh, but so said my new mule-skinner friend "Jimmy."

So perhaps I can take some solace in knowing that I have been traded for a particularly excellent specimen of equine flesh . . . does that sound better?

My true friend, Martha, is to marry a fearsome-looking fellow, aptly named Tangle Hair, whose wildly unkempt hair causes him to look quite like one of the maddest of the mad inmates from the asylum. But he, too, is by all accounts a distinguished warrior.

In one of the oddest circumstances of this bizarre situation our brave Negress Phemie has been chosen by a black man among the savages. Indeed, that is his name—Black Man. It was explained to us by the camp interpreter, a half-breed Frenchman-Sioux named Bruyere, that Phemie's prospective husband was captured from a wagon train of escaped Negro slaves when he was only a child. Brought up among the Cheyennes, he is considered to be as much one of them as if he were natural born to the tribe. He speaks no

English and is treated in all ways as an equal. Perhaps in this regard the savages are more civilized than we. He is a handsome fellow, quite a bit taller than most of the others, well over six feet I should guess, and I must say he seems to be a fine match for our Phemie . . . forgive me if I appear to ramble on Harry . . . exhaustion and terror will do that to a girl . . . I try only to give some order and definition to this desperate affair . . .

Helen Elizabeth Flight, our artiste in residence, has been chosen by a famous Cheyenne warrior named Hog. "Yes, well I expect I'll keep my professional name," she says with great good humor. "That is to say, Helen Hog has rather a dis-agreeable ring to it, don't you agree?" However unattractive his name, Mr. Hog is a fine-looking fellow, taller and broader of shoulder than most of the others.

Sweet little Sara is to wed a slender young man named Yellow Wolf, a youth who appears to have barely reached adolescence. But again I must say that the Cheyennes seem to have chosen wisely, for the boy is extremely shy of coun-tenance and altogether smitten with the girl—can hardly take his eyes off her. Perhaps he will succeed where we have failed in bringing Sara out of her silent, fearful world.

Captain Bourke tells us that among the savages madness is considered a gift from the gods, and as such the insane are accorded great respect, even reverence in their society. Thus some of our group should be held in very high esteem by our hosts, possibly even regarded as idols! Indeed, there was spir-ited competition among several of the savage men over which of them gets poor Ada Ware as his wife. A former asylum inmate herself, suffering from Melancholia, Ada would hardly be considered a "catch" by men in our own society. But ac-cording to the interpreter, Bruyere, the savages believe that she is some kind of holy woman because of her black attire. They have had just enough exposure to our sundry religions to have things all in a muddle.

Our valises were objects of great mirth to the Indians. Those less dignified among them grasped them by the handles and made quite an exaggerated show of carrying them around for the amusement of their foolish compatriots, and then all fell down laughing and rolling on the ground. Truly these people are like unruly children! I was pleased to see that my own intended did not participate in this nonsense, but merely watched sternly.

Poor Daisy Lovelace was involved in a terrible scene with the fellow who chose her to be his bride. As the man was collecting her belongings, he tried to take from her her beloved pet poodle, Fern Louise. Daisy, who I suspect had been taking her "medicine," clutched the little dog to her breast, and said, "No you don't, *suh*, you do not so much as touch my *Feeern Louuuise. Evah.* You *heah* me? *Nevah, evah* do you lay a finger on my *darlin' dawg.*"

But the fellow reached out again, quick as a cat, and snatched the little thing from Daisy's arms, then held it up by the scruff of its neck and made quite a show of displaying it to the others, who gathered laughing to watch as the poor thing flailed the air helplessly. I confess that I do not much care for Miss Lovelace, and care even less for her wretched little poodle, but I hate to see any animal mistreated, and when Daisy tried to take back her pet, I went to her aid. "Give her back that dog!" I demanded of the savage. The fellow seemed to understand what I was after and only shrugged and dropped the poor old thing in the dirt as casually as one discards a piece of trash. The little dog sprawled to the ground but quickly regained its feet and began to run round and round in circles, which only made the savages laugh harder. But as if by centrifugal force, Fern Louise suddenly shot out of her circle in a straight line toward the savage who had so rudely abused her, latched on to the man's foot, snarling viciously and shaking her head like a tiny demon from Hell. Now the savage began hopping about comically and hollering in pain, trying without success to shake the tenacious little poodle loose, which scene caused the others ever greater mirth.

"Hang on, Feeern Louueeesse!" Daisy Lovelace called out triumphantly, "That's right, *honey, hang on to the niggah!* You teach the damn *heathen* not to fool with you, *darlin'."* Finally exhausted from its efforts, the little dog released its hold on the savage, and trotted, panting and slavering pink bloody foam, back to her mistress. Meanwhile, the savage had fallen to the ground, clutching his wounded foot and making piteous howling noises—which elicted no sympathy whatsoever from his compatriots, who found his distress hilarious beyond compare. Indeed, the episode provided much needed comic relief for all of us, and the poodle Fern Louise has gained immeasurably in our esteem.

Because the horse trade was merely a formality to the authorities, the Army has supplied each of us with a good American horse to ride into Indian country, and with proper Army saddles to which we strapped our bags and the few small luxuries which we were permitted to carry with us. Anticipating the difficulty that we would encounter riding any great distance astride such saddles wearing dresses, the soldiers have also thoughtfully outfitted those of us who accepted them with specially, if hastily, tailored cavalrymans' breeches. Suffice it to say that in matters of fit some of us were more fortunate than others. In any case, those among our women who refused these came to regret their vanity almost immediately once we were under way. For their part, the savage men were as agitated by our breeches as they were amused by our valises and made much disproving grunting on the subject. As they don't wear trousers themselves, one can only assume that they've never before seen women so attired.

I have my precious notebooks and a good supply of sturdy lead pencils that Captain Bourke presented to me—for he wisely felt that ink would be a difficult commodity to obtain where we are bound. The Captain has also lent me his cherished copy of Shakespeare to carry with me into the wilderness. Knowing what it means to him, I could hardly accept it, but the Captain insisted. Together we wept, Harry, wept and held each other in the sorrow of our parting, a luxury you and I were never allowed.

Yes, this I offer as a final confession to you, Harry—my first love, father of my children, wherever you are, whatever has became of you . . . you to whom, until last night, I have remained faithful . . . Yes, the Captain and I were quite swept away by passion, our emotions raw . . . we could not help ourselves, nor did I wish to . . . what strange propensity is it of mine, Harry, to involve myself with unsuitable men—a factory foreman, an engaged Catholic Army Captain, and now a savage chieftain. Good God, perhaps I really am mad . . .

As a desperate eleventh-hour attempt to forestall the inevitable, a hastily formed committee of our women called upon Colonel Bradley to see if we might be permitted to spend one last night at the camp. Emotions were running high, and I feared a mass defection. The Colonel in turn passed along our request to Chief Little Wolf, and he and several of the other head Indians conferred over the matter. Finally the great Chief returned and announced their decision: the horses had been delivered as agreed upon and now we must accompany them. There was still plenty of daylight left in which to reach their camp, and apparently the Indians saw no reason to delay our departure for another day. Colonel Bradley explained that if he did not release us to them as agreed upon his actions might be construed by the Cheyennes as an attempt to renege on the bargain we have struck. In which case, there would almost certainly be trouble. As the entire purpose of this bold venture is to try to avoid further trouble with the savages, the Colonel regretfully denied our request for one final night in the bosom of civilization. Well, this is what we signed on for, isn't it?

We have been joined at the last minute by one Reverend Hare, a corpulent Episcopal missionary who arrived here only yesterday from Fort Fetterman, and who is to accompany us into the wilderness. He is a most unusual-looking fellow who must weigh at least 350 pounds, and bald as a billiard ball. In his white clerical gowns, the Reverend looks like nothing so much as an enormous swaddled infant. He rode in on a huge white mule that fairly groaned under the missionary's weight.

Captain Bourke could only shake his head at the Episcopalian's arrival and mutter something under his breath about the "well-fed Protestants." The Captain is evidently familiar with the Reverend's evangelical activities among the savages, and has complained privately that the President's Indian Peace Plan has all the various denominations squabbling over the souls of the savages like dogs over a steak bone. Accordingly, the Reverend, a "White Robe," as the Indians refer to the Episcopalians, has been dispatched by his church to bring the Cheyennes into the fold, thus preventing their souls from being captured by the "Black Robes" as the Romanists are known. One of the first pronouncements that the enormous Reverend made was to voice his opinion in front of Colonel Bradley and Captain Bourke that it would be preferable in the eyes of his church for the savages to remain heathens than to be converted by the Catholics, a remark that, believe me, did not sit well with my Captain.

Still, we have been informed that Reverend Hare has worked among the Indians for a number of years and is something of a linguist, speaking several of the native tongues fluently, including Cheyenne. His function then will be to serve as both translator and spiritual advisor to our strange assembly of lambs going off to slaughter.

And it was in just such a spirit that we rode out from Camp Robinson with our prospective husbands. Some of our women were wailing as though this were a funeral procession rather than a wedding march. For my part, I tried to maintain my composure—in spite of Captain Bourke's disapproval I have vowed to keep a positive face on this adventure, to keep foremost in my mind the thought that this is a temporary posting; we are soldiers off to do duty for our country and can at least look forward to the day when we might return home. Closest of all to my heart, Harry, I keep the memory of our precious children, the dream I shall harbor forever in my breast of one day returning to them; this dream will keep me alive and strong. I have tried from the start to hearten the others with the same comforting thought: that one day we shall return again to the bosom of civilization—free women at last.

So I rode at the head of our procession, proudly alongside my intended, nodding slightly to Captain Bourke, whose own consternation with the occasion was written clearly in his countenance. I started to lift my hand to him in a farewell wave but I saw that he had cast his dark eyes to the ground and did not look at me. Did I detect shame in his averted gaze? Catholic self-flagellation? That in our one mo-

ment of passion he had betrayed his God, his fiancée, his
military duty? Did I detect, perhaps, even a glimmer of relief
that the wanton instrument of his temptation, the Devil's
own temptress, was being taken away to live with savages—
the fitting punishment of a vengeful God for our sweet sins
of the night. Yes, all that I witnessed in John Bourke's down-
cast eyes. This is a woman's lot on earth, Harry, that man's
atonement can only be purchased by our banishment.

But I did not bow my head. I intend at all costs to maintain
my dignity in this strange new life, and if I am to be the wife
of a Chief, I shall fulfill that role with the utmost decorum.
Thus before our departure I instructed my friend Martha
and those of the others who seemed most fearful—instructed
them with the advice given me by my muleskinner friend,
Jimmy, aka Dirty Gertie, who herself has experience among
the heathens: "Keep your head high, honey, and never let
them see you cry," but, of course, this advice was more difficult for some to implement than others. I, personally, have
resolved never to display weakness, to be always strong and
firm and forthright, to show neither fear nor uncertainty—no
matter how fearful and uncertain I may be inside; I see no
other way to survive this ordeal.

Within a short time most of our women seemed to resign
themselves to our fate. Their wailings subsided to an occasional choked whimper and there was very little conversation
among us; we were like children, speechless and awestruck,
being led passively, meekly into the wilderness.

What a strange procession we must have made, riding in
a long lazy line—nearly one hundred strong, counting Indians and brides—our passage winding and undisciplined
compared to our recent military processions. To God, if he
should be watching over us, we must have resembled a trail
of ants as we rode across the hills. Up into the pine timber

on the slopes and down again through densely overgrown river bottoms, where our horses forded streams swollen with spring runoff, the muddy rushing water tapping our stirrups. My horse, a stout bay whom I have named Soldier after my Captain, is calm and surefooted, and picked deliberately through the deadfall and then broke into a gentle trot up the rocky slopes to gain the ridges above, where the going was easier.

It was a lovely spring afternoon, and we were all somewhat consoled by that, by the notion that no matter how foreign and uncertain our future we still lived under the same sky, the same sun still shone down upon us, our own God, if such we believed in, still watched over us . . .

The faint sweet acrid scent of woodsmoke on the air announced the Indian encampment long before we reached it. Soon we could see a light haze from its fires in the sky above, marking the camp. A group of small boys greeted us on the trail, chattering and making weird cooing noises of amazement. Some of the smallest of the children rode enormous leggy dogs the likes of which I have never before seen— shaggy wolfish beasts that more closely resembled Shetland ponies than they did canines. The dogs were decorated with feathers and beads, bells and trinkets, and painted to mimic the men's war ponies. Now I felt more than ever that we were entering some other world, one possessing its own race of men, its own creatures . . . and so we were . . . a fairy-tale world existing in the shadows of our own, or perhaps it is our world living in the shadow of this one . . . who can say? A few of the bolder boys ran up to furtively touch our feet, and then scampered off chattering like chipmunks.

The pack of urchins ran ahead to announce our arrival to the camp, and then we could hear a great commotion of rising voices and barking dogs—a cacophony of village sounds, all of it foreign to us, and, I confess, all of it terrifying.

Throngs of curious women, children, and old people gathered as we entered the camp. The tents—tipis, they are called—appear to be set in roughly circular formations, groups of four or five of them forming half circles which in turn form a larger circle. It was a colorful, noisy place—a feast for the eyes—but so strange that we were unable to take it all in and were further distracted by the hordes of people who approached us babbling in their strange tongue and all trying to touch us gently about the legs and feet. Thus we rode the whole length of the camp, as if on parade for the residents, then turned at the end and rode back again. There rose such shouting and chattering among the heathens, such noise and chaos that my head began to whirl, I hardly knew what was happening to me. Soon we were separated from one another and I heard some of our women calling out in confused desperation. I attempted to call back to them, but my words were lost in the din. I even lost sight of poor Martha as the families of the savages claimed us, absorbed us, one by one, into their being. My head spun, all was a blur of unfamiliar motion, color, and sound . . . I seemed to lose myself.

Now I write to you, my Harry, no longer from the safety of an Army tent, but by the last fading light of day and by the faintest glow from the dying embers of a tipi fire in the center of a Cheyenne warrior's lodge. Yes, I have entered this strange dream life, a life that cannot be real, cannot be taking place in our world, a dream that perhaps only the insane might truly understand . . .

I sit now in this primitive tent, by the failing fire, surrounded by sullen squatting savages, and the reality of our situation becomes finally quite inescapable. Riding out of

Camp Robinson this afternoon, it occurred to me for the first time that I may very well die out here in the vast emptiness of this prairie, surrounded by this strange, godforsaken people . . . a people truly like trolls out of a fairy tale, not human beings as I know them, but creatures from a different earth, an older one. John Bourke was right. As I look around the circle of this tipi, even the chokingly close walls of my old room at the asylum suddenly seem in memory to be somehow comforting, familiar . . . a square, solid room with four walls . . . but, no, these thoughts I banish. I live in a new world, on a new earth, among new people. Courage!

Good-bye, Harry, wherever you may be . . . never has it been more clear to me that the part of my life which you occupied is over forever . . . I could not be further away from you if I were on the moon . . . how odd to think of one's life not as chapters in a book but as complete volumes, separate and distinct. In this spirit, tomorrow I shall begin a new notebook. This next volume to be entitled: *My Life as an Indian Squaw.* I will not write to you again, Harry . . . for you are dead to me now, and I to you. But I did love you once . . .

HEF

⇸ NOTEBOOK III ⇷
My Life as an Indian Squaw

"*I fell then into a deep slumber and I had the strangest dream . . . at least it happened like a dream . . . It must have been a dream, for my husband was now in the tent with me, he was still dancing softly, noiselessly, his moccasined feet rising and falling gracefully, soundlessly, he spun softly around the fire, shaking his gourd rattle, which made no sound, danced like a spirit being around me where I lay sleeping. I began to become aroused, felt a tingling in my stomach, an erotic tickle between my thighs, the immutable pull of desire as he displayed to me.*"

(from the journals of May Dodd)

✕

12 May 1875

Good Lord! Four days here, no time to make journal entries, exhausted, nearly insane from strangeness, sleeplessness, lack of privacy. I fear the Captain was right, this entire experiment is insane, a terrible mistake. Like moving into a den with a pack of wild dogs.

First of all, how utterly perverse is the notion of sharing a tent with one's future husband, his two other wives, an old crone, a young girl, a young boy, and an infant! Yes, that is how many live in our quarters. How, one might fairly inquire, are conjugal relations to be managed? Privacy, such as it is, is maintained by the simple fact that no one ever looks at the other, much less speaks. It is the most peculiar feeling, like being invisible. And I can hardly describe the odor of all these bodies living in such proximity.

I am being attended to by the Chief's "second" wife—a pretty girl not much older than myself whose name, according to Reverend Hare, is Feather on Head. As mentioned Little Wolf appears to have two other wives, but the older one serves largely the function of domestic help—she cooks and cleans and has yet to so much as acknowledge my presence in the lodge. This one's name is Quiet One, for she almost never speaks. Although she goes about her business as if I don't exist, my woman's instinct senses her hatred of me as keenly as if she were holding a knife blade to my throat. Indeed, I have had the same nightmare every night since we arrived. In my dream I awaken and the woman is crouched over me, squatting like a gargoyle, holding a knife to my throat. I try to scream, but I cannot, because to move is to cut my throat on the blade. I always wake from this dream unable to breathe, gasping for air, choking. I must watch out for this one . . .

Our women have been immediately pressed into action doing the most demeaning women's work around the camp— we are like children taught by our Indian mothers, little more than slaves if the truth be told. It was our understanding that we were to be instructing them in the ways of the civilized world, not being made beasts of burden, but, as Helen Flight has pointed out, of what use are table manners to those without tables. Indeed, the savage women seem to be taking full advantage of our situation as newcomers by making us do all the hardest labor. We haul water at dawn from the creek, gather firewood for the morning meal, and spend our afternoons digging roots in the fields. God, what drudgery! Only Phemie seems to have escaped the daily chores—I do not as yet know how she has managed this, for I have barely seen her. The camp is large and spread out, and we are all working so hard that it is all we can do to eat a morsel or two of revolting boiled meat from the pot and collapse on our sleeping places at the end of the day. For my part, I will cooperate with our hosts for a time, but I have no intention of being made a slave, or a servant, and several of us have already voiced our complaints to Reverend Hare about this treatment.

For their part, the savage men appear to spend an inordinate amount of time lounging around their lodges, smoking and gossiping among themselves . . . so that it occurs to me that perhaps our cultures are not so different after all: the women do all the real work while the men do all the talking.

14 May 1875

We are told that the savages are plotting some sort of group wedding ceremony which involves little more than an elaborate feast and a dance, but these plans have been complicated by the presence of Reverend Hare, who feels obligated to conduct a Christian ceremony. Speaking of whom, while it would be very useful, indeed, if the Reverend made himself available to translate and help us adapt to our strange new life, he is truly one of the most indolent individuals I've ever encountered and has spent most of our first few days here lounging like a minidiety on his buffalo robes in the tent he shares with one of the Cheyenne holy men—a fellow named Dog Woman . . . which peculiarity of name I shall attempt to explain in a later entry. Truly so much has happened, our senses have been so constantly assaulted by one bizarre occurrence and sight after another, and I am usually so exhausted, that I don't see how I shall ever be able properly to record this experience . . .

In any case, the Reverend has got things in an even greater turmoil; under the agreed upon arrangement we have the option of "divorcing" our Indian "husbands" after two years. But evidently certain of the denominations who are participating in this scheme under the auspices of the Church Missionary Society do not permit divorce—which presents a bit of a problem if we are to be married in a Christian ceremony. Such nonsense! It would seem to me better for all concerned if we merely entered into the heathen union—after all, "when in Rome . . ."—under which there would be no future legal or religious obligation. In any case, until all of this is sorted out no marital relationships are to be consummated—although I for one say, let's get down to the business at hand.

I have, I should here mention, quite put John Bourke out of my mind and am prepared to be a dutiful wife to my Chief. This is easier said than done, but it is clear to me that if I am to keep any hold at all on my sanity, I must not dwell on what might have been . . . to do so would be to go truly mad. It is the one lesson I learned well at the asylum—to live each day as it comes, day by day, and to dwell neither on regrets of the past nor worries about the future—both of which are beyond my power to influence. This lesson should be well applicable to life among the barbarians, for in a genuine sense I feel as though I have simply entered another kind of asylum—and this one the maddest of them all.

A few more words about our daily routine: in the morning the men gather at the creek to take a swim together. The women do not seem to observe this daily ritual, but occasionally go down to the creek in the afternoon to take a kind of cloth bath—which is hardly sufficient after a day of the filthiest labor imaginable. Personally, I enjoy a daily bath, something I missed more than anything at the asylum and during our long journey. And so on our third morning here I followed the Chief from the lodge. He has so far paid me little attention—has hardly spoken to me or even looked at me—let alone made any amorous advances toward me.

I have brought with me among my few meager possessions my old bathing costume that I once wore another lifetime ago at Sunday outings with Harry to the beach on Lake Michigan. It was in a trunk among my effects at the institution and it was partly as a sentimental gesture that I packed it with me here. However, I also had in the back of my mind just precisely this matter of bathing in the wilds. I had no idea what provisions the savages made for personal hygiene, but I assumed that we would be reduced to something as basic as a dip in the creek, and I certainly had no intention of appearing before everyone in a natural state. When I saw that the men made this swim every morning while the women hauled water and firewood, stoked the fires, and prepared the morning meal, I determined my own clear preference to join the men at the creek. Indeed, as a young girl I was rather an accomplished swimmer—a recreation that I deeply missed after my incarceration.

Thus I awoke early this morning and, beneath my buffalo robes, dressed in my bathing costume. (I must say, lack of privacy notwithstanding, the bed of pine boughs, buffalo robes, and trade blankets is not altogether uncomfortable.) When the Chief slipped from our tent for his morning dip I followed him to the creek. There the other men had gathered at a pool formed by a beaver dam, chattering away like schoolboys and taking deep preparatory breaths prior to plunging into the frigid (as I quickly discovered!) water. When I first joined them they issued a kind of collective murmur of disapproval, more of a grunting actually. Then one of them made some sort of a remark—I'm certain now that he was making reference to my bathing costume, and they all began to laugh, a horribly unattractive guffawing which soon had them clutching their sides and rolling on the ground like morons. Only Little Wolf maintained his chiefly composure.

The men's rudeness angered me and, I confess, wounded my vanity. I have always believed that my bathing costume shows my figure to its best advantage. Nor am I accustomed to being made an object of ridicule. I'm certain I blushed deeply, and I had to fight back tears of shame and rage. But I refused to be defeated by their idiocy. Instead, I gathered

myself and walked out to the end of a log over the beaver
pond, and executed the most graceful dive I could muster
into the icy depths—praying all the while that it wasn't too
shallow! Truly, I thought my heart would stop from the
shock when I hit the water! I swam deeply and when I broke
the surface the men were no longer laughing but standing all
together watching me with expressions of some admiration.

Now this afternoon I learn, via Reverend Hare, that the
Indian name given to me is *Mesoke* which means "Swallow,"
rather a charming name I think, and one for which I feel very
fortunate. For instance, the Reverend tells me that our large,
gregarious friend, Gretchen, has been named something un-
pronounceable that he translates as Speaks with Big Voice—
which, I suppose, is a variation of our own more vulgar
"loudmouth." My, but these are a literal-minded people . . .

After my dip, which once I had adapted to the frigidity of
the water was magnificently invigorating, the men suddenly
seemed too shy to enter the pool themselves . . . perhaps
they objected to swimming with a woman. One by one, they
drifted away to another section of the creek until only Little
Wolf was left watching me. I suspect that I had violated some
ridiculous code of heathen behavior by trying to swim with
the men. How preposterous! It rather reminds me of the
stuffy men's club in Chicago to which Father belongs . . .
Yes . . . well, with that thought in mind I believe I'll call this
The Savage Men's Bathing Club!

Little Wolf finally slipped into the water himself. He
wore only a breechclout—an immodest article of clothing
if such it can be called, little more than a flap of leather
hanging from a string tied loosely about the waist. It barely
conceals his . . .

Let me describe the Chief. He is a slender man, rather fine-
boned and small-muscled, dark-eyed and dark-complected.

His skin is extraordinarily smooth and unlined, the color of deeply burnished copper. He has very high cheekbones, that seem nearly Asian, perhaps Mongolian, and his hair is perfectly black, glossy as a raven's feathers. He is actually quite handsome in a "foreign" sort of way, and he appears to be a man of the utmost dignity and bearing. I have yet to see him behave in anything other than the most chiefly fashion. I do find him to be a bit stern of countenance. In fact, as he waded into the water I thought to myself, "I would like just once to see my intended smile." And, lo and behold, at precisely that moment, as if somehow he had read my mind, I thought that I saw the flicker of a smile cross the Chief's face, though certainly, I suppose it may just as easily have been an involuntary grimace in reaction to the icy waters.

Mr. Little Wolf plunged underwater, sleek and graceful as a river otter, came to the surface, shaking himself lightly like a dog, and exited the pool without another glance in my direction. Frankly, I was a bit disappointed as this seemed the perfect opportunity to become acquainted away from the others with whom we are in such constant proximity. Not that I expected, or indeed encouraged, romantic advances in the frigid waters of the swimming hole, but it would be lovely if the Chief at least spoke to me.

15 May 1875

We have determined to hold daily meetings in small groups, scattered about the camp. These are in order to share our experiences and, we hope, aid one another in the transition to savage life. The meetings are supposed to be organized by Reverend Hare, but, as I mentioned, His Corpulence seems to have permanently esconced himself in the lodge he is sharing with the Cheyenne holy man Dog Woman. Let me explain . . . Not only does this Dog Woman reputedly have the ability to turn himself into a canine, but he is also what the Cheyennes call a *he'emnane'e*—half-man/half-woman. I do not know if the holy man is one who simply dresses like a woman or is actually hermaphroditic and has the organs of both sexes, but a stranger creature I have never before encountered; in her/his buckskin dress, brightly colored shawl, and leggings he/she makes a very convincing, if not particularly attractive, woman. This is all terribly confusing and only reinforces the sense we are experiencing of having entered another world peopled by a different species of human beings. Again I cannot forget John Bourke's words to this effect.

This Dog Woman creature seems to be much respected by the Cheyennes and has been chosen to provide quarters to Reverend Hare. The two holy men, one savage and one civilized, one hugely fat and one got up like a woman, make an odd couple, indeed! They, too, have a cronish old woman—Sleeps with Dog Woman is the manner in which Reverend Hare translates her name, which only confuses the issue further—who lives in their tipi and takes care of them, a kind of live-in servant, I suppose.

The Reverend has sufficient experience living among the Indian tribes of the Middle West that he hardly seems inconvenienced by the lack of amenities and appears to have already made himself quite comfortable here. While one might expect the big man to soon shed some of his excess poundage, the Reverend manages to have some culinary delicacy or other constantly at hand, having arranged for food to be carried to him by the Indian women of the camp.

They arrive at his tent in a steady procession all day long bearing various dishes which they present to him as solemnly as if making offerings to an idol. I can't help but feel that the Reverend is taking some advantage of his position as a holy man.

Well, at least he speaks a bit of the Indian tongue, for which we are all grateful. The language barrier is proving to be a real hindrance to our settlement here; I am working diligently to learn the sign language of which I now know several useful gestures.

Our best intentions to meet daily notwithstanding, the constraints and pressures of our new lives here are already beginning to make themselves felt. After only a few days I sense our community ties loosening. As I mentioned, we are often simply too exhausted after the day's labors to assemble, and the camp being quite spread out makes it difficult for us to keep track of one another or to get news to and from each other. It is all I can do to steal a few minutes alone with those among my closest friends. The Indians have a camp crier, an old man who makes the rounds of the camp each morning calling out the day's "news" and "activities," and I have suggested that we do likewise for our women.

I confess that I was both shocked and thrilled when I finally saw Euphemia at our meeting yesterday. As I may have mentioned I have not seen her with the other women during the chores. Now she strode in like a princess, having already given up her civilized attire in favor of Indian garb—a deerhide dress stitched with sinew thread, moccasins, and leggings. I must say, the costume quite becomes her; she is completely striking.

Several of the women gathered about her to admire her costume. I went immediately to her and grasped her by the hands. "I have been so concerned about you, Phemie," I said. "I thought you might be ill. Why have I not seen you working with the others?"

Phemie laughed her deep rich laugh. "Oh May," she said, "I did not come here to be made a slave again. I already escaped once from that life, and when I did so I made the promise to myself that I would never toil for another. I'm a free woman. From now on I choose my work."

"And how were you able to manage that?" I asked. "While the rest of us do women's chores?"

"A simple act of refusal, an assertion of my freedom of choice," Phemie said. "I've decided that I should like to be a hunter, not a digger of roots, and so I explained to my husband that my efforts shall be devoted to that end. What can they do to me—put me in chains? Whip me? Let them try. I will always carry scars on my back from the whip and a brand as a reminder of a slave's life among tyrants, and I will not allow this to be repeated."

"Good for you, Phemie!" I said. "We must use your example in our meeting today."

"Let me show you something else, May," Phemie said, pulling her rawhide dress up to her waist to reveal that she was wearing a Cheyenne chastity string. We had each been presented with one of these ungodly devices by our women tentmates on the first day of our arrival. Apparently all the young Cheyenne girls wear them. It is a small rope which passes around the waist, is knotted in front, two ends passing down between the thighs, each branch wound around the thigh down nearly to the knees. Now several of the more prudish women present (I swear some are so prissy that I cannot understand whatever possessed them to sign up for this program!) gasped in offended modesty. But Phemie paid them no mind. "No one visits here without a key," she said in her melodic voice, and she laughed. "I wish that I had had such a contraption when I was in bondage. Many nights at the whim of my master there was no sleep at all for this nigger girl. But now I'm in charge of this part of my life, as well."

"God, Phemie," I said, "you're actually wearing the ghastly thing! The old crone who lives in our tent tried to get me to don mine, but I refused. It looks terribly uncomfortable."

"And she didn't force you, did she?" Phemie pointed out. "You see, May, these are a democratic people, after all. As to the subject of comfort, it is certainly no less comfortable than the corsets into which many of you strap yourselves daily."

"But we are here to procreate, Phemie," I said, "not to protect our chastity."

"Yes, but that moment, too, I shall decide for myself," Phemie said.

I must say, contrary to the popular reports in the newspapers and periodicals of the immoral, lurid, and rapacious savage, this hardly seems to be a carnally oriented society. By all accounts at our daily meeting, none of the other women have yet even been approached by their prospective husbands. Under the circumstances a chastity string seems quite superfluous . . .

"*Right ya* are, May," said cheeky Meggie Kelly on the subject. "I been trying to get me laddy's weapon charged since we got here, but he'll have *noone* of it. Shy as a bunny he is." In a kind of uncannily perfect symmetry, the twins have themselves been paired for matrimony with twin savage men. The four of them together look like some kind of strange mirror image. Twins are considered by the savages to bring good luck to the people, and as a result seem to have a certain special status. Naturally the Kelly girls have been in no hurry to disabuse our hosts of this superstition, as their major responsibility seems to be to saunter around camp with their twin fiancés, letting all the others admire them.

At Meggie's remarks several of us laughed, but the Reverend hushed us sternly. "I will remind you ladies that you are not yet married in the eyes of our Lord," he said. "And that fornication is forbidden until the marriage union is thus sanctified."

"*Aye*, in the eyes of your Lord perhaps, Reverend," said Susie Kelly, "but you're a damn Protestant! Doesn't mean a thing to us unless a holy Roman priest conducts the ceremony. And then me and Meggie'd be stuck here in the wilderness married for the rest of our life raising a brood of heathens. Two years is the bargain we *stroock*. And then Meggie and me has got important business back in Chicago. Right Meggie?"

"Right as rain, Susie," said Meggie, "but let the fat old heretic marry us in his devil's church. Like *ya* say, wouldn't be binding to a *coople* of good Catholic girls *loyke* us."

Now the Reverend turned very red in the face and began to stammer. "I will not be spoken to in that manner, young lady. I demand respect. It is the Episcopal Church, the only true faith, the true house of the Lord, that has been charged by our government with the task of saving the souls of the heathens!"

"That's a damn shame, it 'tis, Father, for the souls of the heathens, then," said Meggie, uncowed by the Reverend's wrath, "because everyone knows that Protestants go to Hell!"

"Blasphemer!" shouted the red-faced Reverend, pointing at the redheads as one. "Blasphemer! Satan's spawn!"

It occurred to me that the job of making Christians of the savages will certainly be complicated by the fact that we can't even agree on a common God among ourselves.

"I for one agree with Susan and Margaret," I spoke up.

"The wedding ceremony is a mere formality and should not be binding to any of us. The fact is that we have been sent here to bear children by the savages, and the sooner we have fulfilled our part in this bargain, the sooner we will be free to go home if we so choose. I say, let's get on with it."

"And under whose authority, Miss Dodd, have you assumed the moral leadership of our contingent?" asked Narcissa White, who rarely misses an opportunity to undermine my efforts at maintaining unity among our women. I'm certain that her jealously of me is further fueled by the fact that Chief Little Wolf chose me to be his bride, while Miss White was herself taken by a man named Turkey Legs—a gangly, aptly named young fellow without any real stature in the tribe.

"Why, under no one's authority at all," I replied, surprised at the charge. "I try only to do my part to expedite our mission here."

"Your part, my dear," she said in her most sanctimonious way, "does not include advising the rest of us on matters of moral conduct or the sanctity of the marriage union. It is my responsibility as official representative of the American Church Missionary Society, and that of Reverend Hare as spiritual agent of the Episcopal Indian Commission, to render decisions on all such spiritual questions. Although it is doubtless true," she added in her insufferably insinuating tone, "that you have more practical experience in carnal matters."

At this last, a general tittering ran among the others. All know by now the reason for my incarceration in the asylum—the accusation of promiscuity alone sufficiently damning to ruin a woman's reputation, especially among other women. Too, it is possible that Captain Bourke and I were spied upon in our moment of passion . . .

"As the mother of two children," I answered, "I should certainly hope to be more knowledgable on that particular subject than a fat priest and a zealous spinster," I answered, "which hardly makes me an expert."

To which rejoinder, my own supporters laughed heartily.

"I think that some of us had not understood," I continued, "that our mission here was to be directed by the church. We were under the impression that our first authority was the United States government which hired us to bear children by the savages."

"Partly true," said Miss White. "But the government has in turn given over responsibility for the Indians to the care of the church and the Missionary Society. We are the ultimate authority here."

"Ah, go *wan ya* beggar," said Susie. "There isn't any authority out here."

I looked at the Reverend, who had returned to his bowl of food, his denominational outrage evidently slackened by the morsels of meat that he placed in his mouth with his fingers, like some kind of wilderness emperor.

Now he wiped his greasy mouth with the back of his hand, and smiled, the picture of fatherly benevolence. "My dear madams," he said, calmly, "the Episcopal Church has been charged with ministering to the souls of heathens—as well as to seeing that they are eventually settled under God's protective wing on the reservation."

"But the Cheyennes do not have a reservation," I said.

"They will have one soon enough," he said. "We are even now working toward that end. Then our real work begins."

"We were all told that our purpose here was to give birth to Cheyenne babies as a means of assimilating the savages," I said.

"Yes, that, too," admitted the Reverend, with a shrug.

"Washington's idea. After which the Cheyenne children, yours included, will, at the earliest possible age, be sent to church-affiliated boarding schools which we are presently in the process of establishing across the region. This is all a part of the President's Indian Peace Plan. In this manner, the children's first influence at an impressionable age will be civilized white people and good Christians—*Protestants*, I might add. The hope of the church and the State is that being half-Caucasian by blood, your children will have a distinct spiritual and intellectual advantage over the purebred heathens, and that the savages will in turn peacefully follow this superior new generation into the bosom of civilization, and down the true path of Christian salvation. I am merely here to provide you with spiritual guidance." At this, the enormous Reverend again made a slight emperor-like incline of his head, which caught the morning light and glistened like a glazed ham.

"And the Kellys and I are only suggesting that we get down to the business at hand," I repeated.

"As Christians," said Narcissa White, "some of us may choose for ourselves a higher path upon which to elevate the savages from their lowly lot."

"Your prospective husband gave a horse for you, just like all the rest," I pointed out.

"I certainly have no intention of compromising my chastity with a heathen for a horse," she answered. "I intend to teach my husband that the true path to Christian salvation lies on a higher plane."

"Ah *yooor* a grand lady, aren't ya, Narcissa," said Meggie Kelly, "and won't *pooor* Mr. Turkey Legs be in for a rude surprise on his wedding night when he tries to dig his spurs into that stony *coontry*!"

"And what about you, Phemie?" I asked.

Phemie chuckled again. Truly I envy her calm. Nothing seems to bother her. "When I'm ready, May," she said. "And if I like my new husband and believe that he will make a good father to my children, then yes, I'll remove my chastity string. However, as he is both a heathen and a nigger, under the circumstances it will be difficult for me to give birth to the superior half-Caucasian child of which the Reverend refers to as the church and government's ideal."

"Aye, Phemie, and we won't be *'avin'* no Protestant babies, neither," said Susie Kelly. "Of that ya can be damn *shoore*. Right, Meggie?"

18 May 1875

Phemie was correct in saying that the savages are a democratic people, and using her example I have begun to make tiny inroads in liberating myself from the drudgery of women's chores. It seems useful if one displays some other talent, even if it is only perceived as such by the savages. Like those scamps, the Kelly girls, who are largely excused from manual labor for no better reason than that they are twins! In this same way the savages are fascinated with my notebook and may even be ascribing some supernatural quality to my writing in it—which may yet prove useful to me. Yet I will not be a shirker, for it would be unfair to the others and to my fellow tentmates if I did not do my fair share.

I have this also to say on behalf of the savages: they are a tremendously tolerant people, and though some of our ways and customs appear to amuse them to no end, they have yet to be condemnatory or censorious. Thus far they seem to be merely curious, but always respectful. The children are particularly fascinated with our presence and stop whatever

they are doing to stare at us when we pass with round dis-
believing eyes as if we are enormously odd creatures to
them—and, indeed, I suppose we are! Sometimes they come
forward shyly and touch our dresses, only to run away giggling. Often they follow us about at a slight distance, like a
pack of hungry dogs. I brought with me a little hard candy
from the supply store at Fort Laramie and often I carry a
few pieces in my pockets to give to the children. They are
precious little things, brown and full of healthful vigor. They
seem for their age more mature, healthier, and better behaved than Caucasian children of comparable years. They
are too shy to speak to us, and take my offerings of candy
with great solemnity and then run off again posthaste chattering like magpies. I feel that the children may prove to be
our bridge to the savage way of life and theirs to ours, for all
children are good, are they not? All children are children finally—it hardly matters to which race or culture they
belong—they belong first to the race and culture of children.
I so look forward to learning this difficult language that I
may speak to these tiny savage elves. How I love the sight of
them! What joy, mixed with sorrow, they bring to my heart
when I watch them playing their games about the camp. For
I cannot help but think of my own dear babies . . . How I
long to hold them in my arms . . . and how I find myself beginning to look forward to bearing one of these little heathens myself!

Speaking of children, I have tried as well as I can to keep
watch over little Sara. A most extraordinary thing has occurred. We have heard the child speak, just a few words, and
not in English, but in the Indian tongue—it is either that or
pure gibberish, for neither Martha nor I was able to make
any sense of it. Her young fiancé, Yellow Wolf, seems to understand her perfectly, and so I can only assume that he is

teaching her his language—though I still cannot make her to utter one single word of ours. Isn't it strange? And wonderful . . . Perhaps romance is blooming here among the savages after all.

For her part Martha seems to be having some problems adjusting to the savage life and inevitably her own high expectations of romance with her fierce, unkempt warrior Mr. Tangle Hair, have been somewhat disappointed. "He seems to be a kind fellow, May," she said to me while we were digging roots with the other women yesterday morning. "But I do so wish he would groom himself." Then she paused in her work. "Something I've been wondering—after our marriage am I to be known as Mrs. Tangle Hair? Because you do know what the savages call me now, don't you? Reverend Hare has just translated it for me. They call me Falls Down Woman. It is because I'm so clumsy."

The savages do seem to seize upon some obvious physical characteristics in their choice of names, and, in fact, poor Martha is a bit clumsy—constantly stumbling and falling.

"It's only because you insist on wearing your high buttonshoes with the tall heels, Martha," I said. "These were fine on the boardwalks of Chicago but are entirely inappropriate for walking on the uneven ground of Nature. And they are certainly not intended for laboring in the root fields. Why just look at them!"

"I know, of course you're right, May," Martha said, "I've practically ruined them . . . but . . . but" and I could tell the poor thing was about to break down . . . "they remind me of home." And then she began to weep, terrible shuddering sobs. "I'm sorry, May," she blubbered, "I'm just tired . . . I'm homesick. I don't wish to be known as Falls Down Woman, or as Mrs. Tangle Hair. I want to go home."

"Well, dear," I said, trying to console her, "that you can't do right now. But you could teach your future husband to comb his hair. And if you're unhappy with your own new Indian name, we'll just see that it's changed."

"And how shall we do that?" asked Martha, wiping her nose with a handkerchief, her sobs subsiding.

"It seems to me that the Indians are forever changing names on the least whim or fancy," I said. "Perhaps if you perform some deed or other, or adopt some new habit, or even simply don some article of clothing—wear one of your scarves over your head, for instance. Then, no doubt they will begin to call you Woman who Wears Scarf on Head—"

"Why on earth would I wish to be named that?" Martha asked, rather petulantly. I'm afraid that the general strangeness and the homesickness we are all feeling, coupled with the exhaustion of our labors and the frequently sleepless nights, have caused all of our moods to be a bit erratic.

"I only use that as an example, Martha," I said. "Tell me, what would you like to be called?"

"Something more romantic—your name, for instance, Swallow—*Mesoke*—it's quite lovely in either language. Or the one they call Woman Who Moves Against the Wind. How much more charming that is than Falls Down Woman."

"Well then, we must think of a name that pleases you and that somehow suits you . . . God this is filthy work, is it not?" I said, pausing, and throwing down the crude little spadelike implement that the savages fashion out of wood and stone for this chore. "It's ruining my fingernails—look how cracked and dirt-encrusted they are. Had I known we were to be doing work as fieldhands I'd have brought with me a proper pair of gloves and a spade. Soon they'll be calling me Needs Manicure Woman."

"But who gives out these names?" asked Martha, unamused by my attempt at humor—and to my way of thinking somewhat preoccupied with the matter. "How is it that they come into general usage?"

"As I make it out, they just occur," I answered, "for the most banal reasons. Someone sees you stumble and fall down, for instance, in the high-buttoned shoes that you insist on wearing, and the next time your name comes up in general conversation, they say, 'Oh, you know the one I mean—the woman who falls down.'"

"Why can't they simply call me by my Christian name—Martha?"

"In case you haven't noticed, my friend," I said, "we are not presently among Christians. Now, let's put our heads together and think of a suitable name for you, and then we shall launch a campaign to bring it into general usage."

"But we are unable even to speak the language," Martha said. "It's hopeless." And I feared that she was going to start crying again.

"No matter," I said. "We're learning the sign language, and we can always enlist the assistance of Reverend Hare—assuming, that is, that we can get his enormous Episcopalian backside off the buffalo robes. In any case, as I have said, these names seem to come about more as a result of actions or physical characteristics."

We considered the matter for a while as we continued to dig the damnable roots. Finally I had an idea. "How would you feel about the name: Woman Who Leaps Fire? Personally, I find it rather enigmatic . . . romantic."

Martha brightened perceptibly. "Why yes! I like that very much. Leaps Fire Woman! And I think I know what you are going to suggest."

"Exactly," I said. "From now on, every time you come to one of the fires smoldering outside the lodges, or for that matter, inside Mr. Tangle Hair's own lodge, simply leap over it. You are bound to earn the new name. What else could be construed from such an action?"

Ah, but here is the unfortunate result of our seemingly well-laid plan; Martha is not athletically inclined, a fact which I should have considered. The first fire she came to after she left me, she attempted to leap in the witness of a number of the savages, but, partly because she was still wearing those damnable high shoes of hers, she stumbled and fell directly into the fire pit and was no sooner covered head to toe in black oily soot. The Indians do have an uncanny knack for choosing names and this morning, according to the Reverend, poor Martha is referred to by two names: Falls Down in Fire Woman, and, the even less attractive Ash Faced Woman. I'm afraid that she will never live this down . . . how lucky for me that I made my impulsive dive into the beaver pond . . .

19 May 1875

My dearest sister Hortense,

It occurs to me that I have not written to you for an entire month—certainly the strangest month of my life! How much there is to tell you. But first how is dear Walter? And the children? Father and Mother? Do send news, won't you . . . ah, if only you could . . . if only I could have news of my babies . . .

Of course mail delivery is somewhat spotty out here on the frontier, but you might try addressing your correspondence to: Madame Little Wolf, Queen of the Savages, or, less formally, to Swallow, in care of the Cheyenne Nation, Somewhere in the middle of Nowhere, Nebraska Territory, USA . . . yes that should find me posthaste . . . Hah! . . . if only . . .

Truth be told, I have no idea where we are. Another world

certainly . . . Sometimes I try to imagine all of you back in Chicago comfortably ensconced in the bosom of civilization, sitting in Mother's drawing room at teatime, for instance . . . I must concentrate so hard to conjure the image, truly my imagination fails me, just as you cannot possibly imagine the life I am leading . . . not in your wildest dreams, my sister . . . not even in your wildest nightmares can you possibly envisage this Indian village, these people, this landscape.

Let me describe to you a bit of the daily routine of camp life among the savages. The three Mrs. Little Wolves, yes, there are three of us—the old one, the young one, and, most recently the Caucasian one, though as yet we are only betrothed (the Chief is, it occurs to me, what my Harry would have undoubtedly called "one lucky redskin")—all inhabit the same tipi, a lodge it is grandiloquently called in the periodicals but it is certainly not to be mistaken for Father's hunting lodge on the lake—it is actually nothing more than a large round tent, possibly fifteen feet in diameter—you've undoubtedly seen artists' renderings of these primitive habitations— made from buffalo hides and painted with crude aboriginal designs. The floor is earth, there is a fire ring in the center, and our "beds," if such they may be called, are animal skins spread atop tree boughs and leaves, each with a wooden-framed backrest for reclining in a sitting position if one wishes . . . somewhat like a divan. Well, I must admit, finally, that this arrangement is not entirely without its comforts once one grows accustomed to life without furniture and to sleeping on the ground.

There are, I may have neglected to mention not only we three women, and the Chief himself, but a young girl, named Pretty Walker, presumably the Chief's daughter by his first marriage, a young boy who looks after the horses and who I take to be an orphan, and an old crone, who looks exactly like the witch of childhood nightmares, with a large hooked nose and who serves the function of tent organizer and enforcer; she stands guard immediately inside and to the left of the entranceway to the tent, and brandishes a large wooden club at the slightest infraction of a multitude of complicated tipi "rules and regulations" with which I am still not completely familiar.

And finally, completing our big happy family is an infant child, the progeny of the second wife, Feather on Head. The child is so perfectly quiet that I actually lived in the lodge for several days before I was aware of his existence. Indian babies do not cry as do our own; it is quite extraordinary, they are rather like deer fawns, not uttering a sound to give them away. Too, I think his mother may, out of some sort of protective maternal instinct, have intentionally kept the child hidden from me for the first few days of my residency . . . oh, Hortense, when I discovered the baby, or I should say, when Feather on Head finally revealed him to me, how my heart ached, a bittersweet ache of joy at the sight of this tiny infant, and of longing for my own two dears . . . how clearly he brought them back, their pinched smiling faces . . . will I ever see them again?

The child took to me immediately; as you know I have always had an affinity for babies—hah! yes I know, both with bearing them and with caring for them . . . He smiled up at me, truly a little cherub, brown as a chestnut, his eyes as bright as copper pennies, and when Feather on Head witnessed her son's and my obvious mutual affection she became instantly warm toward me. She softened and smiled shyly and we have since become quite friendly, my first friend so far among the Cheyennes! Although perforce our ability to communicate is yet limited by the language barrier. Feather on Head is helping me greatly with my sign language, and although I am trying to make some sense of the Cheyenne tongue itself, I think that I shall never be able to speak it. It is a language that often appears to be without vowels—a language of the crudest sounds rather than words—hisses, grunts, and ululations—strange noises that seem to issue from some older and more primitive earth than the one you and I inhabit. Or I should say than you inhabit . . .

I have recently discovered that a few of the savages do possess an extremely limited command of the English language and even more of them appear to be decently proficient in a kind of bastardized French—which they first learned some years ago from the old-time French fur trappers and traders, and which has been passed down as a kind of patois, barely comprehensible to us but certainly more so than their native tongue. How I wish you could hear their accents, dear sister! The first time this abomination assaulted my ears I didn't even recognize it as the French language—but at least it sounded vaguely familiar. Fortunately, there is one French girl among us, a very pretty dark-haired girl named Marie Blanche de Bretonne, who was touring America with her parents when they were tragically killed by thieves in our fair city of Chicago. Truly, no one is safe any longer in this world. While still in shock and mourning, the poor girl, alone in a strange city, stranded thousands of miles from home, signed up for this program. Like many of our little group, I'm afraid that she is having second thoughts about the matter . . . In any case it was through Marie Blanche that we first discovered the Cheyennes' ability to speak French, if indeed we may call it that. Why, Hortense, truly it would be enough to make our childhood tutor, Madame Bouvier, turn over in her grave. You remember what a stickler she was for pronunciation? how she would rap our knuckles with her pointer when we got it wrong, and say "Zat eees eencarrect, mademoiselle" . . . But I digress, *n'est-ce pas?* I must stop recalling the past, which comes back to me so vividly when I write to you, as if this new life is but a dream and you, still living in the real world, are trying to pull me back . . . too late, alas, too late . . . would that it could be so . . .

As you might imagine it is hardly an enviable position to find oneself in the home (the word "home" I'm afraid does not properly conjure our bizarre living arrangements) of another woman—in this case, two women—as the soon-to-be third bride of their husband. The older wife, Quiet One, has been far less accepting of me than young Feather on Head. Some nights I lie awake on my bed (such as it is) in mortal fear that she will cut my throat with a knife if I dare to fall asleep . . .

The situation is awkward to say the least. Indeed the word "awkward" hardly describes it. Yes, well we are people from such different . . . backgrounds . . . God, I sound just like Mother when she would lecture us all those years ago about playing with the servant children . . . I begin to understand that this experience requires a new vocabulary altogether—trying to explain it to you would be like trying to describe the world of Shakespeare to the savages . . . the words don't exist, language fails . . . John Bourke was right . . .

Yes, well let me try again. We live in a tent—why mince words, a tent made of animal hides—three wives, a girl, an old crone, an infant child, a young orphan boy, who seems to have been adopted by the Chief's family and who cares for the Chief's considerable string of horses and sometimes helps the women with the chores, and this man Little Wolf, who is a great Chief of his people.

It is quite a spacious tent, as tents go, I'll say that for it. I have my own charming little corner space . . . if it is possible to have corners in a round tent . . . where I sleep upon a bed of pine boughs, animal hides, and trade blankets. The odors in our "home" are quite indescribable—a word that I find myself using often in my attempts at rendering these little scenes on paper. There are the odors of human bodies, of the earth beneath us, of the animal skins used as bedding, of the smoke from the fire . . . Added to these, if the wives have been cooking (which they seem perpetually in the process of doing, for the savages do not seem to observe the custom of breakfast, dinner, and supper at regular hours as we do, but rather eat whenever they are hungry so that there must always be food available) there is generally also an odor inside the tent of food being prepared. Sometimes the cooking scents are actually appetizing, at other times the stench rising from the pot is so perfectly revolting that I can hardly bear it, I feel that I shall be sick and must stumble outside and gasp fresh air and I know that I shall go hungry that day. As you know, Hortense, I have always been interested in the culinary arts as a recreational pastime, but I have not yet offered my services in the "kitchen" such as it is (another excellent example of the inadequacies of language) nor indeed have I been asked to help with meal preparation. However, if I am to live here among these people I fully intend to take a turn at the stove . . . the fire . . . Perhaps I will make my tentmates a lovely little French dish, say a delightful Coq au Vin . . . Harry's favorite repast . . . though, of course, the first question that presents itself is where might I obtain a decent bottle of French burgundy wine? Or for that matter, any bottle of wine . . . Hah! . . . But now I allow myself to drift off again into thoughts of that old life, which can only make this new one so much more precarious and difficult, and . . . insupportable.

Now then, dearest sister, on the brighter side. It has finally been determined that we are to be wed with the others in a group ceremony tomorrow evening. Reverend Hare, an enormous Episcopalian missionary who has accompanied us into the wilderness, will be performing the Christian services. Would that you were here to act as my bridesmaid! Ah, how I love to imagine the family all gathered together . . . staying in our . . . guest tent! Father thin-lipped and appalled, Mother alternately weeping and swooning in abject horror of the heathens. Why, we'd be administering smelling salts to her every quarter hour! God, what fun it would be! I, who have always had such a talent for shocking the family, have this time truly outdone myself, wouldn't you agree?

As I understand it this mass wedding is an unprecedented event and one that does not fit neatly into any of the established ceremonies of the Cheyennes. For the savages, the giving of horses, a feast, and a dance are all that is required to seal the marriage union, it being a simple agreement between the two parties—much as Harry and I took up our life together. Being neither of a particularly religious bent myself, nor, as you know, much interested in the institution of marriage, I find this arrangement to be quite adequate.

However, the addition of Christian nuptials into the upcoming ceremony has got things all complicated both among our women and among the Indians. The savages are unable to reach consensus on even the smallest matters without hours of incredibly laborious deliberation. Now after much "powwowing" and smoking of pipes with Reverend Hare (in this one regard it strikes me that men of all races are similar), the parties seem finally to have come to terms.

In this same way, the savages are absolute sticklers for protocol—some of their customs so peculiar as to simply defy description. Hardly a day goes by that I don't violate some bizarre cultural tabu or other. For instance, it appears that when seated in the lodge the well-brought-up Indian maiden is expected to sit with her feet pointing to the right—except in the case of one particular band to which some of our women have gone and which is encamped slightly separated from the main camp and in which the women are noted for sitting with their feet pointing to the left. Yes, well, I have absolutely no idea how or why these preposterous customs became established in the first place, but the savages take them with the utmost seriousness. My Captain Bourke says that these are due to their innately superstitious nature. On my very first day here, I immediately cast my feet in the wrong direction and there suddenly issued from the women in our tent all manner of disapproving clucking and general distress. The old crone went so far as to wave her stick at me, jabbering like a mad hen. Of course I pay no attention to the position of my feet and shall continue to sit in the lodge with them pointing in whatever direction I damn well choose—regardless of the deep anxiety this appears to cause my tent-mates. So you see, Hortense, just as in my "old" life, I am already a fly in the ointment of savage society, already rocking the conventional boat, already considered to be something of a scandal . . . which has always seemed to be my mission in whatever culture I live, does it not?

Ah, but here was a lovely surprise: My fellow wives have sewn for me the most beautiful wedding gown upon which I have ever gazed. It is made of antelope hide—the softest skin imaginable—sewn with sinew thread and intricately embroidered with beads and porcupine quills, and dyed with the essence of roots in exquisite colors and designs. I was completely flabbergasted—and very much touched—when they presented it to me, for it must clearly represent hundreds of hours of the most intensive labor imaginable and would seem to indicate that they have accepted me into their family—and in very gracious fashion, indeed. It is, I understand, common practice for the bride's family to make for her an elaborate wedding dress, but as we are all without our families here, other women of the tribe have taken it upon themselves to dress us properly for the occasion. In fact, all of our other women have also been presented with wedding dresses—in most cases made for them by the sisters and mothers of their intended. I may surely be prejudiced in the matter, but of those dresses I've seen so far, mine is by far the most beautiful, certainly the most elaborately decorated. Perhaps because I am to marry the great Chief, special attention was taken in its creation . . . Even the sullen and unfriendly Quiet One participated in the making of this gown—which is not to suggest that she is warming in any way to my presence.

As you might well imagine, I and most of the other ladies have balked at giving up our own clothing in favor of the savage attire. The clothes and meager personal possessions which we have brought with us into this wilderness represent our last connection to the civilized world, so we are naturally reluctant to part with them—for fear that once we don savage garb, we become perforce savages—not just the brides of savages, but savages ourselves. This is, you understand, an important distinction . . . Some in our group are so intent on keeping up their attire and toilet, no matter how inappropriate these may be, that they can sometimes be seen promenading through the camp—little gaggles of our ladies strolling and chatting and twirling their parasols as if on a garden tour, trying desperately to appear oblivious to our present circumstances. I think that they are quite mad—indeed, some of them really are mad—but while I personally have decided to give up such attempts to forge civilization out of wilderness, I must admit that I have not quite yet resigned myself to dressing exclusively in animal skins.

Fortunately, the Cheyennes are traders, as well as hunters, and some of their attire is not so terribly different from our own. They have available, for instance, cloth and blankets and buttons, and other articles from our world. Indeed, some of the men dress quite ludicrously in bits and pieces of white man's clothing, wearing altered U.S. Army uniforms, and hats—all misshapen and with the tops cut out and eagle feathers protruding from them. This gives the Indians who affect this attire the appearance of children playing dress up; they look more like carnival clowns than soldiers—their outfits bizarre hybrids of the two cultures . . .

I'm pleased to report that my own intended dresses very modestly in traditional Indian garb. The only white man article which he affects is a large silver peace medal around his neck, a gift from President Grant himself.

But I seem to be rambling again . . . where was I? Ah, yes, with the exception of Miss White and some of her more strident followers we are to be married in traditional Cheyenne wedding gowns. We are to be dressed prior to the feast by our Cheyenne "mothers" and "sisters," literally stripped of our civilized clothing and dressed as savages—this is difficult to describe to you, Hortense, and, I'm certain, even more difficult for you to understand, but the prospect is somehow both . . . terrifying and exhilarating.

Without intending to keep you in undue suspense, I shall continue this correspondence after I am officially a bride . . . right now there is much to do.

21 May 1875

Good God, Hortense, so much to tell you, I am only now, two days later awakening from the experience . . . I am still not myself, fear that I shall never again be the same. I have been drugged, my senses assaulted, my very being stripped to its primitive core . . . its savage heart . . . where to begin . . . ?

The music . . . still beats in my mind, throbs through my body . . . dancers whirling in the firelight . . . coyotes on the hilltops and ridges, taking up the song beneath the moon . . .

22 May 1875

Forgive me, dear sister, but I fell back into a deep slumber after my last incoherent ramblings . . . I must have slept the full day and night round and I woke feeling better, stronger, a child grows inside of me . . . is it possible? Or have I only dreamed this, too . . .

Yes, the scene of our wedding night is even more vividly etched now in my mind . . . let me describe it to you:

The moon was full in the sky; it rose early before the sun had set and did not set again until after the sun rose; the moon spent the entire night crossing the sky, illuminating the dancers in an unearthly glow, casting their shadows across the plains as if the earth itself danced . . . all who danced lit by moonlight.

We spent nearly the full day of the wedding in our lodges being dressed by the women, ornaments and totems hung from our clothing and from our hair, our faces painted with bizarre designs so that we would hardly recognize one another later under the pure white moon . . . perhaps this was just as well, perhaps our painted faces were meant as disguises, allowing each of us, savage and civilized alike, to act out these pagan rites in anonymity. It is true that several days later—or so I feel it to be for I have lost all track of time—we "civilized" women are hardly able to look one another in the eye for the madness that overcame us.

The men had recently returned from a successful buffalo hunt—stupidly, it had never occurred to me that the Cheyennes had been waiting for that good fortune to befall them before scheduling the wedding feast, because of course, without the bounty of the hunt, it would be a poor feast, indeed. Clearly, I have as much to learn about the ways of subsistence living as they do about those of civilization.

As it was, individual feasts were held in virtually every lodge in the camp, a kind of large, communal, movable feast. There was a vast amount of food, much of it surprisingly palatable. The first wife, Quiet One, is renowned in the camp for her talents as a cook and outdid herself on this occasion. She roasted the tender ribs and liver of the buffalo over coals, and boiled the tongue, and from another pot served a stew of meat and the wild turnips referred to by their French name, *pommes blanches*. There were other roots and various spring greens with which I am not familiar by name, but all quite interesting to the taste. We "brides" were not allowed to lift a finger—to the point that even our food was cut up for us in small morsels and hand-fed to us by our Indian attendants, as if they were trying to conserve our strength . . . now I understand why.

There was one particular dish that I must tell you about, a dish that most of our women, myself included, were unable to tolerate. Too horrible! Too despicable! Boiled dog! Yes, yes, choked pup! It is considered a great delicacy, saved for just such a special occasion as our wedding. My friend Feather on Head who served the older one as a kind of *sous chef*, performed the gruesome task of wringing the little puppy's neck just prior to cooking—which she did with her bare hands as casually as if she was wringing out a dishcloth. My God! When I tried to intervene, to rescue the poor little thing from her death grip, she merely laughed and pulled away and continued her stranglehold until the flailing puppy was limp and lifeless. It was then scalded in boiling water, scraped of hair, gutted, and roasted over the fire, and all present made such a fuss about its culinary qualities with much satisfied oohing and ahhing and general lip-smacking. I could not bring myself to taste the dog meat—even its odor while cooking sickened me.

Our tipi was crowded with twelve people exactly, the majority of them clearly chosen because they were poor. You would know little about this, Hortense, because you have led such a sheltered and privileged life, but there is a universality to poverty that transcends culture; just as in our own society, there are among the savages both rich and poor—those who are successful hunters and providers who live in well-appointed lodges with many hides and robes and have a good string of horses, and those who have little and depend on the largesse of their neighbors. And never have I seen a more generous, selfless people than these. I believe that those unfortunates who came to our lodge that night—there, you see, already I begin to take a proprietary interest in my living quarters!—were the families of men who had been killed in battle, or possibly the families of some of those poor wretches whom we had encountered at the forts—the drunks and beggars who had deserted their wives and children . . .

one can't help but wonder what we are doing to these people that their lives and livelihoods unravel so with our presence—"spoiled" by contact with us, as the Captain put it . . .

It seems to be a primary duty of my husband . . . how strange to say . . . my husband Little Wolf . . . as head Chief to look after the poor of his people. Several women brought children of various ages with them to the feast; they sat quietly in the back of the lodge, silently accepting the food their mothers passed them.

After all had eaten, the younger children, sated, fell asleep on the robes, the men passed a pipe and told stories, which of course, I could not understand, but to which the older children listened raptly. Possibly it was the effect of the food, or the warmth inside the lodge, or simply the soft murmuring of the men's voices—I confess that I am beginning to find the language less objectionable; it possesses a certain rhythm and cadence that though primitive is no longer so displeasing to the ear—I began to fall into a kind of trance, a state that was like sleep, but I was not asleep, just floating as if in a dream, as if drugged.

Then by some unspoken signal, everyone began to leave the lodges to assemble in the communal circle around which the tents are strategically placed . . . this is, I suppose, something like our own town square, but of course round rather than square. All is round in this strange new world . . . The musicians (yes, well, again I must use the term loosely for they would hardly be confused for the Chicago Philharmonic Orchestra!) and the singers and dancers also began to assemble. Our own women gathered in small clusters to inspect each other's "wedding gowns," to marvel at each other's painted faces and outlandish costumes. My friend Martha was made up to look like a badger—an uncanny resemblance—with a black mask and white stripe down her forehead and nose. I have no idea for what purpose, but the savages have some meaning for everything. For my part half my face was painted black with white stars forming constellations on my cheeks and the full moon on my forehead, the other side of my face was painted all white with a blue river meandering its length. "You are the day and night," Martha said strangely, marveling, she too appearing to be in some kind of narcotic stupor. "You are the heavens and the earth!"

"*Aye*, and we're a pair of foxes we are, Meggie!" said the Kelly sister Susan appreciatively. Surely the red-haired Irish twins were no less identical got up with real fox heads attached to their hair and fox tails pinned to their rears. An uncanny likeness, and knowing something of the girls' wily natures, a stroke of pure genius on the part of the heathens.

But perhaps most striking of our group was the Negro Phemie, her entire face and body painted white with brilliant red stripes running up her arms, around her neck and eyes, her full Negro lips painted crimson, even her hair painted blood red—my God, she was magnificent to behold . . . a savage dream goddess.

Now appeared the holy man they call Dog Woman and his apprentice, named Bridge Girl—also a *he'emnane'e*, as these half-men/half-women are called. Two stranger creatures I have never before laid eyes upon! The young apprentice, Bridge Girl, speaks in the soft, high voice of a female, but is clearly a young boy. The older man, too, is effeminate in both voice and gesture. Yes, well we've seen similar people on the streets of Chicago—Nancy Boys, Father refers to them.

Now these two set about organizing the dancers, which they did with great solemnity and skill. The men/women are said to possess special abilities at matchmaking and are very popular with the young people, their advice in matters of the heart much sought after. For they know everything of both sexes.

Now at last the music began—an entire savage orchestra! Flute players, drum beaters, gourd shakers . . . a primitive symphony, to be sure, that makes for a crude harmony . . . but one with an undeniably rhythmic power. Then the singers took up the song, the eeriest song I've ever heard, the higher notes of the women floating lightly over the deeper tones of the men, a throbbing, steady, repetitive beat like a riffle running into a pool . . . it sent chills up my spine and in concert with the otherworldly music actually caused a number of our women to swoon dead away, they had to be revived by the fire—a huge bonfire that had been built in the center of the circle, flames and sparks leaping into the night sky, licking the heavens . . . I assure you, dear sister, not even the lunatic asylum in full riot could prepare one for this bizarre spectacle . . .

Dog Woman announced the different dances, sometimes gently scolding the young people if they did not perform the steps exactly right. Truly, she reminded me of old Miss Williams at our dancing school in Chicago—you remember her don't you, Hortense? . . . you see, still I clutch these memories to draw me back, to keep me from going completely mad in the face of this assault on our sensibilities . . .

The children sat in the back behind the adults on the outside of the circle, watching raptly, beating time with their hands and feet, their faces shining in the moonlight, the flames from the fire sparking in their slate-colored eyes, flickering golden in their oiled black hair.

Now the huge Reverend Hare resplendent in his white clerical gown made his grand entrance. He held his Bible aloft for all to see. Although the savages cannot read, they know it to be a sacred text—being a people to whom totemic objects are of utmost importance—and many crowded around him trying to touch it. The Reverend called out and the grooms began to appear out of the shadows of the fire, seemed to issue from the flames themselves like phantoms. I am to this day not absolutely certain that we had not been unwittingly drugged during the feast, for we all remarked later on the dreamlike state we felt.

If we brides considered ourselves to be elaborately made up for the occasion, the grooms were even more fantastically painted and adorned. It was difficult even to identify some of them and many of our women had simply to take as an article of faith the fact that the man standing beside them was really their intended. I did recognize my Chief Little Wolf, who wore a headdress with buffalo horns on either side, black raven feathers surrounding his head, ringed by eagle feathers, spilling like a tail down his back. He wore spotless new beaded moccasins, a fine deerskin shirt artfully trimmed with what, I now realize, can only have been human hair. Over his shoulders he wore a buffalo robe that had been painted red and was adorned with all manner of intricate designs. In one hand he carried a red rattle, which he shook softly in time to the music, and in the other a lance trimmed with soft fur. He was a picture of savage splendor, and in my altered state of mind, I felt oddly proud to be standing beside him. Well, after all, isn't this how a girl is supposed to feel on her wedding day?

Over the sound of the music and with the dancers still performing in the background, Reverend Hare began reciting the Christian wedding vows. Whatever else may be said of the man he has a commanding and sonorous speaking voice, which managed to rise above the music:

"Dearly beloved we are gathered together here in the sight of God, and in the face of this company to join together these men and these women in holy matrimony . . ."

And each verse, the Reverend repeated in Cheyenne.

"Into this holy estate these couples present come now to be joined. If any man can show just cause why they may not lawfully be joined together, let him now speak, or else hereafter forever hold his peace . . ."

Did Captain John G. Bourke swoop into the camp at this moment atop his big white horse and snatch me away from these proceedings, carry me off to live in a little house set in a grove of cottonwoods on the edge of a meadow, by the banks of a creek, at which safe harbor I would be re-united with my own sweet babies and bear others by my dashing Captain and there live out my life as a good Christian wife and devoted mother? No, alas, he did not . . . Did I pray fervently that at this very moment in the ceremony of matrimony, my Captain would rescue me thusly? . . . Yes . . . I did, I confess that I did . . . God help me.

"Wilt thou have this Woman to thy wedded wife, to live together after God's ordinance, in the holy estate of Matrimony? Wilt thou love her, comfort her, honor, and keep her, in sickness and in health; and forsaking all others, keep thee only unto her, so long as you both shall live?"

When the Reverend uttered his translation of this last verse, a collective *"houing"* arose from the grooms, a strange noise like an unearthly wind blowing through the assemblage.

"Wilt thou have this Man to thy wedded Husband, to live together after God's ordinance, in the holy estate of Matrimony? Wilt thou

obey him, and serve him, love, honor, and keep him, in sickness and
in health; and forsaking all others, keep thee only unto him, so long
as ye both shall live?"

There was a long pause here before there came from
among us a scattering of "I will's," some of them barely more
than murmurs, remarkable for their general lack of conviction. I know, too, that a number of our women did not answer
the question at all, but left it hanging there in limbo as their
final escape . . .

"And to those whom God hath joined together, let no man put asun-
der. Foreasmuch as these men and women have consented together in
holy wedlock, and have witnessed the same before God and this com-
pany, and thereto have given and pledged their troth, each to the
other, and have declared the same by joining hands; I pronounce,
that they are Husband and Wife; in the name of the Father, and of
the Son, and of the Holy Ghost . . . Amen."

And then it was done . . . A stunned silence fell over our
company of women as the full import of this momentous occasion made itself felt. The grooms, seemingly less impressed
by their new matrimonial state, faded back into the shadows
from whence they came, to rejoin the dancers. Meanwhile
we brides came together in small coveys and in some mental
disorder, to congratulate one another, or commiserate, which-
ever the case might be, over our newly wedded state. Some
wept, but I do not believe that these were tears of joy. All
wondered what was to come now . . .

"Are we truly married, Father, in the eyes of God?" asked
the strange woman, "Black Ada" Ware, of the Reverend. She
was dressed still in mourning for her wedding, her black veil
in place. "Is it so?"

All gathered about, I think hoping that the large Reverend might relieve our minds by telling us that, no, it had been nothing more than a sham ceremony, we were not truly married to these foreign creatures . . .

"Have I married a damn *niggah*?" asked Daisy Lovelace, who had also declined to be attired by our hosts and who wore, by contrast, a stunning white lace wedding gown which she had brought with her especially for the occasion. Now the woman pulled her silver flask from under her dress and took a long swallow.

"That's certainly a lovely wedding gown, Miss Lovelace," said Martha, who seemed still to be in a sort of trance.

"It belonged to my dear departed *Motha*," said the woman. "*Ah* was to wear this gown, myself, when *Ah* married Mr. Wesley Chestnut of Albany, Georgia. But after Daddy lost everything in the *wah*, Mr. Chestnut had a sudden change a heart, if you know what *Ah* mean.

"If *Motha* and *Daddy* could only see their little baby girl now," she said, "havin' entered into holy matrimony with a gentleman with the deeply unfortunate name of *Miistah Bluuddy Fuuuut*" (her husband's descriptive name, in fact, was gained by the actions of her brave little dog, Fern Louise). "My *Gawd*!" And then the woman began to laugh, and suddenly I felt a new sympathy toward her, I understood fully and for the first time why she had signed up for this program; she had lost her fortune, had been left standing at the altar by a cad, and was quite possibly no longer as young as she claimed. For all her ugly bigotry, I began to like Miss Lovelace infinitely better for the touching fact that she had brought her mother's wedding gown along with her on this adventure. It proved that for all her apparent cynicism she still held on to hopes, dreams. And I began to laugh with her at the sheer absurdity of our situation, and soon all of us were laughing, looking at each other, some of us made up like demons from hell, married now to barbarians, we laughed until tears ran down our grotesquely painted faces. Yes, surely we had been drugged . . .

After we had spent ourselves laughing and the strange reality of our situation had once again insinuated itself into our befuddled consciousnesses, we wiped our tears and gathered in little coveys, clustered together for protection like confused chickens—indeed, that's what we most resembled, with our painted faces and our colorfully ornamented dresses.

We were naturally shy to take up the dance, but true to her nature, our brave good Phemie was the first to join in. "I must show them how an Ashanti dances," she said to us in her sonorous voice. "The way my mother taught me." For a moment all the Cheyenne dancers paused to watch our bold and unashamed Negress, as she took her place in the dance line. We were very proud of her. She did not dance in the same style as the Indians . . . in fact she was a superior dancer, her step sinuous and graceful, her long legs flashing beneath her dress, she pranced and whirled to the pulsing beat—but careful to follow the steps to the dance, as specified by a stern Dog Woman—who tolerated no unauthorized variations. A general murmuring of approval ran among the Indians who spectated, and then I believe that the dancing became even freer and more frenzied.

"My, that big *niggah* girl can surely dance," said Daisy Lovelace. "Daddy, God rest his soul, always did say they had special rhythm. *Enabuddy* care for a little sip a *medicine*," she asked, holding out her flask.

"*Aye*, I'll have a wee nip of it, *shoore*," said Meggie Kelly. "Loosens my dancin' feet, it does." And she took the flask from Daisy and took a quick pull, making a small grimace and passing it to her sister. "*T'isn't* Irish whiskey, that's *sartain*, Susie, but under the circumstances, it'll 'ave to do."

And then the Kelly sisters themselves melted into the dance—a more fearless pair of twins you could not hope to find; they hiked their skirts up and performed a kind of lively Irish jig to the music. Which made old Dog Woman crazy with anxiety at the impropriety of their steps!

"*Oh vat de* hell, I *tink* I may as *vell* join *een*, too!" announced dear homely Gretchen, encouraged by the twins' boldness. "I *ben* watching, I *tink* I learn *de* steps now." Gretchen was herself painted up in dark earth tones and wrapped in a rare blond buffalo robe adorned with primitive designs. Indeed, she resembled nothing so much as an enormous buffalo cow. Now she entered the dance line herself, God bless her. "*Yah!*" she called out with her typical gusto, "*Yah!*" and she took up the step with a heavy Slavic polkalike gait, a bovine gracelessness that provided additional humor to the moment. Several of us began to giggle watching her, covering our mouths with our hands, and even some of the native dancers and spectators laughed good-naturedly at her efforts. The savages are not without a sense of humor, and nothing amuses them so much as the sight of someone making a spectacle of herself.

"Lovely! Spiffing good dance!" said Helen Flight, eyebrows raised in perpetual delight. Helen, who has been given the Indian name, Woman Who Paints Birds, or just Bird Woman, was got up very stylishly to look like a prairie chicken hen with artfully placed feathers about her narrow hips and rump. "Unfortunately I've never had the talent, myself," she said. "That is to say, my dearest companion, Mrs. Ann Hall, would never permit me to dance at balls; she felt that I was always trying to lead the men and that I was 'conspicuously heavy of foot'—her words exactly, I'm afraid."

Miss Flight has already proven to be somewhat scandalous to the natives for her habit of smoking a pipe which, like the morning swim, is a savage activity very much reserved for men—and, at that, is one undertaken with much ritual and ceremony. Whereas Helen is liable to fire up her pipe at any time and in any situation—causing the savages even more consternation than when I sit in the tipi with my feet pointing the wrong way! However, because of her considerable artistic skills, which the heathens hold in the very highest esteem, they have chosen to more or less tolerate Helen's smoking. (A primer on savage etiquette would be most useful to us all.)

Narcissa White came now among us, nearly beside herself with Christian righteousness. Evidently her religious beliefs do not permit dancing. "The recreation of the Devil," she objected. "His evil trick to inflame the passions and overcome the intellect."

"Thank *Gawd* for it," said Daisy Lovelace. "What would we do here with intellect, *Nahcissa*?"

Nor had Miss White allowed herself to be dressed in native attire; she still wore her high-buttoned shoes and high-collared missionary dress. "How can we possibly hope to Christianize these poor creatures," she asked, "if we allow ourselves to sink to their level of degeneracy?"

"Narcissa," I said, gently, "for once why don't you stop sermonizing and try to enjoy our wedding reception. Look, even the Reverend is participating in the festivities." It was true that the Reverend had comfortably ensconced himself fireside on a mound of buffalo robes, surrounded by several of the Cheyenne holy men; he was eating as usual, and chatting animatedly with his savage counterparts.

"Quite, May!" said Helen Flight. "We shall have more than sufficient opportunity to instruct the savages in the ways of civilization. At the present time, I say, 'When in Rome . . .' Indeed my conspicuous heaviness of foot, notwithstanding, if you don't mind very much, ladies, I believe I'll give it a try. I have studied the grouse on the lek and this is one step I know." With which Helen, too, entered the dance line. "Oh, dear!" I heard her call with delight as she was swallowed by the native dancers, swept away in their midst under the moon until all I could see of her were her hands waving gaily above her head.

"God help you, people," whispered Narcissa White in a small voice.

"Gawд, Nahcissa," drawled Daisy Lovelace, "Don't be such a *дamn stick in the muд.* This is our weddin' night, we should all be *celebratin'.* Have a lil' drink, why *дon't you."* Daisy held out her flask, and seemed rather drunk herself. "We can repent *tomorah* after we have made passionate *luuuve* to our *niggah Injun* boys tonight," she continued, "because *Ah* have a *дaaahk* suspicion that *tomorah* we shall be most in need of *дeevine* forgiveness . . . But what the Hell, *Ah* believe *Ah'll* take a turn on the dance floor *mahself.* I shall pretend that *Ah'm* attendin' the spring debutante ball at the Mariposa Plantation. It is there that I came out to society and where *Ah* danced away the most glorious night of my life. Wesley Chestnut said *Ah* was the most beautiful girl at the ball . . . and afterwards he kissed me for the first time out on the *veranдa . . ."* And poor Daisy curtsied and held her arms out, as if joining an invisible partner, and said in a soft dreamy voice, "Thank you, *kinд дuh, Ah* don't *maahnд* if I do," and she began to do a slow waltz to the music, twirling in among the dancers, soon lost in their midst.

And so, one by one, each of us, trying to hold on to some precious recollection of our past, even if it was only a familiar dance step—any thin lifeline to keep us from falling completely into the abyss of savagery that was opening beneath us—so we joined, one by one, the dance.

What a sight we must have made whirling madly under the full moon . . . waltzes and jigs and polkas, a lively cancan from our pretty little French girl, Marie Blanche—for you see it did not matter what step we did, for all steps were the same finally, faster and faster, a frenzy of color, motion and sound, all the dancers now like breeding birds on the lek, plumage puffed and ruffled, the cocks' chests swelled, the hens' backsides half-turned teasing the air between them— we danced forward and back, round and round—in the music could be heard the steady booming drumming of the grouse, laid over the pulsing rhythmic heartbeat of the earth, and in the singing could be heard the elements of thunder, wind, and rain . . . this dance of earth. How the gods watching must have enjoyed their creation.

And the music and singing filled the sultry night air, washed out over the plains on the breeze so that even the animals gathered on the hills around to watch and listen—the coyotes and wolves took up the song, the bears and antelope and elk appeared—their outlines distinct on the moonlit horizon, and the children watched from behind the embers of the fire, spellbound, a bit frightened by the power of madness they beheld, and the old people watched, nodding to one another approvingly.

We danced. We danced. The People watched. The animals watched. The gods watched.

Some of the dancers danced all night, for the music played on until the first light of dawn surprised the setting moon. But most of us were claimed earlier by the families of our new husbands; they surrounded us at some point, quietly and without comment, and we followed, meek as lambs, as they led us back to the lodges.

A new tipi had been erected just outside the circle of the Little Wolf family lodges. To this I was taken and at the entrance was made to sit on a soft trade blanket spread on the ground there. Then several of the family members, who included both of the Chief's other wives as well as two young female cousins and the Chief's daughter Pretty Walker, grasped corners of the blanket and wordlessly picked me up and carried me through the entrance into the lodge—much like being carried over the threshold as is our own custom—but by the groom's family women rather than the groom himself. Now I was set down in the new lodge, beside a small fire that burned in the center. The buffalo-hide walls were newly tanned as white as parchment paper and prettily decorated with all manner of primitive drawings, some depicting the hunt, others scenes of warfare, others of men and women in sexual intimacies, of family life, children, and dogs, and still others designs that I could not decipher but were perhaps images of the heathens' gods themselves.

After all had left me alone, I breathed a great sigh of relief—privacy at last! How I hoped that this was to be my own new home. I realized that it was the very first time I had been completely alone since we had arrived here, and what a wonderful luxury it seemed. Exhausted, I stretched out on the soft blanket, before the warm fire, listening to the pulsing music . . .

I fell then into a deep slumber and had the strangest dream . . . at least it happened like a dream . . . It must have been a dream, for my husband was now in the tent with me, he was still dancing softly, noiselessly, his moccasined feet rising and falling gracefully, soundlessly, he spun softly around the fire, shaking his gourd rattle, which made no sound, danced like a spirit being around me where I lay sleeping. I began to become aroused, felt a tingling in my stomach, an erotic tickle between my thighs, the immutable pull of desire as he displayed to me. I dreamed that I saw his manhood grow from beneath his breechclout like a serpent as he danced and I lay on my stomach breathing shallowly and pressing myself against the blanket, feeling that I would explode there. I tried to reach to him but he moved away and behind me and in my dream I could feel him brushing my now naked rump as if with feathers, teasing and brushing so that I became even more aroused. And then, still lying on my stomach I raised my rump toward him, offered myself, and the brushing intensified and I fell again to press against the blanket, a deep pain of longing to be filled. And still he danced lightly, soundlessly behind me, footsteps rising and falling. Now in my dream a noise rose in my throat, like a sound issuing from another, a sound I had never before heard and I raised my rump again higher and made with it slow circular motion, an act of nature, and the brushing of feathers came again and became finally the faintest touch of flesh, a nipping at my neck, the serpent warm and dry fell across my rump, gently rested between my legs with its own pulse like a heartbeat, moving them apart, opening me, entering me slowly and painlessly and pulling back and entering me again and pulling back so that at last I thrust myself backward toward it as if to capture it once and for all, to take it in. And then it entered me deeply, completely, and the strange sound rose again in my throat and my body trembled, shook, and bucked, and in my dream I was not a human being any longer with a separate consciousness, but became a part of something older and more primitive, truer . . . Like animals, Bourke said . . . this is what he meant . . . like animals . . .

There the dream ended and I remember nothing more until I woke up alone at dawn still lying facedown on the blanket, still dressed in my deer-hide wedding dress. I know that it can only have been a dream, an erotic dream the likes of which I had never before experienced. But I also know that, as if by magic, a child now grows inside of me . . .

Well, Hortense, what else is there to say of that night? Would that you could read these words—how shocked you would be by the erotic details of my wedding night! It amuses me to imagine you considering this description over a cup of tea after you've sent Walter off to the bank and the children to school. If only you could know to what depths the family's actions have driven me, finally, surely poor Harry Ames might seem like a less unsuitable mate for your little sister. If only you could know that your accusations against me have led me to a world more lunatic than any you can possibly imagine.

Please give my regards to Mother and Father, and tell them that I shall write to them soon. And kiss my dearest babies for me . . . tell them that not a day passes, not a moment when they are not in my heart and my thoughts . . . and that soon they will have a new brother or sister and one day we shall all be together . . .

I am, your loving sister,
May

HEF

→ NOTEBOOK IV ←

The Devil Whiskey

*"If there is a Hell on earth, being abroad in the camp . . .
that night was like walking through its labyrinths. A
few dancers still staggered by the dying firelight. Others
had fallen down in a jumble of bodies around the fire;
some struggled to regain their feet while others lay
writhing on the ground. Throngs of drunken savages . . .
jostled me as I pushed by. Naked couples copulated on
the ground like animals. I stepped over them, pushed
aside those who came up against me, and, when it was
necessary, cleared a path by swinging my club. It was as
if the whole world had fallen from grace, and we had
been abandoned here to witness its final degradation."*

(from the journals of May Dodd)

><

23 May 1875

So much to report . . . Yesterday, my husband . . . how strange
it sounds . . . my husband, Little Wolf, came to our wedding
lodge riding his horse, and leading mine, which was saddled.
He trailed two packhorses one of which was laden with a
"parfleche"—which is the Cheyenne version of our valise—
a kind of folding case made of sturdy buffalo rawhide into
which household possessions, cooking implements, food supplies etc, are packed. There are several of these parfleches, all
of them elaborately painted, in the Chief's lodge. He is obviously a "wealthy" man among his people, for "our" lodge is
both larger and better appointed than that of many of the others in camp—as befits a great chief. As Captain Bourke had
already explained to us, among the heathens he who owns the
most horses is, by definition, the "wealthiest"—at least partly
for the simple reason that the more horses one owns, the more
goods and the larger lodge one is able to transport from place
to place. Even Father, I think, would appreciate the simplicity
of these savage economics.

Through the use of sign gestures, Little Wolf, his nut brown
face less stern than usual, made it understood that I was to
gather some belongings, that we were going off together.

"On our honeymoon, perhaps?" I asked laughing, but of

course he did not understand me. I hurriedly put a few items of clothing and toiletries into a beaded buckskin pouch that had been left, along with other items, in my wedding lodge. I can only guess that these were gifts from Little Wolf's family, for there was also a full set of Cheyenne woman's clothing which included a pair of elaborately beaded deerskin moccasins, soft as butter, as well as a pair of leggings that fit over the latter, attaching with a strap just below the knee—somewhat like our own garter. The dress itself was made out of a similarly soft animal skin, sewn with sturdy sinew thread, and rather simply and tastefully decorated with beads and brass buttons. It has a slightly smoky, and not at all unpleasant odor from having been smoked over cottonwood coals in the tanning process. As part of our apprenticeship, we have watched the Cheyenne women fashion these garments in all stages. They are marvelously adept at their various crafts, which we are clearly expected to learn ourselves. In fact, one of our more fortunate ladies, Jeanette Parker, had been a professional seamstress in Chicago before being committed to the State Lunatic Asylum for murdering her husband in his sleep with a leather-stitching needle. I do not know if she is insane or not—and do not care—for it sounds to me as though the lout rather deserved his fate. Jeanette has greatly impressed the Cheyenne women with her sewing skills, having even taught them some stitches with which they were unfamiliar—as a consequence she is held in high esteem among them.

Owing to its smocklike construction, and the fact that the sleeves are open, somewhat like a cape, my new native dress is wonderfully comfortable, as are the leggings and moccasins—all have the effect of a kind of second, loose-fitting skin that lies rather sensuously over one's own. Such practical attire makes our own clothes and shoes seem most constricting. I am very nearly prepared to give up the latter altogether. Even our cavalry-riding breeches seem by comparison overly confining.

But I digress: hurriedly I gathered together a few items, mounted my horse, Soldier, and rode out with my new husband.

The other wives watched us away, Quiet One, dutifully standing in front of her lodge, but still unable to bring herself to look at me. These last several days in my own quarters have provided a much-needed respite—for all of us I am certain. I can hardly fault the woman for her resentment of me and can only imagine what my own reaction would be were I in her position. I have learned that the young second wife, my friend Feather on Head, is the older's sister, which is common among the Cheyennes and designed to help alleviate such stress between wives. At the same time not all of the Cheyennes are polygamous . . . theirs is a complicated culture, and we have much to learn about one another.

As we rode through the camp, my friend Martha came out of her tent, looking every bit the blushing bride. We had not seen each other since our wedding night, but from the glow on her face, I had a suspicion that hers had not been a disappointment. "Oh, May," she said now, running alongside my horse to keep up, "we must speak. I was going to come see you today. Where are you off to?"

"I have no idea, Martha," I said. "As you can see I am simply being a dutiful wife, following my husband. If I'm not mistaken, we're off on our honeymoon!"

"A honeymoon? When will you be back?" Martha asked nervously. "What will I do without you?"

"I don't know, dear," I said, "but you'll manage. You've done quite well without me in the past few days, haven't you? I'm sure we won't be away long."

"May, I must ask you," Martha said, the color rising in her cheeks. "How was your . . . your . . ."

I laughed. "My wedding night?"

"Yes! How was it? Was it strange? Was it wonderful?"

"It was like a dream," I answered. "I'm not sure that it really happened."

"Yes!" Martha said. "That's exactly how mine was—like a dream. Were we drugged, May? I feel certain that I was drugged. Was I only dreaming, or did it really happen?"

"How did you feel the next morning?" I asked.

"Exhausted," Martha said, "I was exhausted, but content . . . and I was . . . I was . . ." Now she blushed even more deeply as she hurried to keep up.

"Sore?" I finished for her. "Was there blood, Martha?"

"Yes," she said. "You know that I was a virgin."

"I would suggest then the possibility that it was more than a dream," I said.

"Do you think it is somehow possible, May, that it was at once a dream but also actually happened?" Martha asked.

"Yes," I said. "Yes, I think that's a fine way of putting it. Like this whole adventure, a dream that's actually happening."

Now we were at the edge of the village, and Martha, not wishing to go on further, stopped and said: "One last thing, May, did you see his face, did you . . . did you . . . were you facing your husband at the moment?"

I laughed. "No, I was like the female swallows we have been watching this spring, Martha, with my tail raised in the air."

"Yes," Martha cried, waving as we rode away from her, "yes, that's it exactly! Good-bye then, May, dear friend. Don't be away long; we need you right here."

"You'll be fine, Martha," I called back to her. "You'll be just fine. I'm sure we won't be gone long. Such an adventure, isn't it!"

Martha waved. "An adventure!" she called back.

And then we were away, swallowed by the immensity of prairie. I was not in the least bit apprehensive at leaving the others behind, and felt secure and perfectly safe in the company of my husband. It was a magnificent summer morning, the prairie in full bloom. Wildflowers of all varieties carpeted the rolling plains, the grass was brilliantly green and waved ever so slightly in a soft breeze, the meadowlarks sang, and in the willows and cottonwoods along the river birds of all kinds took up their morning songs.

As the village faded behind us, I turned on a rise to look back and saw the smoke from the morning fires curling above the tipis, the People going hither and yon about their morning business, the dogs barking, the boys herding the horses out into the meadows, the faint sounds of laughter and life, and suddenly I felt the keenest sense of place—of home—the very first time I have thought of it as such. It was as though I had to leave and look back in order to discover this perspective, in the way that one looks away and then back again at a painting to reaffirm its beauty. And when I did so, and for the first time, I was enveloped by a great sense of peace and contentment. I thought to myself "How extraordinarily fortunate I am."

Yes, for all its savage strangeness and hardships, our new world seemed inexpressibly sweet on this morning; I marveled at how cunningly and perfectly these native people had folded themselves into the earth, into the countryside; they seem as much a part of this prairie landscape as the spring grass. One can't help but feel that they belong here as an integral part of the painting . . .

For the first quarter of an hour, Little Wolf rode well ahead of me, leading the pair of packhorses. He did not speak, nor even turn to check my progress. Finally I nudged

my horse forward with my heels and broke into a canter
(never have I more fully appreciated the riding lessons that
Mother made us take as children! for I am quite comfortable
on horseback—a skill that will obviously be of no small use-
fulness here). I pulled up abreast of the Chief, who looked
surprised, and possibly mildly annoyed—as if I were violat-
ing yet another point of heathen etiquette.

"I am a New American woman," I said to him, settling my
mount into the same gait as his, "and I have no intention of
riding twenty paces behind you the whole day long." I know
that Little Wolf could not understand my words but I gestured between our horses, to suggest their position side by
side and then I gestured between the two of us, and I smiled.
And the Chief seemed to consider this, and then he nodded
as if he understood and smiled back at me. Yes, we had made
a genuine communication! I was very pleased.

I believe now that the Chief has orchestrated this sojourn
as a way for us to become acquainted, and possibly also as a
way for him to show me a bit of his countryside. We made
camp early yesterday afternoon in a copse of cottonwoods
along a creek—the name of which I do not know. The Chief
has brought a small hide covering that we strung as shelter
between willow branches in case of rain, though the weather
has remained clear and mild. Beneath this we made beds of
grass, covered by buffalo robes. After we set our camp, I
gathered wood in the creek bottom for the fire, happy to be
afoot again after a day on horseback.

Little Wolf carried a small rawhide bag containing steel,
flint, and a piece of buffalo dung from which he would break
a piece and pulverize it to serve as kindling. It seemed terribly ingenious to me how quickly he could spark a fire, to
which he would add grass and twigs and soon we had a true
blaze over which to cook and take the night chill off.

For our dinner we roasted pintailed grouse that the Chief had killed with his bow earlier in the day, right from the back of his horse, one after the next, when the covey flushed in front of us. Even Father would have been impressed with his marksmanship; I can hardly wait to describe it to Helen Flight; I swear a man (or woman) with a firearm could not have been quicker or truer.

The birds were quite delicious: I stuffed them with tender wild onions and herbs that I had gathered during our day's prairie idyll. Thanks to the education provided by our Indian "mothers" I have become rather adept at identifying some of the edible plants.

This is the first time that we have passed truly alone together, and I think we were both a bit shy at first. However, I have finally devised a means of overcoming the nearly constant frustration of trying to make myself understood, by simply giving up to it. I now babble away in English to Little Wolf, saying whatever nonsense springs to mind—for as he cannot understand me what difference does it make? I must have told him my entire life story last night—I told him about Harry and our children and life in the institution; I told him about Father and Mother, and sister Hortense. I told him about Captain Bourke. I told him everything and I felt the strangest sense of liberation in the unburdening. Little Wolf listened patiently, or at least he appeared to be listening, even if he could not understand, he watched me as if he did, and nodded now and then, and finally even replied, speaking softly to me in his own language, although of course, I have no idea what he said. Thus we sat around our fire half the night, conversing, I in English, and he in his native tongue, far more sparingly for he is hardly what one would call a loquacious man; I am certain that he, too, told me important things about his life, for sometimes he spoke quite animatedly. I listened carefully, trying to fathom a few words, to make some meaning of what he said, but it seemed that I understood him better when I simply let his words wash over me and did not try to decipher them. In this way, we forged a peculiar closeness: I believe that we both spoke what was in our hearts, and perhaps our hearts, if not our minds, understood one another.

This morning the Chief has gone out early to hunt, while I take this opportunity to record these events in my journal. It is a fine morning and the birds sing merrily in the cotton-woods. I am very comfortable wrapped in my buffalo robe and when the sun is a bit higher in the sky and the air warms, I shall go down to the banks of the creek and have my bath . . .

But dear God, I have had a terrifying encounter, my hand still trembles so to recall it that I can barely hold my pencil. Shortly after I made the preceding entry I went down to the creek. I was delighted to discover there a pool formed by a hot springs. Steam rose from it, and when I felt the water with my toe, it was wonderfully warm. My husband must have chosen this camping site for its proximity to the hot springs.

I removed my clothes as I always do now when bathing—having largely abandoned any pretense of modesty, naked-ness being a natural state among the savages. I stepped into the pool, luxuriating in the warmth and silkiness of the wa-ter which had a slightly sulfurous odor and was of a perfect temperature. I floated on my back in a state of the purest relaxation.

Suddenly I had the disconcerting sense that I was not alone, that I was being watched. I lay motionless in the water, my heart beginning to pound with an inchoate but no less genuine fear. Finally I sat up, covering my breasts and looked quickly about me. Then I saw him—squatting as still as an animal on the bank was a man, if such he can be called— one of the most fearsome-looking creatures upon whom I have ever laid eyes. He had long matted hair that hung down almost to the ground where he sat, and thick swarthy features that seemed barely human, like those of a wild boar.

The creature was naked but for a breechclout. His skin was blackened with dirt and he was . . . he was in a state of arousal that was not concealed by this garment. When he saw that I had seen him he smiled at me, exposing blackened teeth like the fangs of the Devil's own dog. Then he grasped himself and nodded at me with a disgusting familiarity. I sank back into the water to cover myself as the man stood, still holding himself thus, his intention quite clear. I was shocked to hear him speak to me not in a savage tongue, but in French. "*Salope,*" he said in a low voice, "*je vais t'enculer a sec!*" I will not . . . cannot translate this for the sheer depravity of it.

Now the wretch started into the water toward me, still grasping his manhood like a terrible weapon of violence. My heart rose in my throat, I could not move, my body frozen with fear. "Please, no," I whispered. "Please don't hurt me." Never in my life have I felt more alone, or more terrified. I began to paddle frantically backwards from the man until I came up against the far bank of the pool. I pressed myself against a large boulder there, with no further to go as the creature approached me. Now I could smell him, even above the mineral odor of the water, could smell his filth, his stench of evil . . . He spoke again to me, words so unspeakably vulgar that I felt the bile rise in my throat, and I was certain that I was going to be sick. Just as the wretch reached out toward me I heard the voice of my husband. Yes, thank God! I looked up to see Little Wolf standing on the bank holding his quirt coiled in one hand. He spoke in a calm, even voice, and although I do not know what he said, I sensed from his tone that he knew this man. He addressed the wretch firmly but without a trace of rancor in his voice.

The man replied in Cheyenne, seemed to speak deferentially, almost obsequiously to the Chief, and began to back out of the pool. But then he stopped, as if he had just remembered something, and he turned back to me and smiled his rotten-toothed wolfish grin. This time he whispered in a guttural but surprisingly fluent English, "I am Jules Seminole," he said, and his voice chilled me to the bone. "We will see each other again. And I will do to you those things I promised." Then he waded from the pool without looking back.

Later I attempted to question Little Wolf about the identity of this horrible creature. "*Scu-sis-e-tcu,*" he said, or so the word by which the Cheyennes refer to themselves as a people sounded to me. And then he made slashing motions with his right index finger across his left which is the sign they use to identify themselves. "Cheyenne?" I asked in English. "How could he be?" Perhaps Little Wolf understood the question in my voice, for he placed his hand in the center of his breast and made a motion across his left side and said again the word "*Sas-sis-e-tas,*" and then he drew his hand across his breast to his right and said, "*ve'ho'e,*" the Cheyenne word for white man. "He's a half-breed, then," I said.

"*O'xeve'ho'e,*" the Chief answered.

26 May 1875

We have stayed in the same campsite for the past several days. After my terrifying encounter with the half-breed Jules Seminole, I had fervently hoped that we would move to another place, or even return to the camp, but we have not. Although my fear has gradually begun to subside, I have taken the man's threat to heart and I do not let my husband out of my sight. Now when he goes to hunt, I accompany him. If he goes to the creek, I follow him there. I have never been of a particularly timid nature, but for the moment, at least, I feel truly safe only in Little Wolf's company. He does not seem to mind my constant presence and, indeed, the more time we spend together, the more genuinely fond we grow of one another. He is a gentle, solicitous man, and very patient with me.

Little Wolf's hunting expeditions have been most successful. We have killed and dressed, and eaten of, pronghorn, elk, deer, and a variety of small game, including grouse, ducks, and rabbit—the savage's life appears to be one of feast or famine, and when food is bountiful they eat almost constantly. I have been cooking over the fire. We have with us in one of the parfleches a few modern utensils obtained from the white man's trading post and with these I attempt to prepare something more interesting than the standard fare of boiled meat. Besides wild onions and dandelion greens in the meadows, I have found morel mushrooms among the trees in the river bottom. These I recognize from Illinois, where they grew in some profusion in the spring and where I used to gather them with Mother and Hortense.

The rest of the meat has been hung in the cottonwoods

well away from our camp, presumably lest bears or other wild creatures should be attracted to it. Besides my cooking duties I have been kept busy learning the finer points of skinning, dressing, and butchering an animal. This, too, is considered to be women's work by the savages, and the Chief has instructed me in the various procedures until I have become, if not precisely expert, at least decently proficient. Fortunately, because Father was himself a hunter, I grew up around wild game and am not in the least bit squeamish about blood and offal. There are those among our group, including my poor friend Martha, who will have some real difficulty adapting to this chore.

The savage life, it strikes me, and particularly a woman's life among them, is one of nearly constant physical effort. There is little time for leisure. Nor has our excursion of the past few days been what most white women might consider an ideal honeymoon! Still it has been an instructive and useful experience.

Never have I been so grateful for my bath at the end of the day's labors—especially in this hot spring. Not only does it give me the opportunity to wash myself of the blood of wild creatures in which I am quite literally "up to the elbows," but it also allows me to scrub the damnable greasepaint from my skin. I and many of our other fair-skinned women have been forced to wear this concoction as protection against the blistering prairie sun. Indeed, many of the savages themselves use the paint for the same reason, and thus I have finally learned the origins of the term "redskin." The paint is made from mixing a brownish red clay, common throughout this country, with fat or tallow. It stinks terribly, and makes one feel perfectly filthy.

Other times the greasepaint is made from a white clay

material, which gives the wearer a kind of ghostly appearance. No one looks more ferocious than our Phemie in the white paint which she favors—although her already dark-pigmented skin requires considerably less than ours in the way of protection from the unremitting sun. My own Scottish ancestry and creamy complexion are a distinct disadvantage in this shadeless wilderness of prairie and sky—as it is for Helen Flight and the Kelly girls and nearly all the rest of us of "old world" ancestry. Thank God for the grease-paint, and for our little copse of trees in this campsite.

Per custom Little Wolf takes his bath in the morning when I, too, join him. In the afternoon, he sits on the bank, watching me as I wash again, guarding me I think from any further advances of the wretch Jules Seminole, who still lurks in my nightmares.

The warm water is a perfect temperature, like bathwater heated on the stove at home, and feels wonderful. This afternoon I swam out to the middle of the pool to float there for a few minutes as is my habit. I turned and beckoned to Little Wolf as I often do, making the sign for swim in the hopes of coaxing him into the water, trying to elicit from him some sense of play. I'm afraid that my husband is, if not exactly a dour fellow, a generally serious one, hardly given to displays of merriment. Perhaps this is only a function of his age and position. I had brought with me on our trip Lieutenant Clark's pamphlet on the Indian sign language, which, while hardly complete, has been enormously valuable to us. We practice the gesture language in the evenings by the fire and the Chief has been quite patient with my efforts—trying to teach me a few words of Cheyenne in the bargain. It is slow going, and I still enjoy babbling away in English as a means of release from the frustration of being unable to communicate properly. Yes, well, it occurs to me that anyone who listens so attentively to my incessant ramblings must be a patient man, indeed!

Of course, because he cannot read, it is impossible for Little Wolf to comprehend the nature of a book, but he marvels at the thing, touches it and turns it over in his hands as if it has magical properties—which in a sense I suppose it does. We are able to engage in rudimentary communications (although to be sure we are hardly translating the Bard into sign language as Captain Bourke and I so amused ourselves in attempting!).

Now finally, after much cajoling on my part, Little Wolf slipped into the water himself. He is a physically graceful man. However, the Indians practice a decidedly rudimentary kind of dog paddle, and so I decided, then and there, to teach him a few swim strokes. First I demonstrated the overhand stroke, which, being an athletically inclined fellow, he picked up quickly. Then I showed him the breast stroke. It was great fun and soon we were laughing like . . . well, very much like a pair of honeymooners! I felt that I had "broken the ice."

Impulsively, I put my arms around the Chief's neck, and wrapped my legs around his waist—he looked terribly surprised, even mildly panicked; I do not know if he feared that I was trying to pull him under, or if he only considered it unseemly of a woman to be so forward, for he tried to pull away from me.

"Don't worry," I said in English, grasping him closer, "I am just playing." But truly although I had indeed begun this wrestling entirely in a spirit of play, I found that I liked the touch of him, experienced an unmistakable stirring at the feel of his taut warm skin. Now I felt with my hands the small hard muscles of his shoulders and arms and with my feet explored the firmness of his legs. I found myself pressing more urgently against him. We have, I should mention, had no physical contact whatsoever since our dreamlike wedding night.

"Oh, dear," I whispered now, "Oh my, I had not intended . . ." The Chief seemed to respond to my embrace; I could feel the tension and reluctance drain from his body. For a moment we floated together thus in the warm, buoyant waters of the spring, my legs wrapped lightly around his waist. Then I began to kiss him very softly about his neck and face and on his lips—the savages are not well versed in the art of kissing, and it was rather like kissing a child, but soon he responded in kind. "Isn't that fine?" I whispered. "Yes, isn't that nice, isn't that just lovely?"

This is an indelicate matter . . . I know no other way to address it but directly. As John Bourke suggested the Cheyennes have not encouraged contact with the whites or with the missionaries until now, and although they have traded with them and know something of their ways, this has not included, at least in Little Wolf's case, any knowledge of carnal matters. What the savages have learned on the subject of sexual intercourse between a man and woman they have learned from watching Nature, as John Bourke put it, from watching animals couple . . . and thus they make love . . . like animals . . .

While I am hardly the authority on the subject that Narcissa White would make me out, I am not ashamed to admit that Harry Ames and I enjoyed an active erotic life, or that I am a woman of powerful passions. Men boast of such feelings— women are sent to lunatic asylums for them. Counting my single indiscretion with the Captain and my own "wedding night," I have now had three lovers in my short life. Does this make me a sinner? Perhaps . . . I do not feel like one . . . A harlot? I don't believe so. Am I insane? Hardly.

Now we floated, entwined in the water, my husband and

I, my arms wound round his neck, my legs about his waist, floated. Our bodies slid easily against each other, comfortable and familiar, the sulfurous water was warm and oily on our skins. Have we not been sent to instruct the savages in our way of life? Should this not include matters of the flesh? Yes, if the Chief can teach me the finer points of fleshing a hide, so perhaps I can reciprocate by teaching him a few secrets of the human flesh—a fair exchange it seems to me between our worlds.

I slid my hand down Little Wolf's back to his buttocks which was smooth and muscled, hard as river rock, and around to stroke him, sleek as a stallion, slippery as a snake in the oily mineral waters. "Put your hands on me," I whispered, although of course, he could not understand me, and I took his hand and placed it between our bodies and ran it over my belly to my breasts. He has very fine hands, strong but at the same time almost feminine, with a gentle touch unlike that of any I have ever known. I kissed him again and this time he kissed me back and I took him again in my hand, guiding him, settling my hips upon him, legs around his waist, the warmth of the springs entering me, filling me inside with heat and light . . .

28 May 1875

This morning, as I make these hasty scribbles, we prepare to depart—I assume to rejoin the village, for Little Wolf is presently loading our packhorses with all of the meat and hides that we have gathered and prepared in our few days here together. With the exception of my terrifying encounter with the one named Jules Seminole, of whom, thank God, we have seen no further sign, it has been a fine excursion, which

I am sorry to see come to an end. We have made, I believe, some valuable progress, Little Wolf and I, in beginning to bridge the gap between our cultures—I do not mean that only as a sly euphemism . . . although there is that, too. I am greatly encouraged and believe now more than ever that there is real hope for the success of our undertaking. Perhaps President Grant's people are right, and the sheer power of American womanhood can knit these worlds together after all. Not only have my husband and I learned to converse on a rudimentary level but we have learned a new respect and a genuine affection for one another. The Chief will be my truest window to the lives of the savages, for within him resides all the qualities so prized by these simple people—courage, dignity, grace, selflessness—and something else of which I have only seen a glimpse, but that I think would be called fierceness. Little Wolf has the character of a natural leader in any culture, and I'm certain that even John Bourke would have a grudging respect for him—and he for Bourke. For truly it strikes me that they have much in common. Captain and Chief . . . heathen and Catholic. Soldier and warrior . . . tied together now by a woman's love.

And yet, in spite of my best intentions I cannot pretend to have the same feelings for Little Wolf that I had for John Bourke, which was a passion such as I have never before known, a love of both intellect and flesh—body, mind, and soul . . . God I feel that I have lived three lives already, with three loves—my first, Harry Ames, a physical love like a spark, to be extinguished by the darkness of my asylum cell; only to be reignited by the implausible light of a new love like a shooting star. Yes, for if Harry Ames was the bright, erratic spark of my womanhood, then John Bourke was my shooting star, burning brilliantly and intensely. And this man Little Wolf, my lodge fire, offering warmth and security . . . he is my husband, I shall be a good and a faithful wife to him. I shall bear his children.

So Little Wolf and I rode back to the main camp on the Powder River, this morning, our last. I have tried to keep my bearings with the help of a compass and an Army map which Captain Bourke presented to me before our departure—I do not know how accurate the map is and I am far from being skilled as a cartographer, but I know at least the major water courses. The Chief and I rode side by side now—as equals, as it should be—and I chattered as we went, remarking on this and that, pointing to the birds and animals and plants, babbling away as is my wont.

Sometimes the Chief answered me, giving me the names for these things, and sometimes, I suspect, just talking himself, as has become our manner together. I think that I am finally beginning to absorb a bit of the language, though I am yet shy about attempting to speak it.

Now as we came in off the vast silent prairie, the village suddenly seemed by comparison to our last few days of solitude to be a veritable city, bustling with human energy and activity. Indeed, a whole new village had sprung up the opposite bank of the river from ours during our absence— nearly one hundred new lodges had been erected since we left.

The camp dogs came out to bark at us as we approached, and then to sniff and nip harmlessly at our heels as we rode through camp. Packs of small children followed us excitedly; some of the little imps I recognized and was happy to see again. How I love the children! How I look forward to having another of my own!

Several of our ladies greeted me by their lodges as we rode in. I was amused to see that in only the few days of my absence it was becoming more and more difficult to tell some of "our" brides from the natives. Since the wedding ceremony many others have adopted savage garb, and indeed some of the Cheyenne women are now wearing "civilized" attire given them by our women.

Gretchen, attired in a buckskin dress, was carrying a pail of water to her lodge, and she stopped to greet me and to admire our game-laden packhorses. "*Yah*, you got a *goot* man there, May!" she said. "I can hardly get *dat* lazy bum of mine to leave *de* tent," but she spoke with some genuine affection in her voice. "All *de* big *galloop* wants to do is 'wrestle' with me on *de* buffalo robes. *Yah*, you know what I mean, May? *Dat* damn savage of mine can hardly get enough of it! I come see you later, *yah?* I wish to speak to you."

Now we rode past Reverend Hare and Dog Woman's lodge, just in time to witness the latter exit the tipi wearing one of our white women's dresses. He is really rather a sweet old fellow and I couldn't help letting a bark of astonished laughter escape at the sight of him. Hah! Dog Woman glared at me, tugging on his bodice with which he seemed to be having some difficulty. I covered my mouth. "*Je suis désolé*," I apologized, for the hermaphroditic medicine man speaks a bit of French. "*Alors vous êtes très belle*! You look perfectly beautiful." This seemed to placate Dog Woman somewhat, and indeed, he/she looked rather proud of her new attire. "*Dites-moi, où est le grand lapin blanc?*" I asked.

"Reverend," I called out, "if you are inside there, you must help your roommate arrange her new dress."

"Is that you, Miss Dodd?" the Reverend's oracular voice boomed from inside the tent. "May I remind that you have missed Sunday services again this week. We've got half the camp coming now. We'll make Christians of the heathens yet!"

"Good for you, Reverend!" I answered. "But you'd best hurry before they make heathens of us. I've been thinking myself of converting to the religion of the Great Medicine. It's beginning to make great good sense to me."

Now the Reverend thrust his bald head, pink as a newborn baby, through the opening of his lodge and blinked in the sunlight. "You are a Godless young woman, Miss Dodd," he scolded me. Then he spoke in Cheyenne to Dog Woman, who answered him.

"Reverend, please ask Dog Woman to tell you the new Cheyenne name the Chief and I have given you," I called mischievously as we rode away. "It came about, as these things do, quite naturally on our trip when I was trying to explain to my husband in the sign language the literal meaning of your Christian name."

The Reverend spoke again to Dog Woman, who again replied. In this way, Reverend Hare first learned his new Cheyenne name, which I predict will spread like a prairie fire through the village.

"You're a Godless young woman, May Dodd!" called *Ma'vohkoohe ohvo'omaestse*—the Big White Rabbit—as we rode on through camp. "A Godless young woman! I shall pray for your salvation! And for that of your artist friend Helen Flight, as well. I urge you go to see her immediately, for she has become in your absence Satan's disciple and beguiles the savages with her wicked arts of conjuring, witchcraft, and thaumaturgy!" I began to wonder if perhaps the Reverend hadn't been getting too much sun on his bald pate.

How disappointed I was to discover that my wedding lodge had been dismantled during our absence, and my possessions moved back into the "family" tipi. Thus the honeymoon really is over. Having already grown accustomed to the privacy of my own lodge, I can hardly abide living in such proximity to all the others again.

As I had expected, Martha was the first to come visit me at the lodge, arriving just after I had made this unhappy discovery. She was full of excitement, inquiries, and news.

"Thank God you have returned safely!" she said, breathlessly. Our Horse Boy appeared at that moment, true to his name, to lead my horse away. He's a dear little thing, brown and lithe as an elf. I patted him on the head, and he grinned at me lovingly. "I have so much to tell you, May, but first I must hear about your honeymoon. How was it? Where did you go? Was it terribly romantic?"

"Let's see . . ." I mused, ". . . we traveled by first-class coach into the city where we stayed in the bridal suite of the finest hotel . . . took all of our meals by room service, made love on a feather bed . . ."

"Oh, stop teasing me, May!" Martha said, giggling. "Where did you go, really?"

"We simply roamed the countryside, Martha," I answered. "We camped for several days in a cottonwood copse along a creek, where we bathed in a pool formed by a hot springs . . . in which we made passionate love—"

"Truly?" Martha interrupted. "Is that true? I never know when you are only teasing me, May."

"Tell me news of the camp, dear," I asked. "To whom do the lodges on the other side of the river belong?"

"To the Southern Cheyennes," Martha said, "our 'relatives' who have come visiting from Oklahoma Territory."

"Yes, that would explain the appearance of the wretch Jules Seminole," I said. And I told Martha of my encounter.

"The southerners have got our men all puffed up and

strutting about like roosters," Martha said. "Soon they're off to make war against their enemies the Crows. They've enlisted Helen Flight to paint birds on their bodies and on their horses in preparation. She's become very 'big medicine,' quite the *Artiste*-in-residence."

"Ah, so that's what the Reverend was referring to," I said.

We determined to go straightaway to Helen Flight's lodge, where we found the artist sitting outside on a stool in the sun painting the image of a kingfisher on the chest of a young man. The kingfisher was exquisitely rendered just in the act of diving into the water. Seated cross-legged on the ground next to Helen, watching her work, was an elderly fellow with long white braids and a dark, deeply furrowed complexion that resembled ancient, cracked saddle leather.

Helen beamed at our arrival, pausing in her work and removing her pipe from her mouth. "Welcome home, May!" she said, enthusiastically. "We've missed you. My goodness, how pleased I am that you've both come! Do sit down. You must keep me company as I work . . . I've been at it all day. I seem to have been 'discovered' by the savages! I can hardly keep up with the demand for my services.

"Ah, but do please excuse me for failing to make proper introductions," she said. "Have you ladies had the pleasure of meeting the esteemed medicine man, Dr. White Bull?"

"I'm afraid we haven't," I said. "Please don't get up, sir," I joked. The old fellow was much unamused, implacable, rather grumpy, in fact. Both he and the young man wore deathly serious expressions on their faces, and barely glanced at us.

Helen popped her short, beautifully engraved stone pipe back into her mouth and took up her brush again. She has fashioned for herself a very cunning palette made from a rawhide shield, upon which the stretched leather has dried as hard as wood. Here she mixes her colors from an assortment of powders and emulsions made from pounding different-colored stones, earth, grasses, berries, clays, and animal bones, according to ancient savage formulas about which Miss Flight could scarcely be more enthusiastic—for she has available to her nearly the entire color spectrum.

"A fine likeness, Helen," I said with true admiration. Indeed Audubon himself would have been envious, for Helen's kingfisher was a work of art, the colors iridescent, flashing from the boy's taut brown skin as if the bird itself were alive.

"Why thank you," Helen said, pipe clenched firmly between her teeth. "Last night young Walking Whirlwind here had a dream. In his dream he was struck by bullets in battle, but his flesh closed up around the bullet holes and he remained unscathed. The boy has never before been to war, and he is naturally anxious about his prospects. Therefore, this morning he went directly to the medicine man, Dr. White Bull, to tell him of his dream—the interpretation of dreams being a major function of the medicine man." At this point Martha and I both looked again at White Bull, who watched intently and rather critically, as Miss Flight applied her paint to the boy's chest.

"Dr. White Bull," Helen continued, "told the young man that his dream was intended to inform him that the kingfisher was his 'medicine' animal. For when that bird dives under the surface of the water, the water closes up behind it, just as in the boy's dream the wounds in his flesh closed up after the bullets entered. Bloody ingenious concept, isn't it? Thus this painting, which I am presently executing upon the boy's chest, is intended to protect him from harm. Of course," Helen said, pausing from her work, and removing the pipe from her mouth, her eyebrows raised in ironic surprise, "I offer no guarantees of magic properties with my work!"

"I should certainly hope not!" I said. "Why it's pure superstition, Helen. And quite useless against real bullets."

"I expect so, May," Helen said. "But I am only an artist fulfilling a commission. Guarantees of magic properties are strictly the province of Dr. White Bull here."

At just this point, and as if on cue, the old medicine man started chanting in a low, rhythmic voice.

"There, you see!" Helen said, delighted. "As we speak my collaborator is imbuing my kingfisher with a full complement of special powers."

Hanging from Helen's tent were dozens of bird skins of every species imaginable, many of which she had collected herself in the course of our journey here and others of which have been brought to her by the savages as specimens for the likenesses which she is being "commissioned" to paint on their bodies, and on those of their war ponies. On the ground around her lodge were piles of gifts which the savages have bestowed upon her for her services—articles of finely embroidered clothing, animal hides, an assortment of "medicine" pipes, jewelry, braided horse bridles, and saddles.

"I do encourage you ladies to carry away any of my goods which might be of interest to you," Helen said now. "I hardly have room for them all. I now own a string of a half dozen horses which I have given to my husband, Mr. Hog. Suddenly I find myself a woman of means. I must say it strikes me as frightfully ironic that I've had to come to the middle of the wilderness to achieve economic success as an artist. Ah, and here comes my next commission," Helen said, as another young man rode up on a horse laden with hides.

"Another crane, I'll wager," Helen said, "a perennial favorite among the savages. Which is of particular interest in view of the fact that many other cultures throughout history—both Eastern and Western, primitive and civilized alike—have been known to ascribe special qualities to the noble crane. In the case of our savages, the bird is highly prized for its courage. For even when wounded and unable to fly, it stands its ground and fights heroically. So you see, by wearing these images upon their breasts the warriors believe that they assume these same characteristics."

"But doesn't it concern you, Helen," I asked, "that in spite of the good doctor's assumption of responsibility for magical properties, you may still be held accountable when your art fails them—as it inevitably must?"

"Ah, but Art never fails anyone, May," Helen said cheerfully. "Magic and 'medicine' may certainly fail, but never Art.

"Furthermore," she said, taking a long, thoughtful puff on her pipe, "is it possible that if a warrior believes in his 'medicine,' he can make it come true? A fascinating concept, is it not? And one that lies at the very core of pagan religion."

"And perhaps of our own," I pointed out, "for now you speak of faith, Helen."

"Quite!" said Helen, with customary good cheer. "That is to say, faith in the power of God, in the power of Art, in the power of medicine men and medicine animals—it's all one, finally, don't you agree, May?"

"Your paintings are magnificent, Helen," I said, "but if I had to wager, I'd still put my money on the power of bullets."

"Ah, ye of little faith!" said Helen, in a light tone.

"So the Reverend says of us both, Helen," I answered.

"Quite," she said. "The Episcopalian accuses me of encouraging the worship of false idols. I've explained to him that I'm only a poor artist trying to make my way in the world."

"By encouraging a finer appreciation of art among the heathens," I added.

"Just so, May!" Helen said. "Art being a cornerstone of civilization. And, in any case, what could be false about a kingfisher? There," she said to the boy, sitting back on her stool to inspect her efforts. She made the sign for finished. "All done. Be a good chap, and run along now. He'll do well in battle, that one," she added with satisfaction.

"Ah, the artist begins to believe her own notices!" I teased.

Helen smiled around her pipe and looked down at the old medicine man, White Bull, who appeared to be dozing in the sun. "Wake up, you old charlatan. Here's our next patient."

1 June 1875

With the presence of our visitors from the south the entire camp has been abuzz with activities for the past several days and has much the festive atmosphere of a large family reunion or a county fair.

I have passed my time calling at some of my friends' lodges and watching the various contests of skill that are everywhere being held between the different bands and warrior societies. These include tests of horsemanship, accuracy with bow and arrow, rifle and spear, running events, etc. Nearly everyone in the camp turns out either to spectate or participate.

As Bourke had warned, the savages are relentless gamblers and brisk wagering takes place at every opportunity. Prior to their arrival at our camp the southerners had been to the trading post, and they have brought with them many items of civilization—blankets, utensils, knives, beads, and trinkets—and with these they wager on games of chance and contests of all kinds.

Right in the thick of things I was not surprised to find those scamps the Kelly twins. I can't help but admire their spirit but truly they are a pair of scoundrels! *Hestahkha'e* the savages call them—Twin Woman as if they are one, for it is so difficult to tell them apart. (Martha tells me that a scandalous report is circulating about the camp that the two switched husbands on our wedding night.)

The girls seem to have set themselves up as something like professional bookmakers, and have themselves made a small fortune in trade goods, hides, and horses by organizing and betting upon various games. Yesterday, for instance they put our own Phemie up against several of the Southern Cheyenne men in a running race. Our statuesque Negress offered a great shock to all, Caucasians and savages alike, when she strode to the starting line wearing nothing more than a man's breechclout.

"Good God, Phemie," I said when I first saw her, "you're practically naked!" Truly she was something to behold, her long gleaming black legs muscled like a colt's, her breasts hard and small as a girl's.

Phemie laughed richly. "Hello, May!" she said, greeting me warmly, for I had not seen her since my return. "Yes, when I was a little girl I always ran footraces naked against the other children. I was the fastest child on the plantation. My mother told me this was how our people raced and fought in Africa. Why carry the extra weight of clothing to slow you down?"

"Right *ya* are, too, Phemie," said Meggie Kelly. "They say that the Irish lads of olden days always did battle naked themselves for that very same reason."

"*Aye*, and for the fact that it struck terror into the hearts of their enemies!" added Susie. "And which of you brave laddies'll run against this poor little *goorl* then?"

Several warriors had stepped up to the line by then. Among the Southern Cheyennes were a number who spoke passable English, this branch of the family having had more contact with the whites than ours. With their assistance as translators the Kellys haggled with the other bettors over the odds—a new concept to the savages.

"*Aye*, but she's only a poor *goorl*, you see," Meggie explained through the translator. "It hardly seems fair does it now that she should compete with equal odds against the big strong men? On account of which disadvantage all who bet on Phemie need only put up half as much as those who bet on one of the lads. And those are excellent odds we're givin' *ya*, too, if I may say so."

"I'll take a piece *a* that action *mahself, you rascals*," said Daisy Lovelace. "*Ah* don't give a damn if she's a *guuurl* or not. *Mah* Daddy always did say that nobody can outrun a *niggah*. Daddy said they got those long legs from runnin' through the jungle *bein' puursued* by lions and other *waahld* creatures. Yessir, *Ah'm* taking all wagers on my dear friend Euphemia *Washin'ton*."

Then the signal was given, and they were off, Phemie's stride worth two of those of any of the savages. She ran as swiftly and gracefully as a pronghorn, and handily won the race, which led to another challenge and another round of furious wagering. Phemie won a second time, all the other runners now utterly shamed in front of their friends and family, and roundly ridiculed by all.

Of interest to note is the fact that the Cheyenne women were as proud of Phemie's victory as we, and made their funny little trilling noise when she ran across the line ahead of the others. Indeed, where certain obvious tensions and jealousies have existed between us since our arrival here, Phemie's success seemed to bring us all closer together for a moment in a new community of women. This can only be a good thing.

3 June 1875

The festivities to mark the southerners' arrival and the beginning of the summer hunts continue . . . Yesterday afternoon an astonishing thing occurred which makes me—a "nonbeliever" if ever there was one—reassess the discussion we had with Helen Flight on the notion of magic.

The Kellys were taking bets on shooting contests with bow and arrow and rifle when a little girl entered the circle where the competition was being organized. The child led an old man by the hand. The old man had milky eyes that appeared to be entirely blind; he was stooped and wizened with age, his thin hair worn in wispy white braids. The girl whispered shyly to one of the southern Cheyennes who in turn translated to Meggie Kelly.

"Oh, sweet Jesus!" said Meggie to her sister. "The dear little thing says her granddad wants to challenge Black Coyote to a shooting contest." Black Coyote is a brash young warrior married to Phemie's new friend Buffalo Calf Road Woman, who is herself a Cheyenne warrior woman. He was widely considered to be the best shot in the camp and had so far handily beaten all comers.

"*Oih* never *hooord* such a thing, Meggie," said Susie with a laugh. "And who'll bet on the old poor fellow? Why look at him—he's blind as a bat."

"The child says her granddad's got big medicine, Susie,"

Meggie said. "Isn't that grand? Says the family'll wager two horses on the old fool."

Susan came closer, and took the girl's chin in her hand. "Oh, child, are *ya* quite sure of what you're askin' us?" she said. "Your old granddad cannot even see the target."

"You're not goin' soft on me are *ye*, Susie Kelly?" said her sister. "If the child's family wishes to wager, I'll not stand in their way. And I'll put some of my own winnings on Black Coyote. Haven't we got a regular string of horses now among our winnings?"

"Aye, that *mooch* we do, Meggie," said Susan. "But this is takin' candy from a baby, is it not? I hate to steal from a little girl who believes in her dear old granddad."

"Well, just to make *ye* feel better about it, Susie," Meggie said, "we'll give 'em long odds. How about we put six horses up for their two? Would that salve your precious conscience, then?"

Now a round target was barked off a cottonwood tree, a black circle drawn with charcoal in the center and the distance paced off. Black Coyote, who is a cocksure young fellow, went first. He was shooting a brand-new cartridge rifle that he had won off a southern Cheyenne in an earlier contest. He aimed casually and fired with quick confidence, his bullet lodging just inside the circle. The spectators all "*houed*" approvingly.

Now the old man stepped up to the line. He held his hand closed in a fist and he opened it to reveal one of our seamstress, Jeanette Parker's, sewing needles. Now there was much *houing* of an astonished nature.

"What's the old fool doin', Meggie?" asked Susie. "Where's his damn rifle?"

The old man held his open hand up to his mouth, pointed it toward the target, puckered his lips, and blew a pitiful wheezing breath of air—hardly enough breath to rustle a leaf. But the needle was suddenly gone from his palm and the little girl pointed at the target. All went to examine it closely and there was the needle sticking in the exact center of the circle—a dead bull's-eye!

"*T'isn't* possible, Meggie," said Susan. "How did the old faker *pool* it off?" Indeed, none of us had ever seen anything like it!

" 'Tis a damn trick they're playin' on us, Susie," said Margaret. "That *moooch* is *shoore*. Got to be rigged somehow."

Now the twins sent a boy to collect their horses to pay off the wager, and while he was gone, they conferred in close confidence. Being no one's fools, they issued a challenge for another contest between Black Coyote and the old man, whose name the translator gave as Stares at Sun. This time they marked a different target on another tree even further away, and all inspected it for any evidence of advance tampering. Many of the savages, who are nothing if not superstitious creatures, had been won over by the old man's magic and this time the wagering was considerably brisker. The twins themselves doubled their bets, with even odds now, and took a number of side bets. They looked to make a killing, and just to further ensure that the old man couldn't play the same trick a second time, right before the contest began they added the stipulation that Stares at Sun must this time use something other than a sewing needle. Clever girls, those Kellys.

Again Black Coyote had the first shot and this time he aimed more carefully before he fired, and his bullet hit the target less than an inch away from the exact center of the circle.

The old man bent down and whispered something to his granddaughter. The child plucked a porcupine quill—which the savages use as ornamentation—off her sweet little dress, and put it very carefully in the old man's open palm. The twins watched closely and suspiciously for any possible sleight of hand.

Again the old man raised his palm to his mouth and, directed by his granddaughter, held it toward the target. He pursed his lips and blew weakly, making a little airless sound like *"pffftt."* Again the little girl pointed at the target, and all went to inspect it, the Kelly girls in the lead so that no further shenanigans could be perpetrated upon them. Incredibly, the porcupine quill was embedded in the precise center of the circle.

"Blooody Hell, Susie!" said Meggie. "The old charlatan has tricked us again! We've been swindled!"

I could only think of Helen Flight's words and wonder if the child's faith in her old grandfather had somehow made his magic work . . .

In any case, we all had a good laugh at the expense of the Kelly twins, and no one minded that they had lost a wager for a change!

4 June 1875

A disturbing encounter today . . . The Kellys have found a veritable gold mine in Gretchen Fathauer, who has been challenging all comers to arm wrestling contests. The girl is strong as a horse and no man had beaten her yet!

This morning Martha and I were standing on the edge of the circle watching as Gretchen handily defeated yet another poor fellow. It was then that I heard a chillingly familiar voice close behind me, *"Je t'ai dit, salope,"* whispered Jules Seminole in my ear with hot stinking breath. *"Je vais t'enculer a sec!"* The wretch so startled me, his filth so filled me with loathing, that I turned on him furiously. "I am not alone here now," I said, "and if you ever touch me, my husband Little Wolf will kill you."

"Good Lord, May," said Martha, frightened as much by my reaction to him as she was by the man himself. "Who is this?"

Seminole laughed, displaying his rotten black teeth. He was dressed in a filthy U.S. Army shirt and a cavalry hat which he removed now to reveal matted hair that spilled in greasy curls down his back and over his chest. "Jules Seminole, *madame*," he said bowing to Martha. *"Enchantée!"*

"Go find my husband, Martha," I said. "Right now." And to Seminole, I said, "If I tell Little Wolf what filth you speak to me, he will kill you."

"Non, non, ma chère," he said, shaking his head in mock sadness. "You do not understand. A Cheyenne is forbidden to kill a member of his own tribe. It is the greatest sin of which a man is capable. Even if he wished to do so, Little Wolf could never kill me, for my mother was Cheyenne, and I am married to the Chief's own niece. He could not kill me no matter what I choose to do with you. It is the law of the People."

"Then he will certainly take his quirt to you," I said, flushing angrily. "Keep away from me. I will tell him what filth you speak."

"You have much to learn about your new people, my sweet *salope*," Seminole said. "A more fearless warrior than your husband does not live among the People, but Little Wolf is the Sweet Medicine Chief. He must always put the interests of the People ahead of his own personal affairs. He is forbidden by tribal law from raising a hand against me, because to do so would be an act of selfishness. Why do you think he did not strike me with his quirt at the hot-water hole? Do you think he did not know my intentions toward you? Do you think he did not see my *vetoo-tse*—that one day soon will split you open like an axe splits the crotch of a sapling tree?"

Now Seminole called out to the Kelly girls. *"Oui,* I Jules Seminole will wrestle the German cow! And I'll wager a barrel of whiskey on it."

"Whiskey, you say?" said Meggie Kelly. "And what would you have us put up in return, fine sir?"

"I'll take the cow back to my lodge with me when I beat her," he said. Then Seminole spoke in rapid Cheyenne to Gretchen's husband, who watched on the sidelines and who is himself a rather buffoonish fellow, known by the name *Vonestseahe*—No Brains. The half-breed pulled out a small bottle from his shirt pocket, uncorked it, and handed it to No Brains, who took a long swallow and made a grimace. But he smiled and nodded and spoke again to Seminole.

"Les jeux sont fait, Mesdames," Seminole said. *"Vonestseahe* bets Jules Seminole his white wife against a keg of whiskey in an arm wrestling contest."

"You can't do that," I said. "You don't have to do this, Gretchen. He can't bet his wife. Susie, Meggie, don't let this happen. One of you run now and get the Reverend."

"What kind of *husband* are you, anyhow?" Gretchen demanded, approaching No Brains with her hands on her broad hips. The man already appeared to be a little drunk from the sip of whiskey. "You bet your wife in a *gottdamnt* arm wrestle contest? What kind of man does such a *ting* as *dat?*" Now Gretchen took hold of her husband's nose between the knuckles of her forefinger and middle finger and twisted until tears ran down the man's face and he fell to his knees in agony. Everyone began to laugh.

"Yah, OK," Gretchen said, releasing his nose, *"dat* all you *tink* of me, is it, mister? OK, *den* I do it. Come on, Frenchy."

She pushed up the sleeve of her dress. "Come on, *den*, I take you on."

"Don't do it, Gretchen," I begged. "I know this one. He's evil. He'll hurt you."

"He *haf* to beat me first, May," Gretchen said. "Don't you worry. You seen me lose yet? When I was a girl my *brudders wuld haf* to come get *der* sister to pull *de gottdamnt* oxens out a *de* mud on *de* farm, because I *yam de* strongest one in *de famly*. I beat *dem* all at *de* arm wrestling. I never lose. Don't worry. Come on *den*, Frenchy. We get down here on *de* ground. I show you how *ve Sviss* do it. Susie and Meggie *vill* be judges, *yah*? OK? I beat you, you give me keg of whiskey. You beat me, I go lie on *de* buffalo robes *wid* you." Gretchen raised her stout index finger in the air. "One time, *dat* is. You don't own me, and I don't stay *wid* you, I *yam* not your wife. Understood? One time."

"*Oui*," said Seminole. And he gave her an evil leer. "*Une fois*. One time is all I could stand with a fat German cow like you."

"*Sviss*, mister," Gretchen said. "I *yam Sviss*. And you not exactly the kind of fellow a girl dreams about *eider*. You stink like a *gottdamnt* hog."

I begged Gretchen again not to go through with it, but she would not listen to me. Now she and Seminole got situated on the ground, positioning themselves and locking hands. The side-betting was furious. "You know," said Gretchen, "*dis* not really a fair contest, because I liable to pass out from *de* smell *a* Frenchy's breath before we even get started."

Then Susie Kelly gave the signal and the struggle began. Gretchen was all business now, and holding her own, her arm seemingly as stout and immovable as a fence post. We all cheered her on, the Cheyenne women as much as we—making their trilling—for everyone likes Gretchen and clearly all are terrified of the lout Seminole and would not wish such a fate on any woman.

But Jules Seminole is a powerful man, his short swarthy arm thick as a bear's. He began to wear Gretchen down, little by little, gaining slowly, steadily, inexorably. Gretchen's face turned red with blood as she strained against him and the veins in her arm and neck stood out like cording. Now the back of her hand was only inches from the ground. Good God, she was going to lose . . .

"You think my breath *est dégoulas*, eh, my ugly cow?" Seminole said. "*Alors*, wait until you put your fat German tongue up my arse."

And from Gretchen's breast there rose a bellow like the sound of a great dying buffalo, a sound filled with equal measures of anguish and wrath, and, as if infused with an inhuman strength, her arm began to regain the lost ground inch by inch. Now the sweat poured from Seminole's apish brow as his advantage slipped away and soon their arms were locked again at the fulcrum where the contest had begun. Clearly neither had much strength left and it was here at this moment where the match would be decided. And now Gretchen spoke, her face swollen like a blood sausage, her voice barely a whisper as if she had no breath left for words. "*Sviss*," she hissed, "I told you French pig, I am *Sviss*!" And then with a final roar, this one triumphant, she slammed the wretch's arm to the ground, their locked hands making a thud and a puff of dust like a dropped stone. All cheered heartily as Gretchen stood and wiped the dirt from her dress. She pushed past her well-wishers to her husband. "*Yah*, you go on now," she said to him. "You go on and collect your whiskey, my *hustband*. But don't you come back to my lodge." And then poor brave Gretchen, her great heart broken, looked around at the crowd of people and added, "Someone tell *dis* man what I say to him. You tell him not to come back home to my house."

5 June 1875

Tonight marks the last night of the past days of games, feasts, and dances commemorating the arrival of the southern Cheyenne. It is true that the savages love nothing so much as an excuse to hold festivities. All of our efforts against it not-withstanding, tomorrow the war party goes out against the Crows, and other parties are off on the hunt.

This afternoon Martha and I arranged a conference in Reverend Hare's lodge with our husbands Little Wolf and Tangle Hair, who is himself the Chief of the Crazy Dog soldier society. The intent of our meeting was to enlist the Reverend's aid as translator and moral arbiter in a final ef-fort to dissuade the men from making war against their neighbors.

The *he'emnane'e*, Dog Woman, organized the seating inside the lodge—he's a prissy old thing, and not before everything was just so did he light the pipe which was passed among the men. The women, as usual, were required to sit outside the circle of men, a heathen custom which I find objectionable—particularly given that this "powwow" was our idea in the first place. I suppose that this is not so different from the way women are treated in our own world. Of course, neither were we offered the pipe.

First I expressed through the Reverend our concern about our husbands going off to war. After he had translated, both Little Wolf and Mr. Tangle Hair seemed amused; indeed, they had rather a fine chuckle over it.

"Horse-stealing raids upon enemies, my wife," said Little

Wolf, speaking through the Reverend, "are the business of young men, not 'old men' chiefs such as ourselves."

"Well then you must advise the young men not to go," I said.

"I cannot do so," answered the Chief.

"But you are the Chief," I said. "You can advise them as you wish."

"The raid upon the Crows is being organized by the Kit Fox society," Little Wolf explained. "I am the leader of the Elks Society and Tangle Hair is the leader of the Crazy Dogs. We are unable to interfere in the affairs of the Kit Fox society. This is tribal law."

"Kit Foxes, Elks, Crazy Dogs!" I said, exasperated. "These are like the clubs of children."

"That I cannot translate," said Reverend Hare.

"And why not?" I demanded.

"Because it's insulting to our hosts," he said.

"As His Reverence has himself pointed out," I said, "our purpose here is to encourage the savages to settle on the reservation. Surely making war against their neighbors does not work toward that end."

"Your government's official position on the matter, madam," explained the Reverend, "is that the heathens are to be distracted from making war upon white people. However any intratribal discord only encourages those who are friendly to us to enlist as scouts against those who oppose us."

"I see," I said, "divide and conquer." I began, then, to understand that not only do we face the obstacle of the heathens' innately warlike nature but also the hypocrisy of our own representatives. "And do you speak for the government or your church, Father?" I asked.

"In this case the two have a common purpose," answered the Reverend.

"Allow me then, please," I said, "to speak to my husband simply as his wife and not as a representative of either your church or our government."

"And what would you like to say to your husband, madam?" asked the Big White Rabbit with a patronizing nod.

"I would like to say: 'Kit Foxes, Elks, Crazy Dogs! These are like the clubs of children.'"

The Reverend smiled benignly, "You are an impetuous young woman, Miss Dodd," he said. "And frequently an irritating one."

"Shouldn't you address me now as Mrs. Little Wolf, Father?" I reminded him. "And isn't your function here to serve as a translator and not a censor?"

"At my discretion, Mrs. Little Wolf," he said. "You must understand that we have interests to protect in this delicate undertaking. That there is a protocol to be observed in all dealings with these people. Believe me, I have a great deal of experience in such matters. One must be diplomatic; one does not order, one must only suggest; one does not insult, one must flatter and cajole."

"Good God, Reverend, you sound more and more like a politician than a man of the cloth," I said.

"I caution you against blasphemy, young lady," he said sharply.

"Then let me rephrase my prior statement in a more politic manner," I said. "Perhaps you will translate the following to my husband: 'We have been sent here by the Great White Father'—No, no let me start over, I loathe that ridiculous term . . . 'We have been sent here by the United States government as a gift. You yourself requested that gift. You asked that we teach you how to live after the buffalo are gone. We are trying to learn from you about your way of life. And, in return, we are trying to teach you the white man's way. Now it is time that you begin to learn these things. That is the reason I have come here to be your wife. As Chief it is your duty to explain to the young men that they must stop waging war against their neighbors.'"

The Reverend translated—or so, at least, I assume. The Chief sat impassively, listening thoughtfully. He took a long puff on the pipe as he seemed to consider my words. Finally he spoke.

Reverend Hare smiled in his irritatingly smug fashion. "The Chief would like to know if white people do not make war upon their enemies?" he asked.

"Why yes, of course they do," I answered, frustrated, for I could see where the conversation was heading.

"He would like to know what difference there is between the Cheyennes making war against their enemies and white people making war against theirs?"

"How do I even know you're translating accurately?" I demanded angrily of the fat Episcopalian.

"Mrs. Little Wolf, please," said the Reverend, raising a pale chubby hand in stern admonishment of my outburst, "do not shoot the messenger."

"Couldn't you just tell my husband that God doesn't want the Cheyennes to go to war against the Crows?" I asked. "Would not that be a fair interpretation of God's position on the matter?"

The Reverend looked at me, the blood beginning to rise in his round, pink, hairless face, darkening his complexion. He spoke in a low voice. "Madam," he said, "may I remind you that it is hardly within the realm of your responsibilities to determine what God does and does not wish for these people."

"Ah, yes, of course," I said, nodding. "That's up to the church and the United States military, isn't it?"

"I warn you, young lady," said the Reverend pointing at

me with a fat trembling finger, "I warn you once and for all not to incur the wrath of God, for the wrath of God is a terrible thing to behold."

"Martha," I said, turning to my friend for support, "please, don't be so timid. Speak up. Tell your husband to discourage the young men from going to war."

"You may repeat Mrs. Little Wolf's sentiments to my husband," Martha said to the Reverend. "Hers is my position exactly."

The Reverend addressed Tangle Hair, who responded curtly. "Your husband says that we should take this matter up with the leaders of the Kit Foxes," said the Reverend. "Which, I'm afraid, is his last word on the subject. And mine."

And this is what we are up against . . . I'm afraid that John Bourke was right about many things . . . that this entire enterprise may have been ill-advised, doomed to failure . . . that we are all of us helpless pawns of higher powers . . . although clearly not high enough.

I scribble these last notes of the day prior to our attending yet another, and, I hope, final feast. I am happy to report that we are not cooking at "home" tonight. Rather we have received an invitation to dine at the lodge of a prominent Chief of the southern Cheyennes, a man named Alights on the Cloud, and then we shall proceed to the dance . . . All this partygoing is beginning to remind me of the Chicago social season, with dinner tonight at the Alights on the Clouds' residence akin to Mother and Father being invited to the McCormicks' estate. I shall give a full report of these festivities tomorrow . . .

7 June 1875

Good God! The flippancy of my entry of two days ago did not presage the coming night's reign of terror . . . a passage through Hell . . . our slender faith in this mission has been shaken to its core . . . our group is in complete disarray, many have vowed to leave here, to return immediately to the safety of civilization—a safety that is, for now at least, to be denied us.

Let me recount, as plainly as I am able, the events that have led us to this dire state. My husband and I attended the aforementioned feast at the lodge of Alights on the Cloud. I was aghast to see upon our arrival that among the half dozen or so other guests was none other than the half-breed wretch Jules Seminole, who was in company with his own wife, a frightened and surely much mistreated girl whom they call by the name Howling Woman . . . yes, well is it any wonder? The poor thing is probably tortured to a state of howling by the miserable lout.

My blood ran cold when first I laid eyes upon Seminole, who leered at me with his disgusting expression of insinuating familiarity, as if we are intimates. Truly, the man makes my skin crawl. My husband hardly seemed to notice, or if he did, said nothing. It is true, I now know, what Seminole told me of the selfless nature of Little Wolf's position among the People.

Because I wished to get out of sight of the wretch as soon as possible, immediately after the feast I told my husband through the sign talk that I could not accompany him to the dance, that I must return to our lodge. However, I was not able to leave immediately, for no one is allowed to enter or depart the lodge while the men are smoking their damnable pipe. It is another of the savages' endless "rules."

While they were smoking, and as usual taking their sweet time over it, Jules Seminole produced a bottle of whiskey. In spite of that which he had lost to Gretchen, he now boasted that he still had several full kegs of the stuff which he had procured at the trading posts en route here. He passed a tin cup around and allowed all the men present one sip of the whiskey. I was disgusted to see that my own husband accepted a drink when the cup was handed to him. And as Little Wolf drank, Seminole looked at me and whispered, "Tonight, my beauty."

All immediately wanted another drink of the stuff, but Seminole only laughed at them, and said that the first taste was free but now they would have to pay for it.

Never have I witnessed a more rapid transformation among the men. Captain Bourke was right on that score, as well—the savages are slaves to whiskey, and have a pitifully low tolerance for it. Many already appeared drunk after the first "free" drink and became immediately belligerent and bellicose. I told my husband again that I was returning to our lodge; I did not care whether the men were finished with their smoke or not, and I began to crawl toward the lodge entrance. There was much *houing* of disapproval from the men at my impropriety, and Little Wolf, acting in uncharacteristically rough fashion, caught me by the ankle and dragged me back. All of the men seemed to find this most amusing and fairly shook with hearty laughter.

But my husband looked at me in a way that I had never before seen, with an expression so debased that it chilled me to the bone. I suddenly no longer knew this man. I wrenched free from his grasp and scrambled as fast as I could out of the lodge and ran back to our own tipi.

Soon the music from the dance began, but it had a different and strangely discordant tone. We began to hear from our lodge all manner of loud shouting and cursing. Our old tipi crone, Crooked Nose, looked at me, shook her head and said, *"ve'ho'emahpe."* Then she made the sign for drinking with her thumb.

Worried for the others I decided to go out again. But when I tried to leave the tent, the crone blocked my way with her club. "Please," I said, and I made the sign for "friends" and for "search." "Please let me pass." The old woman seemed to understand me; she muttered disagreeably, but finally she removed her club from my path.

I skirted the immediate area in which the dance was being held but paused long enough to see that Seminole had set up a kind of makeshift "saloon" there with a keg of whiskey and that a line had formed of men and women holding all manner of drinking vessels and goods with which to trade for the whiskey. These included bows and arrows, carbines, hides, blankets, household goods, beads, clothing, and many other items. It appeared that by the end of the night the wretch would own the entire camp!

Even from a distance I could see that a general state of drunkenness already prevailed and that the *he'emnane'e* had lost all control so that the usually orderly dancing was degenerating into a kind of mad gyration. Those who had been prudent enough not to have imbibed the alcohol were quickly retiring to their lodges, and relatives hurried to cut loose the young girls who are tied together at these affairs with a common rope—a peculiar, but effective, savage custom designed to prevent the girls from being lured away from the fire by young men whose romantic ardor has been inflamed by music and dancing. Or tonight, as was the case, by the devil whiskey.

I hurried on with the idea in mind of finding first Martha, and then as many of the others as possible, so that we might seek refuge at Reverend Hare's lodge—in the same way that one seeks sanctuary in a church. The camp is greatly spread out, and there were several separate dances in progress as I made my way, but it appeared that the whiskey had infected them all.

I reached Martha's lodge and found her there alone in, as I had expected, a state of near panic.

"Good God, what's going on out there, May?" she asked. "It's madness!"

Martha and I made our way to the Reverend's lodge. The situation was deteriorating by the moment—all control appeared to be lost. Bonfires burned everywhere. There was gunfire and brawling, and dancing of the most depraved sort accompanied by a demented music that seemed to issue from the bowels of Hell. We were sickened to witness men dragging their screaming wives and daughters to trade for a drink of whiskey. Fearing for our own lives, we dared not intervene.

When we arrived at the Reverend's lodge, we found that a number of our women were already there, many huddled together, holding each other and weeping in terror. The *he'emnane'e*, Dog Woman, was in the rear of the lodge trying to console and minister to the Reverend, who seemed himself to have suffered a complete breakdown. The latter was in a state of great agitation, and cowered under his buffalo robes like a giant child just awakened from a bad dream. He rocked himself back and forth, wild-eyed and perspiring heavily.

"*Qu'est que se passe avec le Reverend?*" I asked of the hermaphrodite. "*Il est malade?*"

"*Il a perdu sa médecine,*" said the man/woman sadly.

"*Comment?*"

"*Sa médecine, elle est partie,*" Dog Woman repeated. He was very sympathetic and now passed a piece of burning sage under the Father's nose. This was presumably designed to help him find his lost medicine again—or as I would have it, his courage.

I knelt beside the giant, trembling, white-robed priest. "Are you ill, Reverend?" I whispered. "Please, what's the matter with you?" I grasped him by his fleshy arm and shook him hard. "Please, these women need you."

"I'm sorry, Miss Dodd," he said, wiping his brow, and trying to collect himself, "the situation is hopeless, it's the worst possible thing that can occur. I have been among the savages before when they were drinking whiskey. It is Satan's tool to possess their soul. It makes them insane. You cannot imagine the atrocities of which they are capable. You cannot imagine. They know no restraint. The only hope, the only defense, is to hide oneself completely from their sight."

"Good God, man," I said. "This is no time to lose your faith. Pull yourself together. Can't you see that the women need you to be strong?"

"Hide yourself," the Reverend said, pulling a buffalo robe over his head. "Hide yourself. It's the only hope."

Even though the Reverend was clearly incapable of defending them, those women already present chose to stay in his lodge, and others soon joined us until it was quite crowded there—all were too fearful to venture forth again into the mad chaos that prevailed throughout the camp.

Jeanette Parker was there, as was the little French girl Marie Blanche, and the strange, quiet Ada Ware dressed as always in black, her bleak vision of the world seeming to come true. "A lucky thing for us that the church sent the Reverend to look after us, isn't it?" she said darkly. "I feel so much better for having him here."

Now Narcissa White entered the lodge, disheveled and muttering to herself in a kind of self-absorbed hysteria. "There you see, I told them so, we have failed," she said, "Satan rules the night, I told them, I told them so . . ."

"Told them what for God's sake, Narcissa?" I asked.

"Told them to cast Satan from their hearts," she said. "Told them not to copulate with the heathens until the church had done its proper work and God possessed their miserable souls." She looked at me as if seeing me for the first time. "Did I not?" she asked. "Did I not tell you so? Now look, look what you have done, you Godless whore. You have taken up Satan's ministry, and this . . . this is the result!" She hiked her dress up and I saw the thin rivulet of blood that ran down the inside of her thigh. Evidently, Narcissa's husband had decided, presumably under the influence of the whiskey, to exercise his conjugal privileges after all.

"I'm sorry, Narcissa," I said. "Truly I am. But I don't see how you can blame me or anyone else for this. Have you seen any of the others? Have you seen Phemie or Daisy Lovelace? The Kelly twins? Gretchen? Have you seen little Sara?"

"Sinners, each and every one of them," said Narcissa shaking her head. "You'll all burn in Hell."

"Look around," said Ada Ware. "We're already there."

Worried for the others and for my tentmates, I elected to return to my own lodge. Martha, too fearful to let me out of her sight, accompanied me. We hurried as quickly as we could, keeping to the edge of the dance circles and never looking directly at anyone—trying our best to appear invisible.

There we found my other tentmates cowered together on their robes. As I had expected Little Wolf had not returned. The Chief's daughter, Pretty Walker, who is a lovely girl only a few years younger than myself, had also attended the dance, tied to the others. Thankfully she had been freed and now huddled next to her mother, weeping softly. The young wife, my friend, Feather on Head, anxiously clasped her baby to her breast. I knelt beside the frightened girl, and tried to console her. The old crone, Crooked Nose, sat cross-legged on the ground at her designated place just inside the entrance to the tent, holding her club vigilantly across her lap. For once I was very happy to see her on guard there.

An inhuman howling and wailing rose above the camp—gunfire and savage shrieks, the heartbreaking cries of wives and children. How I worried for our women.

"I must at least find Sara," I said. "Just to know that she is safe. You stay here, Martha," I said. "You'll be fine here."

But when I tried to leave the lodge Crooked Nose again laid her club across the entrance and this time she was implacable. I pleaded with her to let me pass, but finally lost patience and said in English, "Alright you old witch, go ahead and strike me down then. I am going out to look for my friends."

I pushed past her club and opened the flap. As soon as I did so my heart caught in my throat, for there standing in front of the entrance to our lodge was Jules Seminole. I heard Martha scream behind me as Seminole grasped me roughly by the arm and dragged me outside. He pulled my face close to his with an iron grip . . . and then . . . then he licked me like a dog . . . he put the tip of his tongue into my nostril . . . it was like a maggot crawling into my body . . . I was certain I would vomit.

"Yes, now show me your tongue, my little *salope*," he said. "Give me your tongue."

"Oh, no," I whimpered, trying to pull away. "Oh God, please no."

And then Crooked Nose caught the wretch a terrific blow

behind the ear with her club, which made a hollow cracking sound like a gourd splitting. Seminole collapsed on the ground like a dead man, blood running from his ear.

"My God, you've killed him," I said to the crone. But I said so triumphantly.

Martha, useless in her terror, sobbed as Crooked Nose and I each took ahold of one of Seminole's legs and with great effort dragged him some distance away from the lodge, where we left him lying upon the ground. God help me, I wished him dead, but when I bent over him I could see that he was still breathing, his ear beginning to swell like a mushroom.

When we were back inside the tipi I took the old woman by her forearm; it was as hard and sinewy as an old tree root. "Thank you," I said. "You saved my life, thank you." Crooked Nose smiled her toothless crone's smile, her eyes crinkled shut. She nodded and made the sign for "wait," and then she dug about in her parfleche by the head of her bed until she pulled another smaller, stone-headed club from beneath her headrest. Clearly the crone takes her job seriously and is well armed for the task. She waved the club in the air and said something to me in Cheyenne, and then handed it to me. I knew exactly what she was saying: *If anyone bothers you again, knock them over the head with this.* I said, *"Hou,"* to show her that I understood her meaning.

"Please don't go out again, May," Martha begged me. "Stay here with us."

"I'll be back, Martha," I said. "I must check on the child."

If there is a Hell on earth, being abroad in the camp yet a third time that night was like walking through its labyrinths. A few dancers still staggered by the dying firelight. Others had fallen down in a jumble of bodies around the fire; some struggled to regain their feet while others lay writhing on the ground. Throngs of drunken savages, men and women, jostled me as I pushed by. Naked couples copulated on the ground like animals. I stepped over them, pushed aside those who came up against me, and, when it was necessary, cleared a path by swinging my club. It was as if the whole world had fallen from grace, and we had been abandoned here to witness its final degradation. Never had I felt more keenly our precarious situation. Never have I been more fearful. I thought of John Bourke, of all that he had told me, of all his dire warnings. Would that I had heeded him. How I longed now for him to hold me again in his arms, to carry me back to civilization safe from the horror.

Then I came upon the most shocking sight of all. It was Daisy Lovelace surrounded by a group of men. She was lying on her stomach, covered in blood, her dress pushed up around her waist. The savages appeared to be taking turns upon her. I yelled and pushed through them as another fell atop her. I swung my club with all my strength and hit the man a solid blow on the back of his head. He groaned and went limp upon her, but before I could push him off, another one grasped me from behind and wrenched the club from my hand. Now they had me down, grappling and pinning my arms. I fought for all I was worth, kicking, biting, scratching, and spitting. They tore the dress from my body. I screamed again. Suddenly I heard the crack of a bullwhip, and then another, and one of the savages who squatted upon me grasped his throat and made a gurgling sound as he was lifted backwards like a child's rag doll.

Then I heard a familiar voice, familiar in tone, but because it spoke in Cheyenne I could not place it immediately. But when the voice came a moment later in English I recognized it.

"*Git* the hell *offa* her, you miserable *stinkin'* heathens!" It was the voice of my old muleskinner friend, Jimmy—my savior Dirty Gertie.

At that same moment two others came to my aid. Another of the savages was lifted off me and I heard Gretchen speak. "I kill you you *gottðamnt* drunken pig!" she said. "You are not my *hustband* no more, I swear to God I kill you!" And she began to kick the man, who was too drunk to walk and crawled along the ground on hands and knees trying to escape her wrath. But Gretchen followed him mercilessly, taking measured aim with a heavy foot that sent him sprawling again and again in the dirt. "You *gottðamn* drunk son of a bitch, what you *tink* you doing? I kill you. You bad man son of a bitch drunken sot. I kill you, you *baðtart*!"

By then Phemie had wrenched my club away from the savage who had taken it, and in the same motion backhanded the man in a perfect arc across the face, laying his nose against his cheek in a torrent of blood. And the whip cracked again and now the remaining men were scrambling to escape this fury of women they had unleashed, stumbling and falling over themselves and trying to crawl away in their drunkenness.

"Are you alright, May?" Phemie asked, her voice so calm as to be almost otherworldly. She helped me to my feet.

"I'm fine, Phemie, but what of Daisy?" I had lost track of the poor thing in the confusion.

Now we saw that she still lay facedown in the dirt where I had first discovered her. We knelt beside her. She mumbled something to us, but we were unable to make out her words.

"We have to take her back to her lodge," Phemie said.

Gretchen now had ahold of her drunken husband's hair and was dragging him the way that a child drags a rag doll as he struggled to get his feet under him. "I *yam* so sorry, May, I *yam* so sorry to everyone," she said, and I could see that she was weeping great tears of grief and rage. "I *yam* so sorry to everyone," she said again. "I take this *gottðamn* drunken pig son of a bitch back home now. I see you all tomorrow, *yah*? I *yam* so sorry to you everyone."

"Now that's an old gal I wouldn't want to mess with," Gertie said admiringly. "I bet that ol' boy'll think twice fore he takes hisself another drink a whiskey."

"God bless you, Jimmy," I said to her, gratefully. "You couldn't have arrived at a better time."

"Aw, you can call me Gertie now, honey," she said, "or whatever the hell else you like. The cat's outta the bag. They found me out at Camp Robinson. 'Nother skinner fella caught me just like you did, squattin' to take a pee. It's a dead giveaway, but there ain't no way 'round it, is there now?"

"What are you doing here, Gertie?" I asked.

"Your Cap'n sent me, honey," Gertie said. "Got a message for you. But let's get in out of this damn mess first. I'll give you a hand with her, then we'll talk. Things seem to be winding down some now. Hell, they was so busy parrying when I got here I was able to ride right into the goddamn camp without even bein' noticed. Ain't they just plumb lucky I weren't a Crow Injun come to steal me some Cheyenne ponies? Why you folks'd be afoot fer the rest of the damn summer."

Gertie was right, the village had begun to quiet down; most of the dancers and revelers had either passed out or returned to their lodges, or crawled down into the willows along the river to sleep it off. Gertie, Phemie, and I half carried Daisy back to her tent. She had regained consciousness and was able to at least shuffle her feet. "Not a word to *mah* Daddy about this," she mumbled. "Mr. Wesley Chestnut has not conducted himself like a gentleman, *takin'* advantage in this manner of a girl when she is slightly tipsy. Not a word to *mah* Daddy, *Ah* beg of you."

Daisy's tipi crone met us at the entrance to their lodge, and we carried the poor thing inside and laid her gently down on her buffalo robes. The crone dabbed at the blood on her face with a cloth dipped in the water bowl, and made small clucking noises as she did so. The little French poodle, Fern Louise, yapped and ran in agitated circles about Daisy's head.

Daisy's husband, Bloody Foot, returned to the lodge moments after our arrival. The little dog seemed to have made friends with his new master and greeted him enthusiastically. To his credit, the man had not been drinking himself, and now told Gertie in Cheyenne that he had been searching the camp all night for his wife. His unpleasant name notwithstanding, he is a fine-looking fellow and was clearly genuinely concerned for Daisy. We did not tell him what had happened to her; but surely he could see.

It was just dawn by the time Gertie, Phemie, and I finally left Daisy's tipi. Promising to meet later, Phemie went to her own lodge, while Gertie and I walked back toward Little Wolf's.

A strange quiet had descended over the camp. The air was cool and perfectly windless, and the smoke from the dying lodge fires rose in thin straight lines above the tipis. Against the lightening horizon, the faint outlines of the bluffs over the river revealed themselves, and the birds took up their morning songs, tentatively at first and then in full voice. As always, the dawn cast a fresh light on the world; an uncertain hope returned. All seemed calm again, peaceful, as if the earth was a ship at sea and had managed to right itself after the storm.

Gertie and I skirted the half circles of family-grouped tipis where the bodies of some revelers still lay prone upon the ground, insensible as corpses. Fearing the worst, I stopped at Sara's lodge, for which I had started out all those hours ago. I scratched lightly on the covering and called for her. To my great relief, the girl came to the entrance, her face still swollen with sleep. She smiled when she saw me. "I was worried for you," I said. "I've been trying to get to you all night. I just wanted to see that you were safe."

She touched the center of her breast with the tip of her right thumb, the sign for "I," and then she extended her left hand, back down, in front of her body, and placed the tip of her right index finger, held vertically, in the center of her left palm, the sign for "safe." "I am safe," the gesture said.

I peered beyond her into the dimly lit lodge and saw her young husband Yellow Wolf, sleeping soundly on the buffalo robes. The child smiled at me again and swept her right hand, palm down from her breast outwards in a kind of chopping gesture, the sign for "good." Her husband was good, I think she meant to tell me.

"That's wonderful, sweetheart," I said. "I was just worried for you. Go back to sleep. I'll see you later."

And Gertie and I walked on.

"How is it that you speak Cheyenne, Gertie?" I asked her.

"Oh, hell, honey, didn't I tell you that I lived with the Cheyennes for a spell when I was a girl? Not this particular band but I'll betcha I know a few a these folks. I had me a Cheyenne boyfriend, too. Yessir, mighty nice young fella, good-lookin' boy, named *He' heeno*, Blackbird, . . . prob'ly would married Blackbird myself but he got killed by Chivington's army at Sand Creek, Colorado, in sixty-four. We wasn't doin' nothin', we was just camped there."

Now people were starting to stir in their lodges. A few wives and old women came outside to assess the condition, and in some cases, the identity of those who lay on the ground in front of their tipis. Some of the old crones kicked the corpses, squawking at them like angry mother hens to drive them away if they did not belong there. Others dumped bowls of yesterday's tipi water on their faces, which brought them awake sputtering and groaning.

"Goin' to be some sorry sickass *Injuns* around here today," Gertie remarked. "Yessir, whiskey goin' to be the ruination of these folks, that you can bet on, sister. Where'd they get it anyhow?"

"The southern Cheyennes came visiting," I said. "A half-breed among them named Jules Seminole brought whiskey."

Gertie nodded darkly. "Sure, I know Jules Seminole," she said. "A bad character, a very bad character. That's one you want to stay as far away from as you can, honey. Take my word for it."

I laughed, albeit without humor. "Yes, so I have discovered."

"He ain't hurt ya, has he, honey?" Gertie said, stopping to look at me.

"No," I answered, "not really." But then I felt the tears welling up behind my eyes, as if the horror of the past night had finally fully descended upon me. "Oh, Gertie," I said and I began to weep, to sob uncontrollably. It was the first time I had wept since this ordeal had begun, and now I could not stop and had to kneel down on the ground and bury my face in my hands.

"It's OK, honey," said Gertie, kneeling beside me and putting an arm around my shoulder. "You go ahead and have yourself a good cry. There ain't nobody around to see you but old Dirty Gertie, and she ain't goin' to tell nobody on you."

"Tell me your news of the Captain, Gertie," I said through my tears.

"Sure, honey," she said, but I sensed a reluctance in her voice. "When we get back to the lodge, I'll tell ya all about it."

"Has he married the Bradley girl yet?" I asked, composing myself. "Tell me now, Gertie."

"You're a tough gal, honey," she said. "I like that about you. I'll tell ya straight. Weddin's set for next month."

"Fine," I said, nodding and wiping my tears. "That's good. She'll make a fine wife for the Captain."

"Honey, I don't know exactly what went on between you two, but I got a pretty good idea," Gertie said. "Just because the Cap'n was already spoke for, and so was you, don't mean it can't happen. I know how it is out here. You feel like you're out on the edge of the world about to fall off and when somebody like the Cap'n comes along, somebody strong and decent, you grab ahold and you hang on for dear life. And just because he's goin' to marry someone else that don't mean he ain't been moonin' around like a lovesick kid hisself since you left."

"And why did he send you here, Gertie?" I asked, regaining my feet. "Surely not to tell me that." We continued on our way.

"He sent me to warn you, honey," she said. "He couldn't trust anyone from the Army, because what I got to tell you would get him in a heap a trouble. He sent me because I know you and because I speak the language and got ties among these folks."

"Warn me of what?"

"You prob'ly heard the rumors 'fore you come out here about gold in the Black Hills?" Gertie said. "Well, the government give that land to the Sioux and to the Cheyennes in 1868 in the Fort Laramie treaty—it's all on paper. All legal as can be. As long as the Injuns don't bother the whites passin' through, all this country from the Black Hills to the

Yellowstone is theirs to roam and hunt—forever. That's what it says right there on the treaty: forever. Well, now word has got out that there's gold in the Black Hills. Just last week, the Army sent out General Custer in charge of an expedition with a bunch of geologist fellas to find out for sure about them reports. Some a my old compadres is skinnin' for 'em—I'd a been with 'em myself if I hadn't got found out fer a gal.

"The scuttlebutt is that if Custer comes back at the end of the summer with his saddlebags full a gold," she continued, "the rush is goin' to be on—in a big way. It's already started strictly on account of the rumors. All them prospectors and settlers and shopkeepers and whores and everyone else who follows the gold rush is goin' to need—is goin' to demand—military protection against the Injuns. Because the Injuns still think that country belongs to them—see? And why shouldn't they? It was give to 'em fair and square. That's the heart of their big medicine country, and they ain't goin' to take real kindly to all them white folks running through it, shootin' it up and scarin' off the game. Now according to what the Cap'n is hearin', Grant's people is fixin' to pull the plug on this whole brides program—for a couple a reasons. For one thing, when the shit storm begins, they don't want a bunch more white women in the way of killin' off the rest of the Injuns. And they sure as hell don't want to get themselves in no situation where the Injuns can use you gals as hostages—then the newspapers would find out about this whole damn mess. How do you suppose that would look for President Ulysses S. Grant? So until further notice you all is the first, an mos' likely the last installment of payment to the Injuns. Now all this is unofficial right now, you understand? The Cap'n is privy on accounta bein' Crook's aide-de-camp, which a course puts him in a tight spot. Now if word gets out among the Injuns that the Great Father in Washington is—number one—backin' out of the brides deal, and—number two—plannin' to take the Black Hills back, well just all kinds a shit's goin' to fall from the skies. The Cap'n don't want you in the middle a that. He wants you to come back to Robinson with me. Right now. After we get a little catnap, we can leave later today."

"All of us?" I asked. "Leave now?"

"Honey, if all you gals was to try to leave at once," Gertie said, "it'd take the damn Injuns about five minutes to track you down and bring you back. And they wouldn't take kindly to it. See, they think you was given to them. And to an Injun a deal's a deal. No, this'd just be you and me, honey. We'd just sneak off and the two of us'd have a pretty good chance a makin' it. Especially after last night. I know this country, and anyhow, Little Wolf might just let you go. It wouldn't hardly look good, see, for the head man to go chasin' off after his wife like a damn jilted lover, if you get my meanin'.'"

"But Gertie, you know perfectly well that I can't leave my friends here," I said. "Especially after what has just happened."

"That's what I told the Cap'n you was goin' to say," Gertie said. "But he said to tell you that the government's goin' to figure out a way to get the others out, too. It's just a matter of time, and in the meantime at least you'd be safe."

"The government being so reliable," I scoffed. "John Bourke must take me for a fool to believe that. Or a coward to leave my friends here."

"Neither, honey," Gertie said. "You know that, but he figured it was worth a try. You think last night was bad, things is goin' to get a lot worse out here 'fore they get better. They'll get over the whiskey, but once the Injuns get things figured out, which after they start to see all the settlers moving into the Black Hills, will be real quick, this ain't goin' to be no place for a lady. You ain't goin' to be safe here."

I laughed. "We're hardly safe now," I said. "Tell Captain Bourke to come out here with a detachment of troops and provide us all safe escort home," I said. "Like a gentleman."

"Like I say, he can't do that, honey," Gertie said. "He's an Army man. He'd be facin' a court-martial for sure if his superiors even got wind of the fact that he'd sent me out here to warn you."

"So what is our position, then—officially speaking?" I asked. "Are we nothing more than sacrificial lambs? An interesting, but unsuccessful political experiment? Missionaries stranded in the line of duty? Or perhaps, easiest to explain, white women gone astray, taking up with savages of our own volition?"

"Yup, that's about it, honey," Gertie said. "Take your pick. Like I say, they goin' to try to figure a way to bring you home, but until Custer gets back with a full report on the gold, and until they figure some way to do that, everyone is just settin' tight. Which, you know, honey, has always been the thing the government does best."

"Shame on them!" I said. "Have they no sense of shame?"

"That's the thing they does second best, honey," Gertie said with a wry smile, "is not to have no sense a shame."

We had reached our lodge, Little Wolf's lodge . . . my home. "You must be exhausted, Gertie," I said, "and hungry. Why don't you stay here, have a bite to eat, and sleep for a while."

"Don't mind if I do, honey," she said. "I got to picket my mule, though, first. I left him tied up on the edge of camp."

"I'll have Horse Boy tend to him," I said. "That's his job, and he's very good at it."

"Whooo-eee!" Gertie said, "Ain't you just the lady a the house! Why you got servants to do all the work for ya!"

All were still in their beds inside the lodge, except for old Crooked Nose, who, I believe, never sleeps. She took me by the arm, her fingers like an eagle's claw, and smiled her toothless grin, which was meant, I believe, as an expression of genuine happiness for my safe return. Gertie introduced herself and they whispered briefly in Cheyenne. It did not surprise me that Little Wolf had still not returned to the lodge—the great man was probably passed out somewhere with his drinking cronies of the night.

I went to Horse Boy's bed and knelt beside him. The morning light was still dim inside the tipi but I could see that the child's eyes were open, catching the faint light from the embers of the fire and shining like gunmetal. I stroked his forehead and he smiled slightly. I held my hands open on either side of my ears and wriggled them, the rudimentary sign language for mule. The boy giggled at my antics, and, I think, thought that I was trying to amuse him. Gertie came over and knelt beside me. "Tell the boy where you tied your mule, Gertie," I said. "He'll fetch it and take care of it for you."

She spoke to the lad, who immediately scrambled to his feet, wide-awake and eager as always to perform his duties. I was finally beginning to understand a few words of the language but was still shy about speaking it. "God, I envy you Gertie. I have a terrible time with the Cheyenne language."

"Like I said, I learnt it when I was just a girl. Always easier to pick up at a young age. But you'll get the hang of it. Just remember that everything's done backwards from the way we say things. Let's say you want to say somethin' like, 'I'm heading down to the river to take a swim,' which in Cheyenne is said—'Swim, river, go there, me.' See? It's all backwards."

Without a sound, Quiet One had gotten up herself to stoke the fire with sticks and to put a small pot of meat to heating. Then she left the tipi to fill the paunch water vessel. The savages observe a curious custom of emptying out water that has stood all night—"dead" water they call it—and filling the vessel from the creek each morning with "living" water.

Soon she was back, and she poured some of the water into a small tin trade pan into which she also sprinkled a handful of coffee grounds. She put the pan on the fire to boil. Coffee is a precious commodity among the savages, and she was clearly serving it in honor of the company—without even knowing, or asking, who the company was; generosity is a universal trait of these people. And so in spite of the trials of the night, life went on . . .

The camp was exceptionally well provisioned at the present time. Besides the whiskey that Seminole had brought with him, the southerners had furnished us with the three most prized commodities among the savages—white man tobacco, sugar, and coffee. All these they had brought as gifts from the trading post—although most had probably been squandered last night on the whiskey.

Now I laid a bed of buffalo robes for Gertie next to mine and brought her a bowl of meat and a tin cup of coffee with a generous lump of sugar in it.

"Hell, this ain't so bad now is it, honey?" she said, making herself comfortable against the backrest I had fixed for her. "I always did enjoy sleepin' in a Injun lodge. Cozy, ain't it? Makes ya feel safe."

"I was beginning to feel so until last night," I said. "I have lived in a lunatic asylum, Gertie, but never have I seen lunacy like that."

"It's just the whiskey, honey," she said. "Plain and simple. It's poison to 'em. Turns 'em plumb crazy."

"How long did you live among them, Gertie?"

"Oh, I don't know, let's see . . .'bout eight years I guess altogether," she said. "I was stole off a wagon train when I was a girl, and I stayed with 'em until after Sand Creek. Someday I'll tell you the whole story . . . when I ain't so plumb tuckered out. But Hell, I liked livin' with these folks just fine. Hated to leave 'em. Yes, ma'am, a person can get mighty accustomed to this life, you understand what I'm sayin'? Besides last night, how are you takin' to it, honey?"

"I've hardly been here long enough to say," I confessed. "And I've hardly had time to reflect upon it, so busy have we been working and learning, adapting to their ways and trying to teach them something of ours. Now that you mention it, it occurs to me that in the past weeks I have hardly stopped to ask myself if I was happy here . . . I had simply resigned myself to it . . . But after the events of the night I shall have to reconsider the question . . ."

"Naw, you don't want to do that, honey," said Gertie, with a dismissive wave of her hand. "Like I say last night was just whiskey talkin'. They'll get over it. You'll get over it. I knew damn well you wasn't comin' back with me. I told the Captain you wasn't no welcher. This is a good band of people you got here. Some of them southerners is a bad influence, that's true. They've spent too much time with the whites, but all in all, if these folks was left alone, things'd be just fine. If the whites'd leave 'em alone, stop lyin' to 'em, stop givin' 'em whiskey, things'd be just fine."

"Stop giving them white brides," I added.

"Yeah, we're always messin' around where it ain't none of our business," admitted Gertie. "An' that's exactly the good thing about the Injun life—you don't have to stop and think about whether or not you're 'happy'—which in my opinion is a highly overrated human condition invented by white folks—

like whiskey. You don't have to think about it any more than
a bear cub or a pronghorn antelope or a coyote or a damn
bird has to think about it. You got a roof over your head? You
warm? You got enough food to eat? You got plenty a good
water? You got a good man? You got friends? You got somethin' to do to keep you busy?"

I nodded affirmatively to each of these in turn.

"You got a Injun name yet, honey?" Gertie asked. "I forgot to ask ya that. Mine was *Ame'ha'e*—which means Flying
Woman because one time I jumped off a runaway horse at a
full gallop and landed right in a damned tree and the Injuns
all thought I could fly. I always did like that name."

"The name they've given me is *Mesoke*," I said.

"Swallow," Gertie said. "Yup, that's a real purty name.
Seems to me that you got everything a body really needs in
life. Hell, honey, you tell me, what more does a person need?"

I thought the question over for a moment and then I said:
"Safety . . . security . . . love, perhaps."

"Aw, hell, honey," Gertie scoffed, "if them first two things
was so important to you, you wouldn't be here. You still be
livin' in that asylum you mentioned. And love? Hell, that's
the easy part! You see that old girl squattin' by the fire?" she
asked pointing to Quiet One. "Now you think she spends
her time worrying about whether or not she's happy? You
think maybe she ain't got enough love in her life—what with
her family, her husband, her children? I'll tell you something.
You know when you'll find out if you been happy here?
You'll find out after you leave. When you really got some
time on your hands to think things over."

"I miss my babies, Gertie," I said. "That's the worst part of
it. Do you know that I have two children? It was for them
that I signed up for this program, to gain my freedom so that
one day I might be with them again. I think of them every

day, try to imagine how their lives are, what they look like now. It helps me to go on. I like to imagine how it would be for them if they came to live with me here, grew up among the savages."

"Oh, they'd plumb love it, honey," Gertie said. "Put the damn whiskey aside, and it's a wonderful life for children. I thought I was goin' to die when they first took me, but after a while I practically forgot all about my real folks. It was like livin' a damn fairy tale. Like I say, where the fairy tale comes to end real fast is when you bump against the white man's world again. That's what happened to you last night. An' that's what happened to me at Sand Creek."

"If I give you a letter to my babies, Gertie," I asked, "will you post it for me at the fort when you return? They would not permit us to send any communication to our families before we left, but perhaps you could post one for me?"

"I'll try, honey," she said. "Sure I will." And she laughed. "You're a long way from mail delivery out here, ain't you?"

"If you liked this life so much, why did you go back to the white world, Gertie?" I asked. "Was it because Blackbird was killed at Sand Creek?"

Gertie was silent for a long time, and I thought perhaps that she had drifted off to sleep. "That was part of the reason," she finally said. "But it was also just because I couldn't get away from the fact that I'm white myself. There's no damn way around that, honey."

And after that we fell silent, as the exhaustion of the night's efforts overcame us. I curled up on my own sleeping place next to Gertie's. I felt like a little girl having a friend spend the night and was especially grateful this morning to have her here with me. She is a rough woman, it is true, and could surely use a bath, but she has a big heart, and what more can be said of a person than that?

The sun had risen, and the camp was going about its business, but it was muffled quiet and safe inside the tipi, the gentle morning sunlight filtering softly through the buffalo skins; the fire was warm and took the early-morning chill off the air, the tent pungent with the mingled scents of human beings and smoke and coffee and meat cooking, the smell of animal hides and earth. All these no longer seemed to me to make for an offensive odor, but rather an oddly comforting one—the smells of home.

Within moments Gertie had started to snore, loud and rhythmic, a snore befitting a muleskinner named Jimmy, but it did not disturb me . . . and soon I drifted off to sleep myself.

15 June 1875

Over a week has passed since our night of terror. I have rested my pen, and with the others thrown myself back into the business of living day to day, trying in the process to repair the dreadful damage done, to refill the empty well of our spirits.

Gertie left this morning, alone, for Camp Robinson. She carried only a letter from me to my children, and a private message to Captain Bourke. In the letter I thanked the Captain for his concern for my welfare but declined his offer to return with Gertie. I wished him well in his new married life. I told him that I was most satisfied in my own . . .

As to the news that she had brought from him, I have not mentioned a word of it to any of the others. Perhaps I err in this decision and should let all decide for themselves what course to follow, but I see no reason to alarm the women about events that are quite beyond their control. To panic them now when all are at their most fragile could only lead to more tragedy and despair. We may have entered into this enterprise as volunteers, but recent events suggest that we are, in reality, captives.

As I had feared, a group of our women, led by Narcissa White—who after the night of drunken debauch and her own violation by her husband, apparently decided to give up her mission here—tried to leave camp the very next day. Just as Gertie predicted, the women's husbands had no difficulty tracking them and returning them to their lodges within a few hours. They wouldn't have gotten far anyway and would only have perished in the prairie or been captured by some other tribe. "If they'd a got caught by the Crows or the Blackfeet," Gertie said, "they'd a found out how cushy life is here with the Cheyennes."

My own husband Little Wolf did not return to our lodge for three days and three nights, nor was he anywhere seen about the camp. He stayed out during that time, alone in the prairie, without shelter, food, or water, sleeping on the ground, doing, I believe, penance for his sins. Perhaps he sought divine guidance from his God.

When he came back in at last he was trailed by a sickly coyote; everyone in camp saw it and everyone remarked upon it—although only we white women seemed to consider this to be a particularly bizarre sight. We are beginning to realize that the savages' world has even a different corporeality than ours, and one quite inaccessible to us.

The coyote was gaunt and losing its hair in patches, and skulked around our lodge for three more days, always keeping a little away. I was frightened of the beast—when I shooed him he skittered sideways like a crab and made a strange hissing sound. Each time that Little Wolf departed the lodge, the coyote followed him, trailed along always the same distance behind. For their own reasons, the camp dogs did not bother the coyote—perhaps they recognized its illness—and they seemed intentionally to keep away from it.

Little Wolf himself never spoke of the coyote, never so much as acknowledged its presence; he remained silent and brooding as if involved in some terrible struggle of his own. He refused even to make the sign talk with me and when I tried to speak to him in English as I had done on our honeymoon outing together, instead of responding in his own language as was our way, he ignored me altogether. There was much speculation in camp about his behavior.

The medicine man, White Bull, told Helen Flight that the coyote was the Chief's medicine animal, that its sickness represented his own sickness and the sickness of the People from drinking the whiskey, and that if the coyote died in the camp, this would be a very bad thing for everyone. But after three days the coyote disappeared—one morning it was simply gone and did not return—and gradually Little Wolf came back to himself.

Other repercussions of that night: a man named Runs from Crow, who was married to our own little French girl Marie Blanche, was killed by a fellow named Whistling Elk—shot dead through the heart. Poor Marie has had a very hard time of it, what with her parents both murdered in Chicago, and now her husband. She is quite beside herself, for she rather liked the fellow. Now Runs from Crow's younger brother, One Bear, has offered to marry her, which is the Cheyenne custom—and rather a civilized one in my opinion. It is my limited experience that French women are, by nature, a practical race, and Marie Blanche, while still grieving for her first husband, is considering the proposal. She will certainly need someone to care for her and her child.

Sadly, the murderer, Whistling Elk, is married to Ada

Ware—as if that poor dark thing didn't already have sufficient cause for Melancholia in her life. The affair is a shocking event for the Cheyennes, as killing another member of
the tribe is the greatest crime of which a man is capable in
their society, and has occurred only rarely in all their history. The murderer, with any members of his family who
choose to accompany him, is exiled and must live alone beyond the perimeters of the village. He will be forever an
outcast, never fully accepted back into the tribe. People
cease to address him, or to so much as acknowledge his presence, and he is not allowed to participate in any tribal activities. He becomes, in effect, an invisible man.

Ada's exiled husband has even been stripped of his name
and renamed Stinking Flesh, for the Cheyennes believe that
one who kills a tribal member begins to rot from the inside
out. By tribal law, Ada is free to leave the man with no formal divorce decree being required, but for the moment at
least has chosen to join him in his banishment. As she is
guilty of no crime herself, she is free to come and go among
us. However, as the wife of the murderer she is considered to
be tainted by her contact with him, and is not allowed to
touch anyone or anyone's possessions. Pots or dishes from
which she eats at the lodges of others must be broken or discarded for fear that they have been contaminated. I need
hardly add that this superstition does not make Ada a popular visitor or dinner guest in anyone's lodge.

"When the doctors at the hospital questioned me about my
illness," the poor hapless thing said at our meeting the other
day, "I told them that I found it unsupportable being married
to an adulterer—especially through the long gray Chicago
winter. It was that time of year in particular that I felt the
full weight of the black dog crouched on my chest, as if suffocating me. And so that winter the doctors consigned me to

a dark room in an insane asylum, where the black dog was my sole company. My husband took the opportunity of my illness and prolonged absence—which was really in payment for his sins—to divorce me and marry his lover. Still the doctors questioned me incessantly: Why was I so sad? Why did I dress always in black? To what did I attribute my Melancholia?

"Now I find myself married to a murderer by the name of Stinking Flesh—who by all accounts is rotting from the inside out . . . and once again I have been exiled for his crime. Now does any among you wonder why I dress in black? Is there no end to a woman's suffering on this earth?" It was the most Ada had ever spoken to us or revealed of herself.

"*Aye*, but look on the bright side then, Ada," said Meggie Kelly. "*Ya* may be married to a *moordoorer* but now that he's an outcast, at least you don't have to worry about the beggar committin' *adooltory* on *ya*, for no one else'll *tooch* him!"

We all laughed; even Ada smiled, for she is not without a sense of humor, albeit a frequently dark one.

"Meggie's right," said her sister, Susie, "and furthermore, dear, I get a *tooch* of the Melancholia *meself* in Chicago in the wintertime, but *ya 'ave* to admit that *thar's* a great deal more *soonshine* in the prairie in the summertime than ever *thar* was in Chicago in winter. It'll be too damn hot for that old black dog in this country, I'll wager. You won't be seein' *mooch* of him out here."

And in such ways we try to bolster each other's spirits.

This next sad fact I am most loath to report: a number of other girls, both native as well as several of our women, were ravaged that night by drunken savages—in some cases, as in that of Narcissa White, the women's own husbands forced themselves upon them. Daisy Lovelace has grown silent and withdrawn since her terrible ordeal, and we are all filled with concern for her. Her husband, at least, is a kindly and patient man and seems to be caring well for her.

Perhaps most unfortunate, the wretch responsible for the entire night of terror, Jules Seminole, remains still among us, unpunished and by all appearances unrepentant. But for a still swollen ear he seems to have recovered from Crooked Nose's blow, and has already several times come by our lodge to leer at me and make his unspeakably degenerate talk . . . I try to disguise my fear of him, but I am terrified of the man, and make every effort not to go abroad unaccompanied.

Little Wolf, too, is aware of Seminole's skulking and unwholesome interest in me, but has thus far managed to keep vigilant control over his temper when the man comes around. As Sweet Medicine Chief, my husband is powerless to do anything other than speak out against Seminole in council for bringing the whiskey among the People. Truly, but for his own fall from grace as a result, Little Wolf's observance of his duties is monklike . . . nearly Christ-like in its selflessness.

17 June 1875

This morning Helen Flight came to visit, to invite me to a dance tonight in which she is guest of honor. The Kit Fox warriors returned yesterday from their raid against the Crows. Having wisely not imbibed in the drinking on that Hellish night, they had held their own private war dance across the river, and off they went the next morning as planned. All of them were by then painted with Helen's fantastic bird designs—the likes of which the savages, whose

own painting skills are limited to the most simple stick figures, had never before seen.

The raid was a great success, and yesterday the Kit Fox
warriors came whooping into camp with the usual fanfare,
driving an enormous herd of Crow ponies. Not only had the
men captured many enemy horses, but also they had not lost
a man.

"I'm afraid, *Mesoke*," Helen told me this morning, "that the
Fox chaps are giving me full credit for the success of the venture, after all. 'Medicine Bird Woman'—they call me now
'*Ve'kesohma'heonevestsee*'—a frightful mouthful isn't it? So
please do continue to call me by my short name, Bird, won't
you?"

"Of course, *Ve'ese*," I answered. (Some of us are making a
concerted effort to speak the Cheyenne tongue, and names
are an easy place to start.)

"Yes, well one bloke has already been 'round to present
me with three Crow horses and to tell me the story of his
great success in the raid," said Helen. "I should say—to sing
and dance the story. I'm sure you'll see the performance
again tonight if you would be so good as to accompany me
to the dance. I had the chap painted with the image of a
snipe and he showed me how he and his horse had been able
to zigzag through the bullets and arrows of the pursuing
enemy just as the snipe flies, thus avoiding all injury. All the
while as he danced and sang this tale, he held his arms out
like bent wings and made the specific winnowing sound of
the snipe in territorial display. Quite extraordinary, I should
say. Haunting actually . . . never seen anything quite like it.
That is to say, he sounded so like the bird, it was as if he had
actually become the snipe."

"Perhaps I must revise my opinions of the efficacy of your
magic, Helen," I said. "You may make of me a believer yet."

Speaking of which Reverend Hare's staggering loss of faith that terrible night—the dismal failure of his own "medicine"—has greatly diminished his influence among both our women and the savages—who despise more than anything the display of cowardice. They reason that if the Reverend's medicine is so puny in the face of that of his archenemy—the evil God Satan—against whom he is constantly preaching, then what kind of power does the Father's Great White Spirit really have? However childlike in nature it seems, the savages' theological reasoning has a certain simplistic logic. The influence of gods being only as good as their earthly representatives, at the moment Helen Flight's magic seems to hold greater sway among all . . .

The word about the camp is that tomorrow we depart on the summer hunts. I do not know where we go, or for how long . . . I do not know if John Bourke, or Gertie or the Army itself will be able to monitor our movements. This imminent departure to live the life of nomads seems yet another separation, yet another step further into the wilderness—leading us not closer, but seemingly always further away from our eventual return . . .

Having missed my monthly cycle, I am more than ever certain that I am pregnant now. The prospect of being a mother again fills me with both joy and trepidation. Now there are two of us to worry about . . .

→ NOTEBOOK V ←

A Gypsy's Life

"Now we move out again, the horses slipping down off the knoll, following the People, who follow the buffalo, who follow the grass, which springs from the Earth."

(from the journals of May Dodd)

7 July 1875

We have been on the move for weeks—thank God for the calendar I brought to mark off the days or surely I would have lost all sense of time, for, of course, the savages do not observe our calendar, and time itself passes differently among them—impossible to explain this . . . only that there is no time . . .

We have been traveling mostly westward and sometimes north—that much I know for certain—hunting and moving, we follow the buffalo herds.

At present I sit atop my horse Soldier on a slight rise overlooking the green plains below. The sweet child, Horse Boy, light as a feather, his brown skin warmed like a biscuit in the sun, rides up beside me on the saddle as he frequently does. I have grown ever fonder of the boy. He is my little man, my protector, and I his.

Several of us women ride abreast; in this case, I, Martha, Phemie, Helen, and Feather on Head. This traveling time is our best, and in some cases only, opportunity to visit and catch up on each other's news—because, when we are in camp there is too much work for all to do.

For the same reason, I shall try to keep this poor record while on the move, and have taken to strapping my notebook to my back so that when I have a moment to pause thus I can make a few scribbles on the page. Presently I rest my notebook against my little man's back as I write.

Now we watch as the entire band, possibly two hundred lodges strong with the southerners among us, moves out across the prairie, horses and dogs and travois, some people afoot, others riding, with the warrior guards appearing now and then on the distant horizons, before disappearing again into the folds of the land like ships at sea into the swales—it is a sight to behold! How many white people, I wonder, can lay claim to having witnessed such an exodus? Have ever participated in it?

The Cheyennes are a wealthy people and, particularly since the raid against the Crows, we have many horses. Some of the women and older children walk alongside the packhorses or alongside those that drag the travois, occasionally snapping their quirts to move them along. Others ride atop the packs themselves—two or three little girls together on one horse, they play games and chatter away like chicks in the nest. Some of the smaller children ride the huge camp dogs, others ride ponies. From the time that they are able to walk, Cheyenne children are comfortable on horseback, and their little hammerheaded prairie ponies, which are quite distinct in appearance from our own, are superbly eventempered, well trained, and biddable. Some of the older people, especially if they are ill or in any way infirm, and some of the youngest children who still need to be tended to by adults ride atop the travois—while the infants ride on baby boards strapped to their mothers' backs. Sometimes the baby boards are hung from the pack saddles or the travois poles themselves, where they dangle and bob gently with the movement of the horses much to the comfort and amusement of the infants themselves, who smile and gurgle, and, when they are not sleeping, watch all of the proceedings with wide-eyed interest. In this manner they absorb the nomadic prairie life as naturally as sunlight. The Indian children rarely cry. They are superb, perfect little creatures—but then what children aren't? I think constantly now of our own babies—for many of the others have announced their pregnancies. Our government may have lost faith in our mission, but how can a prospective mother not be filled with hope for the future?

I am in a bright mood today. The constant travel of the past weeks, though hard and frequently exhausting work, rather agrees with me. It occurs to me in response to the conversation I once had with Captain Bourke in which he asked, rhetorically, "Where is the savage's Shakespeare?" that possibly the reason the aboriginals have made scant contributions to world literature and art is that they are simply too busy living—moving, hunting, working—without the luxury of time to record the process, or even, as Gertie suggested, to ponder it. Sometimes I think that this is not such a bad state . . . and yet here I am, trying to steal a few moments whenever possible that I may faithfully report these events.

I take this opportunity to study the four of us—representatives of our group as it were. Such a ragtag assembly we make! We are nearly natives now, all but indistinguishable from our fellow Cheyenne women, and finally, almost as dark of skin (and Phemie, of course, darker!). Even my fair complexion has gone brown as a chestnut though I am still careful to wear the greasepaint as much as possible.

Weather permitting Phemie dresses still in men's breechclouts and little else, the scandal of her bare breasts long since accepted.

With the increasingly warm weather Helen has given up

her heavy knickerbockers and has had our seamstress Jeanette Parker fashion a buckskin suit for her, with fringed blouse and trousers. It is a decidedly eccentric outfit for a lady, but suits Helen perfectly—she looks every bit the frontiersman, especially with her ubiquitous pipe clenched between her teeth.

Like me and my friend and fellow wife, Feather on Head, Martha wears the simple loose-fitting antelope hide dress that the native women favor.

Now we move out again, the horses slipping down off the knoll, following the People, who follow the buffalo, who follow the grass, which springs from the Earth.

14 July 1875

However peripatetic our wandering of the past weeks may seem, there is a genuine method to it. The camp organizes and moves with marvelous efficiency. I am reminded of Mother's stories of the gypsies of Europe. Of course, now I understand why my bridal lodge had to be dismantled—I could hardly have managed it by myself. This is communal life in the purest form. Like a hive of bees, or a colony of ants, all participate for the good of the whole.

The women do all the work of packing the parfleches, dismantling the lodges, rigging and loading the horses and travois, and at the end of the day's travel, remaking the camp in exactly the same formation as the last. In our lodge, the old crone Crooked Nose oversees this process, squawking at us like a cranky magpie while brandishing, at the slightest infraction, a willow switch from her arsenal of weapons. On the morning of our very first move she actually lashed me across the back of the legs with her damnable switch; I was, presumably, packing incorrectly.

"Ouch!" I hollered, leaping at the sting; she'd hit me hard enough to raise a welt. I turned furiously on the old woman, who, instantly recognizing my wrath, began to shrink away from me. I moved toward her, shaking my finger; I put my cupped hand on my throat and pointed at her again and said: "You may be in charge of this operation, you old hag, but if you ever do that to me again, I'll wring your damn buzzard's neck!" I was speaking English, of course, but I was also speaking the universal language of women, and the old crone understood me well. She has not lifted her switch against me again.

The men devote themselves to the hunt, the various military societies to guarding the camp and protecting us as we travel. So far we have had no encounters with enemies nor seen any sign of them but for a few abandoned campsites. It is said that we have recently entered Crow and Shoshone country, and all have noticed an increased vigilance on the part of the warrior societies.

Altogether, having more or less accepted my woman's lot, I would admit that the division of labor among the aboriginals is an equitable one. Far from being a casual pastime as it was for Father and his friends, hunting is quite literally a matter of life and death—extremely difficult and frequently dangerous labor. Already this summer we have had one man trampled and killed when he fell off his pony in the middle of the chase. Another was severely gored by a buffalo bull, but survived (the fellow's name has now become Buffalo Not Kill Him), and a third was badly injured when his pony stepped into a badger hole at full gallop and broke its leg (this man now known as Horse Breaks Leg). Still I have not failed to notice that the men embark upon their hunting expeditions with a somewhat keener sense of anticipation than we women are sometimes able to muster for our camp chores and moving activities. Although even these are generally accomplished in a spirit of good cheer and cooperation.

To her own and to the savages' credit, our Negress Phemie, *Mo'ohtaeve'ho'a'e*, which translates interestingly to Black White Woman, is permitted to accompany the men on the hunt. Although women are not allowed membership in council, the Cheyennes are surprisingly egalitarian in recognizing special talents, and Phemie has clearly proven her venatic prowess.

At the same time, women in the tribe wield a great deal of influence in daily affairs and are regularly consulted on all subjects that concern the welfare of the people. My own Little Wolf, for example, values the advice of a prominent medicine woman, Woman Who Moves Against the Wind, above that of all the other medicine men, and, while he hardly agrees with my views on all subjects, he nevertheless listens to them with great respect. Perhaps our own society might learn something from the savages about relations between the sexes.

The scouts have consistently found good-sized herds of buffalo at nearly every place we have been. Thus the men have had excellent hunting, and the larder is full. The buffalo have been further supplemented by elk, deer, pronghorn, a variety of small game, and trout—the streams hereabouts so choked with fish that if one is quick about it one can scoop them up on the bank by hand—another job for the women and children. We have already amassed an abundance of hides, both for the comfort of the tribe and to trade later at the agency trading post for the precious commodities of cof-

fee, sugar, tobacco, cloth, gunpowder, trinkets, cooking utensils, and what other white man luxuries strike the savages'
fancies.

Some days I actually find myself hoping that the hunters
will not locate game, for its very fecundity makes more labor
for everyone. At the expense of my hands which begin to
look prematurely like the hands of a crone, I have become
competent in all aspects of skinning, butchering, scraping
and tanning hides, drying meats, and cooking over the fire—
although as to this last, not all members of our family have
fully appreciated my culinary efforts.

I have also made a tenuous peace with the old wife, Quiet
One—we are hardly friendly, but she tolerates my presence
and no longer do I fear for my life at her hands. However,
she still becomes sullen every time I insist on taking a turn
at the fire—obviously she feels that I am trying to usurp her
position as first wife and head cook. Frankly, I should think
that she would be grateful for relief from the chore.

If sometimes I find myself complaining about our daily
labors, others among our group are shirking their fair share
of work altogether. Since her unsuccessful attempt to "escape" Narcissa White has made it plain to our host/captors
that she is here against her will and refuses to cooperate in
any way whatsoever. The grand scale of her missionary efforts has been similarly reduced. Having largely given up on
saving the souls of the savages, whom she has deemed as yet
too crude and unformed to be properly Christianized, she
has now turned her attentions to teaching them to be obedient servants to their future white masters.

"She wants to teach them to be slaves, first," Phemie has
observed. "Then, as my people have done, they will turn to
the white God for spiritual salvation. It is the manner in
which conquerors have always created a force of laborers."

Toward this end, Narcissa has taken two savage girls under her wing and is trying to teach them certain "civilized" domestic duties—to curtsy and carry her possessions for her, to say "yes, ma'am" and "no, ma'am" and other such things which appear comical, and even mildly insane, in the middle of the wilderness.

Many of the People do own utensils—pots and pans, tin dishes, and even some poor silverware obtained at the trading post, though some still eat with their fingers.

"After they are settled on the reservation," Narcissa explains, "my instruction in such matters will serve them well. For they will always be able to find employment at the forts in the homes of the officers, and in the white towns and settlements that spring up after the frontier is once and for all secured from the heathens that civilization may extend her noble boundaries without constant fear of their vicious depradations." (Speaking of which, Narcissa has never forgiven her husband for the "involuntary" consummation of their marriage—does not allow him in the lodge, and refuses to say whether or not she is pregnant.)

I have no idea why her "servant girls" go along with this treatment, perhaps simply out of curiosity, or mere politeness, for the savages are both curious and polite in abundance. However, I predict that as a rule these people will make poor domestic help.

Now we have reached our afternoon destination, chosen by an advance guard of scouts, and announced by the old camp crier who rides the length and breadth of our procession, spread out by the end of the day over a distance of several miles.

Regardless of whether our new campsite is intended to accommodate us for one day or several, the women set up each as a perfect replica of the last—with every family and each lodge in the same position relative to the whole. The full tribal circle opens always to the east, to face the rising sun, as does each family circle, as does each individual lodge entrance. This is both a religious and practical consideration, for one awakens to the warmth of the morning sun, and by leaving the lodge flap open in the morning the sun lights, warms, and freshens the whole tipi. The symmetry and order is quite lovely—a kind of art form.

Well before sunset, we have the entire village in place and settled—just as if it had been here for weeks or months. Fires burn, food cooks, children play, men smoke and hold their councils—and, as always, women work . . .

1 August 1875

We have been camped for the past six days along the Tongue River, the single longest encampment since we began traveling. It is a lovely spot situated in a natural bowl at the base of the mountains, well protected from the wind and elements. The small valley is green and lush, with ample grass for the horses, surrounded by low hills and bluffs, the river lined by huge cottonwoods whose leaves rustle softly with the slightest breeze.

I walk down to a pool on the river each morning at first light, my favorite time of day, before the camp is fully awake, to fetch the morning water. The wrens have just taken up their lusty morning songs and warblers flicker like bright yellow flames in the green willows' branches. Often ducks, geese, and cranes flare off the water at my approach, and sometimes a doe deer with a fawn bounds away, tails flagging through the undergrowth. At the river's edge, swallows swoop from their nests in the sandy cliffs to skim insects from the surface, and rising trout make concentric rings upon the pool. I drop my paunch vessel into the cool, moving water and as it fills to tug heavily downstream, I feel a part of this world, pulled like the vessel itself to fill up with this life.

This is the best time to make these scribblings in my journal, a few minutes stolen from the beginning of the day, before the bustle and commotion of camp life begins. I sit on my rock overlooking the pool on the river, the air cool and still, the bluffs still shadowed, the sun not yet risen above them, the constant prairie winds not yet come up . . .

Sometimes Helen Flight joins me at dawn on my rock to sketch the bird life. If we sit very quietly, sandhill and whooping cranes might come back into our pool, blue herons and night herons, geese and ducks of many varieties. She holds her sketch pad open on her lap, pipe clenched firmly between her teeth, eyebrows raised as always in delighted anticipation, as if something perfectly extraordinary is taking place. Periodically when I pause in my writing she gently lifts my notebook from my lap and makes a quick study of a bird in the margins of the page—a swallow swooping for insects on the water, or a Kingfisher perched on a tree branch, holding a fish in its beak. "Perhaps *Mesoke*," she says, handing it back to me, "you and I should consider a collaboration of our own, *A Woman's Life among the Savages of the Western Prairies* we might entitle it, letterpress by Mrs. May 'Swallow' Dodd Little Wolf, with illustrations by Mrs. Helen Elizabeth 'Medicine Bird Woman' Flight Hog."

"A splendid idea, Helen!" I answer lightly. "Certain to become a classic in frontier literature!"

"Unfortunately human figures have never been my artistic forte," Helen says. "That is to say, I've always been more comfortable drawing animals—specifically birds. Once I undertook a full-length portrait of my companion Mrs. Ann Hall of Sunderland, who, gazing upon it for the first time, exclaimed: 'Why, Helen, you've got me looking exactly like a roseate spoonbill!'"

Besides Helen's company, if I sit long enough on my rock, we may be joined by Gretchen, Sara, Martha, Daisy, or Phemie—often a number of us get together here—a kind of morning girls' club, I, its self-appointed president.

Daisy is happily much recovered from her night of terror at the hands of the drunken savages, and considerably softened around the edges. Oddly (although under the present circumstances of our lives what can any longer be considered odd?) she has become quite close friends with Phemie since her "accident."

"Did *y'all* hear the news about my dear friend, Euphemia Washington?" Daisy asked us this morning, holding her little poodle Fern Louise in her lap. "She has just been asked to join the Crazy Dogs warrior society—an event without precedent among the savages. And *Ah* do not mean as a ceremonial hostess at social events. *Ah* mean as a *full*-fledged warrior woman. The very *fuust taame* in the history of the tribe that a woman has been so honored—and a *whaate* woman to boot. Aren't *y'all* so proud? Fern Louise and I are, aren't we, darlin'? We believe it is a great honor to us all, *havin'* come about naturally due to Miss Phemie's prowess on the games field and in the *huuunt*."

Now little Sara beams and chatters away in Cheyenne, laughing with Pretty Walker, the daughter of Quiet One and Little Wolf, who often accompanies me to fetch the water. The Indians call Sara Little White Girl Who Speaks Cheyenne, for she has been the first among us to learn their language fluently; they can hardly appreciate the full irony of the fact that prior to speaking Cheyenne she was mute! Now she has blossomed like a wild rose under the prairie sun—happier and healthier than I've ever seen her. I can hardly believe that she is the same frail and frightened child who clung so desperately to me on the long train ride west. She and her slender young husband, Yellow Wolf, are inseparable, thick as thieves—two people have never been more deeply in love.

Speaking of which, dear Gretchen, *Moma'xehahtahe*, she is now called, or Big Foot, has reconciled with her foolish husband, No Brains, whom she has well cowed and completely under her thumb—or her foot, I should say—since the dark night of whiskey drinking earlier this summer.

He is an indolent, vain fellow with a well-deserved reputation as a poor provider for his family. Often Gretchen must heave him out of the tent with strict instructions to *"Brink home dinner you bick lazy dope!"* and on the all too frequent occasions when No Brains has returned from the hunt with an empty packhorse, we have witnessed a bizarre, albeit not unamusing spectacle: a contingent of angry family members, led by Gretchen herself, followed by the man's mother and any children who happen to join in, chasing the fool through the camp with sticks. *"Yah!* You great *bick stupit* idiot,"* Gretchen, red-faced with Swiss wrath, hollers at him, kicking him in his buttocks and smacking him roundly about the head and shoulders with her stick, as the children lash at his legs. "How you expect to support a family if you can't even *brink* home meat to put on *da* table? *Vee* must depend on your *gottdamnt brudder* and your *udder* friends to feed and clothe us. I *vill* not be a charity case! I always *vork hart* for my own living and I not take handouts now! You *stupit* silly jughead! Look at you, you all *drest* up, you got all *dat* fancy stuff, and you could not bring home meat if the *da* *gottðamnt* buffalo falls dead at your feet! You great *stupit* nincompoop!"

And poor No Brains stumbles through the camp, trying to escape Gretchen's Big Foot, while warding off the others' battery of blows until inevitably he stumbles and falls to the ground where he is set upon by the smallest children who strike him with their little sticks and shout insulting epithets at him, laughing gaily all the while. Let it not be said that the hunter's life on the prairie is an easy one.

And yet in quieter moments, when we meet, as now, on our rock above the pool of the river in the still of the morning, Gretchen, as placid as a dairy cow, expresses her great fondness for this same buffoon. She is, I think, grateful to have a husband at last, and only wants him to make something of himself.

"I admit *ðat* he is not *ða* brightest fellow, in *ða* whole *vorlð*, *ðat* is true," Gretchen says in his defense. "But before *ða* children come, I *vill* teach *ða* big ninnyhammer how to be a *goot hustband* and provider. I know I *yam* not a pretty girl myself, but I always *vork hart* and I make a nice home for my family *vedder ðey* be Indian people or white people—it don't matter to me. I am a *hartvorking*, tidy person, and I *vill* be a *goot mudder* to my children—and a *goot vife* to my *hustband*. *Dat* is how I was taught by my own *mudder*. And, you know girls, *ðat* fellow of mine he may be *ða* biggest pumpkinhead in *ða* whole tribe, but he is still my man . . . you know, and he likes me . . . *yah*!" she covers her mouth and giggles. "He likes me lots," she adds striking her robust breast with a flat hand. "He loves my *bick* titties! All he wants to do is to roll in *ða* buffalo robes with me!" And we all laugh. Bless her heart.

Now the camp begins to stir, and others come down to the water's edge to fill their water paunches, and the men, the members of the Savage Men's Bathing Club, arrive at the water for their morning dip, and we can hear them splashing about up- or downriver, and the birds begin to lift off, flushed by the human congress in their domain, the deep sounds of hundreds of heavy wings all along the river, the cacophonous cries of the rising birds like a discordant natural orchestra—yakking and honking and wailing and warbling—fading away to be replaced by the voices of women, children, and men. In the distance, the camp crier begins his rounds . . . calling his messages in a high shrill voice, marking the end of this quiet, best time of day . . .

Sometimes I send Pretty Walker back with the water paunch while I stay on writing or visiting with my friends. She is a lovely thing—the boys can hardly keep their shy eyes off her—slender and long-legged like her father, moves with the grace of a dancer, is not so sullen and suspicious as her mother—an eager, open-natured child, with bright, intelligent eyes. She enjoys the company of us white women, and we have been teaching her a few words of English, while she, in turn, helps us with our Cheyenne. Most of us are less self-conscious about speaking the language now, and can make ourselves understood on a rudimentary level—which, as these people are hardly given to complicated philosophical discourse, is usually quite sufficient. Pretty Walker has been most useful to us in this regard, and we have great fun with her, although I'm afraid that our budding friendship has not entirely met with the approval of her mother.

I have avoided this next topic for the fact that it so exceeds the bounds of propriety, but I must here make mention of one of the most difficult adjustments that we have had to make. That is in the matter of toilet facilities. Fortunately, ours is a very cleanly tribe—unlike some of the others. One might well imagine the stinking mess that would accumulate in a camp of two hundred people if everyone simply went off to do their business at random in the bushes. We have in our recent travels come across the vacated campsites of other tribes—the stench announcing their location from miles away.

The Cheyennes have devised a relatively hygienic solution to this—although one that does not afford a great deal of privacy. In each camp a central area is established, always placed downwind of the village, where all are expected to do their business. Young boys are assigned to guard these communal latrines and to make sure that waste is immediately buried. This is a boy's first job after which he graduates when older to guarding the horses. Latrine duty and the burying of feces is done not only for reasons of basic sanitation, but also because there are many dogs about the camp and, given the opportunity, dogs will . . . forgive me, please, for this is a vile subject . . . roll in, and even eat, human excrement.

For our part, we white women have made certain improvements on the latrine system. Little Marie Blanche, our French girl (who has, after all, "married" her murdered husband's brother), was quite appalled by the whole thing. The French, being accustomed to irregular bathing, have devised many clever means of hygienic compensation, and thus Marie Blanche has insisted that water vessels, to serve the function of "bidets," be installed and maintained by the "B.M. boys," as we call them. Thus in this one small—but to a woman, essential—area I think perhaps we have taught the savages something useful. But surely I've said enough on a subject which requires no more graphic description . . .

Despite my present acceptance of our lot, even a certain contentment, I have had an uneasy premonition of late—an indefinable sense of gloom lurks in the background of my general good spirits. I wonder as I strain to see the page in the silvery half-light of dawn, if something were to happen to prevent my return to civilization, who would ever read these words? What would become of my dear children, Hortense and William, should I be unable to make my way back to them? I pray that the letter Gertie took for me will reach them, but how can I know that Father and Mother will ever show it to them when they are old enough to read? Such thoughts fill me with unease. Whatever is to become of me, I should be greatly consoled by the knowledge that my children might one day learn something of their mother's life among the savages, might understand that however eccentric she may have been—however stubborn, foolish, and impetuous—she was not insane . . .

7 August 1875

My recent gloomy premonitions have come more horribly true than ever I could have imagined, for the worst catastrophe possible has befallen us. On this, our darkest day yet, I and several of my compatriots find ourselves in a desperate predicament.

The day began as peacefully and uneventfully as any other. At dawn I sat upon my rock overlooking the pool on the Tongue River near our camp. I was just preparing to unstrap my notebook from my back. Helen Flight sat on one side of me, waiting for the light of day to be favorable for sketching; Martha, Sara, and little Pretty Walker sat on my other side. The Kelly twins, too, had joined us and were squatting on the water's edge about to toss a hook and line into the pool after trout for their breakfast. Gretchen had just lumbered down to fill her own water paunch and squatted now beside the stream.

We all sensed, I think, at exactly the same moment that something was amiss, for the birds which had already taken up their morning song went suddenly silent—a lull broken by the sound of several dozen ducks and geese getting up all at once off the water just downstream from us. We looked up from our respective tasks but no sooner had we done so, than in a heartbeat's time we were each descended upon at once, filthy hands clamped over our mouths, knives held at our throats, arms like iron bounds rendering us immobile. The single sound that could be heard over the wing-beats of the rising waterfowl was a heavy thump from a stone war club and a miserable groan as our friend Gretchen collapsed in a heap at the water's edge.

So well orchestrated was our abduction that, as I look back on it now, I believe our attackers must have been watching us, perhaps for several days—assessing our comings and goings, gauging the force necessary to carry us off. And Gretchen, with her great size and obvious strength, must have appeared more to them than they believed one or even two men could comfortably handle, and thus they had rendered her, and her alone, unconscious.

So quickly, stealthily, and powerfully were we overcome, that there was no question of resisting. We knew that if we dared struggle or tried to cry out, our throats would be instantly cut. Now each of us, helpless and paralyzed with terror, was half-dragged, half-carried, downstream from whence our abductors must have come. One particularly large and fearsome-looking fellow hoisted Gretchen over his shoulder and carried her as if she were a sack of potatoes. I did not know yet to what tribe these men belonged, but they were as a rule taller and rather fairer-skinned than our own Cheyennes, were dressed some of them in flannel shirts of white man manufacture, and several wore black Army hats with the tops cut out and the sides wrapped in feathers and variously colored cloth.

At a shallow ford downstream they carried us across the river, where several younger boys waited in a grove of cottonwood trees, holding a string of horses. Among these I recognized a number of our own mounts. Here our hands and feet were bound with rawhide thongs and cloth gags tied over our mouths, and we were very roughly thrown across the pommels of the saddles like so many fresh-killed deer carcasses. One of our savage abductors then climbed up behind each of us.

I do not know exactly how long we traveled thus—it must have been several hours at least, but seemed far longer so great was our pain and discomfort. I was certain that they had killed poor Gretchen for she remained unconscious, and, from the little I could turn my head to look, appeared lifeless where she lay across the pommel. Not until what must have been a full hour had passed was I relieved to hear a moan of life issue from her.

After the hard and agonizing ride, during which we could do nothing but reflect helplessly upon our situation, we arrived at last at a small camp of a half dozen or so makeshift lodges—little more than stick lean-tos covered with canvas— clearly the temporary encampment of a hunting or war party, for there were no women about, only several more young men who met us when we rode in. Now once again we were handled with extreme roughness, thrown off the horses' backs to sprawl in the dirt. This seemed to excite the savages to much laughter and taunting in their unfamiliar tongue.

At last they untied our hands and feet and removed the gags from our mouths. Mine had been so tightly bound that my mouth was split and bleeding at its corners. When free I scrambled on my hands and knees to attend to little Pretty

Walker, the youngest and most terrified among us. The Cheyenne children are brought up on tales of being captured thus by other tribes—like the boogeyman stories of our own culture—and this was clearly the girl's worst nightmare come true. *"Ooetaneo'o,"* she wailed in terror. *"Ooetaneo'o."*

So frightened was she that I could not understand what she was trying to say, until Sara spoke up. "Crow," she translated. "She says that these men are Crow." Only later did I realize that it was the first, and the last, time that I would ever hear our Sara speak a word of English.

We all knew the Crow to be the archenemy of the Cheyenne—and a loutish-looking bunch at that with their half-white man clothing and preposterous Army hats, they swaggered and gloated and made merry at our despair. Poor Martha, scared witless herself and in a state of evident shock, began repeating: "They're going to kill us, they're going to kill us all. I know they're going to kill us . . . they're going to kill us all . . ."

Finally, Meggie Kelly spoke sharply to her. *"Showt* up, Martha," she said. "If they were plannin' to kill us, they'd a *doon* so by now. They'd not have gone to all the trouble of carrying us away *loyke* this."

"Aye, Meggie's right," said her sister in a low voice, "They'll not *moorder* us yet. First they're going to *folk* us. Look at that one there. He's *sportin'* a wood, he is."

It was true that one of the men was in a state of erection beneath his breechclout, and the other men, now noticing his condition, laughed and urged him on.

Now the wretch grabbed my little Sara by her hair, and began to drag her toward one of the crude huts. It was less a conscious selection of the girl than that she happened to be in the nearest proximity to him. "No," I screamed, and I grasped the attacker's leg, "not her, please, not her. Take me."

"*Aye*, ya filthy beggar," said Susie Kelly, taking ahold of the man's other leg, "or me! Let that child go, goddamn *ya*!"

Our pathetic entreaties seemed to elicit much further merriment among the man's cohorts. After a short struggle the savage shook loose of Susie's grasp and then caught me square in the jaw with a kick that sent me sprawling. All but Martha, who was too frightened to move, and poor Gretchen, who lay upon the ground half-conscious and groaning, tried to come to our aid, but the savages held them back.

The fiend who dragged her now released his grasp on Sara's hair, fell atop her, and began to force apart her legs. The girl wept and struggled against him. Never as long as I live will I forget the look of silent intensity on her young face, the tears of sorrow that ran down her cheeks. I knew in that instant that this same unspeakable fate must have befallen her as a child growing up in that awful asylum—that her muteness had been her final strength, her final testimony to the cruelty of this world. Held on the ground now by another of them and helpless to stop the crime, I began to weep myself, to plead, to beg, to pray to God . . .

I do not know where the knife came from. Some said later that it belonged to the Crow and that Sara took it from his belt, others that she had it concealed all along beneath her dress. But I saw the flash of steel as it came up in her hand and she plunged the blade into the man's neck as he lay atop her. He made a surprised gurgling sound and clawed wildly at the knife handle, finally pulling the blade free as a great geyser of blood shot like a fountain from his neck. But with his last breath before he bled to death and fell lifeless atop her, he drew the knife across our dear Sara's throat, and in a terrible instant the life drained from her eyes.

❊ ❊ ❊

Now darkness falls and we sit huddled together upon the ground inside one of the rude stick shelters. Here we try to console one another, weeping softly and whispering together. Several of the younger savages squat in front of the entrance, guarding us, but they have not bothered to bind our hands again for all fight has left us. After they murdered Sara, the filthy brutes violated the rest of us in turn . . . we all simply endured, silently, their vicious assaults . . . I managed only to save the child Pretty Walker from this fate, distracting her would-be assailant by offering myself a second time in her stead . . . I have my notebook, strapped all along to my back, open in my lap and here I make these wretched and perhaps final entries . . .

"Why do you still write in your journal, May?" Martha asked me a moment ago in a small, hopeless voice. "What difference does any of it make now?"

"I don't know, Martha," I said. "Perhaps I write to stay alive, to keep us all alive."

Helen Flight laughed bleakly. "Yes," she said, "I understand perfectly, May. Your pen is your medicine and as long as you're exercising it, you are elsewhere engaged, you are alive. In spite of everything, we are all still alive . . . that is to say, except, of course, for dear little Sara."

We all looked at the child's body, which lay cold and stiffening, where we had dragged her to the rear of the hut.

"I do not wish to live any longer," Martha said. "Perhaps Sara was the lucky one. Surely death would be a blessing after what has befallen us . . . and what we have to look forward to."

"Aw stop *yer* damn whinin', Martha," said Meggie Kelly. "Susie and me are going to 'ave our babies, and we plan to be alive for that event. Isn't that so, sister?"

"Right, Meggie," said Susie. "We're goin' to be mothers

we are. The lads are goin' to come for us, I just know they will."

"Yes, I believe so myself," said Helen. "Chin up, Martha. We've been used abominably ill, it's true, but our husbands aren't going to allow the Crows to just walk off with their wives. Your own husband, Tangle Hair, is, after all, head man of the Crazy Dog soldiers—May's husband, Little Wolf, head man of the Elk warriors, of which society my own Mr. Hog is second-in-command—and a most capable fellow he is, too, if I may say so. I'm quite certain the chaps have already set out to rescue us. That they will swoop down at any moment and exact their vengeance against these criminals."

Brave Gretchen, who was still barely sensible from the terrible blow she took, and whom the savages had at least spared in their ravishment, now raised her head weakly from where she lay beside us. "*Yah* and don't forget my *hustband* No Brains, either," she said. "He come for me. I know he *vill.*"

We are allowed no fire and the night air is chilly and so we close in together for warmth and what little comfort we can offer one another . . .

8 August 1875

Yes, thank God! Helen was correct, we have been saved, delivered to safety, returned to our own people! The Crow thieves—kidnappers, murderers, rapists, fiends—are dead. Our warriors killed even some of the young men among them . . . of that I am sorry, for they were little more than boys, though I believe that several escaped in the ensuing melee . . .

The attack came just at dawn after the darkest twenty-four hours of our lives. The Crow guards must have first been silently eliminated, for our other captors were still asleep inside their huts when our brave warriors stormed the camp. The Crows had barely time to exit their shelters before they were struck down, butchered amidst their own cries of surprise and the bloodcurdling shrieks of our men. My husband Little Wolf himself led the charge, seemed not like a man at all but like a God of vengeance, an animal, a bear, fearless, without mercy. He carried a shield and a lance as he rode, striking down the enemy like the wrath of God itself. Truly he was, at that moment, my knight in shining armor.

We women stayed huddled in our shelter but could see the terrible carnage from the open entranceway. Riding right alongside the men, but for her breechclout naked atop her white horse, was our own brave Phemie. The Crows must have been paralyzed with terror at the sight of this howling warrior woman bearing down upon them, drawing her bow like a mythic goddess of war to drive an arrow through the heart of an enemy and then with another bloodcurdling cry, to smote a second with her club. Good God, what a vision . . .

All of our husbands had come for us, just as Helen had predicted, yes, even No Brains, who was finely dressed for battle in an elaborately ornamented war shirt but whom I feel certain held back until the initial charge was over and then came in to count coup upon the already dead and stricken enemy.

The boy Yellow Wolf was the very first to enter our hut and when he saw his beloved bride laid out there cold and dead, a more piteous howling of grief I have never before heard. He went to her, gathered her corpse in his arms, and pressed her to his chest. All of us wept anew for our friend and for her young husband's splendid grief.

Leaving the boy to his private mourning, we exited the shelter to search out our own husbands amidst the chaos of death and dying. The scalps of enemies were being taken . . . other mutilations occurring . . . the scene had an unreal, dreamlike quality to it—as if we were there and yet not there . . . truly we are all of us savages now . . . anointed together in this bloody sacrament of revenge . . . for we took pleasure in our enemies' death and mutilations, and shall never be the same for it . . . we have seen the savagery in our own hearts . . . have exulted in blood and vengeance . . . have danced over the scalps of enemies . . . all that we have done, God help us . . .

The Cheyenne men tend not to be demonstrative in matters of conjugal affection, but when the Kelly girls saw their own twin husbands they ran to them in joy, leapt upon their ponies like sprites, wrapping their legs about the young men's waists, hugging them about the shoulders and kissing them wildly on their faces and necks. "God bless *ya*, lads," they said. "God bless *ya*. We knew *ya'd* come for us. We knew you'd save *yore* dear blessed wives."

Gretchen, much recovered from her injury, but still wobbly and weak-kneed, found her own buffoonish husband, who was afoot leading his horse. No Brains was all puffed up like a cock with his recent coups and himself waved a bloody enemy scalp for all to see.

My husband Little Wolf sat his mount, quiet and still as is his way, watchful and surveying the scene like the dominant wolf of the pack. When he spied me with his daughter Pretty Walker beside me, he rode directly to us and slipped from his horse.

The child began immediately to weep, threw herself into her father's arms.

"Neve'ea'xaeme, nahtona," Little Wolf said, holding her. "Neve'ea'xaeme, nahtona. Do not cry, my daughter."

And then he looked over the child's shoulder at me. "Ena'so'eehovo, Mesoke? They raped her, Swallow?"

I shook my head, no, and to the next question in my husband's eyes, I cast my own eyes to the ground, and began to weep myself, "Nasaatone'oetohe, naehame, I could not stop him, my husband. Nasaatone'oetohe."

Little Wolf smiled gently at me, and nodded and when he spoke, I think, it was for the comfort of us both. "Eesepeheva'e," he said. "Eesepeheva'e. It is all right now."

Riding back into our camp this afternoon, we were greeted by the joyful trilling of our women as all ran out to meet us. But when the family of Yellow Wolf saw him bringing up the rear, leading a horse with the body of Ve'ho'a'o'ke laid across it, a high keening arose from some of the women, and spread throughout the camp.

9 August 1875

This morning we buried Sara and the unborn child she carried. Her body was dressed in her Cheyenne wedding gown and wrapped in a white buffalo hide, covered with rocks in a shallow grave on the prairie.

There had been much discussion among all concerned about whether the girl should have a Christian or a traditional Cheyenne burial. Of course, Reverend Hare and Narcissa White argued for the former. But others of us believed that the only true happiness our Sara had ever known in her short life on this earth had been among these people. And we wished for her soul to go to the place the Cheyennes

call *Seano*—the place of the dead—which is reached by following the Hanging Road in the Sky, the Milky Way. Here
the Cheyennes believe that all the People who have ever
died live with their Creator, *He'amaveho'e*. In *Seano* they live
in villages just as they did on earth—hunting, working, eating, playing, loving, and making war. And all go to the
place of the dead, regardless of whether they were good or
bad on earth, virtuous or evil, brave or cowardly—everyone—
and eventually in *Seano* all are reunited with the souls of their
loved ones.

"Heaven," I said to the Reverend Hare. "*Seano* is just like
our own Heaven. What difference is there, Father?"

"A substantial difference, Miss Dodd," said the Reverend,
"for it is not a Christian heaven and any soul can gain entrance there without regard to baptism, without reward for
virtue or punishment for sin. Such a place does not exist,
cannot exist, for how can there be a heaven unless there is a
hell?"

"This earth, Reverend," I said, "is both a heaven and a
hell. No one knew that better than our Sara. She should be
allowed a simple heathen burial by her husband."

But the Reverend remained, as I knew he would, implacable on the subject. "The child was baptized in the only true
church," he said, "and her body must receive the holy sacra-
ments so that her soul may enter the Kingdom of Our Lord."

And so, finally, both services were conducted, one by Reverend Hare and the other by Yellow Wolf and his family,
who carried Sara's body to its final resting place, leading her
saddled horse, which to all of our shock the boy killed there
beside her grave, drew a knife across its throat—just as his
young wife had died herself—so that the horse fell to its
knees with a pathetic trumpeting of air escaping its severed
windpipe. "*Ve'ho'a'o'ke* must have her horse," Yellow Wolf ex-

plained as the horse toppled over on its side and the light faded from its eyes, "to ride the Hanging Road to *Seano*."

Thus Sara's soul rode her horse wherever she wished to go—a choice of heavens—and all were satisfied.

11 August 1875

Our funeral procession left Yellow Wolf sitting cross-legged beside the grave of his bride. For two days and two nights, we have heard the boy's wails of mourning carried on the wind.

I need hardly say that it has been a difficult time for us all . . . not only dear Sara's tragic end but our own debasement at the hands of the Crows has changed things among us, and within us, things that we can as yet only faintly comprehend.

But for hollow platitudes, the Reverend offers us scant comfort and we have, as always, only each other for solace . . . and thank God for that.

And so we have made a pact together, each of us, never to speak of that night, or the following day, neither among ourselves, nor with any of the others. We cannot change what has happened and so we must go forward away from it.

Our Cheyenne families have taken us back into their generous bosoms, caring for us with great solicitude and kindness, without a hint of reproach—which seems to be the domain of a few of our own women alone. Of course, Narcissa White treats us as if our little group had somehow enticed the Crows to carry us away, that whatever humiliation we may have suffered at their hands was just punishment for our sins and confirmation of her own righteousness.

Since our ordeal I have hardly let my husband out of my

sight—truly he is my savior and protector, a good, brave man. I feel a greater attachment to him now than ever, though in a strange way more as a daughter than as a wife. I have taken, the past few nights since our return, to slipping under the buffalo robes with him, after all in our tent sleep—not, of course, for the reason of sexual intimacy, but only to feel him beside me, to curl next to him and take comfort in the smooth warmth of his skin, the fine wild smell of him. The old wife Quiet One has been extremely kind to me; I know that she is aware of these nightly visits but does not begrudge me them. I believe that she knows of my efforts to protect her child, Pretty Walker, who since our return, has herself slept in her mother's bed. The child and I have both now seen the boogeyman in the flesh and are more than ever afraid of him.

20 August 1875

By my estimation I am now approaching the third month of pregnancy. I do not believe that my baby has been injured and for that I am grateful. Martha and the Kelly girls, too, seem healthy in their terms. As does Gretchen. Thank God.

Of my closest circle of friends only Phemie and Helen Flight seem not to be with child. Helen, of course, has already confessed to me about having lied to the medical examiner regarding the matter of her fertility in order to be accepted into this program.

"Mr. Hog is really a most agreeable fellow," she says now, "but he has since our marriage been possessed of the unfortunate male notion that unless he impregnates his wife he is something less than a man. He used to inquire of me almost daily, by rubbing his stomach hopefully, if I was yet with child, and when I answered in the negative . . . well, then he would wish to try again! I must say, it got to be a dreadfully tiresome business. However since our abduction and safe return he has made no further overtures toward me. I am able henceforth to concentrate my efforts solely on improving my 'medicine.'"

For her part Phemie is still wearing her chastity string, and merely chuckles deeply. "Like you, Helen, I have an occupation," she says. "I am a hunter, and now a warrior, which is hardly a suitable profession for a prospective mother. Moreover from the time that I was a child men have forced themselves upon me whenever they so desired. I am very fond of my husband, *Mo'ohtaeve'ho'e*, and one day perhaps I shall have his child. But I shall decide when I am ready."

As for the rest of us, we have the comfort of all being pregnant together, so that we may share the experience, commiserate, make plans. By our estimation our babies will be born next February, and although we worry about the prospect of being far along in our terms throughout the cold winter months, hopefully we shall be more permanently encamped then. We may even expect to be living at one of the agencies with a doctor and hospital nearby—for there has been talk among some of the men in council recently about going in this year.

23 August 1875

A very ugly thing has occurred today, the repercussions of which will be felt for a long time to come. Hearing shouts of distress from Reverend Hare and angry cries from a mob of savages, a number of us hurried in the direction of the Reverend's lodge. There we came upon a shocking scene.

A man named *Hataveseve'hame*, Bad Horse, was driving the naked Reverend from his and Dog Woman's lodge with a quirt. The Reverend—huge, pink, and hairless—was sobbing and trying to protect himself from the man's lashes, which were raising angry red welts all over the fat man's body. A number of people had gathered, including other members of Bad Horse's family. Bad Horse's wife, a short, squat woman named *Kohenaa'e'e*, Bear Sings Woman, came from the Reverend's lodge carrying their young son—who was also naked, although, especially among the children, such a natural state is not in the least bit unusual. Still it became clear what had occurred, for the Reverend in his confused blubbering combination of Cheyenne and English was trying to explain that he had only been giving the boy instruction in his catechism. Which explanation did not placate the furious father, who continued to drive the Reverend with vicious blows of his quirt.

I stepped up beside Susie Kelly who, with her sister, had joined the small crowd of onlookers. "Should we do something to help him?" I asked, for my dislike of the man notwithstanding, it was a pathetic sight.

" 'Tis a family matter, May," Susie said. "The old hypocrite got caught *booggerin'* the boy. *'Appens* all the time, you know, amongst the Catholics. When Meggie an' me was growin' up in the orphanage, the old priests used to *boogger* the lads *bloody*. Isn't that so, Meggie?"

"Right, Susie, a sad thing, it 'tis, too," said Meggie. "For lads that take it up that chute that way become angry men, that's been my experience. I don't believe they've ever seen such a thing among these people. Even the old Nancy Boys amongst them like the Father's roommate don't fool with the young lads. They say the old *he'emnane'e* are celibate."

"He's a lost soul," I said of the pathetic Reverend, "who may not deserve, but still requires, mercy."

"*Noothin'* to be *doon* for him, May," said Susie. "They won't kill the old *booger*. They're just goin' to teach him a *goood* lesson."

And indeed, the outraged parents' fury soon abated, the family went home with their son, and the crowd dispersed. Then the twins and I went to our fallen spiritual advisor, who lay curled upon the ground, reduced to a quivering mass of torn red flesh. We helped him back into his lodge, where old Dog Woman, clucking his concern, ministered to his wounds.

I'm afraid that the Big White Rabbit's disgrace among the People is final, and irrevocable. I must say, beyond the fact that some of us have fulfilled our end of the bargain by becoming pregnant, we do not seem to be having much success in instructing the savages in the benefits of civilized ways.

28 August 1875

We are on the move again. This time and for the first time since our arrival we are dividing into several groups and heading off in different directions. The game has dispersed and so must the People, for it is easier for smaller bands to feed themselves than one large band all together.

This separation has caused a great deal of anxiety among our women. Martha is nearly hysterical with worry as she and her husband Mr. Tangle Hair belong to a different band than my family, and as a consequence we will be separated— possibly for weeks . . . possibly longer.

"I cannot leave you, May," the poor thing said this morning

when we learned of our imminent departure. "Oh, dear God, what shall I do without *you*?"

"You'll be fine, Martha," I tried to console her. "You'll have others in your group."

"For how long are we to be apart?" Martha asked. "I cannot bear the thought. What's to become of us?"

"You must stop worrying so," I said. "You worry yourself sick and then everything turns out fine after all, does it not?"

Martha laughed. "My friend," she said, "if you call the events of the past months, and especially those of the past weeks, 'fine,' truly you possess a serenity that will never be mine. I cannot survive without you to give me strength."

"Don't be silly," I said. "Of course you can, dear. We will be together again soon enough."

"How can you know that, May?" she asked. "How can we know that we'll ever see each other again?"

"There you go worrying again," I said, trying to be light-hearted. "You are soon to be a mother, and I have always been a believer in the old saw that anxious mothers give birth to anxious babies."

"Of course you're right, May," she said. "But I cannot help myself. I am anxious by nature. I never should have come here to the wilderness . . . I'm too much of a mouse, terrified of everything . . ."

"After what you have been through, Martha," I said, "you have every right to be terrified."

"But you are not, May," she said. "I would give everything to be like you—intrepid and unafraid. I know that we are not to speak of that night, but I must tell you this . . . I must tell you how proud I was of you . . . and I'm sorry, I'm so sorry I didn't help you when they murdered Sara . . ." Now Martha had begun to weep. "I was so frightened, May. I wanted to come to your aid, but I could not, I could not move. Perhaps if I had been able to help you the wretch wouldn't have killed her . . ."

"You must never think that, Martha," I said, sharply. "And you must honor our pact not to speak of that night. There was nothing any of us could have done to save the child."

"Yes, but you protected Pretty Walker," Martha said. "I would never have had the courage to do what you did, May."

"Nonsense," I said. "Enough of that, Martha."

And then she put her arms around me and hugged me with all her might. "Tell me something to give me courage, May."

"I can tell you one thing only, my dearest friend," I said. "And then we will not speak of it again. You must promise me that."

"Yes, of course, I do."

"I was just as terrified as you that night, as everyone else," I said. "I have been from the beginning of this experience. But I've learned to disguise my fear. I made the vow to myself on our very first day, that whenever I was most afraid for my life I would think of my babies, my Hortense and Willie, and I would find peace in knowing that they are safe, I would seek serenity in the image of their little hearts beating calmly. That's what I thought of when the savages set upon me that night. I realized that the worst thing that could happen to me was not that I should be killed—but that this baby I carry would die. And thus I submitted. And I endured. Just as you and the others endured. Because we are women, because we are mothers some of us, and others mothers to be. And some, like Helen Flight, are just plain strong. Do you remember what Helen said once in our discussion on the subject of a warrior's medicine? That if they believed strongly enough in their own power, perhaps they are protected by it?"

"Yes, I remember," Martha said, "and you said it was pure poppycock! Pure superstition!"

"Yes, I did," I admitted, and I laughed. "And truth be known, I still think so! But you must remember, Martha, that you survived that night yourself, you submitted and endured, and by doing so you saved your baby. Your power as a woman, as a mother, is your medicine, and it saved you. Take your courage from that. Do not be afraid of our separation. Have faith that it is only temporary, that you will be well protected by your husband, your family, and the friends who accompany you, and that you and I shall be reunited again in due time."

6 September 1875

Our band heads south. We are told that we are returning to Fort Laramie to trade at the post there for sufficient provisions to see us through the coming winter. Little Wolf also wishes to discuss with the fort commander the matter of the remainder of the white brides that have been promised to his young warriors by the Great White Father. I have neither tried to disabuse him of this notion nor said a word to him of Gertie's report to me on the subject. There have already been disgruntled murmurings of late among some of the Cheyennes that once again the whites are reneging on a treaty provision, for, of course, no more brides have been sent since our arrival—and clearly no more will be.

This will be our first contact with civilization since we were given over to the People in May . . . only five months. But it seems a lifetime. After all that we have endured I am filled with a strange trepidation about the prospect of returning to the fort. Of course, I cannot help but wonder if

Captain Bourke will be still stationed there with his new bride. I have had no more word from him since Gertie's visit earlier in the summer. And since that time we have been almost constantly on the move.

Presently we are extremely well supplied with buffalo robes and hides, elk, deer, and antelope skins, so much so that nearly all of our horses are fully packed and more of the People are afoot. There is talk among the young men about launching yet another horse-stealing raid against the Crows. Others talk of stealing horses from some of the white settlements we pass on the way to the fort. The "old men chiefs" such as my husband council against this, for they believe that we are at peace with the whites.

I, myself, am largely afoot, for my own horse Soldier has been pressed into duty carrying parfleches of household goods. And so I walk to lessen his burden. I do not mind to walk, in fact in some ways prefer it. Whatever one may say about the hardships of this nomadic life, we are all of us women in magnificent physical condition. I had hardly realized how sedentary and soft of muscle I had become during my long incarceration in the asylum; one begins to take the inactivity for granted and nearly forgets the joys of healthful outdoor exercise. The first weeks among the savages every muscle and every bone in my body ached with fatigue. But now I am fit as a fiddle. So it is with the other women, some of whom I hardly recognize any longer. Almost all have lost weight, and are darker of skin and sleek as racehorses. I believe from this experience that Caucasian women should also discover the healthful benefits of this open-aired life of physical activity.

I'm happy to report that Helen Flight and her husband are included in our little band as are Phemie and the Kelly girls. Of my closest friends Gretchen, Martha, and Daisy

Lovelace are all headed off in separate directions. Poor Ada Ware has loyally remained with her murderer husband and continues to live on the periphery of the Dull Knife band, who themselves are off, God knows where. It is much like keeping track of separate flocks of geese, and while not wishing to alarm poor Martha on the subject, I have no idea how or when we will be reunited.

Both the unfortunate Reverend Hare and Narcissa White have elected to join Little Wolf's band—presumably because ours is headed to the fort. After the former's disgrace, he trails some distance behind us on his white mule, like a penitent or an outcast himself. I never cared for the man, but I feel some pity for him now. I won't be surprised if, after we reach the fort, we will be seeing the last of him. As to Narcissa, after the conspicuous lack of success of her own mission, I have a suspicion that she, too, may be plotting a defection.

Most of the southern Cheyennes have already departed back to their own country, while a few accompany us to Fort Laramie and from there will continue south. I am deeply distressed to report that after a much welcome absence of nearly two months the damnable wretch Jules Seminole is again among us. I hope that we will have seen the last of the lout after we reach Fort Laramie, when he will surely continue on south with the rest of his people. After my experience at the hands of the Crows I am less able than ever to tolerate his presence.

"*Exoxohenetamo'ane,*" I finally said to my husband the last time the man came skulking around our lodge. "He talks dirty to me."

Little Wolf's face darkened in rage. And there the matter rests.

Our smaller group is able to move with even greater dispatch, breaking camp early every morning and traveling hard until nearly dusk. I do not know how many miles we cover each day. The country itself is quite pretty—rolling prairie grassland cut periodically by river courses, the water low now after the dry summer, the whorled grasses already beginning to turn their autumnal shades of yellow. A chill fall wind blows down out of the north reminding us all of the coming winter.

Keeping the Bighorn Mountains to the West, we move roughly south by southeast, across the Tongue, where Hanging Woman Creek flows into it, to the junction of the Clear River and the Powder, following the Powder down to the Crazy Woman Fork and then east and south toward the Belle Fourche. At least this is how I mark the watercourses on my Army map, though some have different names among the whites than the Indians. Beyond the Belle Fourche, the buffalo-grass prairie gives way gradually to a series of desolate, arid buttes, rocky canyons, and dry creek bottoms. We hurry across this inhospitable desert, for the only water to be found here is brackish and alkaline, and impossible to drink.

One day we were just able to make out the faint outline of the Black Hills rising up on the eastern horizon, and the next day we were close enough to see the pine-studded slopes but these we kept to our left as we headed south on the prairie's edge.

10 September 1875

A war party of Oglala Sioux has ridden down out of the Black Hills to intercept us. Fortunately these people are close allies of the Cheyennes, and members of the party have relatives in our own camp. Even though they had identified us as friends, the warriors made a spectacular entrance, quite clearly designed to impress us—which it most certainly did—with their faces painted like demons, they were dressed in all manner of elaborately beaded and adorned attire, yipping and wheeling their horses—a more ferocious-looking bunch I have never before seen.

It has been my observation that the savages are showmen of the first order who spend a great deal of time on their personal toilet and appearance and no more so when they prepare for war. The old medicine man, White Bull, has explained to Helen Flight that a warrior must always look his best when going off to wage war in the event that he is killed in battle. For no warrior wishes to embarrass himself by being underdressed when he goes to meet his maker, the Great Medicine. "So you see, May," said Helen Flight with perfect delight, "it's an artist's dream come true, for not only do I adorn the warrior for his protection in battle, but I adorn him so that he might make a good impression on the Great Medicine. That is to say, what more can the artist hope for than to have her work viewed by God in his heaven?" I hardly need mention that Helen, although she professes to be an Anglican, is nearly as irreverent as I.

Although there is much intermarriage between the Sioux people and the Cheyennes, Little Wolf does not speak their language, and does not generally care for them. He believes that their women are unvirtuous. Truly my husband is very much of a tribalist and has kept himself and his family separate from these allies, almost as much as he has from contact with the whites.

Nevertheless, after the warriors—perhaps thirty in number—had finished their display of horsemanship and fierce posturing before us, the Chief emerged briskly from our lodge to speak the sign language with the leader of their party—an enormous fellow named, as I understood it, Hump.

Naturally, before anything important could be discussed between the two Chiefs, the entire Sioux contingent had to be invited to eat and smoke. Not to extend such an invitation would be considered impolite. Several families opened their lodges to the warriors, after which a general council was held in the Medicine Lodge. When all the formalities were completed, and the ceremonial pipe lit, the Sioux at last explained that the intent of their war party was to launch a series of raids against the white gold seekers and settlers who were invading the Black Hills.

Speaking through a Cheyenne interpreter, the Sioux Chief, Hump, then asked Little Wolf if the Cheyennes would join them in a war against the whites. The Black Hills, Hump said, belonged to both the Sioux and the Cheyennes, had been given to them "forever" in the last great treaty talks.

Little Wolf listened politely to this request and then answered that he was quite familiar with the terms of the treaty but that, as the Sioux could plainly see, ours was only a small band with more women and children among it than warriors and that at present we were on our way to do business at the trading post, not to wage war against white settlers.

"Perhaps the Cheyennes will not fight the whites because the soldiers have given you these pale women," Hump said, waving his arm toward us. "Perhaps the white women have made you soft and afraid to fight." At this evident *bon mot* some of the Sioux warriors present made insinuating snickers.

My husband's face darkened and I could see the muscle in his jaw rippling, a sure sign of his well-known temper rising. "The Sioux are certainly aware of the Cheyennes' ability to make war," Little Wolf said. "We claim that we are the best fighters on the plains. It is a foolish thing for the Sioux to say that we are afraid. Ours is not a war party, but a trading party. I have spoken. And that is all I have to say on the subject."

With this Little Wolf stood and left the Medicine Lodge. I followed him home. The next day the Sioux were gone.

14 September 1875

Yesterday we reached Fort Laramie. A more distressing return to the bosom of civilization I can hardly imagine . . . we are all left now to ponder the question of which world we really inhabit . . . perhaps neither.

We struck our camp as far away as we could from the hangs-around-the-fort Indians, whose appearance and behavior was, if anything, even more shocking to us after living among the Cheyennes these past months. Truly contact with our white civilization has caused nothing but ruination and despair for these unfortunate souls. A number of them, ragged and thin, came straightaway to our camp to beg from us.

After we made camp, Little Wolf himself led our trade contingent to the fort grounds to conduct our business at the trading post there, our packhorses well laden with hides. A few among our group chose to accompany their husbands to the fort, but others had grown suddenly shy faced once again with the prospect of confronting civilization after these many months in the wilderness.

As I look back now with the luxury of twenty-four hours of hindsight, I realize that I, myself, was impulsively bold in my own insistence upon going to the fort with my husband. So anxious was I to catch a glimpse of civilization that I had hardly given a thought to how we would appear to civilized people. I think, too, that in the back of my mind, I must have hoped to catch sight of John Bourke, or at least to hear some word of him.

Phemie and Helen, equally unselfconscious, also elected to go into the trading post, as did the Kelly girls—whose swagger is undiminished by any circumstances. Both the Kellys and Helen Flight, I should mention, have become rather wealthy women by savage standards—the former by the ill-gotten gains of their gambling empire, and Helen for artistic services rendered. Helen hoped to trade her goods for gunpowder and shot for her muzzle loader, as well as for additional painting supplies and sundry "luxuries" of civilization.

"And I intend to post a letter at last to my dear Mrs. Hall!" she said, with great excitement. I, too, had prepared a letter to send to my family, although I felt certain that we would be forbidden still by the military from posting these communications.

Our old crier, *Pehpe'e*, identified us to the fort sentry, and after some delay the gates swung open and a company of Negro soldiers galloped out to meet us. With snappy military precision, they formed lines on either side of our little trade contingent to escort us inside. For all their soldierly discipline, the black men could hardly take their eyes off our Euphemia. *Nexana'hane'e* (Kills Twice Woman) as she is called since our rescue from the Crows, rode her white horse beside her husband Black Man, who rode a spotted pony. It was a mild day and she was bare-chested as is her summer habit, wearing nothing but a breechclout, her long legs bronzed and muscled, adorned with hammered copper ankle bracelets. She wore copper hoops in her pierced ears, and a necklace of trade beads around her neck and looked as always perfectly regal—more savage than the savages themselves.

Although it must certainly have been in violation of military regulations, one of the soldiers nearest Phemie couldn't resist whispering. "What you *niggers* doin' with these people?" he asked. "Are you prisoners?"

Phemie chuckled deeply. "We live with these people, *nigger*, that's what we're doing," she said. "These are our people. My husband is Cheyenne and does not speak English."

"Cheyenne!" said another soldier behind the first. "*Whooo-eeee*, woman! You is one crazy *nigger*!"

As we entered the fort we could see that a small crowd of curious onlookers, civilians and soldiers, had gathered to observe our procession. Little Wolf rode at the head, followed by a half dozen of his warriors in a tight cluster, followed by the string of packhorses led by the women and some boys, several more warriors bringing up our rear. I, too, was afoot, leading Soldier and two other of our packhorses, walking abreast with Helen Flight, who led her own four horses in a string. I was dressed as usual in my antelope hide dress with leggings and moccasins. I usually wear my hair braided in the Indian fashion now—having found this to be more practical. My fellow wife Feather on Head is very adept at the process. For her part, Helen had her pipe clenched firmly between her teeth, wore her English shooting hat, buckskin trousers and jacket, and carried her muzzle loader in a sling over her shoulder. The Kelly twins sauntered boldly behind us, leading their own string of horses equally well laden with hides.

Only now, incredible to say, does it fully occur to me what a bizarre spectacle we must have presented to those assembled, and even now I flush with embarrassment in recounting the scene.

What other reception we might have expected, I do not know. My own foolish pride blinded me to the fact that far from looking the part of heroic explorers returning in triumph to civilization, we must have appeared in truth not merely comical, but utterly ludicrous.

A number of the soldiers' wives were included in the group of curious onlookers and there arose among them an astonished murmuring which gave way to an excited chattering and pointing as our procession moved past. *"Look, look there, those are a pair of the white girls, the redheads,"* we heard them say. *"Look how filthy they are! Why they look like savages themselves!"*

"Good Lord, that nigger girl is half-naked!"

"And look at the outfit the Englishwoman wears, the painter, doesn't she look like a buffalo hunter!"

"Isn't that fair-haired girl with the braids the one that was so saucy with John Bourke last spring? From the look of her, she's gone completely wild!"

"Wait until the Captain sees her now!"

These last remarks were like an arrow to my heart; and just as suddenly I knew that I did not wish to see Captain Bourke . . . prayed not to see him . . . How could we have been so proud, so foolish? My cheeks colored, I burned with shame, I cast my eyes to the ground.

"Tiny minds, May," said Helen Flight with her usual good cheer, having obviously witnessed my distress. "They have no sense of manners or decorum whatever. And they are to be paid no attention whatever. Tiny, tiny little minds. Let them not concern us, my dear friend. Why you're the smartest little picture of a lady here! And don't you forget it. Keep your head up now, my dear! An *artiste* must never bow her head to the tiny minds. This is a lesson my dearest companion, Mrs. Ann Hall, taught me long ago. Never bow to the tiny minds!" And then Helen, God bless her, her eyebrows

raised in delight actually took off her hat and waved cheerfully to the astonished crowd of onlookers.

Her words gave me strength, and I lifted my head again.
Still, I continued to pray that the Captain was not here at
Fort Laramie after all to witness my humiliation, to see me
"gone wild."

But then, for some reason, the mood seemed to change
among the onlookers, as if their barbed curiosity spoken in
tones loud enough for all of us to hear was not sufficient re-
proof for our transgression of all things wholesome and
Christian. We had almost reached the trading post when
someone hissed, *"Whores!"*

And someone else: *"Dirty whores!"*

*"Why do you bring your filth here among decent God-fearing
Christians?"* another said.

Perhaps because she has lived with such intolerance
and prejudice for most of her life, the unflappable Phemie
knew just how to react to it; she began to sing one of her
"freedom songs," as she calls them. Her rich, melodic voice
rose above the ugly epithets, covered and finally silenced
them:

> *I've been buked and I've been scorned,*
> *I've been buked and I've been scorned, children*
> *I've been buked and I've been scorned,*
> *I've been talked about sure's you born.*

And though I am certain now that they must have been
punished later for it, several of the Negro soldiers who escorted us joined her in the next verse. They shared the community of racial memory and knew the song well. And they
sang as if to protect all of us in their charge:

There'll be trouble all over this world,
There'll be trouble all over this world, children,
There'll be trouble all over this world,
There'll be trouble all over this world.

We were all of us heartened by the singing, given courage by the deep men's voices in harmony with our own Phemie's contralto which rose above the others like that of an angel— a black angel. And we all sang the third verse, which we had heard Phemie sing countless nights in her lodge:

Ain't gonna lay my religion down
Ain't gonna lay my religion down, children,
Ain't gonna lay my religion down
Ain't gonna lay my religion down

Now we had reached the post store and our procession halted as the trader, with a half-breed interpreter in tow, came out to confer with Little Wolf. As we waited, and for the first time, I took the opportunity to look back at them, to gaze into the crowd at some of the individuals who had witnessed our arrival here in such low mean spirit. They had fallen silent now and regarded us with sullen looks of suspicion and . . . hatred.

Hardly had I begun to peruse their faces than my eyes met those of Captain John G. Bourke . . .

HEf

→ NOTEBOOK VI ←

The Bony Bosom of Civilization

"How strange to recall that six months ago we departed Fort Laramie as anxious white women entering the wilderness for the first time; and now, perhaps equally anxious, we leave as squaws returning home. I realized anew as we rode into the cold wind on this morning that my own commitment had been sealed forever by the heart that beats in my belly, that I could not have remained even if I so wished."

(from the journals of May Dodd)

14 September 1875, Fort Laramie (continued)

This would seem an appropriate place to begin a new notebook, for perhaps it was at the very instant upon first laying
eyes again upon John Bourke that I understood beyond a
shadow of a doubt that he was lost to me . . . and I to him.
That I had crossed over, finally and irrevocably, to take up
residency in "the other world behind this one" as the Cheyennes call the world that exists on the other side of our own.

The Captain could not disguise his horror when our eyes
first met, could not hide the flicker of revulsion that crossed
his face. We stared at one another thus for a long time before he finally turned his gaze away with something like
relief—as though he had decided that he must have been
mistaken, after all; that I could not be the person he had at
first taken me for.

In the tumult of emotions I felt in seeing him again, I do
not know which was more painful to me—the Captain's dis-
gust or his dismissal.

In an attempt to calm the racing of my own heart, I
turned my attention to our immediate business here: we began to unstrap our hides from the packhorses and let the
bundles slide to the ground, where they fell with a heavy

thud—a line of thuds and a cloud of dust billowing up beneath the horses' legs.

The proprietor of the trading post was a short, bandy-legged Frenchman by the name of Louis Baptiste, who now made his way from bundle to bundle, inspecting, counting, jotting figures in the columns of his ledger book. Baptiste had a large hooked nose and small, close-set eyes, and the Indians called him *Pe'ee'ese Makeeta*—Big Nose Little Man.

When Big Nose reached Helen Flight, she said to him: "I shall be negotiating my own trade, sir, independent of the gentlemen. And I authorize Susan and Margaret Kelly to represent me in this matter."

"I only *beezness weeth* the braves," said the trader, "*jamais avec les squaws.*"

"On what grounds, may I ask, sir?" Helen inquired pleasantly.

Now Baptiste looked her up and down, his small eyes narrowed meanly. He grinned. "*Mais peut-être vous avez une petite squaw* under your buffalo robes, *madame, non?*"

Helen's smile never wavered. "These are my goods," she said evenly to the man. "And I should be pleased to let those young ladies right there"—she pointed to the Kelly twins—"conduct my business for me, thank you so very much, sir."

By now Susie and Meggie had sauntered forward. "*Aye*, Frenchy, you'll be dealin' with me and sister here," said Susie.

Louis Baptiste raised his palms as if matters were quite out of his hands. "*Comme j'ai dit, mesdames,*" he said, "I do *beezness* with the braves. *Toujours. Jamais avec les squaws.*"

"Yes, well no doubt they are easier to swindle than the women," observed Helen drily.

I spoke up myself then. "We are representatives of the United States government," I said, "officially dispatched by President Grant to instruct these people in the workings of the Caucasian world. This would seem to be an excellent opportunity to begin their economic education."

Baptiste aimed a stream of tobacco juice between his legs; some of it didn't clear the hook on the end of his nose and dripped from it like rusty water from a leaking faucet. He snorted and wiped his nose with the back of his hand, which he then proceeded to study as if it were a matter of the greatest import. "*Oui*, I know who you are, *mesdames*," Big Nose said with a nod. "You are the white squaw brides of *les sauvages, n'est-ce pas?*" He shook his head with something between astonishment and regret. "*Moi*? I have an Indian squaw woman myself—Arapaho. I find that they are less trouble than white women," he said. And then he shrugged. "Yes, OK, *ça va*. Why not? You may come in the store, but *beeg* Chief he makes deal for everyone." Baptiste moved on down the line of bundles, counting and jotting figures in his notebook.

"Frightfully unattractive little man," said Helen Flight. "Impertinent, too. Never have cared for the French, personally."

"Nor I," said Meggie Kelly. "But he'll not be gettin' the better of the Kelly girls in a trade, I can tell *ya*. Right, Susie?"

Several army officers, including Captain Bourke, had gathered inside the store. Now they stood behind Baptiste, who sat at a long table with his ledger book open before him. Little Wolf was seated across from him, flanked by two of his young Elk warriors standing behind him. Unaccustomed to furniture, the Chief sat stiffly on the edge of his chair. Helen, the Kelly girls, and I stood just inside the door. I was surprised to find that being inside a building after all these months gave me a most peculiar sense of claustrophobia.

John Bourke did not look at me. Indeed, I had the distinct sense that he was trying very hard not to. My heart ached as I watched him . . . I could not help but remember the last time we had seen each other . . .

Big Nose tapped his ledger with a pencil and said, "OK, I *geeve* you four sacks flour, two sacks sugar, one sack baking soda, one sack coffee, six plugs tobacco, one bag wolf poison—"

Before the interpreter, a half-breed hangs-around-the-fort named Little Bat, could finish his translation to Little Wolf, I had pushed forward. "Nonsense," I said. "Those hides and other goods represent an entire summer's worth of labor. What you offer us in trade wouldn't see a dozen of us through half the coming winter."

Captain Bourke looked up from behind the table, seeming at first surprised and then embarrassed by my outburst; he colored and looked down.

"Supply and demand, *madame*," said Big Nose with a wolfish grin. "*Beeg* Chief he understand that. Too many buffalo '*ides* this year. That *eez* my offer. Take it or leave it."

"*Ah, ya beggar!*" said Susie Kelly. "*Ya* think we're damn fools, do *ya*? Too many buffalo hides, *me* foot! Never *haird* a *sech* a thing. The buffalo are *scar*-cer this year than ever before, and you know it as well as we do."

"I am sorry, *mesdames*," said Baptiste, raising his hands. "But that *eez* my offer. If *theez* don't seem fair to you, I suggest you may take your '*ides* to the trading post at Camp Robinson. There *mon chèr ami*, Jules Escoffey make you not nearly such a good deal, I think. *Moi?* Compared to Jules I *yam* Santa Claus."

"What of gunpowder and ammunition?" asked Helen Flight. "We shall require those items for hunting."

"*Non, non, madame,*" said the proprietor, shaking his head. "*Je suis désolé*, I am sorry, no ammunition or gunpowder may be any longer traded to *les sauvages* by order of General

George Crook. *C'est vrai, n'est-ce pas, Capitaine?*" he asked, turning to Captain Bourke behind him.

"That is correct, yes," Captain Bourke answered. Now he turned to me and nodded with stiff military formality. "Please explain to your husband, madam," he said, "that the Great Father in Washington has determined that for the Cheyennes' own welfare gunpowder and ammunition will no longer be available to them as articles of trade. In lieu of such items the Great Father is offering a variety of farm implements at wholesale prices."

I could not help letting an astonished bark of laughter escape. "Farm implements?" I said. "Wholesale? Excellent! Yes, well those items will certainly be of great use to us. Why what possible need shall we have for gunpowder and ammunition to procure fresh game when we shall have a 'variety of farm implements' to see us through the coming winter?"

"*Aye*, isn't that grand though!" said Meggie Kelly. "And are we expected to plant potatoes before the *folking* ground freezes?"

"As to the Great Father's paternal concern for the welfare of his Cheyenne children," I continued in a rising voice, "I imagine that although we are no longer allowed to trade our hides for gunpowder and ammunition, if we wished to trade, say, for a keg of rotgut whiskey capable of poisoning the entire tribe, such merchandise might still be available to us?"

Big Nose bared his wolfish teeth beneath his huge hooked nose. "Oh, *mais oui, madame*," he said, "I throw in a keg of my best *wheesky* if that's what the *Beeg* Chief wishes."

Throughout this conversation, Little Wolf sat impassively, listening to the translation of the interpreter. Now I spoke to him in Cheyenne, surprising myself at the fluency of my anger. "The *vehos* are trying to cheat us," I said. "Our goods are worth ten times what Big Nose offers."

Little Wolf only nodded. "*Pe'ee'ese Makeeta* always tries to cheat us," he answered. "But the People have acquired a taste for sugar and coffee; these goods are important to us, and so we make the best trade that we can manage."

"And you do understand that by order of the Great Father in Washington," I said, "there is to be no more gunpowder or ammunition allowed the People? Instead they offer us farm implements."

Now Little Wolf looked genuinely surprised. As I suspected the interpreter, Little Bat, had not conveyed this last piece of information to him. "Farm implements?" Little Wolf asked. "Of what use are such things to the People?"

"Of no use," I said, "until such time as the People move to the agency and become farmers."

Little Wolf waved his hand in a dismissive backhanded gesture, in the manner that one shoos flies. "We are hunters," he said, "we are not farmers. Tell the soldiers that we have no use for farm implements, that we must have rifles and ammunition." And to Big Nose, he said, "Henceforth my wife, *Mesoke*, and the other women will conduct this trade." With this Little Wolf stood from the table and with his usual great dignity left the room, followed by his soldiers.

Now the Kellys pressed forward to make their case with Big Nose. "There's *noothin'* else to be *doone* now, Frenchy," said Susie, "than to do some '*beezness*' with the squaws, is there, *ya* little cheatin' bastard?"

I took this opportunity to approach John Bourke, who was gathering papers off the table, making quite a show of distracted busy-ness, all transparently designed to avoid having to confront me.

I did not allow him the luxury. "Why does the Army participate in this travesty, Captain?" I asked. "What possible interest does it serve to swindle these people."

The Captain bowed politely. "Mrs. Little Wolf," he said, as if addressing a stranger. "I'm afraid that this is not a matter which I am presently at liberty to discuss with you. Good day," he said, touching the brim of his hat and walking past me.

Before he could do so, I grasped him by the arm. It was, I am aware, a presumptuous act on my part, but I could not help myself. "John," I whispered, near to tears from my racing emotions, "for God's sake, John, it is I, May. Why won't you talk to me, why can't you look at me?"

The Captain stopped and raised his eyes to meet mine, as if seeing me for the first time. "Good God, May," he whispered.

"What did you expect, Captain?" I said. "That I would be dressed in my Sunday finest? Need I remind you that we have been living in the wilderness among savages? I'm sorry if my appearance offends you."

"No, May," John Bourke said. "Forgive me. You offer no offense. You look . . . only . . . very different than I remembered you . . ." And then as if torn by some great internal conflict, his brow furrowed in a storm of anguish, the Captain added, "Please excuse me, madam, I must take my leave. Perhaps we will have an opportunity to speak at a later date." I watched as he strode quickly from the store.

Later that day, my old friend Gertie rode her mule into our camp. I went out to greet her in front of our lodge, alerted to her arrival by the noises of the small pack of children and dogs at her heels. She was roughly attired in woolen trousers and a man's coat several sizes too large for her, wore a red bandanna around her neck and an old cavalry hat that had been refashioned to a style quite beyond Army regulations, and was jauntily festooned with eagle feathers.

"Damn, honey," Gertie said to me, sliding off her mount,

"it's a lucky thing I got a chin strap on this here old hat of mine, or I'd a been relieved of it for sure by now. There ain't nothin' an Injun likes more'n a hat, an' don't ask me why."

Gertie reached into a pocket of her coat and pulled out a handful of hard candies, which she passed out to the children, who chattered gaily and crowded closer around her. "Shoo, now," she said to them, "scoot! I want to talk to the Missus in peace. No, I *awready* told *ya, ya* can't have my *goddamn* hat!" Gertie removed her hat and slapped it against her thigh, raising a cloud of dust. Her hair was sweated and matted greasily on her head, flattened and whorled like the bedding place of a deer in high grass. Her face was streaked with dirt. It was not the first time I have noticed Gertie's lack of attention to matters of personal cleanliness; indeed she possessed a distinct odor that could compete with that of any unwashed savage. I gave her a big hug nevertheless, for I was very glad to see her.

"Damn, but ain't this here a dusty godforsaken country, honey?" she asked. "Coyote ugly, too. I prefer that grass country up north where you been summerin'. You know I trailed you half the goddamn summer with the half-breed scout Big Bat Pourrier. Not a bad sidekick as half-breeds go, old Big Bat. Good tracker, and he never once tried to make no play on me, if you get my meanin' . . ."

I was less astonished by this latter bit of information than the former. "Why did you do that, Gertie?" I asked. "Follow us all summer?"

"The Cap'n asked me to keep an eye on you, honey," she said. "He was awful worried about you, especially after I reported back to him last time—after the little whiskey party. I told him you was makin' out just fine. I figured they would a drunk up all their whiskey that night. One thing about Injuns is that if there's any whiskey around, they'll drink it all up just as fast as they can. Once it's gone and they can't lay their hands on no more that's the end of it. That's about how I figured it would go."

I nodded my head. "But you stopped trailing us after we made our encampment on the Tongue, is that correct?" I asked.

"Yup, figured by then things was goin' real good for you," Gertie said, "so I come back to report in to the Cap'n."

"And since you seem to be in the regular employment of Captain Bourke, Gertie," I said, "may I assume that you've come now with news from him?"

"You can assume exactly that, honey," Gertie said. "He wants to see you. Wants you to meet him underneath the south side of the Platte River bridge this evening after supper. Wants you to wear your white woman duds so as not to attract attention in case anyone spots you two together."

I laughed. "Yes, I suppose it would hardly do for the good Captain to be seen fraternizing with a squaw. Especially the Big Chief's squaw. Unfortunately, I have no white woman clothing, Gertie. I've given them all away. They seemed . . . shall we say . . . unsuitable to our present circumstances."

"Sure, I know just what ya mean, honey," Gertie said. She looked down at her own outfit. "Hell, I suppose I could loan you my duds. I ain't much for dresses, white woman or In-jun, but I'd sure be willin' to swap you for a spell."

"That's very kind of you, Gertie," I said quickly, "but it won't be necessary." Although forced to give up many of the standards of civilized hygiene which I once took for granted, I was still not prepared to don Dirty Gertie's aromatic out-fit. "The Captain will simply have to receive me in my ev-eryday squaw attire. Please relate to him that I will be at the bridge at the designated hour."

"Will do, honey," she said. Then she scuffed her boot in

the dirt. "Well hell, ain't ya goin' to invite me in to set a spell? I figured we'd have some visitin' to do, you and me? Catchin' up."

I smiled tenderly at Gertie, realizing that in my distraction at the idea of seeing John Bourke again in private, I had hurt her feelings, treating her as a messenger rather than a friend. "Of course we do," I said. "I didn't mean to be rude, Gertie. Please, do come in, the ladies will be happy to see you again."

"Honey, 'fore we set down, with the others," Gertie said, "why don't we get one thing over with first, private like. I got a hunch you have a question you're wantin' to ask me."

"A question?" I asked. "You mean regarding John Bourke?"

Gertie nodded. "He broke off his engagement to the Bradley gal, if that's what you're wonderin'," she said. "She went back to her mother in New York."

None of the few pedestrians or drivers of the occasional wagon that passed along the road paid the least bit of attention to one more squaw woman, wrapped modestly in a Hudson Bay trade blanket, as she made her way across the rickety Platte River bridge. On the far side I looked about quickly to be certain that I was not observed and then ducked down the narrow footpath through the willows toward the river's bank.

John Bourke was already waiting for me there. As yet unobserved, I stopped to watch him for a moment, to try to still the pounding of my heart. He stood facing the slow torpid river, his hands clasped behind his back, apparently lost in a reverie. Because I could not bear to see the look of disappointment in his face that I had not metamorphosed back into the comely and properly dressed young white woman with whom he had once recited Shakespeare, I spoke first.

"Do not turn to look at me, Captain," I said.

"Why do you ask this?" he inquired, starting, but he did not turn.

"Because I am as you last saw me," I said. "I am still attired as a savage and I cannot bear the look of revulsion on your face."

And then he did turn. And looking thoroughly distraught, his dark brow riding low over his eyes in a storm of self-reproach, he said: "Forgive me, madam. My behavior toward you was intolerable. It was a shock to see you again after so many months."

I laughed. "Ah, yes, a shock," I said. "Indeed! And to see me then dressed as the enemy. How difficult that must have been for you, Captain!"

"You have every right to be angry with me, madam," he said. "I should not have expected you to be otherwise attired. However, I hope you will believe me when I tell you that it was not revulsion that you saw in my face."

"No?" I asked, approaching him. "And what was it, Captain, that I mistook for revulsion?"

He moved toward me and took my hands in his. His fingers were strong and rough but his touch as gentle as I remembered it. And his eyes softened as he looked into mine with a look that I also remembered. "Heartbreak, perhaps," he said.

"Heartbreak?" I asked, the blood rising to my cheeks. "I'm afraid that I don't understand you, Captain. Heartbreak at my descent into paganism?"

"No, May, heartbreak that you now belong to another man," he answered, "to another people. Once, for the briefest moment, you belonged to me. I let you slip away. What you saw in my face was the look of a man filled with regret for his failures, with self-loathing for his own weakness."

Then I went forward into John Bourke's arms, or he brought me into them, I do not know which . . . I think that neither of us had intended this to happen, particularly not he, whose moral rectitude would hardly allow the embrace of a married woman, but we are like magnets, he and I, and clung to each other, and did not speak . . . for there were no satisfactory words to be said.

I squeezed my eyes shut to keep from spilling tears, but still they fell about his neck and I felt their wetness on my cheek. "John," I whispered. "Dear John. How could we have known . . ."

"I had you, May," he said, "and I let you go. For that I shall never forgive myself."

"And I left you, John," I said. "There could have been no other way. There can be no other way."

The trade blanket had fallen about my feet and as the Captain's arms enveloped me, there was little between the soft, supple skin of the antelope hide from which my garment was so loosely fashioned and my own skin. We could feel each other . . . the at once familiar contours of our bodies fitting themselves into one form, one being . . .

And then at the same moment we both released our embrace. And into my breast rose the terrible weightless sense of falling from a cliff.

The Captain spoke first, with a kind of husky ferocity in his voice, "This cannot be, May," he said. "You are married to another."

"Of course it can't, John," I said, and I thought my flushed heart would explode in a thousand pieces, "for I am also having his child."

At this he smiled, and stepped toward me again, as if the fact itself released us for that moment from our need for one another. He placed his large hand, his fingers spread, upon my belly as gently as if he were touching the child itself. "I'm very happy for you, May," he said. "Please believe that."

I put my own hand atop his. "Four months so, I make it, John. Isn't it strange where life leads us?"

"'What fates impose, that men must needs abide;'" he quoted, "'It boots not to resist both wind and tide.'"

"God, I've missed you, May," he said. "I've never stopped thinking of you."

"Nor I you, John," I said. "And what of your fiancée? What of Lydia Bradley? Gertie tells me you've sent her back East."

"Honor dictated that I could not in good faith any longer marry her," he said. "I had fallen in love with you, May. I had lain with you."

"Oh, John, you torture yourself with your damnable sense of honor," I said, "your inflexible Catholic doctrine. She was a pleasant enough young lady, and would have made you a good wife. And you, her, a fine husband."

"Always the practical one, aren't you, May?" John said. And he smiled his old crooked wry smile, his weathered eyes crinkling in the corners. "'Pleasant enough' is faint praise. In any case she was far too sensitive to be wife to an old Army rat such as myself."

"She'd have been the luckiest woman on earth, John," I said.

"And you, May?" he asked. "How has your luck been running? Tell me, are you in love with your husband? Are you happy in your 'arranged' marriage?"

"I make those three separate questions, Captain," I said. "To the first I would answer that my luck has been mixed. To the second that, yes, I love and honor my husband, Little

Wolf. He is a good man and a fine provider for his family. But I am not 'in love' as I think you mean. I do not love him as I once loved you . . . for how could that be so?

"And finally to the question of my happiness, as our mutual friend Gertie once put it, I would answer that 'happiness is a highly overrated human condition invented by white folks.'"

Bourke laughed then, the rich deep laugh that broke my heart to hear again. "A line worthy of the Bard!" he said. "She's a fine piece of work, our Gertie, isn't she though?"

"Yes, she is," I said, "and she's been a dear friend to me."

"But your life among the savages, May?" he asked in a more serious tone. "How does it go for you? You know that I've been worried sick about you."

"And have sent Gertie to watch over me," I said. "I know, John, for which solicitude I am deeply grateful. She arrived the first time at a propitious moment . . . and left the second time only a moment too soon . . ."

The Captain's face filled again with darkness. "What do you mean by that, May?" he asked. "Gertie said that you were in good health, adapting well to your new circumstances. Has something happened?"

"I was, John, and I have," I said, aware that any description of our abduction by the Crow horse thieves could only needlessly torture him. "It is only that, as you yourself warned us, it is a strange and sometimes terrifying life we lead among these people. One of our girls, my little friend Sara, has been killed in an accident."

John touched my face tenderly with the back of his hand. "I'm sorry, May," he said. "I know how you cared for her."

"Other than that we have, most of us, endured," I said.

"I should say that you've at least done so," he said. "Why just look at you, May, fit and brown as a native. If anything you are even more beautiful than I remembered you. I think life in the out-of-doors must agree with you."

"I admit that it has benefits, as well as its discomforts," I said. "Mostly, John, it's been like living a dream, like a suspension of real life. But coming back here and seeing you again . . . I have been abruptly awakened from the dream."

"Your dream is not over yet, May," Bourke said in a serious tone. He turned his back to me and looked out over the river. "You know that I have asked you here for another reason than my desire to see you again."

"I suspected as much, Captain," I said. "Gertie informs me that the government is abandoning us."

"No, not abandoning," Bourke said quickly, turning back to me. "Not as long as General Crook has anything to say in the matter."

"And *does* General Crook have anything to say in the matter?" I asked.

"The Army has been put in a thankless position, May," he answered. "The pendulum has swung even further since Gertie brought you my news this summer. The geologists with Custer's expedition have since returned with glowing reports about the gold discovery in the Black Hills. Parties of miners, their passions inflamed by the prospect of easy riches, are even now making their way toward the region. The Army has been charged with the impossible task of trying to intercept them in order to defend the terms of the Fort Laramie treaty. Of course, this situation is untenable and cannot continue. Public sentiment, fueled by a righteous press, demands that the Black Hills be made safe for white settlers, and the Indians driven from the land."

"Driven from the land?" I asked. "But they believe that they own the Black Hills—indeed, do own them. The Sioux have already been to see us, John. They are forming war parties against the invading miners. It's only a matter of time until some of our people join them."

"Yes, and for this reason and upon the recommendation of Inspector Watkins of the Indian Bureau," the Captain said, "the War Department has been instructed to bring in the remaining free savages, both Sioux and Cheyennes, and to see to their settlement on reservations, which plan is effective immediately."

"I begin to understand why the Army is in collaboration with that wretched little Frenchman," I said. "You sanction the swindling of the savages in trade in order that, like obedient children, they be forced to throw themselves upon the mercy of their benevolent Great White Father."

"Exactly so," said Captain Bourke, nodding. "A peaceful resolution that can be greatly expedited by you and your friends—by encouraging your husbands to give themselves and their families up at the agencies with as much dispatch as possible."

"And, of course, the decision to deny them any further arms and ammunition," I added, "has been made as a precaution in the event that our efforts toward this end fail?"

The Captain did not avoid my eyes when he answered. He nodded glumly. "A campaign under the direction of General Crook is currently being organized—its purpose to round up all those hostiles who have not voluntarily complied by the first day of February 1876. As Chief Little Wolf's wife, May, you are in a unique position to facilitate the process—and possibly save many lives by doing so."

"Ah, so now you've come to believe that the Brides for Indians program is a useful one after all," I said.

"I believe as I have from the beginning," said Bourke, "that it is a contemptible and immoral program that has put

you and your friends at tremendous risk. But it is nevertheless in place, you are in the field, and, yes, can now be useful."

"My husband is under the impression that as long as the
Cheyennes remain on the land that has been given them 'forever' by official treaty, they commit no trespass," I said.

"President Grant has recently dispatched a commission
to negotiate the purchase of the Black Hills and the surrounding country from the Cheyennes and the Sioux," said
the Captain.

"And if they choose not to sell?" I asked.

"As you may have learned in your travels with them, May,"
he said, "the savages are hardly united among themselves—
even one tribe such as yours has many different factions and
many leaders. Rest assured that the President's commission
will find someone among the Sioux and the Cheyennes who
will be willing to negotiate this sale—after which time all
others who remain on the land will be considered trespassers
by the United States Army."

"God, it's despicable, isn't it?" I said in a low voice.

"But necessary, I'm afraid," said the Captain. "It is the
inevitable course of history."

"And if we are unsuccessful in persuading the Cheyennes to come into the agency before the appointed date," I
asked, "will you hunt us down, then John? Shall we be enemies?"

"That must not happen, May," said the Captain firmly.
"I'm telling you this in order to avoid any such unthinkable
situation. Your husband, Little Wolf, has already requested
an audience with General Crook. Perhaps you can exercise
some positive influence over the chief."

"My husband wishes to discuss the matter of the remaining brides that have been promised him by the Great White

Father," I said. "The Cheyennes may be heathens Captain, but they can count, and the shortage has not escaped my husband's attention."

"You must convince Little Wolf," said Bourke, "that after the savages are peacefully settled on the reservation, they will receive the remainder of their brides."

"Now you ask me to lie for the government, John?" I said, my temper flaring. "To lie to my own husband in order to cover your vile deceptions?"

"Not my deceptions, May," Bourke said quickly, "nor those of General Crook. As you know, we were never consulted by the government and would never have sanctioned this program if we had been. I do not apologize for our role in this affair. We have been charged with protecting those of you who are already afield and at risk. I will arrange for General Crook to meet with your husband. The General is a man of honor who has always dealt fairly with the savages. He will make no promises about delivery of the brides, but he may use the issue as a carrot-on-a-stick. It remains to you to help convince your husband to turn his people in to the agencies before next winter. There they will be given everything they need—food to eat, a roof over their heads, and their children—*your* children—will be educated by Christians, taught to read and write, to farm—to plow and hoe and subdue the Earth as the Bible teaches us we must. Whatever political situations may have changed, May—however you may have changed, do not forget that this was your original mission. To assimilate the savages—to bring them to the bosom of Christian civilization."

"You have heard, perhaps, how our portly Episcopalian brought the children to his ample bosom?" I said.

"I have," said Bourke, coloring, and I could see his temper rising again like water coming to a fast boil. "The Reverend Hare has been recalled by Bishop Whipple, who promises a full investigation of the charges."

"A full investigation is quite unnecessary," I said. "We all know what happened. Are you aware that such acts with children are unknown to the Cheyenne culture? Not just rare—but unknown. As an amateur ethnologist, I should think that you might be interested in this fact. We have much to teach the savages, don't we, John?"

"The Church Missionary Society is looking into finding a Catholic priest to return with you to serve as your spiritual advisor among the heathens. Your husband has, very sensibly I might add," the Captain added with a sly smile, "specifically requested a 'Black Robe' this time."

"Excellent," I said in deadpan tone. "Then our little boys will be safe."

"Good God, May!" Bourke said, shaking his head, and uttering an involuntary laugh. "You're the most irreverent woman I've ever known!" But he laughed again, a deep, delighted belly laugh. And I laughed with him.

We hugged each other quickly before parting, not daring to linger in the other's embrace, lest we allow ourselves once again to become one.

18 September 1875

Little Wolf had his audience with General Crook. None of us white women were allowed to attend or even to leave our camp as several members of the press, including a Mr. Robert E. Strahorn of the *Rocky Mountain News* in Denver, had recently arrived at the fort. It was deemed undesirable by the authorities that we be seen by the press, or identified as affiliated in any way whatsoever with the government or the military. In any case, after our initial reception by the fort residents, we have most of us avoided further contact with the whites. It is rarely spoken of, and the newspapers avoid the subject like the plague, but there are other white women, most of them alcoholic, who have taken up residency among the hangs-around-the-fort Indians. These unfortunate souls are referred to as "fallen whores"—and as such, we are passed off.

All I know of the meeting with Crook is what little I have learned from Little Wolf himself and from Gertie, who eavesdropped beneath the window outside. As Captain Bourke had suggested, the General would make no assurances about delivery of the remaining brides. He could only say that if the Cheyennes agreed to come into the agency before winter, the matter would be taken up again with the proper authorities. This was the kind of white man talk that confused and angered Little Wolf, for in his mind the matter had already been agreed upon, the deal struck.

The General further promised that if the Cheyennes came into the agency, they would be generously cared for by the Great Father.

"Yes," replied Little Wolf, "I have been to the Red Cloud Agency, and I have seen there the generosity of the Great Father. There is no game left in that country and, like the brides that were pledged to the Cheyennes, only a small portion of the provisions that were promised has been delivered to them. So the Sioux have been forced to slaughter their own horses to eat. We have lived free all summer on our own land and we have plenty of meat to see us through the winter. Why should we go to the agency when we have everything we need and live as free people on our own land?"

Little Wolf's logic, simple and childlike, is at once relentless and irrefutable. Even General Crook, an old hand at negotiations with the savages, was somewhat at a loss to explain to what advantage it was to the Cheyennes to come into the agency before winter. The meeting was thus concluded unsatisfactorily.

In the matter of trade negotiations—and in a somewhat brighter vein—Big Nose Little Man had met his match in our Kelly twins. The little wretch's own greed for our hides finally undermined his tenuous alliance with the military who hoped to see us sooner destitute, and we made out rather favorably, after all. At the same time, a flourishing illicit trade and any number of unscrupulous dealers operate outside the fort grounds and from these Little Wolf obtained the rifles, ammunition, and gunpowder we required.

My husband is not stupid and understands that the decision by the Great White Father to withhold arms and ammunition from the Cheyennes is meant to render the People defenseless. As in the matter of the brides due him, it is clear that Little Wolf "smells a rat." Perhaps not incidentally, among the contraband munitions acquired from the illicit traders, our band has purchased a full case of new carbines.

19 September 1875

Yesterday several of our prominent medicine men went into the fort to take up a challenge offered, I was deeply ashamed to learn, by Captain John G. Bourke and several of his Army compadres. The Indians call Bourke "Paper Medicine Man," for as Crook's adjutant he is seen always scratching away in his books.

Had we not been avoiding the fort we white women might have known sooner about the nature of this disgraceful business, and put a quick end to it. As it was I did not learn

of it until a boy came running to Little Wolf's lodge to say
that the Sweet Medicine Chief must come to challenge the
white man's "medicine box," that he must come immediately
to save face for the People, for none of our medicine could
defeat the box.

I had no idea what the child was talking about but I decided to accompany my husband to the fort to find out. We
arrived just in time to witness the latest defeat of yet another of our medicine men at the hands of this so-called
"medicine box." This was little more than an old discarded
electrical battery that the idle soldiers had rigged up so that
when turned by a hand crank it would send a shock through
whatever fool was holding the poles. Next to the battery the
soldiers had placed a pail of water and in the bottom of the
pail a shiny silver dollar.

Now they much amused themselves by challenging any
takers to reach into the pail and remove the silver dollar—
with the stipulation, of course, that the contestant be holding
the pole from the battery in one hand when he did so.

One after another, our medicine men, chanting their medicine songs, attempted to reach into the pail and remove the
dollar. As the soldiers merrily sang their own "medicine
song"—the Irish ballad "Pat Malloy"—one of them, John
Bourke himself, cranked the handle of the damnable machine, which of course shocked the poor savages into submis-
sion with a terrible charge of electricity. Thus the medicine
men were each, in turn, humiliated in front of the spectators.
Some bravely tried a second time, but of course, were helpless
against the thing.

At first Bourke did not see me among the crowd, and I
pleaded with my husband. "Do not do this," I said. "This is
not 'medicine,' it is another white man trick. You will be hurt
and disgraced in front of the people if you try."

But others of the tribe urged Little Wolf forward to prove the power of the Sweet Medicine, and the Chief felt obligated to do so.

Still Bourke had not spied me, and when my husband stepped up to the machine, the Captain said: "Ah, and does the great Chief Little Wolf himself wish to challenge our medicine box?" In Bourke's tone of merriment, I detected an undercurrent of malice, which deeply disappointed me.

I could resist no longer and now came forward myself. "Is this how you gentlemen amuse yourself, Captain?" I asked. "By humiliating innocent people? Perhaps you should run along and find some puppies to torture."

Several of the soldiers laughed, but in slightly embarrassed tones, like children caught misbehaving. "Or to eat like the stinkin' heathens," one of them snickered under his breath.

"We're just having a little fun, ma'am," another said. "It's the heathens themselves who keep asking to try their medicine against ours. No harm intended. It's only a game."

Captain Bourke had himself blanched at my words, more in surprise at seeing me there, I think, than at my reprimand. For when he spoke, he did so with no trace of apology in his voice, but with a kind of cocksure defiance.

"We are teaching the savages, in a relatively harmless manner, that their superstitions are helpless against our own superior powers," he said. "It's a lesson better learned here, madam, than elsewhere, I can assure you."

"I see, Captain," I said. "And now you will teach this lesson to my husband, Little Wolf, the Sweet Medicine Chief, the Cheyennes' most esteemed leader and fearless warrior. And the People will learn for certain how powerless they are against the white man."

"Only if the Chief wishes to test his medicine against

ours, madam," the Captain said, his dark, shadowed eyes boring into mine.

Little Wolf took one of the poles in hand, and the soldiers began to sing their ditty—"Pat Malloy." My eyes never left those of John Bourke, as he began to turn the crank on the battery and took up the song himself. Little Wolf did not chant but only touched the Sweet Medicine pouch that he wears against his breast, a kind of talisman, and began to put his arm into the pail. Just as he did so, the Captain, still staring at me and singing in a hearty voice, left off turning the crank, and my husband reached into the pail and with impunity removed the silver dollar from the bottom. Now all those assembled began to cheer wildly, as I and the rest of the women made our joyful trilling noise.

John Bourke stood from his seat at the machine, nodded to me with a slight smile, and walked briskly away.

20 September 1875

A change of weather is in the air, and we prepare for departure. The mild early-fall temperatures which we have enjoyed these past few weeks have fallen precipitously overnight. Lying in our lodge last night I could hear the north wind blowing down; it made an ominous rumbling sound like a freight train. And though I was warm under my buffalo robes, I felt the chill of winter in my bones.

This morning my friend Gertie came visiting a last time. "You heard the news of your compadre, Narcissa?" she asked.

"I have not," I answered, "but nothing would surprise me."

"She's in the fort hospital," Gertie said. "They say she lost her baby, miscarried, but I know one a the nurses, and she says the doctor pulled it for her."

"Pulled it?" I asked. "You mean to say she had her baby aborted?"

"That's what I'm hearin'."

"I was wrong, Gertie," I admitted. "I am surprised. None of us even knew she was with child."

"Nurse says that Narcissa begged the doctor to do it on account a her husband forced himself upon her," Gertie said, "an' she couldn't stand the idea of givin' birth to a heathen's baby."

"And she will no doubt be stayin' at the fort to recuperate," I said, "rather than returning north with the rest of us."

"You got it, honey," Gertie said with a nod. "Medical leave. Says her mission can be better served anyhow if she stays here to prepare the way for the heathens' settlement on the reservation. You get my meanin'?"

"Perfectly," I said. "A rat from a sinking ship. That's the part that doesn't surprise me. We all knew the woman was a hypocrite. I just never thought that she would go to such great lengths."

"Somethin' else you might want to know, honey," Gertie said. "She's tellin' folks that you an' some a the others has been on the warpath, that you gone plumb wild yourselves, took some Crow scalps, maybe even . . . maybe even . . . relieved some Crow fellas of some body parts, if you get my meanin' . . ."

"I see," I said. "And to whom is she spreading these rumors?"

"Anyone at the fort who'll listen," Gertie said. "You want to talk about it, honey?"

"No," I answered. "I cannot, Gertie. Only to say that

while we were encamped on the Tongue this summer, a group of us were abducted by Crow horse thieves. It must have been shortly after you left. I didn't want to tell you about it because I knew that you'd blame yourself for not being there to look after us. Young Sara was killed in the incident. The rest of us were rescued by our husbands. That's all I can tell you."

Gertie nodded. "Sure, I understand, honey," she said. "I won't ask ya about it again. I just thought you should know what the missionary gal was tellin' folks. It don't make a damn bit a difference to me, see? I been there myself. I know what it's like."

"Thank you, Gertie," I said, grateful that she would not press me on the matter.

"Mostly I come to say good-bye, honey," Gertie said. "We're fixin' to head out ourselves. I don't know where, they never tell us nothin'. But it must be a mighty big expedition, because they give me back my job skinnin' mules, and if they're desperate enough to hire known gals as muleskinners, they must be takin' every damn mule and every damn wagon in the whole country. We're supposed to be ready to march tomorrow morning. My guess is Crook is repositioning some a his troops further north on account a the trouble in the Black Hills. Word is that the Sioux under Crazy Horse and Sitting Bull has been harassing the miners and settlers in that country. I don't know where your folks are headed, honey, but if I had any choice in the matter, I'd sure want to avoid that country. Thing is, when it comes to identifyin' Injun bands, the Army can't tell the difference between buffalo shit and sirloin steak. Even their Injun scouts half the time can't tell the different bands apart. At least not from a distance, and by the time they get up close enough, it's almost always too damn late. So the Army takes the position that any Injuns they come across in hostile territory is a hostile—guilty 'til proven innocent."

"And the Captain hasn't told you anything more specific, Gertie?" I asked.

"I ain't seen him, honey," she said. "When it comes to the movement of troops he'd be skating on awful thin ice to be tellin' military secrets to an old muleskinner, if you get my meanin'.

"But I did hear about that business with the battery," she continued. "You know it took some balls on the Cap'n's part not to juice old Little Wolf when he had the chance. The Cap'n lost face with his own men when he backed down."

"He didn't back down," I said. "He just didn't turn the crank on the machine."

"All the same to the soldiers, honey," she said. "It was their chance to whup the big Chief with their stronger medicine—to teach him a lesson—and the Cap'n let 'em down."

"It was a damn battery, Gertie!" I said. "That's all it was. It was just a damn electrical apparatus!"

"Sure, honey, I know what it was," she said, "but that's just how men are—'I got a bigger battery than you.' He did it for you, honey. You know that, don't you?"

"I know that," I said, "and it was a decent thing for him to do. If you see the Captain, Gertie, will you thank him for me." I laughed. "And if he needs reassurance on the matter, you may tell him that his battery is every bit the equal of the Chief's."

Gertie grinned. "That's what they like to hear, ain't it, honey?" she said.

22 September 1875

On such short notice the authorities failed to locate a priest to take the place of our disgraced Reverend Rabbit, but somehow they managed to find a Benedictine monk to accompany us. We have no idea where the strange fellow came from and know nothing about him except that he rode into our camp yesterday evening on a burro and introduced himself as Anthony—explaining that he had taken his name from Saint Anthony of the Desert, the fourth-century Egyptian hermit monk, and that, like his spiritual namesake, he was seeking a remote spot in the wilderness in which to found his own monastery, and that if we didn't mind, he would be pleased to accompany us.

"Good God," I said under my breath to Helen Flight beside me, "first they send us an overweight Episcopalian pederast on a mule, and now comes a gaunt Benedictine anchorite on a donkey. I think we can see how the authorities value our spiritual needs."

"*Ya've* come to the right place, if you're lookin' for remote, *Broother* Anthony that's for *shooore*," said Meggie Kelly greeting the fellow. "Me an' Susie are a couple a good Catholic *goorls* ourselves. An' we're 'appy to 'ave ya along—right, Susie?"

"Right as rain, with me," said Susie.

"Quite," said Helen. "Anthony of the Prairie we shall dub you! Splendid addition to our little group, I should say."

It is just dawn now as I make this entry. We are to break camp later this morning. I am presently huddled under my buffalo robes and blankets as Quiet One stokes the morning embers. *"Eho'eeto,"* she whispers when she notices me watching her. *"It is snowing."*

I pull my covers tighter around me. I badly have to make my morning water, but I cannot bring myself to leave the warmth of bed, and shall try to distract myself for a few more moments in these pages.

True to Gertie's report, yesterday we watched as two large companies of cavalry, each with mule-drawn pack trains, departed the fort, one headed northeast toward Camp Robinson and the other northwest toward Fort Fetterman. These had to be General Crook's forces, and Captain John Bourke must have been among them. I suspect that Crook had deployed his troops intentionally while we were still present to witness their strength, so that our band might report back to the others.

I take only some small comfort in knowing that we have at least the fall and part of the winter to come into the agency; that much was made clear by both Captain Bourke and General Crook. I intend to speak with the others when we rejoin them so that we may make a united effort to convince our husbands, and perhaps just as importantly, the women of the tribe, of the wisdom of giving ourselves up. But I fear that after a generally peaceful summer and in a time of tribal prosperity, it may be more difficult to make the People understand why they must relinquish their freedom and vacate land that is theirs "forever"—a word clearly less flexibly defined by their culture than ours.

I begin to worry for us with the coming of winter—especially with our babies on the way. Having been blessed throughout this past summer with a generally mild climate, we "brides" have experienced very little discomfort as a result of inclement weather—other than for the nearly constant prairie winds, which do sometimes provoke anxiety and irritability—and in poor Martha's case have greatly exacerbated her hay fever. Now with this first sudden blast of arctic air blowing down out of the north country I dread the prospect of our confinement. Certainly a more permanent shelter at the agency—perhaps even a real house—seems an attractive proposition compared to a long winter in a tipi. For all that, I must admit that the Indian tipi is marvelously well designed—stays remarkably cool in the heat of summer and quite cozy thus far with this first true cold weather of the season. And with the morning fire burning, it warms quickly.

Now Feather on Head with her dear baby boy—whom I call by the name Willie, after my own sweet William—has joined me under my buffalo robes. It is a game I have taught my tentmates; sometimes in the cool of dawn they steal into my bed and I nuzzle the baby, who smells like a wild prairie plum, and we all of us giggle like children and often fall back asleep in each other's arms, curled together like sisters, the baby nestled between us. Sometimes Pretty Walker joins us, her mother, Quiet One, not objecting to these sisterly intimacies. Over these past chilly nights the first wife has resumed her rightful place under the robes with her husband, and I have sufficiently recovered from my own night-terrors to relinquish the position. Truly we are all of us like a pack of dogs, seeking the comfort of another warm body next to ours. Sometimes my little Horse Boy, too, will crawl under the robes with us—although I find of late that he is growing too old to snuggle innocently with the women!—the other day I felt the imp pressing an arousal urgently against my leg! I flicked his little thing, hard as the stub of a pencil, with my finger, causing the child to squeal and quite effectively discouraging his ardor.

Now we girls whisper and giggle under the robes; we trade English words and phrases for those in Cheyenne. The baby coos between us. A happier child I have never before known—he rarely cries and when he does Feather on Head pinches his nose and he stops almost immediately. In this way the Cheyenne mother trains her infant to a perfect animal silence.

It is warm and pungent under our coverings, and we are safe together and none of us wishes to rise to face the frigid air and the crisp fresh snow outside. None of us wishes to pack our belongings today and begin travel in the cold and the snow. But then we hear the old camp crier and all are silent for a moment as we listen for the day's news: *"The People will prepare to depart this morning,"* he cries out. *"We leave for our winter camp to the north. Today we go home. Pack your belongings, take down your lodges, this morning the People will prepare to move."*

Still we do not rise, we snuggle tighter under the buffalo robes until the old crone begins her shrill squawking . . . *"Everybody out of bed, up!, it is time to pack, we leave today."* And if any hesitate she has her willow switch handy and we hear her swacking the covers—any excuse for the old hag to draw on her arsenal of weaponry. Finally Feather on Head slips out from under the robes, suddenly serious again with the often grim business of womanhood in tribal life, which offers scant opportunity for such idle lounging; this morning she leaves her baby in the bed with me—she knows I will care for the sweet Willie, and thus she is free to begin her chores unencumbered. For a few more precious minutes I nuzzle the infant until he coos, coos like a pigeon. But I can wait no longer to make my water, nor can I tolerate any longer the squawking of old *Vohkeesa'e* and so I too, with great reluctance, put away my notebook, and finally slide out from beneath the warmth of my buffalo robes to face the trials of the day. I slip little

Willie out behind me and hang him in his baby board, which leans up beside Feather on Head's sleeping place. He does not make a sound in protest, but I think that he looks at me regretfully, as if to say, *"Don't leave me here, don't leave me, auntie."*

When I step out through the lodge opening, the sun is just cresting the eastern horizon, but contains no hint of warmth this morning. The temperature must be well below freezing, the snow crystalline and sparkling and not yet trampled but for one distinct set of footprints heading down toward the river. It is the track of Little Wolf who rose early for his daily morning swim, which he and the others in the Savage Men's Bathing Club continue to take no matter what the weather. Now I follow his prints, stopping in the willows on the way to squat and take my pee, which steams yellow in the snow, melting down quickly to reveal the wet red earth beneath. And then on down to the river where I strip, first removing my leggings and moccasins before giving up the warmth of the heavy buffalo robe I wear and then quickly shedding my dress. Without hesitating, without giving myself time to so much as contemplate the terrible frigidity of the water I wade into the river, quick as I can, the breath catching in my throat, and I make a shallow dive, and come back to the surface gasping, trying to draw a breath out of my frozen breast and emitting a small choked cry of shock! Good Lord, it is cold!

I rush from the water and wrap the buffalo robe, which still holds some trace of the tipi's warmth, round my naked body and grab my dress, moccasins, and leggings and I run, back to the lodge, barefoot through the snow, my feet numb by the time I arrive. I burst through the opening, laughing and making *brrrrrr* sounds much to the delight of my tent-mates. The baby dangling from his baby board gurgles delightedly at my grand entrance, his eyes wide. "Yes, *etoneto!*" I say using the Cheyenne word, then the English: *"Coooold! Brrrrrr!"* And the girls, Feather on Head and Pretty Walker, cover their mouths and giggle their soft shy giggles that sound like riffles on a spring creek. And the baby gurgles happily. And the old crone squawks, but even she and the usually undemonstrative Quiet One can't help now but give up small smiles at my antics . . .

In this way our day begins. I think only of my duties. Today we leave. I am a squaw.

23 September 1875

The breaking of camp proceeded somewhat slower yesterday with the cold weather, and it was midmorning before we were finally under way. By then the wind had come up out of the north, and directly into this we rode all day.

Thankfully, all who wanted them had horses for the return trip, for we traveled unencumbered by the several hundred hides with which we arrived here, and the trade goods we bartered for took up somewhat less packing space.

I rode most of the day alongside my friend Helen Flight. Our strange new spiritual advisor, Brother Anthony, trailed behind us on his little burro, the fellow's long legs dangling, his feet very nearly reaching the ground, the poor donkey breaking periodically into a rough-gaited trot to keep from falling too far behind.

With the Kellys' canny representation, Helen had managed, after all, to procure some new painting supplies from the "horrid little frog" as she refers to Big Nose. It seems that some of the garrison wives also enjoy dabbling in the arts as a means of passing the endless days when their husbands are off on expeditions, and so the Frenchman stocks a few such supplies. She has replenished her store of charcoal and sketch paper, and has even obtained a precious roll of painter's canvas. The dear thing also purchased two new notebooks, which she presented to me as a gift. I was terribly grateful to her for I am filling these pages at an alarming rate, and may soon have to stop writing altogether for they are becoming rather cumbersome to transport.

Helen kept a pipe clenched determinedly between her teeth as we rode into the frigid wind; it poked out through her scarf, but she had little success keeping it lit. We both were well covered, I in an extra layer of fur-lined moccasins and leggings and a kind of muff affair, made out of silky beaver fur, to keep my hands warm, and she with a new pair of gloves and men's boots for which she had traded at the store, and also wearing native fur and hide leggings. We both wore heavy coats of buffalo hair which we were particularly grateful to have had made for us during the summer by our camp seamstress Jeanette Parker. On our heads we each wore cossacklike hats of beaver fur pulled low over our ears; these last, an Indian fashion and very snug. Both of us also wore woolen scarves over our faces. In these confining outfits conversation would have been difficult in the best of circumstances—all but impossible with the wind blowing directly into our faces so that the words seemed to be pushed back down our throats before they had time to escape. We would try to holler back and forth and then would look at each other helplessly to see if we had been understood. Finally we gave a kind of mutual shrug and contented ourselves to ride in silence, with nothing but our thoughts for company, hunkered low on our horses, trying vainly to make our profiles as small as possible against the ceaseless wind.

How strange to recall that six months ago we departed

Fort Laramie as anxious white women entering the wilderness for the first time; and now, perhaps equally anxious, we leave as squaws returning home. I realized anew as we rode into the cold wind on this morning that my own commitment had been sealed forever by the heart that beats in my belly, that I could not have remained even if I so wished.

Nor can I make room on this page or in my own heart for further thoughts of John Bourke. I push him from my mind. This is no act of easy omission on my part; I do not consign him casually to a forgotten past. It is rather an act of will—a kind of self-performed surgery on my soul . . . the bloodiest of mutilations. Having seen him again, having been held in his arms for that brief moment, having felt again his strong tender hand upon my stomach, the cutting away of him is even more painful this time . . . for in our parting I sense a new finality . . .

I write these few lines from our first night's camp out of Fort Laramie. It did not seem as though we made much progress today, as if the wind itself restrained us. In spite of the fact that I was warmly attired, I felt frozen to the bone by the end of the day—the prairie wind cuts like a razor through any clothing—and the warmth of our lodge this evening seems especially luxurious.

Little Wolf killed an antelope today on the trail and tonight we dine on the fresh backstrap—the most tender and delicious in my opinion of all wild meats. I invited Helen and her husband, Mr. Hog, as well as our new monk Anthony to join us for dinner—which remark as I read it back sounds somewhat more elegant and formal than the occasion warrants.

The guests scratched on the lodge covering at roughly the appointed hour, and were seated in the place of honor by the fire. After Little Wolf had blessed the meat by raising a piece to the four directions, and to the heavens and the earth, and then set it on a little platter off to the side of the fire for *He'amaveho'e*—the Great Medicine himself—to dine upon (although, of course, it is quickly consumed by one of the dogs, which act everyone pretends not to notice), we all fell to eating with hearty appetites. The savages take their meals in a rather serious spirit—perhaps as a matter of life and death—and there is very little conversation around the dining circle.

But Helen and I tend to flout that particular convention (among others, to be sure!), and thus we chattered away, trying to make our new guest feel as much at home as possible in his strange new surroundings.

"Do tell us, Brother Anthony," Helen asked, "are you interested in Nature?"

"It is my life," answered the young Benedictine, with soft reverence in his tone. "I am blessed by all of God's creations."

"Splendid!" said Helen. "That is to say, an appreciation of Nature is nearly a requisite to spiritual survival in the wilderness.

"I don't suppose, if I may be so bold to ask," Helen asked, "that you're a sporting man?"

"A sporting man?" asked the monk.

"No, of course you're not," Helen said, "it's just that this time of year—although at the moment I must say it feels quite like the dead of winter—that is to say, it is the autumn that gets my blood to coursing with thoughts of the hunt—stalking the uplands, the thunderous flush of wings, the crack of guns!

"Indeed, I should like to invite you all very soon over to Mr. Hog and my lodge for a game bird dinner. Do you like to cook, Brother Anthony?"

"I am a baker," Anthony answered softly. I was rather

warming to our monk, whose manner is one of great simplicity and quiet attentiveness. I think that he shall do well
among these people, that he may be useful in reminding us
all that God's work on earth is best accomplished in such a
spirit of humility.

"A baker! Splendid!" said Helen, her eyebrows popping
up. "That is to say, to my mind there's nothing more useful
than a man who can bake. Yes, indeed, fresh-baked bread
will be a wonderful addition to our menus," she went on.
"You know the natives have gone wild for the stuff—no pun
intended. And we are now well supplied with flour and baking powder. Yes, I dare say we'll do a good bit of interesting
cooking this fall, wouldn't you agree, May?"

Thus we ate our antelope, chatting and listening to the
wind howling outside. It remained snug inside our tent with
the fire burning; the wind sliding around the tipi without
entering—an advantage to its round design.

When all had finished eating, Little Wolf extracted his
pipe and smoking pouch, while Helen, never timid about being unconventional, packed her own short-stemmed pipe
with tobacco and lit it from a small stick held to the fire.
Then all settled comfortably against their backrests, as
Horse Boy and the old crone slipped off to curl up on their
sleeping robes.

Even the usually gregarious Helen fell silent and contemplative. The only sounds inside the lodge came from the small
cracklings of the fire, and the wind blowing outside. It was a
moment of near perfect serenity, and I took the opportunity
to study my fellow tentmates, Feather on Head holding her
baby, and Quiet One, for once not cleaning or cooking or
moving about, just sitting quietly next to her daughter Pretty
Walker, both of them staring into the fire. Little Wolf, seated
on the other side of them, puffed reverently on his pipe, which

he would then hand over gently and with some ceremony to our contemplative guest Anthony, who in turn passed it along to Helen's husband, Hog.

As I looked about, I tried to imagine what the others were thinking of on this night. Surely Helen, like me, had felt the tug of civilization in our short time at the fort, and I think we both wondered now if we would be able to get all the way back when the time came.

Perhaps our Indian families thought about the coming winter, or in Little Wolf's case, about the uncertain future of the people with whose welfare he is forever charged. Perhaps they thought only of the next day's journey, of the friends and family with whom they would soon be reunited.

Surely our new monk prayed to his God to show him the way in this strange new world; I smiled at him when I caught his eye so that he might know that he was among friends.

From his bed, Horse Boy stared into the fire, his bright gunmetal-colored eyes reflecting the flickering flames. Perhaps he thought only of his horses on this cold autumn night, for soon he would bundle himself up in a blanket and leave the tent to sit up with them, guarding against thieves and wolves, before being relieved by another boy just before dawn. Such a hardy race of people these are! God love them . . .

After a time Helen and Hog, who is himself a quiet and dignified fellow, and seems genuinely fond of his eccentric artist wife, rose to return to their own lodge. Although I offered to make a place for Anthony to sleep the night in our lodge, he declined, saying that he had a blanket with him and that he was quite accustomed to sleeping upon the bare ground. It was a part of his devotional labors, he said.

I went outside with the guests when they left, to do my business before bed. Especially with winter coming on I must teach the savages the utility of a chamber pot—a clever white man invention that has some real application to tent living!

Although I had wrapped myself in a blanket, I felt the sting of wind on my cheeks as I exited the tipi. We were camped in the crook of a small creek surrounded only by high, treeless plains—uninteresting and lonely country, with nothing to break the wind, which comes whipping down off the ridges to assault our little grouping of tipis huddled here together, so small and defenseless. How tiny we are, exposed to the huge elements! No wonder these people are superstitious in the face of it. No wonder they try to curry favor with the gods of the four directions, with the gods of Earth and Heaven, with the spirits of wild animals and weather at whose mercy we live. And no wonder, by the same token, that the white man builds his forts and houses, his stores and churches—his flimsy fortifications against the vastness and emptiness of earth which he does not know to worship but tries instead to simply fill up.

Now I pull my dress to my waist and squat alongside a low-growing sagebrush, the only available protection from the wind, and a thin one at that. The most "uninteresting of vegetation," Captain Bourke calls it, and I suppose it is, although at least it has a strong and to my nose not disagreeable scent, and there have been times when I have rubbed it on my body as a kind of hygienic measure—the savage version of French perfume, I should say.

There is no moon tonight and the wind has scoured the clouds from the sky and the heavens shine above me. As I squat to pee I look upward at the billions of stars and planets in the heavens and somehow my own insignificance no longer terrifies me as it once did, but comforts me, makes me feel a part, however tiny, of the whole complete and perfect universe . . . and when I die the wind will still blow and the stars still shine, for the place I occupy on earth is no more permanent than the water I now make, absorbed by the sandy soil, dried instantly by the constant prairie wind . . .

28 September 1875

We take our time making our way back to the Powder River country, describing a circuitous route in the process. The Indians have a peculiar way of traveling that might seem to a white person unplanned and quite random. In this case, the scouts lead the way, the People follow—first north and then veering as if by sudden change of plan to the east and the pine-timbered hills around Camp Robinson, where this journey truly began all those months ago. But this time we skirt the camp itself, and avoid the few white settlements that are springing up around it. These are mostly a hastily contructed and seemingly haphazard grouping of shacks and lean-tos, with sod roofs and mud streets; there is nothing graceful about them and it is difficult to recognize in their shantytown appearance the refined hand of civilization—or for that matter any particular improvement upon the raw countryside itself.

There are cattlemen moving into the country around Camp Robinson, and one day as we were passing through some of our young men went out on a hunting party and killed and slaughtered several beeves. I tried to explain to my husband that the cattle belonged to the settlers and that by killing them we would only bring trouble down upon the People, but Little Wolf answered that the settlers had driven off the buffalo and killed out the game in this country and that the People must eat as they travel. In any case, he said, he could not control the young men who went out to hunt and found cows where once there had been buffalo. As is so often the case, I found it difficult to mount an effective argument against Little Wolf's plain logic.

But at the feasts that followed this hunt, the diners made faces of disdain and much grunting of disapproval at the taste of the beef—and I admit that it is not so flavorful as the wild buffalo to which even I now confess a preference.

From the hills above Robinson we made a short visit to the nearby Red Cloud Agency, where Little Wolf powwowed with some of the Dakota leaders, including Red Cloud himself. They discussed the government commission, which was presently at the Army camp trying to negotiate the purchase of the Black Hills, and which included our former Reverend's superior, Bishop Whipple. Little Wolf chose not to attend these meetings, as did many of the Sioux, for the simple reason that neither he, nor they, had any intention of "selling" the Black Hills, even if authorized to do so, which, of course, none are.

However, as usual, the Indians are very much divided on the question. Perhaps because he is already settled on his own agency, Red Cloud himself seems to be in favor of the sale—even though his people have been so poorly provided for by the Great White Father that they seem nearly destitute compared to ours. At the council, Red Cloud told Little Wolf that so many white miners had already invaded the Black Hills that it was no longer possible to stem the tide, that the tribes might as well receive something for the land, rather than nothing, for one way or another, it was being taken from them, in the same way that the whites took everything. After much, sometimes rather heated, discussion and smoking of pipes, no real consensus on the matter was reached.

This division and inability to mount a united front is, as John Bourke suggested, one of the greatest disadvantages that the Indians face in their dealings with the United States government.

While camped briefly at Red Cloud, we were visited by the agent there, a smarmy, unctuous fellow named Carter, who came to our lodge in an effort to enroll Little Wolf's band on the agency rolls. When I spoke to the man in English, he was quite taken aback, having paid me no mind as "just another squaw." Evidently he had no knowledge of the Brides program, for he assumed at first that I must be a captive white woman, and even offered to rescue me! The man became ever more agitated when I explained to him that I was married to the Chief, and that there were others like me also living with the Cheyennes of our own free will. I quite enjoyed Agent Carter's discomfort and did not feel it necessary to elaborate on the subject of the program which had brought us here.

"Ma'am, you're awful pretty to be in such a terrible mess," he said solicitously, assuming me to be among that unfortunate class of "fallen whores," who in their descent from respectable whoredom had, as a last resort, attached themselves to the savages. And then he told me that he knew a woman who had recently opened a respectable "boardinghouse" in the little town of Crawford, which has sprung up near Robinson. Her establishment is frequented by soldiers at the camp, mail and freight carriers, muleskinners, miners, and the general riffraff that has attached itself to our western outposts—although to hear this fellow tell it, a far more genteel clientele than the savages whom we had been forced to service, and who, he assured me, were not allowed to so much as set foot in Mrs. Mallory's place, let alone fraternize with her girls.

At this I took real umbrage; I explained to the man again that we were wives, not prostitutes—married in the eyes of the church and our own government—that we were here of our own free will, and that, indeed, such a demeaning institution as prostitution did not even exist among the Cheyennes. And I further suggested to him that if he didn't leave our lodge at that very moment, I would inform my husband of his insults and he would very likely be skinned alive as punishment and possibly roasted over a hot fire for our heathen supper to boot! I am happy to report that a faster exit has never before been accomplished!

3 October 1875

From Red Cloud Agency we moved north into the Black Hills; Little Wolf wished to see for himself the influx of whites into the area, and also wishes to make a ceremony at *Novavose*—Medicine Lodge—before winter sets in. This place, called Bear Butte by the whites, is a perfectly symmetrical flat-topped mountain on the northern edge of the Black Hills—sacred ground to the Cheyennes. As I learn more about their beliefs, it strikes me that one reason the savages had not more enthusiastically embraced Reverend Bunny's efforts to convert them to Christianity is that they already have in place an elaborate and to their way of thinking perfectly satisfactory religion of their own—complete with a messiah character, named *Motse'eoeve*—Sweet Medicine himself, a kind of prophet and instructor who, rather than coming from such a distant and incomprehensible place as Nazareth, hails right here from *Novavose*—the very heart of the Cheyennes' own country. Is it any wonder they don't wish to give this land up?

According to legend, Sweet Medicine appeared to the

People here long, long ago and told them that a person was going to come among them. This person was going to be all sewed up (the Indian manner of saying wearing white man clothing), and that he was going to destroy everything that the People needed to live—he would come among the People and from them take everything, including the game and the earth itself.

While the Indian religion may be rife with superstition, Sweet Medicine's prophecy is lent some credibility by the fact that it is so clearly coming true in our own times.

Regarding matters of spirituality, our anchorite, "Anthony of the Prairie," is already becoming, as I had predicted he would, quite popular among us all. The Cheyennes immediately accepted him as a holy man—for his spirit of simplicity and self-denial is something that they greatly admire—as they do his daily recitation of liturgies, for the Indians are inordinately fond of any form of chanting and religious observance.

I must say that I look forward to our other white women meeting Anthony as well, for I take from him myself a certain strength. He is a quiet, devout man, and yet has a rather mischievous sense of humor. Although I have never been of a highly religious nature myself, I can't help but have the feeling that he has come among us for some reason, and will serve some valuable purpose. Good Lord . . . perhaps I am finding faith after all!

As to the Black Hills, prettier country I have never before seen, timbered with pine, fir, and juniper, and teeming with game of all variety. Thankfully, the weather has turned mild again, perfect autumn temperatures that seem to promise some brief respite from the coming winter. All of our moods have improved immeasurably with the warmer climate and this new, beautiful country. I think we were all rather dispirited by our short visit at the Red Cloud Agency, which seemed so poor, the people there so dejected. Is that, then, to be the inevitable grand end of our mission?—to bring our own people from freedom and prosperity to this state of abject impoverishment and inactivity—hardly assimilated so much as simply confined . . .

Since we left Fort Laramie I have had several conversations with my husband about the necessity for him to give up his People at one of the agencies. I have, toward this end, invoked the name of his child whom I carry and that of all the other expectant mothers, pointing out that if born on the agency, these children will not only be safe from harm but will also have the advantage of attending schools, which will enable them, in turn, to help teach the People the new white man life. "This is what you wanted," I say to Little Wolf. "This is what you requested when you went to Washington."

And Little Wolf will only answer that the People are quite prosperous at the moment and have managed to keep away from the whites, and he does not wish to give up this good life just yet. As to your children, he says, they will belong to the white tribe soon enough, but they should have the opportunity to know something about their fathers' world, as well, about how it was to live in the old way—even if this is only for the first year of their lives. They have plenty of time later to learn the new white man way of living.

"We will look back on this life that we have now," Little Wolf said softly, "and we will think that no people on earth were ever happier, were ever richer; we have good lodges and plenty of game; we have many horses and beautiful possessions and I am not yet prepared to give this up to live in the white man way. Not yet. Another fall, another winter, perhaps one more summer . . . then we shall see."

The Cheyennes have a different conception of time than

we do; such things as calendar deadlines and ultimatums mean little to them; their world is less static in this way than ours, and does not lend itself well to temporal matters beyond those of the seasons.

"But the Army won't give you that time," I tried to explain to Little Wolf. "This is what I am telling you. You must take the People into the agency this winter."

I wonder now if it was partly for this reason that Little Wolf brought us to Red Cloud, to see the sobering future we can expect for our children in such a place. For truly if that is what we have to look forward to, our present freedom, however temporary, seems more precious than ever.

5 October 1875

All of our efforts to avoid encounters with the invading miners notwithstanding, we have seen much evidence of them in the Black Hills. We have cut the trails of several large wagon trains moving through the country and have come upon a number of new settlements along the way. Our scouts have also reported the presence of Army troops in the region. Under strict orders from Little Wolf, our warriors have harassed no one, and we passed so stealthily that I doubt the whites were even aware of our presence. However, Phemie told me that some of the young men, including her own husband—Black Man—had slipped off to join a war party of Oglala Sioux who were making raids upon the immigrants. Nothing good can come of this, I know.

8 October 1875

We have been camped for several days in the vicinity of the mountain called *Novavose*—at which site the savages are holding all manner of religious observances; there is feasting and dancing and vision seeking and the almost constant beating of drums; many of the ceremonies are too elaborate and too complicated to one unversed in the religion to understand or even attempt to record; there has been much fasting and sacrifices made and other self-imposed hardships endured by the men—including sundry bodily mutilations by the younger men, such revolting practices as piercing their breasts and tying themselves to stakes, or to painted shields (Helen's artistic talents again very much in demand!) which they then proceeded to drag about the dance circle in excruciating pain. Whatever accommodations and adaptations we have been able to make to their life and religion—and these have been considerable—no civilized person can find these primitive customs of self-mutilation to be anything less than repugnant. However, our monk Anthony has been extremely interested in these practices and is taking copious notes on all of the heathens' religious observances. He believes that they might have some application to—perhaps even roots in—Christianity itself. Wishful thinking on the part of the holy man, I should say, but then, I suppose that is, after all, his job. On Anthony's behalf I shall also say that he spreads the Gospel of Jesus very gently among the People, with none of the Reverend Hare's fire and brimstone or threats of damnation, and none of Narcissa White's evangelical zeal. Rather he visits from lodge to lodge in such a spirit of honesty, humility, and generosity that the People hardly know that they are being preached to. He is, I think, our best hope yet for the salvation of their souls . . . if salvation they require . . .

Yesterday, Little Wolf's primary advisor, Woman Who Moves Against the Wind, came to our lodge to tell the Chief of a vision she has had. She is a very strange creature, with wild black hair and a peculiar light in her eyes that is like the reflection of flames from a fire. She lives all alone, and because she, too, is a holy person, her needs are met by other members of the tribe. The men bring her game and the women keep her supplied with other necessities. She is considered to be a seer, one who lives with one foot in the other world—the "real world behind this one." My husband the Chief holds her advice in very high esteem.

Now she sat cross-legged and whispered to Little Wolf: I sat as close as possible behind them and strained to hear her. *"In my vision, I saw the People's lodges consumed in flames,"* she began. *"I saw all of our possessions stacked by the soldiers in huge piles and set afire—everything destroyed, everything we own consumed by the flames. I saw the People driven naked into the hills, where we crouched like animals among the rocks."* Here the woman wrapped her arms around herself and rocked back and forth as if freezing. I felt the chill of her words myself. *"It is very cold,"* she continued, *"and the People are freezing, many dying, many babies freezing blue as chunks of river ice in their mother's arms. . . ."*

"No!" I suddenly cried out, as if involuntarily. "Stop that talk! It is nonsense! I do not believe in your visions, they are nothing but pure superstition. I do not listen to such talk! Someone run and find Brother Anthony for me, he will tell us the truth." But I realized as soon as I said it that I was speaking English, and both Little Wolf and Woman Who Moves Against the Wind only looked at me somewhat impatiently, as if waiting for my outburst to be over. Then they huddled closer and I could no longer hear their words.

10 October 1875

Shortly after the seer left our lodge, Little Wolf, without a word to anyone, himself departed. Only later did I learn that he had climbed to the top of the butte to seek his own vision. The Chief is a solitary man and clearly has much on his mind, and presumably he went off to think over what the medicine woman had said.

Little Wolf returned to our lodge after three days and three nights. Of his vision quest he said simply, "I have made offerings to the Great Medicine that he might protect the People from harm. But I had no sign from him."

14 October 1875

From Medicine Lodge we make our way north and again west, moving silently across the undulating plains. After these several days of religious observance the people are reserved and subdued, exhausted by their ceremonies, and—having seen firsthand the continued invasion of the whites into their sacred land—anxious about their future. All have by now learned of the apocalyptic vision of Woman Who Moves Against the Wind. And all know that while Little Wolf made offerings to the Great Medicine, he failed in his own vision quest. This is not considered to be a good thing.

❀   ❀   ❀

We do not travel hard after our visit to *Novavose* but continue to meander our way back toward the Powder River country. The fine autumn weather continues. The cottonwoods and box elders and ash turn yellow and red in the river bottoms, and the plains roll out before us—a sea of grass, now golden and ocher, the plum thickets in the coulee a deep shade of purple. There is much game along the way—great herds of buffalo already coming into their heavy winter coats, which hang beneath their bellies nearly to touch the ground; there are antelope by the hundreds, deer, and elk in the fall rut so that the bugling of the latter can be heard across the plains like the trumpets of the Gods. The geese and ducks and cranes are on the move, huge flocks that blacken the sky and fill the air with their honkings and cries. Truly it is a spectacle to behold. "We are blessed by God," said Anthony in his pure simplicity as we watched the sky one day. And who can deny it?

Great coveys of pintailed grouse squirt up ahead of our horses, fan off to the horizon like fall seeds spread on the wind. Helen is thoroughly rejuvenated by the shooting and delights our Indian companions with her prowess with the shotgun. She has given some of them instruction in its use, but I am proud to see that none of them can match her shooting skills.

These have been fine days of easy travel and perfect weather, the People quietly harvesting the plenty of the earth—the fall before the winter, the calm before the storm that, since Medicine Lodge, some whisper is coming.

18 October 1875

It was a true homecoming when we reached the winter camp—the other bands had been arriving for several weeks, coming from all directions like spokes on a wheel running to the hub. Some bands had already come in and left again, having decided to make their camps elsewhere. Some have already elected to go into the agencies for the winter, for word has spread from the scouts and between the Sioux and the Cheyennes of the Great Father's recently issued ultimatum that all the free Indians must give themselves up at one of the agencies by the first day of February or pay the consequences. "Three Stars," as the Indians call General Crook, has promised that those who comply early will be favored with the best land for their reservations and a greater share of provisions. Winter at the agency, with all of their food and other needs supplied by the Great White Father, has been promised to be an easy path for all who willingly take it.

We found upon our return that among those who have gone into the agency are a number of our own women and their husbands. Like all of us, they had become increasingly anxious about the prospect of childbirth in the wilds without real doctors and especially in the wintertime. And who can blame them?

With several months yet to go, I remain generally sanguine about my own impending childbirth. I had very little difficulty with either of my former pregnancies, and gave birth to both my children at home with only a midwife in attendance. Still, regardless of what immediate course of action Little Wolf decides for our band, I am pleased that others have already chosen to go into the agency; this can only be a good thing, and our white women will serve as a kind of advance guard to smooth the way for the rest of us when we go—which by all consensus is now only a matter of time. I am certain that before the winter is out the rest of us will succeed in convincing our husbands to "surrender" to "the inexorable march of civilization," as Captain Bourke rather grandly calls it.

So we rode into camp yesterday afternoon, alerting the others to our arrival by singing our song, the song of the Little Wolf band; all the People sang, even the little children, a joyful song of coming together and friendship. I had myself learned the words and sang as we rode in, as did Phemie, Helen, and the Kelly girls. A lively chorus we made of it, too!

The winter camp has been set in a lovely grassy valley formed by the confluence of Willow Creek and the upper Powder River. It is well protected from the wind and elements, defined by rocky pine-studded bluffs on one side of the river, climbing to timbered foothills, and on the other a network of ravines and coulees that rise to the rolling benches and tablelands of the prairie, and on to the faint outline of the Bighorn Mountains against the distant horizon. The valley appears to have everything we need for the moment— sufficient grass for the horses, running water, and an ample supply of cottonwood for our fires. Several large herds of buffalo have also taken up winter residence in the general vicinity and presently feed as placidly as domestic cows on the rich fall grasses.

In this place we will settle for a time—and make our plans for the future. A welcome settling it will be after the constant travel of the past months.

Martha was beside herself with joy at our return. Even from a distance as we rode in and I made her out, I noticed that she was looking quite large with child herself. She waved excitedly to us as we rode down into the valley off the bench above, singing our song, our horses picking their way carefully down the slope. She jumped up and down, clapping her hands like a child. Then I watched as she did something extraordinary; she slipped a rope bridle over the head of one of the horses tethered beside her lodge, grasped it by the mane, and swung onto its back like an Indian! She wheeled the horse and galloped out to meet us! Good God, I thought, can this be my same friend, Martha, who when first we arrived here could hardly take a step without tripping and falling down? Hah! The one they call Falls Down Woman?

She was breathless when she rode up, but hardly more so than I at the sight of her. "May, oh May," she said, "I cannot tell you how pleased I am to see you home! I had begun to worry so for you. Where have you been? You must tell me all about your travels. And I, too, have news for you. Much has happened since you've been away. But first, I must know—did you go all the way to Fort Laramie? Did you dine with the officers? Did you see your Captain?"

I couldn't help but notice how hale and healthy Martha looked. The added weight of pregnancy becomes her; indeed, I'd never seen her look as well. Where, upon our departure all those months ago, she was still mousy and frightened, she has actually grown quite pretty in the interim—her cheeks rosy, her arms brown and strong. I laughed in astonishment and happiness. "All that in good time, dear," I said, "we will have a long visit after we have made camp. And I am so pleased to see you, too. But good Lord, Martha, look at you, you look like a wild Indian! And riding bareback like a trick rider—hardly a proper activity for a pregnant woman!"

"I've never felt better, May, I think that pregnancy and the wilderness life agree with me . . . You were right—I was fine without you . . . I suppose I have become a wild Indian!"

And then we both laughed and rode into camp side by side, chattering away like schoolgirls.

HEF

→ NOTEBOOK VII ←

Winter

"When the end of the village was reached we were to charge at full gallop down through the lines of 'tipis,' firing our revolvers at everything in sight. Just as we approached the village we came upon a ravine some ten feet in depth and of varying width, the average being not less than fifty. We got down this deliberately, and at the bottom and behind a stump saw a young boy about fifteen years old driving his ponies. He was not ten feet off. The youngster wrapped his blanket about him and stood like a statue of bronze, waiting for the fatal bullet. The American Indian knows how to die with as much stoicism as the East Indian. I leveled my pistol . . ."

(John G. Bourke, from his memoir,
On the Border with Crook)

＞＜

1 November 1875

We arrived at winter camp in timely fashion, for two days
ago the first snows came. Fortunately, we had nearly a fortnight of mild weather previous to this and the men made a
number of successful hunts. Now the larder is full with all
manner of game—fresh, dried, and smoked, and we seem to
be exceptionally well supplied.

A frigid wind blew down from the north for an entire day
before delivering the full brunt of the blizzard. And then the
snows marched across the plains like an approaching army,
blowing horizontally, at first lightly but soon so thickly that
even going outside to do one's business was to risk becoming disoriented and lost in the maelstrom. Fortunately the
camp itself is situated so as to be partially protected from
the worst of the wind and drifting snow. After another day,
the wind began to subside, but the snow continued, falling
straighter now, until the air was windless and the flakes, as
big as silver dollars, fell steadily. For two days and two
nights it snowed thus. And then the wind came again and
blew the skies clear and as suddenly stopped. The mercury
plunged and the stars in the sky glittered coldly off the fresh
snow, which had drifted in huge sculpted mounds across

the rolling prairie so that it appeared as if the earth itself had shifted, reformed itself with the storm.

Of course we were very much "housebound" during the storm and there was no visiting among us for those several days. All stayed as much as possible in their lodges; and though ours was warm and snug, the confinement became, finally, quite tedious. After the wind abated I did venture down to the river one morning for a bath, which cold as it is, I do not intend to give up—this activity, at least, allowing me to get out of the "house" however briefly.

5 November 1875

The weather continues clear and cold, but at least we are able to get about now to visit. I should mention that an inventory of our numbers since our band's return from Fort Laramie reveals that well over half of our women chose to move with their husbands and "families" to the agency for the winter— good timing on their parts as a move now with the snow would be virtually impossible. Gretchen and her doltish husband No Brains are still among us, as are Daisy Lovelace and Bloody Foot, of whom Daisy has grown even fonder. "Ah *nevah* would have believed *mahself*," she says, "that I could fall in *luuuve* with a *niggah Injun* boy, but *ah'm* afraid that this is exactly what has happened. I don't care if he is *ðaaaak* as *naaaght*, Ah *luuuve* the man, and I am proud to say that *Ah am* carryin' his *chaalð*."

As to Phemie, especially since our visit to Red Cloud, she and I have been in some conflict about the matter of enrolling at the agency, and have had several heated discussions on the question. For my part, I argue that such a move is inevitable and in the best interest of the People—while she equates the reservation system with the institution of slavery itself.

"My husband *Mo'ohtaeve'ho'e* and I have discussed the matter," Phemie says. "He does not remember our people's slavery for he has lived most of his life as a free man. Thus we have decided that we will not surrender to the agency. My days of enslavement to white folks are behind me."

"Phemie, there is no slavery on the reservation," I argue. "The People will own the land and will earn their livings as free men and women."

To which Phemie answers in her melodious and imperious manner. "I see," she says. "Then the Cheyennes will enjoy complete equality with the whites, is this what you are telling me, May?"

"That's right, Phemie," I answer, but I hesitate just long enough that she senses my lack of conviction on the matter.

"And if the People are equal to the white tribe, why then are they being restricted to reservations?" Phemie asks.

"They are being asked to live voluntarily and temporarily on reservations as a first step toward assimilating them into our own society," I answer, and already I know that I am walking right into the trap she lays for me.

Phemie laughs her deep, rich chuckle. "I see," she said. "And if they do not 'volunteer' to live on the reservation? Then am I to understand that they may remain on this land which belongs to them and upon which they have been living for many hundreds of years and where some of them, myself and my husband included, are quite content to remain?"

"No, Phemie," I answer, abashed, assuming the role now, involuntarily, of Captain Bourke, "they cannot live here any longer. You cannot. If you try to stay here past the February deadline, you will be breaking the law and you will be punished for it."

"The law made by the whites," Phemie says. "The whites being, of course, the superior race, who make these laws in order to keep the inferior in their place. That, May, is, by definition, slavery."

"Dammit Euphemia!" I answer in frustration. "It's not the same thing at all."

"No?" she asks. "Explain to me then the difference."

And, of course, I cannot.

"My people were once forcibly removed from their homeland," Phemie continues. "My mother was taken from her family when she was just a child. All my life I have dreamed of going back for her. Now, living among these people, I have in a sense done so. This is as close as I will ever get to my mother's homeland, to my family. And I have promised myself, May, that one way or another I will live from now on as a free woman, and I will die, if necessary, to protect that freedom. I could never tell these people that they should surrender and go to live on reservations or at agencies, because to do so is to take from them their freedom, to make of them slaves to a higher order. That, my friend, is my position on the matter and nothing you can say to me will change my mind."

"But Phemie," I plead, "why then did you sign up for this program? You are an educated woman; you must have understood that the process of assimilation that we are facilitating is, inevitably, a process whereby the smaller native population is absorbed into the greater invading one. It is the way of history, has always been."

"Ah, yes, May," Phemie chuckles, seemingly amused at my distress, "*your* version of history, the white man's version. But not mine, certainly, not the history of these, our adopted people. My history, my mother's history, is one of being torn from homeland and family and enslaved in a foreign land.

Theirs is one of being pushed from their own land and slaughtered when they refuse to give it up. Absorbed? Assimilated? Hardly. Our common history is one of dispossession, murder, and slavery."

"Perhaps you're right, Phemie," I say. "Which is precisely our purpose here. To see that history does not repeat itself, to prove that there is another way, a peaceful solution in which both races learn from the other, learn to live in harmony together. Our children will be the final proof of this commitment, and the true hope for the future. Let us say, for example, that my son were to grow up to marry your daughter. Think of it, Phemie! Their offspring would be part white, part black, part Indian. In this way we are pioneers, you and I, in a great and noble experiment!"

"Oh May," Phemie says with real sadness in her voice. "The plantations were full of mulattos—people of mixed blood and of all shades of color. I myself am one. I am half-white. My father was the master. Did this make me free? Did this make me accepted by the 'superior' culture? No, I was still a slave. In many cases our lives were more difficult for being of mixed blood, for we were considered neither black nor white, and resented by both. Your Captain was right. You've seen the half-breeds around the forts. Do they appear assimilated to you?"

"They come and go among the two races," I said, without conviction. "But they were all born to women of the exploited culture, fathered by the exploiters. We women hold the key, Phemie, we mothers. We couple with the Cheyennes of our own free will; we bear their children as gifts to both races."

"For the sake of your children I hope you're right," Phemie said. "You asked me a moment ago why I signed up for this program. As I told you months ago on our train ride here, I signed up to live as a free woman, to serve no man, to be inferior to no one. I shall never give up my freedom again, and I shall choose to have children only when I know that they may live as free men and women. If I have to fight first for their freedom, so be it. And to be born on a reservation is not freedom."

And thus Phemie and I go round and round . . . I, advocating peaceful surrender in the interest of future harmony, an idealistic vision of the future perhaps . . . and one, it is true, without precedent in human history. And Phemie advocating resistance, intransigence, militancy—in the process inflaming her husband and her warrior society against the idea of going into the agency, against the invading white man, against the soldiers.

But we have time yet—a long winter to grapple with these questions—to reach some consensus. As always sentiment among those remaining in the camp runs decidedly mixed on the matter of going in. Some of us are making small inroads persuading our own families that this is the only reasonable course of action. Due to the great influence that women hold in the Cheyenne family, I have been concentrating my own efforts on my fellow tentmates. I describe to them the many marvelous inventions of the whites—with some of which they are already familiar—the many comforts they will own in civilization, the conveniences and advantages which are so dear to a woman's heart. . . . For win the women's hearts and those of the People will soon follow.

10 November 1875

Today Gretchen and I have broken yet another barrier between the sexes. If only temporarily . . .

We have all long envied the custom that the men observe of the "sweat lodge." This is a special tipi which serves the same function as a steam house in our own culture, except that this one seems also to hold special religious connotations—and women are strictly *verboten*, as Gretchen puts it. A large fire is built in the center of the sweat lodge, upon which rocks are laid until they are heated nearly red-hot and then water poured over the rocks to create steam—this whole process attended to by a medicine man who also frequently speaks some cere-monial mumbo jumbo and passes a pipe for the men to puff contentedly upon. The participants themselves sit in a circle around the outside of the fire, until they are perspiring freely and when they can bear the heat no longer run outside and roll around in the snow or leap into a hole chopped into the now frozen river. They then return to the sweat lodge to be-gin the process anew. This strikes me as both a healthful and a hygienic recreation—particularly in the wintertime.

The other day I was visiting with Gretchen in her lodge and she happened to mention—somewhat longingly I thought—that her husband, No Brains, was presently performing a sweat-lodge ceremony. She told me that in the old country her people observed exactly this same practice through the long, dark, northern winters—without the religious overtones, of course, and with no prohibitions upon the sex of the partici-pants. Gretchen's own family had brought the custom with them to America and built a sweat house on their farm in Illinois—which they enjoyed all year.

"Oh, May, *der is nutting bedder dan a goot* steam bath, I tell you *dat*," Gretchen said, shaking her head mournfully.

"And why should we not be able to take steam baths our-selves?" I asked.

"Oh, no May," she said, "*de* men not allow women in *de* sweat lodge here. My *husband* he tells me *dat*."

"Why not?"

"Because, it is only for *∂e* men," Gretchen said. "It is just *∂e* way *∂e* People says so."

"Gretchen, what good reason is that?" I said. "Let's you and I march right over there now and have a sweat bath ourselves!"

"Oh, no I don't *tink* so, May," Gretchen said, "I don't *tink ∂at be ∂ech a goot* idea . . ."

"Of course it is, it's a wonderful idea," I insisted. "And think how invigorating it will be! It is time we taught these people that any activity that is suitable for the men should also be enjoyed by the women. What's good for the goose is good for the gander!"

"*Vell*, OK, May, *vhat ∂e* hell," said Gretchen. "*Vatch* you going to wear in *∂e* sweat house, May?"

"I'm going to wear a towel, dear," I answered. "What else would one wear in a sweat lodge?"

"*Yah*, May, me too," said Gretchen, nodding. "*Dat's* a *goot* idea."

Many of us had brought cotton towels with us when we first came here, a luxury that the Indians have also discovered, and which item is now available at all the trading posts. Thus I fetched my towel from my lodge and went back to meet Gretchen so that we might make our assault on the male bastion of the sweat lodge together.

Truly, living in such close proximity, a sense of modesty regarding our physical bodies is hardly at issue among most of us any longer—and no one pays the slightest attention whether one is clothed from head to toe or half-naked. Going about with one's breasts free seems quite natural. And so Gretchen and I stripped off our dresses, giggling like schoolgirls plotting a prank, wrapped our towels around our enormous pregnant waists, and dashed through the snow to the sweat lodge. We scratched on the covering to the opening. "Hurry up, it's freezing out here!" I cried in my best Cheyenne. I believe now that the medicine man was so shocked to hear a woman's voice demanding entrance, that he opened the flap just a crack out of pure curiosity to see who might have the audacity to challenge this "men only" institution. And when he did so, we did not hesitate for a moment but burst through the opening into the wonderful humid warmth of the sweat lodge, laughing and quite pleased with ourselves. At our sudden appearance, there arose from the men seated around the fire a great grunting of alarm. The medicine man himself, old White Bull, whom I find to be a tiresome and humorless old bag of wind, was not in the least bit amused by our uninvited entrance, and began to speak sternly to us, waving at us a rattle that the Cheyennes use to ward off evil spirits. "You women go away," he said. "Leave here immediately. This is a very bad thing!"

"Not bad at all," I answered. "It's perfectly delightful. And we're staying until we have ourselves a good sweat!" With which Gretchen and I sat ourselves down right in front of the fire.

Several of the men, the most stringent traditionalists, stood and left the sweat lodge, grumbling and grunting indignantly as they did so. Gretchen's husband spoke sternly to her. "What are you doing here, wife? You shame me by coming here in this manner. This is no place for women. Go home!"

"You *gest be quite* you *bick* dope!" she answered (we have all remarked on the fact that Gretchen even speaks Cheyenne with a Swiss accent!), shaking her finger at her husband, her enormous naked breasts flushed pink as scalded suckling pigs in the steamy heat. "A man don't talk to his wife like *ðat*, mister! You don't like *ðat* I come here *ðat gest* too damn bad, *ðen* you can *gest* go home yourself!" The man was instantly cowed by his wife, and fell silent, much to the evident delight of a number of the other sweat bathers. *"Hemomoonamo!"* someone hissed. ("Henpecked husband!") *"Hou,"* said another, nodding. *"Hemomoonamo!"* And they all snickered softly in amusement.

This bit of humor helped to settle the men, and the sweat-lodge ceremony continued much as if we were not there. Indeed, I think it served the men's purpose simply to pretend that we were not there. After Gretchen and I had both broken into heavy perspiration, and the heat inside the lodge had become nearly unbearable, we crawled to the opening where old White Bull let us out and then we ran buck naked to the river, squealing like crazed children, Gretchen running with her heavy lumbering gait, her massive breasts swinging like well-loaded parfleches.

A thin skin of new ice had already formed on the opening of the water hole and through this we plunged, gasping and trying to catch our breaths, exiting again as quickly as we could and running back lickety-split to the sweat lodge. An ill-advised activity, perhaps, for pregnant women, but Indian babies must be hardy to the elements.

But this time, of course, stodgy old White Bull did not answer our entreaties at the entrance, would not untie the lodge flap. "We are freezing out here!" I cried. "You, old man, let us in there right now!" But he did not answer and finally, lest we really did freeze, we ran back to Gretchen's lodge, where we dried ourselves by her fire.

"You know what we shall do, Gretchen?" I suggested. "We shall build our own sweat lodge for the women. Yes, it promises to be a long winter, and we have plenty of hides and nothing but time, so we shall all band together to sew our own sweat lodge, and when we are finished, there will be no men allowed! It will be strictly a girls' club."

"*Goot* idea, May!" Gretchen concurred. "*Dat's* a damn *goot* idea. No men *allowt*! Girls only!"

And so this is how we shall pass the winter. Making what diversions for ourselves that we can, pranks and make-work projects like our sweat lodge, anything to keep ourselves active. For the days, shorter each in their stingy measure of daylight, can seem interminable if one spends them sitting in the dim lodge. We have our chores, of course, going for the living water in the early morning, and gathering firewood—neither of which activity I object to as at least they get me out of the damn tent. And there is always cooking to be done and food preparation and cleaning and sewing and all the other, sometimes dreary projects of wifedom. But these, too, also serve to prevent idleness.

We remaining white women have become, if anything, even closer in our sisterhood. Without the constant activities of traveling—dismantling and reassembling the lodge, packing and unpacking—we have more time to meet regularly in one or another of our lodges, where we consult each other on the progress or lack thereof that we each make in our efforts to convince our families to go into the agency before February.

In our daily meetings we also compare our respective pregnancies, plan our upcoming births, and offer each other what moral support we can. We gossip and argue, laugh and weep, and sometimes we just sit quietly together around the fire, holding hands, staring into the flames and embers, and wondering at the mystery of our lives, wondering what is to come . . . happy that we have one another, for the winter promises to be long and lonely . . .

We are all much comforted by the presence of Brother Anthony of the Prairie and frequently meet with him in his own spare lodge, which he has erected on the edge of the village. It is a very simple, immaculately clean affair, as befits a monk, and often we sit by his fire and recite the daily liturgy with him.

"In this place I shall build my hermitage in the spring," says Anthony in his soft soothing voice. "In these hills above the river I shall be blessed to have everything I require, for a man needs little to commune with God, but a humble shelter and a pure heart. Later with my hands I shall begin the work of building my abbey. I shall be blessed to have other men of humble minds and simple hearts follow me here, and here we shall pray and study and share the word of God with all who come to us."

It's a lovely image and often we all sit together in contemplative silence and imagine it. I can almost see Brother Anthony's abbey in the hills, can imagine us all worshiping quietly there, can imagine our children and our children's children after us coming to this place . . . it is a fine comforting thought.

Beside reading, reciting the liturgies, and instructing us in his Bible, Anthony is teaching us and the native women to bake bread—a fine occupation in the winter and one that fills our tents with wonderful aromas.

The weather continues mostly clear and crisp, with thankfully little wind, and when the sun is up and shining off the pure white prairie, all is very beautiful.

10 December 1875

Nearly a month has passed since my last entry. Time, of course, is not the issue, rather the general torpor of the season and the corresponding lack of interesting occurrences has caused me to rest my pen—to husband and store what little I have to report. Would that we could hibernate like the bears! How wise they are to take their long winter naps and not awake until spring.

The Cheyennes themselves do not appear to suffer from boredom. How lucky they are, for they possess a kind of unlimited patience so that if we are tentbound for days in blizzards, they wait them out without complaint, with a kind of perfect animal-like stillness. Besides simple games that they play, and a bit of gambling among the men, there is little in the way of entertainment—other than storytelling, from which we learn something of the history of these fine people. Of course, they do not read books.

We white women have all read countless times the few volumes that we brought with us or were able to obtain on our last trip to Fort Laramie. I have nearly reduced the Captain's cherished volume of Shakespeare to tatters from my many readings of it, and, of course, much as I may have wished to hoard it for myself, I have made it freely available to the others. Besides our daily visits with Anthony one of our few recreations has been to meet in groups in one or another of our lodges and read the Bard together, passing the book around the circle, each of us reading a different part. But the light is poor in the lodges, especially with the days now so short.

Our women's sweat lodge is now complete and in full operation! It is a perfect delight and we white women have been holding our "councils" there. Hah! We have even encouraged some of the younger and bolder Cheyenne women to join us. Both my tentmates, Pretty Walker and Feather on Head, have attended, with extreme shyness at first, but now more enthusiastically. We have a little girl who tends our fire and keeps a supply of water in the buckets to pour on the hot rocks, and all are welcome—if they are women, that is! We sit, for the most part naked, sweating freely and then dashing for the river. Helen Flight often smokes her pipe and sometimes passes it among the others in a kind of pantomime of the men's dour councils. The Cheyenne women, when they join us, consider this smoking to be quite scandalous, even sacriligious, and will scarcely touch the pipe let alone partake of it.

12 December 1875

I am huge with my baby! Big as a house! I believe that mine is by far the biggest belly in our group! Even Gretchen, herself a hefty woman to begin with, does not seem nearly as large as I. Surely this savage baby of mine is going to be a giant! Fortunately, in spite of the additional bulk I am carrying, I have had a very uneventful pregnancy, almost no illness and, other than the simple act of packing the enormous thing around, very little discomfort. The Cheyennes have all sorts of remedies—teas which they brew from various roots, herbs, flowers, leaves, and grasses—some of which are not disagreeable to the taste; these they give to pregnant women—who are doted over and cared for by the other women, really to the point of distraction.

Much game remains in the vicinity, and the clear weather has been conducive to the hunt, so that we continue to have a steady supply of fresh meat. All of which makes for plenty of work for both men and women so that at least there is less idleness among us—there is always skinning and butchering and tanning to be done.

I have learned to embroider hides with trade beads, and this activity I enjoy—it is a pleasant, time-consuming craft, often peacefully pursued in a group. We sit by the fire, chatting and gossiping and passing the time. Now that most of us white women are so much more proficient in our use of the native tongue, we have achieved a greater intimacy with our fellow Cheyenne wives. Although they have a quite different way of looking at the world than Caucasians, I find that as women we have nearly as much in common as separates us by culture; every day we learn more about one another and have a greater mutual appreciation and respect. Thus we all share the same daily cares and worries, the same labors. And with our pregnancies—for some of the Indian wives are also pregnant—we share the burdens, the responsibilities, and the joys of impending motherhood.

And in our increasing ability to better communicate we also share the fresh glue of humor. At first the Cheyenne women found our white women's irreverence toward the men to be quite scandalous. But now our small jests and banter about the male race in general seems to delight them, seems to unite us all in a new bond of sisterhood. Together we nod and *"hou"* and giggle enthusiastically as, with a little prompting from us, the Indian women discover . . . no, not "discover" . . . I mean to say "acknowledge" the female's natural superiority to the male.

In spite of her reserve, I am sometimes even able to elicit a tiny sly smile from Quiet One. Like many who speak sparingly she is keenly observant of all that takes place around her. The other day, for example, Little Wolf was holding council in the lodge with several other heads of state in attendance, including the old Chief Dull Knife, and a fellow named *Masehaeke*, or Crazy Mule (he was named this by our Sioux neighbors because one time he rode into their camp on a mule, and one of them said, "Here comes that crazy Cheyenne who rides the mule"). Crazy Mule is a tiresomely long-winded fellow and I always dread when he attends the councils because on he drones—on and on—the only good thing about it, I suppose, being that his voice has the effect of a sleeping potion and instantly puts the children into a deep slumber. I have even sometimes observed Little Wolf and others among the council dozing off while the man is speaking. In any case, the other day, Crazy Mule was going on in his usual fashion and I noticed that Quiet One was looking at me in the shy way she has of observing people from the periphery. I smiled at her and held my hand up to the fire to cast a shadow puppet on the lodge covering above old Crazy Mule's head. Opening and closing my thumb and fingers I made my shadow puppet to be yakking on like the man himself. This woke up the assemblage! There was much stifling of laughter from those who could observe my chattering shadow puppet, and even Quiet One allowed herself a smile large enough to warrant covering her mouth demurely with her hand.

According to Captain Bourke in an opinion expressed to me during our brief meeting at Fort Laramie, the only true hope for the advancement of the savage is to teach him that he must give up this allegiance to the tribe and look toward his own individual welfare. This is necessary, Bourke claims, in order that he may function effectively in the "individualized civilization" of the Caucasian world. To the Cheyenne such a concept remains completely foreign—the needs of the People, the tribe, and above all the family within the tribe are placed always before those of the individual. In this regard they live somewhat like the ancient clans of Scotland. The selflessness of my husband, Little Wolf, for instance, strikes me as most noble and something that hardly requires "correction" by civilized society. In support of his own thesis, the Captain uses the unfortunate example of the Indians who have been pressed into service as scouts for the U.S. Army. These men are rewarded for their efforts as good law-abiding citizens—paid wages, fed, clothed, and generally cared for. The only requirement of their employment, their allegiance to the white father, is that they betray their own people and their own families . . . I fail to see the nobility or the advantage of such individualized private initiative . . .

18 December 1875

A disturbing accident has occurred. Yesterday our Quiet One invited several people to our lodge to partake of a feast of bread that she had just baked. Somehow she confused a bag of arsenic powder for that of baking soda. The Cheyennes obtain the arsenic from the trading post and use it to poison wolves.

The results of this mix-up can be readily imagined. By the grace of God, or perhaps, the grace of the Great Medicine, no one died—but for a pair of hapless dogs who were given bites of the bread in order to confirm the fact that it was indeed poisoned. By then several of the guests had already been stricken. I sent Horse Boy to summon Anthony and some of the others, and together we prevailed upon the afflicted to vomit. Thank God I and none of the other pregnant women had ourselves partaken of the bread, for it would surely have cost us our babies.

All have now recovered, although for everyone, it was a long and painful ordeal. Little Wolf himself became deathly ill. I feared deeply for his life and sat up all night with him. Of course, poor Quiet One was completely distraught at her part in the near catastrophe; and I have tried to comfort her as much as I could.

The event has served as a catalyst to a council being called to discuss this question of poisoning the wolves—a practice the Cheyennes only recently learned from the white agents, who have advised them that by poisoning the wolves, there will be more game for the people. Since its use has become more widespread among the Indians, all have noticed across the prairie the carcasses not only of wolves, but also of coyotes, eagles, hawks, ravens, raccoons, skunks, and even bears, for the poison kills everything that partakes of the arsenic-laced meat or that feeds off the carcasses of its victims.

Our lodge was crowded with a number of prominent chiefs, dignitaries from the various warrior societies, esteemed medicine men, and our own Brother Anthony. Several of our women were also in attendance, the latter, along with a number of Cheyenne women, seated as usual outside the council circle of men.

After the ceremonial pipe had been smoked by the men, the first fellow to speak up was an old medicine man, *Vo'aa'ohmese'aestse*, whose name, unless my Cheyenne is worse than I think, translates to something like Antelope Bowels Moving.

"It is unfortunate," began the old man, "that Little Wolf's wife confused the wolf poison with the soda for making bread." At this there was much assorted *"houing"* from the assemblage. "Wolf poison is not something that the People should eat in their bread," he continued with a great deal of pomposity. "However, properly used, the poison is a good thing, for it kills the wolves so that there will be more game for the People." Now the old man nodded smugly, and looking extremely self-satisfied with this reasoning, as those assembled *"houed"* enthusiastically.

I could not help myself, and although I knew it was

unseemly to do so and would possibly even embarrass my husband, at this point I jumped up from my place and said: "If it is true that there will be more game after we kill the wolves, why is it that our relatives at the agencies who have been using the arsenic for some time now have no game in their own country?" (Of course, I offer this far more fluent English translation of my remarks.)

Now there arose a small uproar of grunting among the assemblage expressing general disapproval—whether specifically of my remarks or at the fact that a woman had spoken in council at all, is hard to say.

"*Vehoae* . . ." Little Wolf said with a smile to the assemblage, "*eohkesaahetseveoxohesaneheo'o.*" Which roughly translated means, "white women . . . nothing stops them from saying whatever they are thinking."

At this point the "little chief," Black Coyote, spoke up. He is a fine-looking fellow, but with a bit of a reputation as a hothead, and a warmonger, and particularly known for his dislike of white people. "*Mesoke* is right," he said now. "Instead of using the arsenic to poison wolves, we should use it to poison white people. We should make many loaves of poison bread and distribute these among all the whites. We have much more to fear from them than we do from the wolves."

"Well, I didn't say that exactly," I tried to interject over the mixed *houing* of approval from Black Coyote's more militant followers, and the grunting of dissent from his detractors.

"The People have always lived with the wolves and the little wolves (coyotes)," Black Coyote continued. "It is true that sometimes we kill them with arrows or rifles, but there has always been enough game for all of us to share. It was not until the arrival of the white man that the buffalo and the other game began to disappear. The wolf is not our enemy. The white man is our enemy."

This time the young warrior's words were greeted with more *houing* than grunting as he seemed to be winning over the audience.

"I should like to hear what *Maheo'neeestseveho'e* has to say on the subject," Little Wolf said. This is one of the names the Cheyennes use to refer to Anthony, and means something like "holy-speaking white man."

Anthony spoke softly. He has learned basic Cheyenne in a remarkably short time. "Christ gave the blessing of bread to provide sustenance, not to kill men," he said to Black Coyote. And to the assemblage in general he said, "God put all of the beasts on the Earth for His own divine purpose. He gives abundantly for all to share."

A long silence ensued as all soberly considered Anthony's simple but eloquent remarks.

Finally my husband, Little Wolf, raised his hand and spoke in his usual thoughtful way—without flourish or fanfare, but with plain reason and good sense. "*Mesoke, Mo'ohtaveo'kohome* and *Maheo'neestseveho'e* are all correct," said the Chief. "We have always lived with the wolves, and it is true that far more Cheyennes have been killed by the white soldiers than have ever been killed by the wolves." (There was a smattering of *houing* here.) "The wolves and the little wolves have always followed the People wherever we go, eating the offal and cleaning the bones that we leave behind from our hunts. This is not a bad thing, for all thus returns to the earth, and nothing is wasted. Sometimes, it is true that the wolves kill buffalo calves, and deer and elk calves. They kill old and weak animals, this is also true. But the wolves must have meat. If the Great Medicine intended that only the People should be allowed to eat meat, why would he have put wolves upon the earth? With this poison we not only kill the wolves and the little wolves but many other animals who have been our friends and neighbors. I have eaten the poison myself and almost died. I believe that the Great Medicine himself gave me the poison to eat so that I might know that it was a bad thing. It is the white man way to kill all the animals, to drive them away. It is not the way of the People, for we and all the other animals have lived here together, we have always shared, and until the white man came there has always been enough for everyone. Therefore, we will no longer permit the arsenic in this camp. That is my decision."

25 December 1875

Christmas morning! I awoke thinking of my children, feeling the pull of memories . . . the remembrance of Christmas past . . . when I was a child myself and the day still held such promise . . . with St. Nick in his reindeer-drawn sleigh on the roof of our family's house . . . and he would bring me a doll and some sweet candy . . . I had only two Christmases with my dear daughter, Hortense, and only one with sweet Willie before they took me away from them . . .

I woke this Christmas morning, vowing again that one day we would all be reunited, that I will tell my children the stories of their mother's life and adventures.

It has begun snowing again, snowing and blowing, and again we find ourselves tipibound by the weather. But I refused to be so restrained on Christmas Day, and so I rose quietly, dressed warmly, and managed to slip from our lodge before anyone else stirred. All of us sleep more with the snow and cold and short days—in which sense, I suppose, we do hibernate. I took my notebook—strapped to my back—and off I went to visit Martha this Christmas morning.

The wind blew fiercely as I made my way to Martha's lodge, the snow enveloping me in a whirlwind of white that stole my breath away. I could barely see beyond my own nose and at one point I became disoriented, lost all sense of direction, and felt a rising sense of panic. For that moment I was a prisoner of the white wind. But then the driving snow parted just enough that I could make out Martha's lodge coverings—for all of our lodges are painted with different and distinctive paintings.

Martha herself met me at the entrance, surprised to see me so early and out in the storm. "Merry Christmas!" I shouted to her, but she could hardly hear me over the howling of the wind.

"Merry Christmas," I repeated breathlessly after I had entered. It was dark, warm, and snug as a cocoon inside. I shook the snow from my buffalo coat and Martha helped me out of it. The two of us facing each other were like a pair of matching bookends, our protruding bellies touching beneath our antelope skin dresses.

"Christmas?" she said. "Dear God, May, I had completely forgotten. Christmas . . . Come sit by the fire, I'll make coffee for us."

Martha's husband, *Momehexaehe*, still slept in his place before the fire. I have come to know the fellow rather well as Martha and I spend so much time together and his head of frighteningly disarrayed hair notwithstanding, he is a very pleasant, easygoing fellow.

Now Martha and I both sat ensconced on robes, leaning against backrests, which position at least relieved some of the discomfort of our conditions. She stoked the fire with sticks and set a small pot of coffee to boil.

I had made a small gift for Martha—a pair of baby moccasins that I had sewn myself from a butter-soft antelope hide. "I've brought you a little Christmas present, my dear friend," I said, handing her the baby boots which I had enclosed in an embroidered deerskin pouch.

"A present?" Martha said in a small heartbroken voice. "But May, I have nothing for you. I had completely forgotten the day!"

"It makes no difference, Martha," I said. "What's important is that we are together on this day, safe, warm, and healthy."

And then poor Martha began to weep softly—she wept and wept, and I could not make her stop, could not console her.

"What's the matter, Martha," I asked. "Why are you crying?"

But she could only shake her head and weep; could not catch her breath to speak between her pitiful sobs. Finally, when she had calmed herself enough, she said in a tiny choked voice, "I'm sorry, May, I don't know what came over me. Learning that it is Christmas today made me suddenly so desperately homesick and lonely. Not that I have not been happy with my husband, for truly I have, but sometimes I do so miss home. Don't you ever wish that we were home, May? Don't you ever think of it?"

"Every day, Martha," I admitted. "I think of my children, every day of my life. But I do not have a home any longer except for the one that I have right here. Open your gift now, Martha."

She did so, and touched the baby boots lightly with her fingers, tracing the beads, lovingly. "Oh, May, they're absolutely beautiful. These are the most beautiful baby shoes I have ever seen. Thank you. I'm sorry that I have nothing for you on Christmas." And she began to weep anew.

"Hush," I said. "I'm glad that you like them, dear. But please don't cry anymore."

"Do you think that Santa Claus is going to come down

the smoke hole in the tipi today?" Martha said, smiling and wiping the tears with the back of her hand.

"I feel certain of it!" I said. "And why shouldn't he? Weren't we always told that Santa visited all children all over the world, wherever they lived. Next year he will visit our new babies, Martha. Think of it! Their first Christmas!"

"I hope that we go to the birthing lodge together, May," Martha said, "that we have our babies at exactly the same time, you and I. But if I go before you, will you promise to come and be with me?"

"Of course I will," I said, "and if I go first, which judging from the size of this enormous belly of mine, I surely will, then you must promise to attend to me."

"I promise," she said. "Oh, May, what a fine friend you have been. Merry Christmas!"

"Merry Christmas to you, Martha," I said. "Let us sing a Christmas hymn together, shall we?"

And so the two of us began to sing . . . while outside the blizzard raged, the wind moaned and howled like a living being, the snow roiled around the lodge, hurtled against it, spinning past to drift out across the prairie. Martha and I sat warm by the fire; we had much to be thankful for on this Christmas morning and we sang with full hearts, with hope and courage for the future:

Oh come all ye faithful,
joyful and triumphant,
Come ye, oh co-ome ye to Be-ethlehem . . .

And now I write these notes by Martha's fire, as she dozes contentedly beside me. Mr. Tangle Hair also sleeps, as does their crone at the entrance. All is quiet and warm inside, and we are safe . . . perhaps I too shall sleep . . .

23 January 1876

I have done something very foolish and in the bargain risked not only my own life but also the life of my unborn child—and of all those who ventured out to rescue me in the storm. It has been nearly a month since my "accident" and only now am I strong enough to sit up and write. God, how could I have been so careless!

After visiting with Martha on Christmas morning, I dozed off for a time as I reported in my last entry of that day. When I woke, Martha and the others were still asleep. I did not know what time it was and so I crawled to the lodge entrance and peered out to find that while the storm still blew, there was light yet in the sky. I decided that I would make my way back to my own lodge, before darkness fell. I tore a piece of paper from my notebook and wrote a note to Martha and then I bundled myself up in my buffalo coat and slipped out into the storm.

If anything the storm had intensified. But stubbornly I told myself that our lodge was only a short distance away, that if I simply walked slowly in a straight line I would certainly come upon it. After all, I had made it here this morning, had I not? But after only a few steps, a strange and terrifying phenomenon occurred. The maelstrom of wind and snow enveloped me in its own world of chaos. Suddenly I knew no direction—not east or west, north or south, not left or right, not even up and down. I was completely disoriented. I shall turn back, I thought to myself desperately, I can't have come far. But, of course, I did not know where "back" was. Now I felt the panic overcome me; I fought against it, tried to put one foot in front of the other, but in my state of mental confusion even that proved difficult to do. The snow stung my face and eyes, felt like a million tiny lashes of a whip, cut through my buffalo coat as if I were naked. I had an over-powering urge to lie down, to curl up for warmth until the storm passed, but I knew in what was left of my disarranged mind that if I did so I would surely die there. I staggered on, holding my arms out before me like a blind woman, hoping that I would come across another lodge—any lodge. I tried to cry out but I could barely hear my own words over the screaming of the wind. Tears of terror and pain from the stinging snow streamed down my face to freeze on my cheeks. Finally, I could no longer draw breath from the wind and my own panic; I had no strength to go on. I sank helplessly to my knees in the snow, grasped myself with my arms and rocked back and forth. "Forgive me, child," I whispered to my unborn baby, "forgive me." I fell onto my side, curled up in a tight ball, and felt the sleep of death stealing over me. I knew then that I was going to die . . . but suddenly I was warm and comfortable and I began to have the most extraor-dinary dream.

I dreamed that I was walking in a beautiful river bottom in the spring, the cottonwoods were in full leaf and the sweet yellow clover was in bloom and the grass across the prairie was as green as the fields of Scotland. I was following a young girl who walked ahead of me, and in a moment I rec-ognized her—it was my dear Sara. I began to weep with joy at seeing her, and I hurried to catch up. Sara turned to wave to me, and I could see that she, too, was pregnant. She smiled and called back to me in Cheyenne. "It is so beautiful in *Seano*, *Mesoke*," she said. "I shall have my baby here and later you will join me. I will meet you and show you the way here along the Hanging Road. But it is not quite time yet for you to come.

You must go back now." And she turned and began to walk away from me again.

"Wait, Sara," I called out. "Wait for me, dear, please . . ." But I could not catch up to her and she disappeared ahead of me . . .

I do not know how long I slept, but when I woke at last I was in my own bed in my own lodge. My little Horse Boy sat beside me, my little man, his small hand warm as a biscuit upon my cheek. I reached out to see that he was real, cupped his cheek in my own hand. *"Mo'ehnoha hetaneka'eskone,"* I whispered to him.

The boy regarded me solemnly when he saw that my eyes were open, then smiled down at me.

"Mo'ehnoha hetaneka'eskone," I whispered.

"Mesoke," he said.

And then the others gathered excitedly around me and I was startled to see among them my old friend Gertie.

"Name'esevotame?" I asked, speaking unconsciously in Cheyenne.

"Your baby's fine, honey," Gertie said, "but he's mighty lucky and so are you. What the hell were you doin' wanderin' around out there in the blizzard, anyhow? Are you plumb crazy?"

I smiled weakly. "Some people used to say so. How did I get home?" I asked.

"Your little friend here found you," Gertie said, indicating Horse Boy, "found you half-covered in a snowdrift and drug you home all by hisself, although I don't know how the skinny little bastard managed it what with the extra person you're packin' along in there." She placed a hand lightly on my stomach, smiled, and stroked my belly gently.

"Did you ever have children, Gertie?" I whispered weakly. "You've never said."

"Never did, honey," she answered, "never much cared for the little bastards." But I could tell that she didn't mean it. "This little Horse Boy, though, he's OK, and he sure enough saved your fool butt."

"He's my little man," I said.

For days I faded in and out of consciousness. I had contracted pneumonia from my ordeal, with the attendant fever and delirium. I woke and slept, woke and slept, with no sense of time. Through it all I was aware of the steady stream of people who came and went from the tipi, old Crooked Nose overseeing the visitors like a stern head nurse.

My little man Horse Boy hardly left my side, and sometimes curled up on the robe to sleep beside me. Medicine men chanted and passed burning sage under my nose, rattles and other totemic objects around my head. Anthony read passages to me from the Bible, my friends and family were there— their faces blurring one into the next. Martha sat with me, and Gertie, Feather on Head, Helen, Euphemia, the Kelly twins, Quiet One, Gretchen, Daisy, Pretty Walker—all were there. And in my dreams I saw little Sara.

Sometimes the women sang softly to me. Feather on Head and Pretty Walker sang Cheyenne songs, the white women and the Indians taught each other their songs, and my sick-bed became a place of joyous singing—until the old crone chased everyone off with her stick.

Always when the others had left, my husband Little Wolf was by my side, sitting silently, motionless as a statue so that when I woke, I was never alone, and when I saw him there I felt always safe, knowing that nothing bad could ever happen to me or to my child as long as my husband was here to protect us. If I was cold and shivering from fever, he would lie down beside me and fold me in his arms to warm me.

I slept and I woke and I slept, I thought that I should

never be able to keep my eyes open for more than a few minutes at a time.

But after a time the fever passed and slowly I began to regain my strength. Now I feel the baby move inside me, and I tell myself that all is well.

At the moment I sit propped up against my backrest, scribbling these notes by the dim light of the fire. Feather on Head sits quietly beside me . . . my eyes grow heavy again . . .

26 January 1876

Good God, I can hardly believe the turn of events . . .

After my last entry I drifted off to sleep with my notebook propped against my enormous belly. I woke several hours later, woke with a jolt—the unmistakable tightening of a labor pain. "It cannot be," I whispered to myself. "I am weeks early." And I knew that something must be wrong. Little Wolf sat beside me, and Horse Boy curled against me. I touched the child's shoulder gently, and he woke with perfect animal-like alertness. "Please," I whispered to him, "run and get Martha." And to my husband I said, "The baby comes."

The women came quickly to lift me on my bed and transport me to the birthing lodge—where all Cheyenne babies are born and which gratefully had already been erected in preparation for our group parturition.

The skies were clear as they carried me there, the night air windless and frigid. I lay on my back, borne aloft by the others, looking up toward the heavens at the millions of stars. A shooting star blazed across the sky at that moment. I took this to be a good omen, and I prayed upon the shooting star, prayed that my baby would be born healthy and strong.

A fire already burned in the birthing lodge, tended by

Woman Who Moves Against the Wind. The tipi was very clean and beautifully appointed with fine, newly tanned, and exquisitely embroidered hides and blankets, the walls freshly painted with various symbols and a number of Helen Flight's lovely bird designs. "In this way," she had said while painting them, "each of you may choose in turn your own medicine bird for your child." For mine I chose the mighty wren—*ve'keseheso*, little bird—for its beautiful song, its industriousness and courage.

Now the women laid me gently down on a bed. The Medicine Woman came to my side to examine me, much like one of our own doctors. *"Eane-tano,"* she said to the others.

"Yes, I'm in labor!" I said. "And is the baby healthy?"

"Etonestoheese'hama?" the woman asked, turning to Martha.

"Why don't you ask me that question?" I demanded. "I can tell you perfectly well how far along I am. Just as the others."

"Enehestoheese'hama," Martha answered.

"No, that is not correct, Martha," I said, sharply, "I'm early. I can't possibly be full term yet."

"Close enough, dear," she said, all efficiency now. "You've always been a leader among us, and now you lead us into motherhood. Perhaps your fever has brought on the labor early."

I was still very weak from my recent illness and feared that I had little strength left to spare for the rigors of childbirth. But now the pains came sharply and regularly. The sweat poured from my face. I was certain that something must be wrong with my baby.

The women bathed my brow with damp cloths and spoke their encouragement to me while trying to make me as comfortable as possible. But when at last the time came, I was too exhausted, too weak, I had not the strength left to push; I felt myself fading away, losing consciousness, slipping back into the same wonderful dream I had had before . . . I longed so to go back there, where it was peaceful and green, to be with my little Sara . . .

I found myself in the same beautiful river bottom in the springtime, with the cottonwoods leafing out and the sweet clover blooming yellow in the meadows and up ahead my little Sara, waving to me. "Not yet *Mesoke*," she called back. "You must stay a little longer, for your baby needs you."

And coming from a great distance away, I heard the voice of Woman Who Moves Against the Wind. *"Ena'tseane,"* she said calmly. *"She is dying in childbirth."* And I wondered who she was talking about.

Ahead of me Sara smiled and waved me back. I wanted so desperately to join her.

"No! No! She cannot be dying," screamed Martha from the distance, "May, your baby is coming, May, you must wake up, you must help!"

And Sara said to me, "It is still not time, *Mesoke*. Another time I will bring you to *Seano*. But now you must go back and bring your daughter into the world."

And then I came awake with a choke and I felt my baby's struggle between my legs as she fought to gain the light.

"Oh, God," I said, gasping for breath, "Oh, my God, *name'esevotame, name'esevotame* . . ."

"Yes, May!" Martha cried. "Yes, your baby is coming! Push, push hard now, here it comes!"

And then I felt her come free, the wet slickness of her head sliding across the inside of my thigh, the sharp unbearable pain followed by the sweet release as Woman Who Moves Against the Wind took hold of the infant and brought her forward into the world. She lifted my daughter and smacked her on the rump, and my little Wren gave a hearty wail of indignation. Thank God, thank God . . .

I fought to remain conscious, but I felt myself slipping again into a deep exhausted slumber, too weak to raise my head, too weak even to look at my child.

"*Ve'ho'me'esevotse,*" said the woman with a tone of wonder in her voice, "*Ve'ho'me'esevotse.*"

"What does she mean, Martha?" I whispered, so spent that I was barely able to speak. "Gertie, tell me what does she mean? Why does she say that? Is my baby healthy?"

"*Ve'ho'me'esevotse,*" repeated Woman Who Moves Against the Wind, as she wiped and swaddled the baby. The other Cheyenne women gathered curiously around and inspected the baby. "*Hou,*" they said in voices filled with astonishment, "*Hou, ve'ho'me'esevotse, ve'ho'ka'kesoas!*"

"Tell me!" I gasped with my last bit of strength. "Why do they keep saying that? What's wrong with my baby?"

"Take it easy, honey, your baby's just fine," Gertie said, "a great big healthy girl baby. But, honey, the medicine woman is right, she ain't no Indian baby, she's a *ve'ho'me'esevotse,* just like she said, a white baby, like them others is saying—*ve'ho'ka'kesoas,* a little white girl if ever I seen one."

"'Tis God's own truth, May," said Susie Kelly, "the lass is as pale and rosy-cheeked as an Irishman."

"Scots-Irish, I'd say," added her sister Meggie, wryly.

"That is to say, dear," Helen Flight whispered, "your baby appears to be Caucasian."

"Oh, my God," I murmured, giving myself up at last to the death of sleep that dragged me down—and grateful for it I was, too. "Good God, I've had John Bourke's child . . ."

For nearly two more days I slept, waking only long enough to nurse my baby, though sometimes I woke and the child was at my breast already, placed there by Woman Who Moves Against the Wind or one of the others. She was a beautiful child, and from the moment I first laid eyes on her there was never any question in my mind of her parentage. She had Bourke's nose, Bourke's deep-set intelligent eyes. She was John Bourke's daughter, of that I was certain.

The women fed me broth until I had regained some of my strength, cared for me again as they had before, and finally today I am able to sit up for a time and record this experience in my journal.

Only minutes ago my husband Little Wolf came to see his daughter for the first time. It was a moment that, for obvious reasons, I have been dreading. He sat beside me and looked for the longest time at the baby in my arms. I could only imagine what he must be thinking; I was filled with shame and remorse at my infidelity to this great, kind man—although we had not yet even met at the time of my indiscretion with John Bourke.

Finally Little Wolf reached out and with the greatest tenderness put the back of his fingers against the baby's cheek. *"Nahtona,"* he said, and it was not a question, but a simple statement.

"Hou," I answered in a tiny, tentative voice. "Yes, my husband, your daughter."

"Nahtona, emo'onahe," Little Wolf said, smiling at her, his face filled with fatherly pride.

"Yes, she is, isn't she?" I said. "Your daughter is very beautiful."

"Epeheva'e," he said, nodding with great satisfaction. "It is good that *He'amaveho'e* has given to me, the Sweet Medicine Chief, a white baby to teach us the new way. Woman Who Moves Against the Wind has explained this to me. It is just as the monk said it would be. This baby is the

vo'estanevestomanehe, our Savior. *Maheo* has sent the white baby Jesus to lead our People to the promised land."

I was deeply touched by Little Wolf's naive acceptance of the child as his own, and I could not help but smile at his muddling of Biblical affairs. After months of listening first to Reverend Hare's sermons, and then to Brother Anthony's quiet explanations, the People have ended up with a strange hybridized religion based partly on their own beliefs and partly on those of Christianity. Perhaps this is as it should be and, surely, makes as much sense as any other.

"My husband," I said gently, "the baby Jesus was a boy child, not a girl. This is not the Savior, this is only our little baby girl. Our daughter. Your daughter and my daughter."

"*Hou,*" he agreed, "I understand. This time the Savior is a girl child. That, too, is a good thing."

I laughed then and spoke in English. "I'm not exactly the Virgin Mary," I said, "but if that's the way you want it, my husband, why the hell not!"

28 January 1876

And so it is that my baby girl, John Bourke's daughter, is considered throughout the camp to be a sacred child—*vo'estanevestomanehe*, the Savior—given by *Maheo*, God Himself, as a gift to the Cheyenne people, a white baby who will lead the next generation of Cheyennes into the new world. A steady stream of visitors have come to see her, to marvel and *hou* approvingly at her milky white skin; many bear gifts for her. Surely Captain Bourke himself would appreciate the irony!

I had not intended to encourage the deceit, but neither have I disabused my husband of his superstitions. I have spoken to Brother Anthony at some length about this, having confessed everything to him. He agrees, as do the others, that to tell Little Wolf the truth of our daughter's parentage would serve no purpose, and that, indeed, this great event can only further encourage the remaining free Cheyennes to go into the agency. "There are no accidents in the Kingdom of God," Anthony said. "Perhaps your child, May, has been chosen to continue His work on Earth, to spread the word of God among the heathens."

"Don't tell me you believe it yourself, Anthony?" I said, with a laugh. "Can't she just be my daughter? That's enough for me."

Of course, some of my white friends, especially the always irreverent Gertie and Daisy Lovelace, tease me mercilessly about the child, upon whom all dote. Any speculation among the general population about the nature of my relationship with the Captain has been finally laid to rest—but none seem to hold it against me, or even be particularly surprised.

Daisy, herself very pregnant, came the first time to see the child, looked at her with her wry hooded eyes, smiled slyly, and said in her purring Southern voice, "*Why* if it *idn't* the *lil'* baby Jesus, herself. *A've huurd* so much about you, *mah deah. Everyone* in camp is talkin' about you." And she shook her head in amusement. "May, you are the only *guuurl* I have *eveh* known, who after havin' committed, if not exactly *udultery*, at least an act of *waaalld* and passionate promiscuity on practically the eve of *hur weddin' naght*, is rewarded for *hur* sins by givin' *buuurth* to a *bastaaad whaate chaald* believed *baah* all to be the baby Jesus. This is an *extraordinary* stroke of good fortune, *mah deah.* How did you *eveh* manage it?"

"Just lucky, Daisy," I admitted with a laugh. "Pure, dumb luck."

"And are you goin' to *infohm* the good Captain that he is a daddy?" she asked.

"If ever he has occasion to see this child, he will certainly know," I replied. "But I am married now to the great Chief Little Wolf, and as far as I'm concerned this child is officially his daughter . . . In any case, imagine how the situation would embarrass the good Catholic Captain among his military friends and cohorts?"

"*Idn't* that just the way of *alll* men?" Daisy said, and she let loose a bark of raw laughter. "It *nevah* occurs to them that they are the very ones who damaged the *guuuuds* in the *fust* place, does it? That was *jest* exactly the attitude of the cad Mr. Wesley Chestnut . . . and all along I thought we were goin' to be married . . ."

"You became with child by him, Daisy?" I asked. "I never knew that."

"Yes I did, and gave her away for adoption," Daisy said, "a decision I've regretted every day of *mah* life since. But this baby *Ah'm* carryin' now? This little *niggah* baby. *Ah'm* keepin' this one come Hell or high water."

29 January 1876

Yesterday offered me the first opportunity since my recovery to speak privately with Gertie, to ask her the question I have been pondering since the first night I saw her here after my accident.

"You rarely come to pay strictly social calls, Gertie," I said, coming right to the point, "and as this is dead of winter, reaching us must have been extremely difficult for you— and a matter of some urgency. Tell me what news you bring."

"Honey, I was just waitin' for things to quiet down some before I was goin' to tell you," Gertie said. "You know, what with your sickness and then the baby comin' the way it did . . . maybe you lost sight of it, but you folks have come right up against the Army's deadline."

"I've had other things on my mind," I said.

"Course ya have, honey," she said, "an' that's why I ain't said nothin' about it. I got news from the Cap'n. I brung you a letter from him. Before you read it, I'd better explain what's up. Crook's army left Fort Fetterman at the beginnin' of the month, headin' for this country. Of course, the Cap'n is with 'em. No telling where they is right now on account of the poor weather, which probably caused them to bivouac up somewhere, but even so they can't be more'n a few weeks away from here. It's a big detachment, honey—this time they ain't foolin' around. They got sixty-one officers with 'em, and over fourteen *hunert* enlisted men. And they're well provisioned, too—they got four *hunert* pack mules, sixty-five packers, a *hunert* and sixty-eight wagons, and seven ambulances. Not only that but they got better n' *three hunert* and *fifty* Injun scouts with 'em—'wolves' the Injuns call 'em when they go over to the other side. You never seen nothin' like it, honey. It's an army itself. They got big bands of Shoshone, Crows, Pawnees—they got Sioux, Arapahos, Cheyennes. Yup, some a your own folks is with 'em. Take a wild guess who's head a the Cheyenne wolves."

"Jules Seminole," I said, without hesitation.

"None other, honey," Gertie confirmed, "an' he's got others with him who are right from this here camp, that got family still here. You know some of 'em on accounta some of 'em just came into the agency this past fall with their white wives. You know that little French gal that was with you, Marie

Blanche?—well her husband is one of the wolves, and so is the one they exiled, you know the fella who's married to the gal who always wears black."

"Ada Ware," I said.

"Yup, that's the one—her husband, the one they call Stinkin' Flesh. A course, they won't have no trouble finding you here. They know right where you are. Like I say, honey, the Army don't send out a force like this unless they really mean business. Too many miners and settlers have been getting picked off in the Black Hills, and folks is startin' to really holler for military protection from the Injuns. They been sendin' petitions to General Sheridan in Chicago and to the President hisself in Washington. Crook's orders are to clean out any hostiles they find in this country. And any Injun who ain't enrolled in the agency as of the first of February is a hostile Injun. And that means you, honey."

The irony of having gone from being a volunteer in the service of my government to being considered a "hostile Indian" did not escape my attention. "But with the weather we couldn't have complied if we'd tried, Gertie," I said. "You know that. Especially with all of our pregnant women."

"Sure, honey, I know that," Gertie said. "But what I'm tryin' to tell ya is that this has all been set in motion already. Listen to me on this: A military campaign, once it's set in motion, has a life of its own."

"We can't leave now," I said. "I have a newborn infant. The others are about to have their babies. These are innocent people. We are innocent people. We haven't done anything wrong."

"Honey, I was at Sand Creek in '64," Gertie reminded me. "Those folks weren't doin' nothin' wrong, neither. Last year Captain Henely and the buffalo hunters jumped the Southern Cheyenne on the Sappa, burned the camp, killed everyone in it. Threw the bodies of the smallest babies in the fire. The Army'll do anything it wants. You put a bunch of raw recruits together in hard conditions in winter, fightin' an enemy they don't understand an' that scares the piss out of 'em—anything can happen. Especially when they got orders."

"That's madness, Gertie," I said.

"I know it is, honey," Gertie said softly. "Cap'n knows it is. But it don't make no difference. That's what I'm tryin' to tell you. Them settlers that the Injuns are killin', those are innocent folks, too. What it all comes down to, honey—always comes down to—is that there ain't enough room for the Injuns and the whites in this country. One thing you can be sure of is that the whites ain't goin' to go away. And the other thing is that the Injuns ain't goin' to win this one, either."

Gertie dug into the front of her shirt and brought out Captain Bourke's letter. "Here, honey," she said handing it to me, "I imagine this letter'll tell you pretty much the same thing as I have."

Fort Fetterman, Wyoming Territory
26 December 1875

Madam: I pray that this correspondence finds you in good health. I have news of the most urgent nature to convey to you, and to the other women with you. Thus I have once again dispatched our loyal intermediary "Jimmy" as messenger.

Your people must decamp with as much dispatch as possible and move immediately south toward Fort Fetterman. You must fly a white flag at all times so that your band may be identified as peaceful by Army troops who will intercept you en route. You will be provided safe escort the remaining distance to the fort where arrangements for your future settlement will be made. As I pen this

correspondence, General Crook prepares to dispatch the largest win-
ter campaign in the history of the Plains Indian wars. As a member
of the General's personal staff, I myself will be traveling with a force
that includes eleven companies of cavalry under the command of
Colonel Ranald S. Mackenzie. Taking into account vagaries of
weather and engagements with hostiles along the way, we expect to
reach the Powder River country no later than the middle of Febru-
ary. We have been advised by our scouts of the general location of
your camp and the number of people contained within it.

I can not too strongly impress upon you the fact that there is not
a moment to spare. Under the direction of General Crook, Colonel
Mackenzie and the other commanders have orders to proceed in the
clearance of all Indians between the Bighorn and Yellowstone rivers
to the Black Hills of the Dakotas. No quarter will be given. All Indi-
ans encountered by Colonel Mackenzie's troops are to be considered
hostile—with the sole exception of those traveling south toward Fet-
terman and flying the white flag of surrender. DO YOU UNDER-
STAND ME? I urge you to depart immediately. Do not delay.

I am your humble servant,
John G. Bourke
Captain, Third Cavalry, U.S.A.

30 January 1876

Of course we all of us were deeply shaken by Gertie's news
and the tone of urgency in Captain Bourke's letter—which
the others have also now read. Even with the Army delayed
by weather for several weeks it is inconceivable that we will
be able to comply with their preposterous demands.

I scribbled a quick note to this effect to Captain Bourke
and insisted that Gertie depart immediately to intercept

Mackenzie's troops with whom he rides. And I have also prevailed upon Little Wolf to fly a white flag on a lodgepole in
the middle of our camp. Surely for all their orders and dire
warnings, the Army will not attack a peacefully encamped
village in the dead of winter? A village in which, they are
fully aware, a dozen pregnant white women reside.

17 February 1876

More than two weeks have passed since Gertie's hasty departure. Still no word back yet, but the weather has remained abysmal, with wind and driving snow. As if in a
chain reaction, the others' babies are coming in such rapid
succession that the birthing lodge operates at nearly full
capacity. Martha and Daisy had theirs on the same day—
two strapping boys, beautiful little nut brown infants whose
parentage requires less divine explanation than does mine.
Indeed, the little fellows make my milky white Irish-Scot
daughter look even paler and more exotic by comparison!

"Oh my goodness!" Martha said when first she saw her
own son. "Look, May, he's inherited his father's hair!" And it
was true, her son was born with a head full of matted tan-
gled black hair! Tangle Hair Jr. we have thus named him.

These were quickly followed by the Kelly girls, who true
to form had their labor and births in perfect synchronization—
twin daughters both. Twin mothers, twin fathers, twin
babies—thus the twins multiply in kind. How extraordinary! "*Roons* in the family," said Susie. The Kelly babies are
strange-looking little things, tawny of skin but with deep red
hair.

All the children so far seem healthy; we have been extremely fortunate to avoid anything resembling complications

during birth. The Cheyennes themselves are quite pleased with these new additions to the tribe and all the women dote on them. Feather on Head loves my little Wren like her own; I can hardly wrest the infant away from her when it is time for her feeding, so attached has the girl become. Indeed, were it not for my milk-swollen breasts I'm not certain that the child would know which of us was her mother. Quiet One, too, seems fascinated by the baby, and Little Wolf still acts the proud father.

22 February 1876

Still no sign of the Army. We have all prayed that Gertie was able to deliver my message to the Captain, and we remain confident that all will end peacefully.

Little Wolf has held a council and most of the chiefs of the remaining warrior bands have agreed that as soon as it is practical to travel we will begin the move toward Fetterman—this decision made, at least partly, as a result of the birth of our daughter. I am very relieved. And proud, for truly we are fulfilling our mission here, after all—facilitating a peaceful resolution. Our anchorite Anthony of the Prairie has also been very helpful toward this end. The People recognize a holy man by his own actions, and the monk's simple faith and self-denial, his fasts and penances are something the Cheyennes well understand and themselves practice as a means of drawing closer to their God.

Anthony has baptized each of our babies thus far and has counseled the People toward the path of peace and harmony. He is a good, pure man, with God in his heart. We had hoped that he might accompany us back to Fetterman, but he remains firm in his pledge to make his hermitage here—to one day found his monastery in the hills above the river. We will greatly miss him. Indeed, a part of me wishes I could remain with him, and I intend to be a regular visitor here, after we are settled on the reservation.

Yesterday, Gretchen had her baby, an oddly small and delicate little thing with none of her mother's bulk. The child's Christian name is Sara.

24 February 1876

These past days have seen a midwinter thaw, with temperatures mild again and the snow rapidly melting. Our scouts have been able to venture farther away from camp and returned today with reports of the movement of Army troops at a distance of several days' riding—which means at least a week's travel for the more ponderous military forces. We still fly our white flag over the medicine lodge, and I am now convinced that Gertie safely delivered our message.

However, much to our dismay we have also learned that some of the restless young warriors of the Kit Fox society have taken the opportunity of the springlike weather to slip away with the intention of making a raid upon the Shoshone tribe to the west. This war party was first exposed by the Kelly twins, whose husbands are themselves members of this particular band and who stole off with the others early one morning—telling their wives that the raid was being undertaken in honor of the new babies, and that many horses would be brought back as gifts to them.

"We couldn't stop the lads," said Meggie. "We tried, but they got their damn *bloowd* up. *Ya* think it'd be *enooof* that they got new babies in the house, wouldn't you, but they got to go off an' steal some ponies to prove their damn manhood."

The raid is utter folly, for the Shoshone, like the Crows, while bitter enemies of the Cheyennes, are close allies of the whites. Evidently the recent councils which resulted in the decision to give ourselves up have also caused some of the young men to embark upon this imprudent action as a last opportunity to taste battle, to prove themselves as warriors. Once again the independent nature of Indian society and the lack of central authority acts against their better interests.

On a personal note, I have been recently discussing with Little Wolf our own future at the agency. General Crook has promised that the Cheyennes will be given their own reservation directly upon giving themselves up. Having signed documents, as did all the others, at the outset of this adventure agreeing to stay with the Indians for a minimum of two years, our real work among them will begin in this next year on the reservation—teaching the People the ways of our world.

"One of the first things you will be required to do," I explained to Little Wolf, "is to give up two of your wives. It is against the white man's law to have more than one wife."

"I do not wish to throw away two of my wives," Little Wolf answered. "I am pleased with all of my wives."

"This is the white man way," I explained. "You must keep only your first wife, Quiet One, and give Feather on Head and me up. She is young enough that she can find a new husband for herself."

"Perhaps she does not wish to have a new husband," Little Wolf said. "Perhaps she is happy to stay with our child in the lodge of her present husband and her sister, Quiet One."

"It does not matter what she wishes; this is the law of the white man," I said. "One man, one wife."

"And you, *Mesoke*?" Little Wolf asked. "You, too, will find another husband?"

"I do not know what I will do," I answered truthfully. "But I could not hope to find a more satisfactory man than you, my husband."

"You will perhaps leave us and take our daughter into the white world where she belongs—as a member of her mother's tribe," Little Wolf said proudly. "If the Great White Father had given us all of the one thousand brides they promised to us, all the children would belong to the white tribe and the People and the whites would thus become one."

"General Crook has promised you that when we go into the agency," I said, "we will take this matter up once again with President Grant."

"Ah, yes," said Little Wolf, nodding, "I am familiar with the promises of white men . . ."

28 February 1876

. . . horror . . . butchery . . . savagery . . . where to begin to tell of it . . . with Meggie Kelly's whisper perhaps, alerting us: "Oh Sweet Jesus," she said as her young husband danced proudly around the fire, displaying to her his unspeakable trophies of war. "Oh Sweet Jesus, God help us all . . . what 'ave ya done, lads? What 'ave ya done? . . ."

And Martha's bloodcurdling scream of recognition as my own blood ran cold, a chill so profound that my heart shall never warm again. John Bourke was right . . .

The Kit Foxes returned this morning from their raid against the Shoshones, rode into camp howling like banshees, herding before them a herd of horses stolen from the enemy. On the surface a harmless enough act, for the tribes steal horses back and forth, a game of boys and often no one on either side is injured or killed. And so we believed it had been on this raid, for the men returned triumphant, with no keening of mourning and leading no horses bearing the bodies of fallen comrades. They drove the herd of Shoshone horses through camp for all to see, followed by the camp crier who announced the requisite celebratory dance.

Our scouts came in just behind the Kit Foxes to report that Army troops are in the immediate vicinity. I suggested to my husband that he dispatch a courier with a message to Colonel Mackenzie to reiterate our peaceful intentions. Little Wolf answered that before turning his and the council's attentions to other tribal matters, he, and I, were first obligated to honor the Kit Fox raid by attending the feast and dance to be held at the lodge of their leader, a man named Last Bull. This is a bellicose, swaggering fellow of whom I have never been fond.

Thus off we went to a tiresome feast with much loud boastful talk from Last Bull. After the meal was finished all repaired to the bonfire, where the Kit Fox warriors each in turn danced their victory, and told their war tales.

It had snowed last night but now the skies were clear and winter's icy grip was again tightening, with temperatures beginning to plummet. But even the cold weather did not deter the proud warriors from their celebration.

I had left the baby in our lodge with Feather on Head caring for her, and after the feast I went back to check on her and to give her a feeding. "You go to the dance, *naveó a*," I told Feather on Head, as I held my ravenous little Wren to my breast. "I would rather stay here with my baby tonight."

"No, *Mesoke*," she answered. "You must take your baby to the dance with our husband; it was said by the crier that the new babies must all be present to witness their first victory dance—a victory in their honor. Our husband will be displeased if you do not return with his daughter for such an act would be very impolite to the Kit Foxes."

And so, reluctantly, I took my baby and met the others at the dance circle.

All of the other new mothers had also been invited, with the Kelly girls seated in the place of honor. Evidently their own young husbands had performed some great deed to honor the miracle of the birth of twin babies, the miracle of all the babies.

So huge was the fire that it cast sufficient warmth to off-set the chill, and, of course, we had our babies well wrapped in furs and blankets. Flames leapt toward the heavens as the warriors began to dance, to recount their tales . . . to raise the first bloody scalps, tied to poles and held aloft and shaken at the Gods for all to admire . . . And some among us cast our heads down, recalling with shame the vengeful satisfaction we had taken in the death and mutilation of the Crows, at whose hands we had suffered so . . . now this memory and its bloody aftermath seemed like a bad dream, not something that had really happened, not something that we had actually done . . . for we are civilized women . . .

Meggie and Susie's twin husbands danced before them as the girls both held their twins bundled in their laps. Between them the men passed a rawhide pouch, and sang a song of their great deed: *"In this bag is the power of the Shoshone tribe,"* he sang. *"We,* Hestahke, *have stolen this power to give to our children and now it is theirs. The Shoshones will never be strong again for we own their power. Tonight we give this power as a gift to our own babies so that they may be strong. For the children of our white wives are the future of the People. They own the power."*

And *Hestahke* held the pouch aloft and shook it and none could take their eyes from it; surely it held some great treasure, some great Shoshone medicine. The man danced and waved the bag in the air, and handed it to his brother who sang again the same power song, and as he did so, he reached into the pouch and took from it a small object and held it out to his wife Meggie as if offering her a precious jewel. I strained to see what it was that he held in his hand, all of us did, unable to look away.

At first I could not identify the object, but then my curiosity began to turn to stone, my blood to run cold for I knew instinctively that it was some ghastly body part or other, some unspeakable trophy of barbarity.

"Oh Sweet Jesus," whispered Meggie Kelly, "Oh Sweet Jesus, God help us all . . . what 'ave ya done, lads? What 'ave ya done . . ."

And now the tears began to run from my eyes, to wash cold across my cheeks. "Please, God, no," I whispered. I looked toward the heavens, the flames from the fire towering into the night sky, its sparks becoming the stars. "No," I whispered, "no, please God, let this not be . . ."

And the man danced and sang, proudly holding his grisly trophy aloft. A soft *houing* of approval and an excited trilling from the Cheyenne women began to rise above the drumbeat. *"In this bag are the right hands of twelve Shoshone babies, this is the power of their tribe and now it is ours. I give this as a gift to our daughters. Our children own this power."* He held the little hand aloft, and I could just make out its tiny curled fingers . . .

Martha screamed, a scream of anguish and condemnation that penetrated the night sky like a siren, cut through the drumbeat and the soft musical trilling of the others. I gathered my baby against my breast and stood, weak-kneed with nausea and horror, from my place beside Little Wolf. My husband himself sat impassively watching the performance . . .

Tears ran from my eyes as I clutched my baby to my breast. *"Me'esevoto!"* I hissed at him like an insane person. *"Babies!* Your people butchered babies! Do you not understand?" I said pointing with a trembling finger. "Do you not understand that one of those innocent babies' hands could just as well belong to your own daughter? Good God, man, what kind of people would do such a thing? Barbarians! You will burn in Hell! Bourke was right . . ."

And I fled, running as fast as I could, cradling my child in my arms as the fresh cold snow squeaked painfully beneath my feet.

I ran back to the lodge, weeping, burst in and fell to my knees. I held my baby to my breast, sobbing and rocking her. "My baby, my baby," were the only words that I was able to speak. *"Naneso, naneso . . ."*

Feather on Head and Quiet One gathered beside me to see what was the matter. Desperate for an answer, sobbing, I asked them please to explain to me how the women of the tribe could permit their husbands to commit such terrible crimes. At first they did not understand my question, for it is not a woman's place to ask such a thing.

"Babies!" I cried. "The men killed and mutilated babies. They cut babies' hands off. These could have been your babies, our babies. Don't you understand? It is a bad thing, a very bad thing that the men did." I wished to say "wrong," but there is no word for such a concept in the Cheyenne language . . . perhaps here lies the difficulty.

Quiet One answered softly, "The Shoshones have always been the enemies of the People, *Mesoke*," she said. "For this reason the Kit Foxes stole their horses and captured their power to give to our children. The men did so in order that the Shoshones could not use their medicine against us and against our babies. In this way the men protect the People, they protect your baby, *Mesoke*. Our warriors stole the power of the Shoshone babies and gave it to your daughter—*Vo'estanevestomanehe*, the Savior—to make her strong and safe."

"You really don't understand, do you?" I said helplessly, finally too drained of strength to weep any longer. "There is no power in a baby's hand." I reached beneath the covering and pulled my daughter's hand free. She clutched my finger in hers. "Look," I said, "look how tiny and frail it is. You see? There is no power in a baby's hand . . ."

There was no question of sleep on this dark night. Like me, the others had immediately left the dance and, as I suspected, many made their way to Anthony's lodge on the edge of the village, seeking whatever sanctuary and comfort the monk might be able to offer.

The celebration itself had continued after our departure, and now we all sat around Anthony's fire holding our infants and listening to the throbbing drumbeat, the music and singing as the Kit Fox warriors told again and again of their great triumph over babies.

We tried to make some sense of it, to console each other, to give reason to the madness, to make understandable what was simply not. The Kelly girls were the only among us whose husbands were members of the Kit Foxes, who had themselves committed the crimes, and the twins were most inconsolable of all. Gone was all their cheeky Irish bravado.

"I want to go home, Meggie," Susie said. "I can't ever bear to look at the lads again, after what they've *dooone*."

"*Aye*, Susie," said Meggie. "*Thar's nooothin'* else to be *doone*, we're finished here, that's for *shoooore*. We'll take the *gaarls* and leave *faarst* thing in the morning. Maybe we can find the Army and give ourselves *ooop*."

But we all shared their guilt and their failure, and even Anthony's quiet strength, calm counsel, and the prayers we said around his warm fire could not take the chill from our frozen hearts.

"What kind of God allows such things to happen?" I asked the young monk.

"A God who demands faith," he said, "who gave His only son upon the cross that mankind might be saved."

"Aye, and we *'aven't* learned a goddamned thing since, *'ave* we now?" said Susie Kelly with a bitter laugh. "We're *gooood* Catholic *gaaarls*, Meggie and me, *Broother*, but such a *tarrable* thing as this stretches our faith mighty thin."

"Now your work among the pagans truly begins," Anthony said. "To these innocent souls we must spread the word of God."

It is nearly dawn now . . . some of the women have returned to their own lodges, others doze fitfully with their babies here in Anthony's lodge. Unable to sleep all night myself, I sit here by the fire, recording these grim events. I look forward now to the arrival of the troops, so that they might escort us safely back to civilization . . .

And even still the drums and the music from the dance continue, the People have danced all through the night . . . a night none of us will ever forget. I prepare now to return to my own lodge . . .

1 March 1876

Yes, truly it is finished now, it is over, the soldiers have come with the breaking light of dawn like the vengeful hand of God to strike us down. I am shot, I fear that I am dying, the village destroyed and burning, the people driven naked into the hills to crouch like animals among the rocks. I have lost track of most of the others, some still alive, some dead, I have taken refuge in a shallow cave with Feather on Head, Quiet One, and Martha. Here we huddle together with our babies as the village burns below, a huge funeral pyre upon which the soldiers pile our belongings, everything that we own and all that we have—hides, furs, and blankets, meat and food supplies, saddles and ammunition—and upon these piles they place the bodies of our dead, and with burning torches set all aflame, they ignite our lodges which burst into flames like trees in a forest fire, the ammunition and kegs of gunpowder inside popping and exploding like fireworks . . . all that we have. Gone. It is the vision of Woman Who Moves Against the Wind come true . . . mankind is mad, all of us savages . . . are we punished for the babies? I cannot find Anthony to ask. I must ask Anthony . . . Anthony will know . . .

I am shot, I fear that I am dying, the breath rattles in my chest, blood bubbles from my mouth and nose. I must not die . . . forgive me my dear William and Hortense for abandoning you, I would have returned to you, truly I would have . . . if I die I pray that you may one day read these pages, know the truth of your mother's life . . . know that she loved you and died thinking of you . . .

I must be quick now, I am so cold I can barely move the pencil across the page, my teeth chatter, the women and children and old people are scattered out among the rocks above the camp, Martha is with me, Quiet One, Feather on Head, our babies . . . I do not know where the others are, some are dead . . . many are dead . . .

As long as I have the strength, I shall continue to record these events . . .

This morning at dawn, just hours ago, I left Anthony's

lodge. I took my baby back to our own where I left her under the robes with Feather on Head. Then I went down to the river to where my little man Horse Boy tends the herd. The music from the dance had at last stopped, all had gone to their beds, silence had finally fallen over the camp. From a distance I heard the horses nickering nervously, I sensed that something was terribly wrong. I began to walk faster, dread rising like bile in my throat, faster, I began to run toward the river . . .

I stopped short when I saw him: Horse Boy stood wrapped in his blanket, stood straight as a statue of stone and there before him, mounted and leveling his pistol at the boy like an executioner, was Captain John G. Bourke. Beside him a lieutenant sat his horse, both their mounts as still as stone themselves but for the clouds of vapor they exhaled in the frozen dawn. Behind them, slipping like quicksilver down the draws and coulees, scrambling over the rocks, sliding down the embankments and bluffs, came dozens, hundreds, of mounted soldiers and Indians. I stepped forward. "John, what are you doing?" I cried out. "Put down your gun. He is only a boy. We are all prepared to surrender. Have you not seen our white flag flying."

Bourke looked at me as if he had seen a ghost, with an expression of shock, giving way to horror, and then uncertainty. He hesitated, the gun trembled in his hand. "Good God, May, our scouts have told us that this is the village of the Sioux, Crazy Horse," he said. "What are you doing here?"

"This is the village of the Cheyennes," I said, "Little Wolf's village. My village. Didn't Gertie tell you? Good God, John, put the gun down. He's only a child."

"It's too late, May," the Captain said. "The village is surrounded, the attack begins. Gertie is with another detachment. Our chief scout Seminole assured us that this is the village of the Sioux Chief Crazy Horse. Run the way we have come and hide yourself in the hills. I will find you later."

"Shoot the boy, sir," said the Lieutenant, impatient beside him. "Shoot him now before he cries out to warn the others."

"Fools!" I cried, "Your shot will warn the others! John, for God's sake, don't do this thing. It is madness. This is the village of Little Wolf. We are prepared to surrender peacefully. We fly a white flag of surrender."

Captain Bourke looked at the boy and then back at me. His dark, shadowed eyes went black as coal. "I am sorry, May," he said. "I tried to warn you. We are at war, the attack begins, I have my orders. I am a soldier in the service of my country. Run and hide yourself."

Bourke steadied the gun with a terrible cold certainty and pulled the trigger. Horse Boy crumpled like a rag to the ground, a bullet hole through the center of his forehead.

For a moment there was no other sound but that of the shot, echoing against the rocky bluffs; as if the earth itself stood still in disbelief. As if God in His Heaven had suspended time . . . John Bourke had murdered an unarmed child.

"Charge!" the Lieutenant beside him hollered, and then the gates of hell opened before us.

I ran, stumbling, slipping, falling in the snow, back to our lodge, just as the troops entered the village from both sides; I could think now only of my baby, I must save my child. All were by now alerted to the presence of the invaders whose horses thundered through the camp. Everywhere was gunfire, the screams of terror and death. My husband Little Wolf ran from the front entrance of our lodge carrying his carbine, he stopped to fire, ran, and stopped to fire, as did many of the other men, trying to draw the soldiers to them that the women and children might escape out the back of the lodges.

I ran into our lodge and scooped my baby into my arms. Quiet One slit the back of our tent with a knife, and held it open for Pretty Walker and Feather on Head, who carried her own child on its baby board. Before I went myself through the opening, I turned to old Crooked Nose. "Come, *Vohkeesa'e*, hurry!" I said to her.

But she bared her gums in a smile and shook her club and said in a calm voice, "You run, *Mesoke*, save your baby. I am an old woman and today is a good day to die."

The old woman stepped out through the front entrance of the tipi and as I ran out the hole in the back, I turned to see her swing her club at a soldier riding past. The soldier lost his seat and flailed the air for purchase before hitting the ground with a thud as the old woman set upon him.

I turned and ran for my life. Clutching my baby to my breast, I followed the others toward the rocky bluffs that surrounded the village. All was mayhem and insanity, screams and gunfire, the hollering of soldiers, the cries of our warriors and wails of terror from our women; I cried out for Martha, for Gretchen, for Daisy, but none could hear me over the general din, nor I them.

I caught one glimpse of Phemie, mounted on a white soldier's horse, completely naked, black as death against the whiteness of snow, galloping down upon a soldier who was afoot and trying to extract his bayonet, which was lodged in the breastbone of one of our women. Phemie carried a lance and gave a bloodcurdling shriek that seemed not human and when the soldier looked up at her his eyes widened in terror as she bore down upon him. I turned again and ran following the others into the hills. As I ran I was suddenly knocked down from behind, sent sprawling as if swatted by a lodge pole; I pitched forward, trying to cushion my baby from the fall. But I regained my feet and ran on.

It was very cold, many of the women and children had run naked from their lodges, without time even to put on their moccasins, some of the women carried infants, trying to shield them from the cold with their bodies. Now in the bluffs, old men and women crouched shivering among the rocks. All looked for caves or depressions in which to hide themselves. Stampeded horses from our herd scrambled wild-eyed through the rocks, their hooves clattering in the dry frigid air. Some people had managed to catch a few of the horses and to slit their throats and then open their bellies to plunge their own frozen feet into the steaming entrails.

It was so cold that I feared for my daughter's life. I held her against my skin inside my coat. Thank God that I had been dressed. I caught up at last with Pretty Walker, Feather on Head, and Quiet One, and together we came upon Martha; she, too, was nearly naked, crouched squatting like a trapped animal in the rocks, holding her son to her breast and rocking him back and forth. The baby was blue with cold. I knelt down and took him from Martha and placed him under my coat. He was like an icicle against my skin. Martha was so cold herself and shivering that she was unable to speak. I removed my coat and wrapped it around her and handed Wren to Feather on Head and also placed Martha's child in the girl's arms. "Hold her against your skin," I said. I took the knife from the sheath at Quiet One's waist and together we caught a mare by the mane as she clattered by. I swung onto the horse's back as Quiet One tried to calm her. The mare slipped sideways and tried to keep her feet, and as she did so I leaned forward onto her neck and drew the knife quickly across her throat. There came a deep moan of escaping air and the mare dropped heavily to her knees. I leapt from her back before she toppled, the snow already darkening black with blood beneath her. Then she rolled onto her side, her flanks heaving, the terror in her eyes fading with the light. I slit open her belly with the knife, her steaming entrails spilling forth, and she tried once to rise but fell back dead and I took Martha's son from beneath the robe and thrust him into the hot belly of the mare. "Thank you," I whispered to her, "thank you, mother."

Now Feather on Head and I helped Martha to the horse and we thrust her icy feet, too, into the entrails and at last she stopped her shivering and was able to speak. "My God, May," she said looking at me, "you have been shot. You have been shot in the back."

Now I knew what had knocked me down, and I unstrapped the notebook from my back; it must have absorbed some of the force of the bullet, which had passed completely through it and was now lodged in the flesh between my shoulder blades. "Oh May," Martha said, and she began to weep, "you have been shot. Dear God!"

"Stop it, Martha," I said sharply. "We must find shelter, we must build a fire."

"There is no fuel," Martha cried. "No, we shall all die here in these rocks. Oh my God, May, you have been shot. Our babies, our babies . . ." and she wept.

"Your son is fine, Martha," I said. "Look how little Tangle Hair recovers in the warmth of the mare's innards." It was true. The baby was slick with blood and entrails so that he looked again like a newborn in a strange reverse birth process. But he was regaining his color and now he squalled lustily. "Look at him! How strong he is," I said. "He will stay warm for hours there. But we must find shelter."

My hands are nearly frozen now, my fingers cramp . . . I

make these last notes from this shallow cave . . . we have no fire . . . we all freeze to death . . . my breath comes painfully in shallow rattles . . . bloody bubbles run from my lips.

Down below the flames from the burning village crackle in the cold dawn. From these rocks we envy the warmth of flames we see but cannot feel. All that is left when the fires burn down are smoldering piles of ash and rubble, the half-cremated bodies of those who did not escape. Surely some of our friends are down there among them, and their babies . . . God, forgive us all . . . God forgive mankind . . .

From these cold rocks we can see the camp dogs beginning to slink back into the village to pick among the ruins for scraps of meat. The still frigid morning air bears the odors of roasted meats, spent gunpowder, scorched hides, burnt flesh. There are still dozens of soldiers about in the village so that we are unable to go back down to scavenge with the dogs, perhaps find a scrap of meat for sustenance, a flame for warmth . . . a blanket . . .

The soldiers continue to pile our last remaining goods, and atop them place the bodies of our dead, setting each pile afire . . . the funeral pyres blaze cold and fast and burn down quickly to their charred remains.

Now and then from the hills around a puny shot rings out . . . from our warriors, but they are poorly armed and have little ammunition to waste.

"Good brave girl, May," Martha says now, her teeth chattering again with the cold. "Good brave friend, you keep writing in your journal, you keep us alive as before, I love you so, my dear friend."

"And I you, Martha."

"It is over, isn't it?" she says in a small chattering voice. "All over, and for what?"

"For these children," I answer. "Our babies must live. They will be all that remain of us, and they will be enough."

"Let us go down now," Martha says, "and give ourselves up to the soldiers. When they see that we are white women they will take us in."

"They've killed us all, Martha," I say, "whites and Indians. But perhaps their lust is sated now. You go if you like. Go now, my friend, take your son. Tell them who you are and beg the soldiers for mercy."

"I'll find Captain Bourke," Martha says. "I'll bring him back. He'll help us. You wait for me here, May."

"Yes, you go, Martha. I'm finished writing in my notebook now, and I must close my eyes for a moment . . . I am very tired . . . our little friend Sara lives in the most beautiful place you've ever seen, Martha, a beautiful river bottom in the spring where the sun shines warm and the birds sing . . . go now, my dear, dear friend. . . . Pretty Walker, Feather on Head, and Quiet One will sit here with me for a while. . . . I shall wait right here for you to return with Captain Bourke . . .

"Yes, go now. Hurry. Take your son. Tell the soldiers who we are and what they have done. Tell them that this is not the village of Crazy Horse, that this is the village of the great Cheyenne Chief Little Wolf. And tell Captain John Bourke this from me—he will recognize it: tell him 'It is a wise father that knows his own child . . .'"

✣ CODICIL ✣

by Abbot Anthony of the Prairie
Saint Anthony of the Desert Abbey
Powder River, Montana
November 15, 1926

＊

What an extraordinary blessing! God is never in a hurry to divulge His secrets! To bestow His gifts! He has all the time in the world on His hands!

For over a half century I have known of the survival of the preceding journals. But I have told no one. Three days ago they were brought to me at my abbey not far from where the events of these final pages took place. They were delivered here by a young Cheyenne man named Harold Wild Plums, who lives on the nearby Tongue River Indian Reservation. I have known Harold since he was born. I baptized him when he was a child. He is the grandson of the author of these notebooks—May Dodd Little Wolf—*Mesoke*, as she was known by the Cheyennes. Harold is son of the one the Cheyennes call *Ve'keseheso*, Wren, or Little Bird.

Over fifty years! How very different the West is today than it was in 1876. I pray that I am a different man, that I have given up some measure of the pridefulness of youth and in so doing have been blessed to draw closer to God in my old age. I am ill, nearly blind, and I do not have long to live. I wait with a heart full of joy and love to go at last and sit for eternity at the feet of my King. He calls to me. I am blessed to hear His voice, to see His hand in all things.

Truly I have been blessed with a perfect life of prayer and toil, of reading and study. With the sweat of my brow, the labor of my hands, the love of my God, I have been blessed to carve out this humble abbey in the hills above the river. Here I began my hermitage those many years ago in a simple hut upon a hilltop. Here I am blessed to live still, surrounded now by twelve other quiet men of humble mind who have joined me over the years.

For over half a century I have been blessed to walk these hills. I have studied the plants and animals. I have lifted rocks from the Earth and planted my garden. I have been blessed to receive my visitors with a hot meal, a warm bed, and a fresh loaf of bread to take upon their journey. I have prayed.

Fifty years ago I was blessed to come here as a young anchorite with May Dodd and her friends among a band of Cheyennes led by the great Chief Little Wolf. Fifty years!

"Is your mother well?" I asked Harold Wild Plums on the day he brought these journals to me. "She has not been to visit me in many months. I have been thinking much of her recently."

"She is not well, Father," Harold said. "She is dying of the cancer."

"I shall walk to the reservation to see her," I answered. "For I am old and nearly blind, but I am blessed to be able still to walk, and I can still find my way there."

"No, Father," Harold answered, "my mother asks only that you read these journals and then write down the rest of this story in the last one that still has blank pages. She asks that I come back next week and pick them up and return them to her."

"Tell me, my son," I said. "I have been blessed to know your mother, Wren, since the day that she was born. But we have never spoken of these journals before. Has she always known that they survived the fires of that day?"

"No, Father," Harold said. "They have been kept all these years as a sacred tribal treasure with the Sweet Medicine bundle. Only a few elders knew about them. Old Little Wolf himself kept them in his possession until he died in 1904, but he never told my mother of their existence. He kept them secretly and illegally for twenty-five years after he was exiled by the People for killing Jules Seminole and was stripped of his position as the Sweet Medicine Chief. After his death they were placed in the Sweet Medicine bundle and only recently, because she is dying, were they given to my mother to read."

"And thus after all these years your mother learns the true identity of her father," I said to Harold. "And you, my son, learn the true identity of your grandfather."

"Yes, Father," Harold said. "We know, and now my mother wishes for you to write down in the last notebook that is not yet full the rest of the events of that day so that she may die knowing the whole story."

"You're a fine boy, Harold," I said to him. "Your mother must be very proud of you. I am blessed to do as she requests. Come back next week, and my work will be finished."

And so God in His infinite Grace and Wisdom has set me this final task to complete on Earth at the end of my own life. He has blessed me by placing this great gift of journals in my temporary care. I read them before, many years ago, when old Little Wolf brought them here to me, to read to him, for he never did learn English.

Now as humble scribe I am blessed to take up the last of these notebooks to write this codicil. One side of the notebook is soaked with the dried blood of May Dodd. I press my lips to it in blessing. I write around the brown, burnt edges of the bullet hole that passes through each and every page, to disappear in the flesh of my friend's back.

❊ ❊ ❊

On the day the soldiers attacked I did not run to the hills with those fleeing. I ran toward the village. There I walked amid the slaughter and burning. In my habit the soldiers did not harm me. God protected me on that day as He has every day of my life, before and since, so that I might spread His Word and offer His Gift of Mercy to all who would accept it.

I tried to protect those who could not flee, the old and the infirm, from the wrath of the attackers. I tried to help those who ran to effect their escape. Where I could I put coverings on the naked children and women. I ministered to the wounded, and offered Last Rites and the Lord's comfort to the dying. I walked amid the death and destruction, the fires of Hell on Earth.

Many died in the village that day, cut down by the soldiers. The Englishwoman, Helen Elizabeth Flight, an extraordinary young woman, died defending her home. The last time I saw her alive, she stood before her tipi, with her feet spread, calmly charging her muzzle loader and shooting at the invading soldiers. She held her pipe in the corner of her mouth. One of the soldiers shot Helen through the forehead and killed her. Later all of her beautiful bird paintings were consigned to the flames. It was a great loss to the world of Art. Helen would have been quite well known had her work survived. All that remains of it are the few sketches included here in May's journals.

The Negro woman, Euphemia Washington, also died that day. She died fighting, but killed many soldiers first. She fought like a demon and terrified the young soldiers. Many of them were just boys. Euphemia had a great calm, but she also had a great anger in her heart. I believe that God would have tamed her anger, for she was a spiritual woman. But He had other plans for her. I remember Phemie less for her anger than for the slave songs of joy, sorrow, and freedom that she used to sing. Sometimes when I am gardening, or baking, or just walking in the hills, I still find myself humming one of these songs. Then I am blessed to recall Euphemia—*Mo'ohtaeve'ho'a'e*, Black White Woman, the Cheyennes called her—and later *Nexana'hane'e*. Yes, the Cheyennes still recall the warrior feats of Kills Twice Woman in their old-time ceremonies. I am blessed by the Lord to recall her songs.

By the time I came upon Gretchen Fathauer she was still alive but mortally wounded. She held her dead daughter to her mighty naked breast and wept great sobs of sorrow. Her husband, No Brains, had run into the hills at the beginning of the attack, leaving his family behind to perish. Gretchen was a dear child of the Lord. I covered her and the infant and tried to make her as comfortable as possible in her last moments. "He left his baby," she sobbed. "*De bick* ninnyhammer forgot to take *de* baby *wit* him when he run away. I tried to save my little Sara, *brudder Antony*."

"Of course you did, my sister," I said to her. I was blessed to administer Last Rites to Gretchen and her child and as I did so I broke down and wept myself.

"It be OK, *brudder Antony*," Gretchen said trying to console me through her own sobs of grief. "*Yah*, it be OK. Me and baby we go to live with Sara and God in *Seano. Tings* be OK *dare. Yah*, you'll *see*." There amidst the brutality and death, God revealed Himself to me in Gretchen's goodness. He gave me strength for the coming ordeal.

The soldiers were by now largely finished with their grim business of destroying the camp. A mournful keening had arisen from the contingent of Shoshone scouts. They had discovered the Cheyennes' grisly trophy bag of babies' hands and had identified these as their own. Their cries of grief were terrible to hear. I stopped on my way to try to comfort them. I did not speak Shoshone, but I blessed the bag and I prayed for the souls of the children.

Some Cheyennes lived that day and were spared by the soldiers and others escaped into the hills. Later that morning I came across Martha Tangle Hair, wandering dazed through the village, holding her baby son in her arms.

"Help me, Brother Anthony," Martha begged when she saw me. "My baby is so cold."

I had gathered a small pile of blankets saved from the fires. I wrapped one of these around her child, and another around Martha.

"I must find Captain Bourke," she said. "Please help us, Brother. May is wounded. She needs help. I must find Bourke."

"Can you show me where she is, Martha?" I asked. "I will help her."

"May is very cold, Brother, she is shot."

Martha led me into the bluffs above the camp, but she had some difficulty finding the place again. At last we came to it. It was a shallow cave in the rocks. I still go to that place. I have been blessed to make of it a small shrine in May Dodd's memory. There my fellow monastics and I sometimes say our liturgies and there we sit in contemplative silence. The Cheyennes believe that everything that ever happens in a place—every birth, every life, every death—still exists there, so that the past, present, and future live on forever in the earth. And so I, too, have come to believe.

I called out to May on that terrible, frigid morning, but no one answered. When I entered the cave, I found her alone there, dead, sitting up against the rock wall. Quiet One, Feather on Head, and Pretty Walker were all gone, as was May's baby, Wren. In that cave, I administered the Last Rites to May Dodd and from her frozen fingers I removed the pencil. Her notebook, this notebook that I am blessed to hold now in my own hands, was also gone.

I led Martha back down to the smoldering village, and there I personally handed her and her infant over to the care of Captain John G. Bourke. It was the first time that I was to meet this man. But I would come to know him well later. He came often here to my hermitage over the years to pray, and I was blessed to help him do his penance.

The night after the attack the mercury dipped below zero. With everything destroyed by the Army, the Cheyennes had no protection from the elements and hardly any clothing. The survivors fled toward the village of the Lakota chief Crazy Horse, who was encamped on the other side of the mountain. I followed and did what I could to help and comfort the survivors.

It was a two-day journey of unimaginable hardship and suffering. Eleven Cheyenne babies froze to death in their mothers' arms the first night, three more the following night—including all of the remaining white children, with the sole exception of May's daughter, Wren.

Perhaps some scholars of religion might be tempted to find here a lesson in the vengeful hand of God. But God is not vengeful, my children. God is full of Grace, Light, and infinite Mercy. God did not kill the Shoshone babies. Nor did He punish the Cheyennes in retribution by killing their babies. Misguided men on both sides slaughtered the infants. And God took the souls of His children to His Kingdom.

Daisy Lovelace and her son, Wesley, God bless them, succumbed to the cold the first night. To them, too, I administered the sacrament of Extreme Unction under a cold full moon, and Daisy and her child went bravely and in peace to the Kingdom of our Lord. The little dog, Fern Louise, lay curled shivering beside the frozen body of her mistress. I put her beneath my habit and she survived. Fern Louise lived with me for several years before dying peacefully of old age in her sleep.

The Kelly twins, Margaret and Susan, lost both of their sets of twins in the course of the two-night march. The anguish of their grief was a terrible thing to behold. They cursed me, and they cursed the Lord in His Heaven for taking their baby girls.

They were a sprightly pair, Meggie and Susie. Besides Martha, they are the only white women of whom I am aware to have survived the ordeal of Mackenzie's attack and its aftermath. After the death of their infants, they went quite mad. They joined various bands of marauding Cheyennes and Sioux and fought like demons against the whites in the final days of the Indian wars. They are reported to have ridden with the warriors when Custer and his men were killed later that summer at the Little Bighorn, and to have taken themselves grisly trophies of war there. I made many inquiries on behalf of the Kelly twins over the years and heard many rumors, but I was never able to learn what finally became of those girls. God bless them both.

Little Wolf himself was wounded seven times on the morning of the attack. He fought valiantly to protect his People as they fled from the camp, and somehow survived. With his wives Quiet One and Feather on Head, and his daughter Pretty Walker, he led his ragged band of refugees over the mountain to the camp of Crazy Horse.

The Cheyennes had nothing left, their spirit was broken. Less than a month later many of them began to straggle into Camp Robinson to give themselves up.

The government quietly arranged for the white women who had gone with their Indian families into the agencies earlier that fall to return to their own homes. Some took their children and raised them in the white world, others left their infants with the Cheyennes to be raised on the reservation.

Martha Atwood Tangle Hair, the sole white woman to officially survive the Mackenzie attack, returned to Chicago with her son, whose Christian name was Dodd. I never saw Martha again, but for many years after we kept up a correspondence. She eventually remarried and had several more children. Except to say in her very first letter to me that she had delivered her friend May's last message to John Bourke, Martha never mentioned the affair again. Nor did I ever learn what arrangement she had made with the authorities to purchase her silence. It is not a monk's business to ask such questions. But silent on the subject she remained. Martha joined our Lord in His Kingdom three years ago.

All know the tragic story of Little Wolf's last years. One day several years later he got drunk and shot Jules Seminole dead in the agency store for making a lewd remark to his daughter Pretty Walker. For this crime one of the great men in Cheyenne history was stripped of his position as Sweet Medicine Chief, renamed Stinking Flesh, and banished from the People.

Little Wolf lived in exile for another twenty-five years until he was well into his nineties. He took up a kind of monastic life himself and went everywhere on foot with his faithful first wife, Quiet One. I often used to see the two of them walking across the hills together. Sometimes I was blessed to have them pitch their tipi for a few days next to my hut. It was there that the Chief first gave me these journals to read to him. I always baked a loaf of fresh bread for Quiet One, and Little Wolf would tease her with gentle mischief about the arsenic incident.

Feather on Head had moved out of Little Wolf's lodge when the Cheyennes were required to give up their practice of polygamy. Eventually she married a young man named Wild Plums, and together they raised the child, Wren, as their own daughter. Of course, the People all knew that the sacred white child was the daughter of the white woman May Dodd and Little Wolf—and the Cheyennes still referred to her in their secret old-time ceremonies as *Vo'estanevestomanehe*—the Savior. They still believed, as Little Wolf had always maintained, that the child was *Maheo*'s gift to the People, that she had been sent by God to teach them the new life that must be lived when the buffalo were gone.

Even though I had read all of May Dodd's journals to Little Wolf, and he knew about John Bourke, he never gave up that faith. It was for this reason that he kept the journals secret and never told his daughter of their existence. Before he died he arranged with the keeper of the Sweet Medicine bundle for Wren to be given the journals at the end of her own life. He was a very great man, Little Wolf. I was blessed to know him on Earth.

John Bourke became a great advocate of Indians' rights, and a harsh critic of their treatment at the hands of our government. His outspokenness in such matters largely cost him advancement in his military career. Eventually he married another woman and had a family of his own. His health had been ruined by those terrible years of Indian wars, and he died in 1896.

John Bourke never claimed May Dodd's child, Wren, as his own daughter. But he always secretly watched over her and saw to her welfare as much as he was able. I know this to be true, because I was blessed to be his agent in these efforts. It was I, Brother Anthony of the Prairie, who prayed with John Bourke, and who counseled him to allow these People, and himself, the final miracle of the child's birth. May Dodd was quite right, the children were all that were left of this grand experiment . . . and they are enough.

Blessed be the children of God!

⇥ EPILOGUE ⇤

by J. Will Dodd
Chicago, Illinois
February 23, 1997

꩜

Abbot Anthony of the Prairie died on the morning of December 7, 1926, just two weeks after he completed the preceding codicil to May Dodd's journals. The Saint Anthony of the Desert Abbey which he founded in the hills above the Powder River is still an operating monastery. It was there, propitiously—perhaps even miraculously Abbot Anthony would surely say—that I began my search when I first came out to the reservation, bearing my own family letter of introduction—the one link that I had between my great grandmother, May Dodd, and the Cheyennes.

The monks at the abbey were very interested in my last name—joyously so—for they know well the legend of May Dodd, and the brothers still say their liturgies and hold their contemplative silences in the rocks where she died. Through them I was put in touch with ninety-six-year-old Harold Wild Plums, said to be the oldest living descendant of the great Cheyenne Chief Little Wolf.

Harold lives with his granddaughter, named, not coincidentally, May Swallow Wild Plums, in a concrete block HUD house in the town of Lame Elk, Montana, on the Tongue River Indian Reservation. Like many such reservation towns in America, it is a bleak place with a distinct third-world feel to it. On an abandoned gutted building across the street from

Harold's house, emblazoned in dripping blood-red spray paint, is the ghetto legend—*Fuck Tha Police.*

I had already learned from the monks that as a young man Harold had attended college off the reservation and had gone on to become a well-known attorney in the Native American community. For many years he worked on the reservation, representing the Cheyennes, often without pay, on a variety of Native American issues.

The letter I brought to Harold Wild Plums, of course, was the one I had discovered in my own family's archives, the letter that had fueled my initial search, and the rumors of which had haunted mine amd my brother Jimmy's childhood. It was the only surviving correspondence from May Dodd to her children Hortense and William in Chicago.

The letter was written in coarse lead pencil, much faded, on a sheet of yellowed paper that had been torn from a bound notebook. It was dated *10 June 1875,* below which date was written, *"Somewhere in Nebraska Territory North of the Niobrara River."*

According to my own family research, on June 10, 1875, Hortense and William, who was my grandfather, were living with May's parents at their home on Lake Shore Drive in Chicago. May herself, by all family records, was still living in the Lake Forest Lunatic Asylum, a private facility for the insane in the countryside on the banks of Lake Michigan thirty miles north of the city. This institution is still in existence, having undergone several name changes over the years in keeping with the fashions of the times, and presently known as "Serenity Dunes." Of course no patient records from the 1870s survive there, but according to the official family history, May would die in the asylum the following winter of undisclosed causes. She is buried in the Dodd family plot in the Lake Forest Cemetery, or at least she has a stone there.

Like all of Chicago's old, monied families ours is a large one, by both birth and marriage, and I have often, over the years, been to the plot for the burials of relatives, including that of my brother, Jimmy, after he was killed in Vietnam. His own grave is not far from that of our great grandmother, May Dodd.

Neither my grandfather William Dodd, nor his sister Hortense, would read their mother's only surviving letter to them until many years after it was written. Not wishing to frighten the children with this mad missive from their mad mother, of whom they knew little—except that she had died when they were infants—May's family kept the letter in a safe deposit box, the existence of which was not revealed to the children until after the death of both May's parents. By then William and Hortense were young adults themselves. Their mother's letter, then, took some twenty years to reach them—slow mail delivery even by the standards of the day. It is a short letter, as if hastily written.

My Dearest Children, Hortense and William,

I have entrusted this letter to my good friend Gertie McCartney, known infamously and variously on the western prairies as "Dirty Gertie" or "Jimmy the Muleskinner." I do not know if this will ever reach you. And if it does, I do not know if you will ever read it. In this way, I feel that sending this letter is much like putting it into a bottle and throwing it into this great sea of grass, all the while hoping desperately that it will wash up one day on your shores.

Even more fervently than that wild hope, I hope and pray daily that you are both well, and that we shall all be soon reunited. I have neither time nor space here to tell you of all that has happened. I am keeping a detailed journal of my journey here so that you may one day know the full story of your mother's life. I can only say now, briefly, that I was unjustly taken from you and committed to an asylum. My love for your father, Harry Ames, was deemed to be my "madness"—of which you are both the cherished result. For that I have no regrets on any score. I do not know what has become of your father. Only perhaps your grandfather can explain this to you—if he has the courage.

Presently I am living on the western prairies with a band of Cheyenne Indians ... oh, dear, how insane that must seem to you ... I am married to a man named Little Wolf, a great leader of his people ... Good God, perhaps this letter is not such a good idea, after all, and will only confirm in your minds that your mother is, indeed, "crazy as a hoot owl," as my friend Gertie would put it. Well, too late for such worries ... I am with child by Little Wolf, and will give birth to your brother or sister next winter. There are others with me here—by that I mean, other white women. We are members of an important government program, of which you will one day learn. I hope then that you will be very proud of your mother. I cannot here say more.

Please know that you are both kept close to my heart, that not a moment passes when I do not think of you, or long to hold you again in my arms. One day soon I will do so—I will come back to you, I promise you that, my dears. Every fiber of my being lives only toward that end.

Please remember me as your loving mother,
May Dodd

Harold Wild Plums was blind but still keen of mind, and his granddaughter, May, read him the letter as I sat on the edge of his ratty, stained sofa. Hearing it read out loud, I understood again how "going West to live with Indians" had become the euphemism it had in our family for insanity.

It was a tale for impressionable children, and I think possibly my brother Jimmy and I alone in the family ever actually believed it.

But all I could think of now, looking around this bleak concrete-block house, a child of privilege myself, was how far away I was from my own world, and how far away my great grandmother must have felt on these prairies. And it was then that I suddenly knew beyond a shadow of a doubt that the story was true.

Harold smiled as the letter was read to him, and nodded. "Yes," he said when she had finished, "those are grandmother's words. Do you recognize her handwriting, May?"

May was an attractive woman in her late thirties. "Yes, Grandfather," she said. "It is the same handwriting as the journals, and the same paper. I'll bet I can find the very page where it was torn out."

"You've got the journals?" I asked in a low voice of wonder.

"May, go and fetch Grandmother's journals from the Sweet Medicine bundle," Harold said to his granddaughter. "Our guest is a relative. He is the grandson of my mother's half brother, Willie. He has finally found us." And then to me Harold looked with his milky blind eyes. "I often thought over the years of searching for my white family," Harold said. And he shrugged. "But I was very busy with other matters. Does your grandfather, William, still live?"

"He died of cancer over thirty years ago," I said.

"Ah, yes," Harold said, nodding thoughtfully. "My mother, Wren, also died of the cancer when she was too young. I do not know why I have lived as long as I have. Perhaps to give you these papers now. That's what Father Anthony would have said." And Harold smiled. "Father Anthony would have said that I am blessed to give you these journals."

At that moment, May came back into the room carrying a stack of old cracked leather-bound notebooks, tied together in a bundle by rawhide thongs.

"Yes, perhaps you would be interested in reading these journals, Will Dodd," Harold said to me.

And very carefully May Swallow Wild Plums placed the bundle in my hands, and with long graceful fingers untied the thongs that bound it.

✦ BIBLIOGRAPHICAL NOTE ✦

In researching and writing this novel, the author gratefully acknowledges valuable insights and information gained from the following works:

Charles L. Blockson. *The Underground Railroad: Dramatic Firsthand Accounts of Daring Escapes to Freedom* (1987).

John G. Bourke. *On the Border with Crook* (1891).

W. P. Clark. *The Indian Sign Language, with Brief Explanatory Notes of the Gestures Taught Deaf-Mutes in Our Institutions for Their Instruction, and a Description of Some of the Peculiar Laws, Customs, Myths, Superstitions, Ways of Living, Code of Peace and War Signals of Our Aborigines* (1885).

William Cronon. *Nature's Metropolis: Chicago and the Great West* (1991).

Thomas W. Dunlay. *Wolves for the Blue Soldiers: Indian Scouts and Auxiliaries with the United States Army, 1860–90* (1982).

Jeffrey L. Geller and Maxine Harris. *Women of the Asylum: Voices from Behind the Walls 1840–1945* (1994).

Brigitte Georgi-Findlay. *The Frontiers of Women's Writing: Women's Narratives and the Rhetoric of Westward Expansion* (1996).

Josephine Stands in Timber Glenmore and Wayne Leman. *Cheyenne Topical Dictionary* (1984).

Gloria Davis Goode. "Get on Board and Tell Your Story," from

Jump Up and Say: A Collection of Black Storytelling, Linda Goss and Clay Goss (1995).

George Bird Grinnell. *The Cheyenne Indians*, 2 vols. (1925).

———. *The Fighting Cheyennes* (1915).

———. *By Cheyenne Campfires* (1926).

E. Adamson Hoebel. *The Cheyennes: Indians of the Great Plains* (1960).

Robert H. Keller, Jr. *American Protestantism and United States Indian Policy, 1869–82* (1983).

John Stands in Timber/Margot Liberty. *Cheyenne Memories* (1967).

Thomas B. Marquis. *Wooden Leg: A Warrior Who Fought Custer* (1931).

Joseph C. Porter. *Paper Medicine Man: John Gregory Bourke and His American West* (1986).

Peter J. Powell. *Sweet Medicine: The Continuing Role of the Sacred Arrows, the Sun Dance, and the Sacred Buffalo Hat in Northern Cheyenne History*, 2 vols. (1969).

Glenda Riley. *Women and Indians on the Frontier, 1825–1915* (1984).

Mari Sandoz. *Cheyenne Autumn* (1953).

Frank N. Schubert. *Outpost of the Sioux Wars: A History of Fort Robinson* (1993).

R. B. Stratton. *Captivity of the Oatman Girls* (1875).

Robert Wooster. *The Military & United States Indian Policy, 1865–1903* (1988).

ONE THOUSAND WHITE WOMEN

by Jim Fergus

Get to Know the Author

- Believing in the Fictional World: Where History Meets Imagination, Where Writer Meets Reader—An Essay by Jim Fergus

- An Interview with Jim Fergus

- A Note on the Author

Keep on Reading

- Reading Group Questions

For more reading group suggestions,
visit www.readinggroupgold.com.

ST. MARTIN'S GRIFFIN

What I've Learned from Reading Groups

Believing in a Fictional World: Where History Meets Imagination, Where Writer Meets Reader

In a very real way, writers depend upon readers to define and interpret our books for us, to tell us what about them resonates, and similarly, what doesn't. In this way, writing and reading become a collaborative process. I owe the wonderful word-of-mouth success of *One Thousand White Women* to the thousands of reading groups across the country who have embraced my novel. It has been my great pleasure to meet with some of these groups, either in person or by phone conference. The give-and-take of these lively discussions has proven to be both gratifying and instructive to me as a writer, and from it I've learned a great deal, both about my readers and about the creative process.

One lesson repeatedly driven home to me from the very first publication of *One Thousand White Women* is how much readers wish to "believe" in a novel, and how generous and forgiving they can be in order to do so. Despite the disclaimer in the Author's Note at the beginning of the novel (who reads those anyway?), one of the questions I am most frequently asked, in some variation or other, is: was May Dodd a real person? If not, was her character at least partially based upon a real person? Were some portion of May's journals actually written by a woman who traveled out West? When I answer no to any or all of the above, and when I explain that May Dodd never actually existed, nor did her journals, I often sense genuine disappointment on the part of the questioner. In fact, some readers want so badly to believe that May was a real person that even my assurances to the contrary will not dissuade them.

In speaking to reading groups, I am always careful to characterize *One Thousand White Women* as "semi-historical" fiction. I did a great deal of research for the novel, beginning with a kernel of historical fact and trying to build around it as accurate a historical and cultural framework as I could.

"These fictional characters became every bit as real to me as actual people; I heard their voices, felt their joy, laughed with them, suffered with them...."

In the process I felt a tremendous responsibility to know the "true" history of the Plains Indian Wars, of the Cheyenne culture and of the actual historical figures whom I portrayed in the novel. And as an essential part of my research I traveled through, and walked, much of the ground where pivotal events in the history of the Cheyenne and in the novel occurred.

I felt an equal responsibility to know as much as I could about the lives and backgrounds of my fictional characters. May's incarceration in a "lunatic asylum," for instance, and the horrifying "treatment" she endured there was based on actual experiences of women in that era. Similarly, each of the characters in the novel began their fictional lives as research material, grounded in some historical context, however slight this may have been.

But *One Thousand White Women* is, by definition, a work of fiction, an act of imagination, and for the liberties I have taken with historical fact I make no apology. Only where my imaginings have come up short do I apologize to the reader. But one of the most wonderful things about reading, and writing, a novel is the sense it can sometimes offer us that the world of the imagination is every bit as real as the "real" world. As I wrote *One Thousand White Women*, as the characters took shape and the story unfolded around them, their world became my reality; I lived with them and grew to love them, or hate them, or pity them, as the case might be. Indeed, these fictional characters became every bit as real to me as actual people; I heard their voices, felt their joy, laughed with them, suffered with them, experienced their trials. And I wept with them in their heartbreak. This is where the collaboration between reader and writer comes full circle, and we become fellow travelers in a fictional world of our mutual creation.

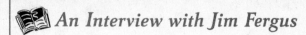

Q: You were a nonfiction writer for most of your career—primarily about hunting and fishing. What inspired you to write fiction?

A: To clarify the first part of that question: I got sort of typecast as a "hook & bullet" writer later in my journalism career, but I actually started out doing general interest journalism—essays, literary and celebrity profiles, interviews, environmental writing, etc.

From the very beginning, from the time I was about twelve years old, I had always intended to become a novelist. All my role models were fiction writers, and after I got out of college I wrote a bunch of short stories and shipped them off to the magazines, certain that I was going to get discovered. And I wrote an unpublished (and unpublishable) novel. It did not take long for me to figure out that I wasn't going to be able to make a living doing this, and so I became a teaching tennis pro, which was the only other thing I knew how to do.

"An old friend of mine who had some money loaned me enough to take a year... and write the novel."

I worked in that profession for a full decade, during which time I wrote yet another unpublishable novel. Finally at age thirty, I had put together a little stake, about $8,000, which in those days still seemed like a lot of money. I retired from tennis and started freelance writing full-time. Of course, the Catch-22 of that business is that in order to make even a modest living at it you have to work all the time; when you're not working on an assignment you're trying to drum up new assignments. It's a very hand-to-mouth existence, not unlike being an itinerant farm laborer, and simply did not allow me any free time for fiction writing. So that old childhood dream was relegated very much to the back burner.

Suddenly I found myself in my mid-forties and it occurred to me that I wasn't any closer to being a novelist than I had been in my twenties. I came upon the idea for *One*

Thousand White Women while researching what I thought
was going to be a nonfiction book about the Northern
Cheyenne Indians. An old friend of mine who had some
money loaned me enough to take a year away from journalism and write the novel.

**Q: You seem to have a great deal of familiarity with the
landscapes as well as the cultures you write about. What
kind of research have you done for your novels?**

A: Well, I always start with the landscape, and the research
here is simply a kind of accrual of experience in a place.
I need to have a certain familial sense of the land in order
to situate a novel in it. In the case of *One Thousand White
Women*, I had traveled extensively in the northern Great
Plains in the course of my magazine work, and I really knew
and loved that country.

With *The Wild Girl* I was less familiar with the landscape of
southern Arizona and northern Mexico. But I had recently
moved to the Southwest and had already spent enough time
down there to know that I would come to love that country, too. The northern Sierra Madre mountains are incredibly rugged and spectacular, and I made several trips down
there, traveling through the Mexican states of Sonora and
Chihuahua. I took a horse pack trip up into the mountains
with a Mormon outfitter out of Colonia Juarez, Chihuahua,
just to get the lay of the land. And in order to be able to
write the scene in which the wild girl is captured. I also
went on a mountain lion hunt on muleback with a rancher
who hunts lions with a pack of hound dogs.

Because of my background in journalism, I tend to be very
hands-on that way; I really need to see and experience these
things before I can write about them. As to the cultural
research, I felt a tremendous responsibility to know as much
as I possibly could about the respective cultures and histories of the Northern Cheyennes and the Apaches in order

to be able to write as truly and accurately as I could about them. For me the research takes as long as the actual writing of the novel.

Q: Some of your most memorable characters are female— May Dodd in *One Thousand White Women*; the wild girl and Margaret in *The Wild Girl*. Do you enjoy writing from a female perspective? What kind of challenges does it present you as a writer?

A: Yes, I do enjoy writing from the female perspective. As a male writer, I find that it takes you completely outside of yourself, offering a kind of clean canvas, a completely fresh point of view free of your own ego, opinions, and prejudices. It's quite liberating in that way.

I've never been particularly interested in writing fiction about myself or in having myself as the protagonist of my novels, and I find that any time a male writer writes from a male perspective, the author's own point of view inevitably bleeds through the character—which is not necessarily a bad thing, either. The challenge, of course, in writing from the perspective of the opposite sex is to try to do so credibly.

Q: When Westerns first became popular, Native Americans were frequently portrayed as savage villains. Then the tide turned and Native Americans were often depicted as noble and victimized. You depict Native American cultures with a great deal of texture and complexity. The Cheyenne in *One Thousand White Women*, for instance, are being decimated by the U.S. government, but they also commit terrible acts of violence against other tribes.

Do you think about the politics of the way Native Americans have been treated when you write, or do you try to put that aside and just tell the story? Do you set out to make a point in your novels?

> *"The challenge, of course, in writing from the perspective of the opposite sex is to try to do so credibly."*

A: One of the things I've heard from Native Americans who
have read my novels is that they appreciate the fact that I try
to avoid portraying them as one or the other of those one-
dimensional stereotypes—either as the villain or the noble
savage. Of course, the truth is that they're human beings
like the rest of us, capable of tremendous savagery as well as
great beauty and spirituality.

The revisionist notion of Native American history has it that
all the tribes were living together in harmony, each in its
own inviolable region, until the evil white man came along
to steal their land and disrupt their perfect way of life. But
the reality is that long before we showed up, these native
tribes were, with some exceptions, warrior societies who had
fought each other for centuries.

As always in nature, the stronger had pushed the weaker
out; they had enslaved each other and committed terrible
atrocities. This is not to forgive or excuse our treatment of
Native Americans, which remains one of the most shameful
chapters in our nation's history.

As to the politics of this, it's hard to write about the subject,
even fictionally, without touching on it, but I certainly don't
set out to write political manifestos or polemics. My main
goal as a novelist is simply to tell a good tale, and if readers
also find a point in my novels, that's fine, too.

Q: You write a great deal about morals. For instance, in
One Thousand White Women May Dodd is judged an
immoral woman, the Cheyenne are judged as immoral savages. In *The Wild Girl*, Billy Flowers is depicted as having
a very clear moral code, for better or worse, in great contrast with those around him. What is it about morality that
fascinates you?

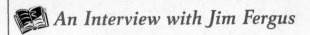

 An Interview with Jim Fergus

A: I'm interested in the sort of quicksilver, subjective nature of morality, the idea that virtually every culture, every religion, and even each era, has its own rather specific set of rules for it. And I also find fascinating the nearly desperate need that human beings have to impose their own particular version of morality upon others, to the point that we're willing to slaughter each other in the name of our own moral codes.

At the same time, we have a tremendous capacity to rationalize our own behavior as moral, no matter how despicable it might be. What is more grotesque, for instance, than the killing of babies and children? And yet every nation does it under the banner of morality.

Q: What do you most enjoy about writing novels? What do you find the most difficult?

A: The first part of that question I'm going to answer with a quote from Gustave Flaubert that I have thumbtacked on the wall beside my writing desk:

"It is a delicious thing to write, to be no longer yourself but to move in an entire universe of your own creating. Today, for instance, as a man and woman, both lover and mistress I rode in a forest on an autumn afternoon under the yellow leaves, and I was also the horse, the leaves, the wind, the words that my people uttered, even the red sun that made them almost close their love-drowned eyes."

How could I say it any better than that? What I find most difficult is creating that universe.

Q: What do you read when you're not writing? Who are your favorite authors?

A: Like many novelists, I'm unable to read fiction when I'm writing it, as we're so easily influenced by other voices. And

because I'm almost always writing I'm afraid I've gotten way behind on my reading, particularly of contemporary fiction.

While I was writing *The Wild Girl*, I actually reread *Anna Karenina*, because I was pretty sure that I wouldn't start writing in Tolstoy's voice. And I was struck once again by what an enormous novel that is (and I don't mean just in terms of page length, though it is a doorstopper). What a truly omniscient performance; the characters of all ages, sexes, classes, professions are all such individuals, so vivid and perfectly rendered, such complete and "real" human beings. I was humbled and stunned all over again by Tolstoy's greatness.

Right now I'm in the middle of writing a new novel, and I recently decided to reread Flaubert's (whom I also revere) *Madame Bovary*. I also love Knut Hamsun. And in terms of living authors, who's greater than Gabriel García Marquez? Although I don't dare read him when I'm writing. My other favorites are too numerous to mention.

Q: Can you recommend some books for fans of your novels who would like to get even more perspective and historical background on the time period, cultures, and events that you depict in your novels?

A: Partly for that purpose, I've included extensive bibliographies at the end of both novels. But if I had to recommend just one book to provide historical background about the Indian wars in both the Great Plains and the Southwest, it would have to be Captain John G. Bourke's *On the Border with Crook*. Bourke was General George Crook's aide-de-camp and a fine amateur ethnographer in his own right. He participated in almost all of the important events and military campaigns against both the Cheyennes and the Apaches. It's an absolutely fascinating true account of that era.

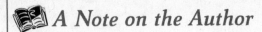

A Note on the Author

Jim Fergus was born in Chicago on March 23, 1950. He attended high school in Massachusetts and graduated as an English major from Colorado College in 1971. He has traveled extensively and lived over the years in Colorado, Florida, the French West Indies, Idaho, France, and Arizona. For ten years he worked as a teaching tennis professional in Colorado and Florida, and in 1980 he moved to the tiny town of Rand, Colorado (pop. 13), to begin his career as a full-time freelance writer. He was a contributing editor to *Rocky Mountain Magazine*, as well as a correspondent for *Outside* magazine. His articles, essays, interviews, and profiles have appeared in a wide variety of national magazines and newspapers, including *Newsweek*, *Newsday*, the *Denver Post*, the *Dallas-Times Herald*, *Harrowsmith Country Life*, *The Paris Review*, *MD Magazine*, *Savvy*, *Texas Monthly*, *Esquire*, *Fly Fisherman*, *Outdoor Life*, *Sports Afield*, and *Field & Stream*. His first book, a travel/sporting memoir titled *A Hunter's Road*, was published by Henry Holt in 1992. Writing in the *Los Angeles Times*, Jonathan Kirsch called *A Hunter's Road* "an absorbing, provocative, and even enchanting book."

Fergus's first novel, *One Thousand White Women: The Journals of May Dodd*, was published by St. Martin's Press in 1998. The novel won the 1999 Fiction of the Year Award from the Mountains & Plains Booksellers Association, and has become a favorite selection of reading groups across the country. It has since sold more than 250,000 copies in the United States. An international bestseller, *One Thousand White Women (Milles Femmes Blanches)* was also on the French bestseller list for fifty-seven weeks and has sold well over 400,000 copies in that country.

n 1999, Jim Fergus published a collection of outdoor
rticles and essays, titled *The Sporting Road*. In the spring
f 2005, his second novel, *The Wild Girl: The Notebooks
f Ned Giles* was published by Hyperion Books. Historical
iction set in the 1930s in Chicago, Arizona, and the Sierra
Madre of Mexico, *The Wild Girl* has also been embraced by
eading groups all across the United States. Winston Groom,
uthor of *Forerst Gump*, called it "an exhilarating and sus-
enseful tale that makes the heart soar."

m Fergus recently completed a long, personal family
istorical novel, *Marie Blanche*, the story of his French
other and grandmother, set in France, England, Egypt, and
merica, and spanning the full 20th century. The French
anslation of *Marie Blanche* was published in Paris by Le
herche Midi in May 2011. The American edition will
ppear in 2012.

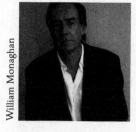

William Monaghan

# Reading Group Questions

1. The Cheyenne are often referred to as "savages," even by the women who voluntarily travel to live among them. During this time period, what is it that makes the Cheyenne savage, and the white "civilized"? Are there ways in which you would judge the Cheyenne in the novel more civilized than the whites? Are there ways in which you consider them less civilized?

2. Were you surprised that Little Wolf, the Cheyenne chief, was so aware and seemingly resigned to the fact that his culture was doomed? How does this differ from our attitudes and assumptions as U.S. citizens?

3. Did you admire May Dodd's rebelliousness? Did you find it shocking that she would leave her children behind? Do you consider her a sympathetic character?

4. Did you find it believable that the U.S. government might undertake a covert project such as the "Brides for Indians" program? Do you think the author had more modern history in mind when he developed this idea?

5. Were you surprised by elements of the Cheyenne culture as depicted here?

6. Do you think that the Cheyenne culture was respectful of women? Consider what might seem contradictory elements—for example, it is a matrilineal society, and yet warriors could have multiple wives.

7. Compare what the Cheyenne culture valued in women compared with what white culture at the time valued in women. Contrast Captain Bourke's fiancee, Miss Lydia Bradley, with May Dodd. In what ways do May and Lydia represent different types of women? In what ways have cultural expectations of women changed since this time period, and in what ways have they remained the same?

8. Did you find it believable that the white women embraced the Cheyenne culture, and willingly married with them?

9. Compare your concept of romantic love, and married love, with the relationship that develops between May and Little Wolf.

0. Were you surprised by the violence among tribes as depicted here? Did it contrast with your understanding of Native American cultures? What similarities were there between the violence among tribes, and the violence between whites and Native Americans?

1. While depicting the slaughter of Native American culture, Jim Fergus also portrays the imminent decimation of the natural landscape. Consider both tragedies. Were they equally inevitable? Are they equally irreversible?